DARK
COVENANT

To Anders,

Ben wish,

Pern Lut

DARK
COVENANT

Peter Luther

To Olga

Second impression: 2007
© Peter Luther and Y Lolfa Cyf., 2007

*This book is subject to copyright
and may not be reproduced by any means
except for review purposes
without the prior written consent of the publishers*

Cover design: Peter Luther and Y Lolfa

ISBN: 0 86243 954 x
ISBN-13: 9780862439545

Printed on acid-free and partly recycled paper
and published and bound in Wales by
Y Lolfa Cyf., Talybont, Ceredigion SY24 5AP
e-mail ylolfa@ylolfa.com
website www.ylolfa.com
tel 01970 832 304

PROLOGUE

The old Queen was dying. The proprietress of the Farthing Works, Mile End, London, received the news calmly, even though she knew it was her death sentence.

She neatly folded her copy of *The Times* and placed it on her bed. She was a voracious reader of all things important and trivial, and would spend several hours that evening with a magnifying glass digesting everything that the Fleet Street gossips had to offer. The Shilling had predicted her life would end with Victoria, that they would bequeath their empires together.

"But mine is strong, strong as houses," she whispered to herself, with a fractional tilt of her head and a half smile. She had long ago consulted a linguist upon the correct elocution of an English governess who had seen service in France, but her East End drawl was still treasured, reserved for her boudoir. "Hers will fall, I wager…"

Her empire was a hoard of money and a workhouse, which was now almost the length of the street, after years of judiciously buying up the adjacent grimy tenements and damp warehouses. Visitors, however, were received up here in the converted set of rooms, lavishly decorated in ivory and gold. When she had done with husbands, only her most faithful devotees were allowed access to these rooms. One such devotee, her accountant, was waiting on her pleasure in the sitting room close by, but she let him linger as she studied her face in the mirror.

She was still beautiful at sixty-two, the odd line and

wrinkle no more than a passing nod to maturity; her eyes, her best feature, were of the deepest green and burned, even now, with ambition. On her dressing tables were many tubs of creams and powders, some with Asian characters and others with exotic symbols, but she had never used any of them. They were there simply to satisfy the curious; they sat beside a wooden head with a wig of thick black hair, which they might assume that she needed. But her hair, like her beauty, owed nothing to artifice.

She looked at the copy of *The Times* with fond expectation. She had a library several doors down and reading had been her passion ever since she had discovered *The Shilling*, the publication that transformed her life. She had found it one night after she had been invited into a hackney, where three young men awaited her, dressed in top hats and giddy on champagne. They sat opposite with vague expressions of doubt and expectation, and she was reminded of three schoolboys awaiting their punishment. The one in the middle was holding a cane with both hands to steady him, holding it level with his chin and making a perfect ninety-degree angle with the floor. Before long the cane tapped the roof of the carriage and the frantic clap of hooves on cobbles went off in her head like an alarm bell.

She had been raped many times, but this torment was something new and something her body, which was going into spasm, found horrific. It was as if they were violating her very soul.

Her heavy make-up was smeared with her tears and her sweat and they noticed her skin. One of them lit a match and another, with a groan of surprise, splashed the remains of the champagne in her face.

"Let me out," she pleaded. "I won't say nuffin... please sirs I won't say nuffin."

Another match revealed the smallpox scars on her

skin; in the glow of the match-light her face shone like the cratered moon, and as she was hauled up, her cheap wig came away in their hands. The one with the cane beat out his self-disgust with swift and righteous blows to her body, to the hoots and catcalls of his friends, before she was thrown out of the moving carriage.

Just as the agony was still vivid, so was the moment… one of those wonderful moments pregnant with change. Such memories were now as specks of gold in the dust of her life.

She had regained consciousness and The Shilling was lying next to her in the street, its pages heavy and sodden in the rain. Her eyes locked on to it even though she was dazed and numb, for she recognised her name on the cover, the two words she had memorised at home and practised before the beak in the criminal assizes. She could barely reach out, the cane had broken several of her ribs, or perhaps it was the fall, she wasn't sure, but the paper in her fingers comforted her.

That was thirty years ago. She smiled and sighed as she turned away from the mirror and called softly to her accountant. The three young gentlemen were framed in portraits, here in her bedchamber and they had startled and gruesome faces. The man in the portrait over her bed, the one who had used the cane, she married some years later. She closed her eyes to relish the memory and opened them as she heard the door.

"Come in my love," she whispered.

The accountant entered with obsequious eyes towards the floor; he was about her age but showing his years, and the reams of papers he was carrying in both arms were giving him trouble. He put them down with relief when he saw that she was in no mood to discuss business. Her fingers were touching the cover of a thick pamphlet on the elegant round table she kept near her bed; she always liked to hover near the bed when she spoke to him, to please him, and to torment him.

"Is it time then, Madam?" the accountant whispered.

She nodded. "Yes, it's time." She tilted her head as she looked at him, expectantly.

"I've put everything in place... everything. I won't let you down. I've always tried to do my best." He was a rich man, but always humble in her presence.

"I know, my love, I know. You've been a trooper. Honest you have."

The accountant smiled gratefully and his eyes wandered to the pamphlet, which he knew to be her proudest possession. The ornate black cover seemed as crisp and off the press as when she had shown it to him all those years ago, when she had shown him the pictures inside that had made his stomach turn. He had been hers ever since. She had promised him that he would be in the next edition, and he believed her.

"My empire will be strong when the Queen's estate is in ruins," she mused. "I'd wager a guinea if I'd wager a farthin'."

The accountant shuffled uncomfortably.

"Madam?"

She took a deep breath, closed her eyes and silently mouthed a three-syllable name. The accountant couldn't make it out; the mistress had been doing that a lot recently, talking to herself.

"So we come to our purpose..." she sighed. "I see a big window. Ah... my little soldjar... did we take it... did we? You're my love, is what you are."

Part One:
Taking The Shilling

1 across	who do you bring?
2 down	to own
3 across	made the fires
3 down	do not accept it
4 across	no rooms
5 down	the process
6 down	she says
7 down	how many now?
8 across	weight hanger
9 down	The Shilling says

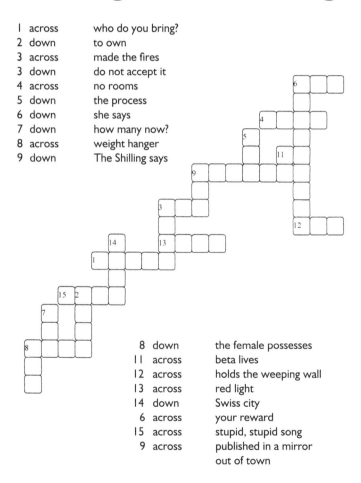

8 down	the female possesses
11 across	beta lives
12 across	holds the weeping wall
13 across	red light
14 down	Swiss city
6 across	your reward
15 across	stupid, stupid song
9 across	published in a mirror out of town

WHO DO YOU BRING?

L ewis lived in a fourth floor waterfront apartment, described as *the Penthouse* in the sales literature and in the mouths of the agents at the point of sale.

An ambitious title, given that it was under 1000 square feet and of cheap construction, but the apartment did have a claim; this was a twenty-foot lounge with a huge semi-circular window, which framed the long industrial dock. Early evening brought a transformation, when the streetlights reflected on the black water and put into shadow the surrounding factories and derelict buildings belonging to the old wharf. To his mind the window had always more than made up for the paper-thin walls and the small lift that occasionally smelled of the neighbour's dog, and went some way to justifying the high price he had paid simply for a view. Money he had had in better times.

He sourly settled back into the leather settee that, along with his view, would be left behind for his creditors. In the past two years he had spent many a wistful evening considering the cold water and passing judgment on his life; the view was calming, but as he now associated it with self-reproach he wondered whether he would miss it. The clank and slide of the lift doors opening broke his reverie and he got up to await the doorbell.

She introduced herself simply as Emily as she strolled into the lounge, without making eye contact. He was looking at his hands, unsure if it was permitted for him to study her too carefully, but he had noted that her blonde hair was natural and straight, her make-up minimal. She was wearing a simple one-piece cloth dress that reached to her knees, something that M&S would sell, which came as a relief because his neighbours always checked out his guests, most probably because there was so few of them. His initial anxiety subsiding, he considered the big worn-out Prada bag being carried in her right hand, which sported a diamond-encrusted Tiffany ring, her only piece of jewellery, and he assessed her as someone with taste who had seen better times. He liked solving puzzles, especially the age-old riddle of first impressions, and he wondered whether his Holmesian theory would hold water.

Emily hovered for a moment then complimented him on his view. On cue, he picked up his Bang & Olufsen remote control and activated his impressive CD changer; the system came to life and the metal dial slid effortlessly down to the fifth disc, one of David Bowie's synthesised Berlin albums.

She momentarily closed her eyes and found a thin smile at this staged display of ostentation, and though he must have been ten years her senior he smarted with the implied charge of immaturity. He asked her whether she often visited the Bay.

"Didn't know this *was* the Bay," she remarked.

"Well, Atlantic Wharf," he conceded, "the Bay's a few miles down the dock. You can see the St David Hotel from here."

"Uh huh."

She sat down, reached into her bag and took out her cigarettes, throwing a glance that asked whether it was okay to smoke and carrying a warning that she was going to smoke whatever he said. He picked up an ashtray from his desk and placed it near her. He only smoked after 6 p.m. on a Saturday, one of his nicotine edicts; he considered his watch, shrugged and collected up his Silk Cut from his desk and joined her.

"What would you like to drink?" he inquired. "I've got red and white wine."

She breathed out smoke, and then as she looked out of the window her eyes narrowed; the view seemed to interest her in the way that grazing gazelle interest a lioness. "Don't drink," she murmured, "not any more."

"Tea? Coffee?"

She tapped her cigarette and turned back to face him. "No, I'm good."

He nodded and groaned inwardly. This was his big act of defiance before he quitted his job on Monday; he had suspected that he would come to regret it but believed he would at least enjoy it.

He had never paid for a call girl before. The agency, Encounters, had seemed quite professional even if it couldn't quite shake off the smell of the backstreet. The manageress was not prepared to give any name other than 'Janet' and spoke with an upper-class accent which occasionally slipped into a Cardiff twang; when he had given his address, in her royal plum she had asked, "And where *to* is that?"

Janet had ventured the opinion that *sir* was clearly a discerning gentleman, who might prefer an 'evening': it would be more expensive, of course, and the young lady would expect an evening meal and a cash tip.

He was regretting his decision now, wishing he had just settled for the 'hour', for the woman appeared moody and he wasn't relishing the prospect of an evening's polite conversation with her. They sat in silence for a time until he suggested that they eat and he led her into the kitchen where he had a Chinese takeaway warming in the oven.

She loosened up a little during the meal, even though she only drank sparkling water. The takeaway was from a good restaurant and she mentioned that she used to cook a lot herself, her own recipes. She declined the chocolate dessert, remarking that she was on a diet and her eyes flickered with some appreciation when he didn't come back with a lazy and predictable compliment.

"You don't mind if I keep eating?" he asked.

She was considering him as she slid over her dessert, and he knew what she was thinking. The observation was invariably delayed, for he grew his hair over his ears and wore baggy shirts, so it took a little while to notice the absence of flesh under his skin and the veins in his neck and arms. His damn metabolism... it was like a demon, which had stalked him all his life.

"You have a problem putting on weight?" she asked casually. She lit a cigarette and seemed interested in him all of a sudden.

He raised his eyebrows as he finished his dessert, leaving a few seconds before answering to register his surprise at her directness. "I eat five Mars bars a day. Seriously, I do. It's the only thing that stops me wasting away altogether."

She was wearing her thin ironic smile again. "We all have our crosses to bear," she murmured.

He shrugged.

"Do you ever wonder how easy it would have been for nature just to have dealt you a few different cards?" she asked. "Fate too..." she pondered, now looking up at her smoke.

He barely heard the comment. He was feeling uncomfortable as he asked her something inconsequential about her history. She answered that she had recently returned from London, where she used to work.

"You mentioned your recipes," he said, still in search of conversation. "Were you a chef?"

She shook her head as she stubbed out her cigarette

then explained that she had worked for a model agency for the last five years or so; she had originally gone to London to try her luck as a model but had found the competition too fierce. Later, she had hooked up with an older man who ran an agency called Circus; he had put her to work as a talent scout.

"That must have been interesting," he lied, unable to think of anything less interesting, finding gangly, spotty teenagers and trying to prize them away from their over-possessive mothers.

"More interesting than you would think," she said slowly, as if she had read his mind and accepted the mental joust. "It wasn't as you would imagine it. Circus was unique... at least, I made it unique."

"Really?"

"Really. The Circus girls were famous... they were breathtaking. More than breathtaking... they were works of art. I did more than just find them, you see. I *nurtured* them."

There was purposefulness in her use of the word... nurtured... that carried a protective strength. He was reminded of the image of the lioness again, but this time with her cubs.

"So why did you give it up?" he asked.

"Circus hit bad times," she replied. "I don't want to talk about it." She lit another cigarette and looked around critically. The dining area was just a pokey extension of the kitchen. "So do you like your Bang & Olufsen?" she asked teasingly, a reference to Lewis' sound system.

"Always loved it," he admitted. "You can wire it up around the house... put a CD on in the lounge and listen to it in bed. Sort of like musical plumbing." He was thinking now about his bedroom and his carefully made bed, with a small knot in his stomach.

"Looks good too, doesn't it?" she remarked. "It's big,

like furniture. I like that. If you have to hide something away, well, you shouldn't have it in the first place."

He smiled, relieved at having found something in common with the woman.

"We had it all the way through our place too," she sighed. "In the apartment in the Montevetro."

He whistled. "You lived *there?* God, it's beautiful, I've seen it in *The Sunday Times*." He didn't believe her.

"We didn't stay there much," she murmured and her eyes were far away. "We preferred the country. And we travelled, travelled all over the place. Italy was our favourite. We'd shop in Venice, St Mark's Square; shop for porcelain and canvas art, and for the glasswork. And Capri... Ana Capri... you walk in the Gardens of Augustus and the flowers mist together and make a perfume. There's nowhere like it. We'd stay in the Quisisana Hotel, the best hotel on the island... there's a quaint town square where you watch the celebrities go by..." Her voice trailed off and she became silent, lost in her memories.

"Sounds marvellous," Lewis said, after a time. "Your... your partner..."

"Anton," she said. "He's Polish."

"Are you still with him?"

She considered her cigarette with an empty expression, and then shook her head slowly. "What's left of my family is still here, in the Vale," she muttered. "I came back to find them."

He nodded, finding a smidgen of empathy with the woman, even though he wasn't taking her story at face value. From the heights of Capri to this, eating a Chinese take away with him on a Saturday night, about to sleep with him, for money. For a moment he hated himself for being part of her punishment.

"Anton's still in there, somewhere," she said to close the story. "I don't know whether I'll ever see him again."

He took a sip of his wine, and then said, reflectively, "You're not the only one who's been unlucky. I've ruined myself in the last year with... well... one thing and another. I'm going to pack in my job on Monday."

"I don't think you will," she responded quietly, still looking at her cigarette.

"Seriously, it's all planned," he confirmed. "I'm going to Spain."

She now turned her vacant gaze in his direction. "You won't pack in your job and you won't go to Spain," she declared. "Things will change. You wouldn't believe the good fortune that's coming your way."

"You read my horoscope?" he joked, uneasily. She didn't answer.

Oh well, he thought. Perhaps blind faith and optimism was all part of the service. He wasn't about to complain.

Emily was generous with her body and she hovered over him for almost an hour, unemotionally administering pleasure and sensation with the patience and ruthlessness of a medieval torturer. Her neck and shoulders glistened with perspiration as she moved but her face was a mask of intense concentration. She didn't smile, politely acknowledged his whispered compliments and gently deflected his attempts to kiss her. When it was finished she rolled over and didn't speak.

He wondered whether she was sleeping or thinking, but he was too shy to ask so he curled up and faced the other way. Eventually he slept, and dreamed of walking onto a sun-drenched balcony, some place far away, in the arms of someone who loved him. His eyes were moist when he woke.

Sunday morning was *his* time and he wanted Emily out of the apartment as quickly as possible. He had already served her two croissants and three cups of coffee, but she was lingering.

"Damn crosswords," she muttered as she put down her pen. She was on the sofa with a magazine that she had pulled out of her bag. It was open near the back.

"I've got *The Sunday Times* if you want a crossword," he offered hesitantly, thinking that she looked a little too much at home.

"No thanks, that crossword's *really* hard. I should be able to do this one, though."

She now stood the magazine up on her thighs and he made out its name: *The Shilling*. There were three smaller words underneath the title: *Fashion, Ambition, Temptation*. The cover was jet black, with ornate white lines creeping up the sides, like monochrome ivy tendrils. "That doesn't look thick enough to be a fashion mag," he remarked. "I obviously don't read the glossies, but I don't recognise it."

She blinked to acknowledge this interruption to her concentration, and then shook out the pages. "No adverts," she answered.

He decided to keep talking, hoping that it would irritate her into leaving. "So how does it stay in business?" he asked.

She blinked again then glanced at him. "It's only available on subscription," she said.

"The Shilling... is that how much it costs?" he joked.

"No, it costs more than that."

"So why's it called The Shilling?"

She put the magazine down with a sigh. "Lewis, will you stop asking me questions about the magazine?"

He smiled. "Why?" he asked.

She considered him for a moment then returned to the crossword, finding her pen. "Because I have to answer all your questions," she muttered, almost to herself.

17

"You do?"

"That's the rule," she confirmed. "And it will take a long time," she added. "Is that what you want?"

Lewis didn't care for her tone, and cared less for her suggestion that she was ready to stay and talk. "Well, just tell me why is it only available on subscription," he murmured sulkily.

"It's old," she answered.

"Old?"

"The publisher is old," she clarified. "This is a recent issue, obviously."

His interest perked up a little at the mention of a historical connection, history being one of his passions. "What, like the Masons?" he queried, not believing a word of it. If this thing had been in circulation for more than two generations it would have been famous: someone had sold Emily a line and she had fallen for it.

"It's something of an exclusive club, if that's what you mean," she said.

"I still don't understand how it pays for itself without adverts and without being on sale on the high street," he said as he tried to make out the price.

She gave a huff of irritation. "The people who subscribe know they can communicate with likeminded people," she answered. "They share their knowledge and their talent. Anton and I paid for our subscription in our gravy days." She paused. "The subscription will come to an end soon," she added sadly.

"Sort of like the internet, but with only a few portals?" he remarked, taking care not to let the conversation wander towards more reminiscences about Anton in Italy.

"If that helps you understand it," she replied smugly. It seemed to him that she was measuring her answers, as if she was playing a truth game where the object was to reveal nothing. "There are some arranged events, and subscribers write in," she continued. "But really it's about the magazine. The articles, the pictures, even the crossword... they're all made for us."

"What, people with fashion and ambition?" Lewis offered, reading the inscription on the magazine.

"Lewis, will you stop asking me questions? Will you let me do the crossword?"

He put up his hands in submission, and then considered her cup balanced precariously on the edge of the sofa; she had finished her coffee but he wasn't going to offer her another one.

"Are you any good at crosswords?" she asked eventually.

"No, hopeless."

"I suspect that you *are* good."

He glanced at his watch. "Cryptic maybe, but my general knowledge sucks."

"Holds the Weeping Wall," she read.

"Geography – no chance."

She frowned. "Well at least have a go."

"Okay. Holds the Weeping Wall. Er, Jerusalem?"

"Three letters, and that's the *Wailing* Wall you're thinking of."

"Then I give up," he said.

She smiled and moved to another crossword clue, not seeming to mind his failure. "Swiss city?" she ventured.

He checked his watch again, this time more deliberately, but if she noticed his signal she didn't acknowledge it. "Okay, Swiss City," he sighed, "that I can do. Geneva?"

"No."

"Zurich?"

"Four letters."

"No idea," he said, without expending any further mental energy. His irritation was noticeable now.

"Now this one you *will* know," she declared. "How do

you spell your name?"

"My name?"

"How do you spell it?"

"Why?"

"How do you *spell* it?" she repeated, with an edge to her tone that startled him.

"L-e-w-i-s," he answered cautiously.

She appeared to check something on the crossword, as if to make sure that the letters fitted, then nodded and got up from the sofa, the magazine in her hand. She came over and planted herself on the armrest of his chair. He caught a whiff of Chanel No 19 and forced back a renewed interest in her as she snuggled her pert bottom into the leather.

She placed the magazine onto his lap, handed him her pen and he glanced at the crossword, which was the strangest looking crossword he had ever seen. She had the same expression he had noticed last night, when she had been looking out of the window; it was distant and predatory, the look that he imagined terrified her little proteges in her model agency. He was starting to feel nervous as he realised she might be a little deranged.

"Write it in please," she said softly, pointing to five boxes. He shrugged and obliged. His mind was in a daze as she took back the pen and his eyes searched out the clue to the answer that he had just completed.

Who do you bring?

"Who do you bring?" he read. "How did you get my name from that?"

Her eyes narrowed. "If you want me to tell you, Lewis, then I will," she warned him.

He shrugged and feigned indifference, which made her smile as she carefully lifted the magazine from his lap and fitted it reverentially into her old and bruised leather bag. "I have to go now," she announced quietly.

"Oh right," he said, jumping up. He had rehearsed this moment and had a fifty-pound tip in an envelope in his desk, all in fives to make it fatter. As he had feared, he found handing over the envelope even more embarrassing than the sex, but she accepted the envelope gracefully, without checking its contents, and with a polite peck on his cheek. He walked her to the lift, uttering a curse in his head as he noticed the smell of dog urine. Inside the lift she pushed the ground floor button and raised her hand in a half salute. Then she looked down. She was still looking down as the lift doors closed. She didn't say goodbye.

He felt both relieved and disappointed as he walked back into his apartment and closed the door behind him, his view and his Bang & Olufsen all his own again. He had an odd feeling that he had needed to say something to her before she left, or that she had needed to say something to him.

So, this was his act of rebellion before he put in motion his life changes tomorrow. Somehow he had needed it to be more important, more significant than just some uncomfortable small talk and a cash transaction. Even the memory of the sex wasn't pleasant and he felt lonely and worthless in his shame.

Lewis... Lewis... what were you expecting? You aren't going to change your life with a prostitute, my friend. Wake up and smell the coffee.

As he slumped on his sofa and reached for his remote control he felt a crackle under his legs. Looking down he found the magazine, which must have dropped out of Emily's bag, and he lobbed it over onto his enamelled coffee table by the window, a place generally reserved for such throwaway items. He lay back and thought intently about nothing in particular, a skill he had mastered long ago for times such as this when he was feeling unhappy and confused.

LEWIS

L ewis ate Sunday lunch in the bar of a fairly fashionable hotel only a few hundred yards away, and lunch was invariably something with French fries, today a club sandwich, and a pint of Guinness.

The bar staff knew him as someone who was always polite but didn't talk. The reason he liked to eat here was so he could read all the newspapers, in company but with no company. The hotel had a hushed and formal atmosphere and there was a subdued silence in the bar area, only broken by whispered conversations and the click of the occasional briefcase being opened by foreign businessmen. A few tourists were dotted around, but they too were forced to enter into the silence and talk without sound.

The Sunday papers had become something of a ritual for him in the last few years, ever since his misfortunes had begun. It was a psychological bluff that he played on himself, that if he read enough papers the news might change. But it was all bad, as usual, for his technology shares showed no sign of recovering. He had made the decision that when he went to Spain, to work in a bar, he wouldn't look at his portfolio again until his return, maybe in three to four years time.

Back in his apartment he disobeyed his nicotine edicts and had his first cigarette of the day; he tried to apply a 6 p.m. watershed on the weekends but he knew that it would be impossible today. At his mahogany desk, which held a flat-screen computer – state of the art before twelve months of progress had turned it into junk – he signed on to check the money channels and saw that he had e-mail.

He saw a shares magazine circular and deleted it. Then he saw an advert from a share tipster and deleted that too. A third e-mail, from 'Farthing.com' he didn't recognise, but as his mouse cursor hovered over the delete button he noticed that the message listed all of the five stocks in his portfolio. He didn't trust any analyst recommendations any more, but he metaphorically shrugged and opened it. Unusually for his computer, the e-mail sprang into life in an instant.

Lewis, welcome.

The market blows, hot and cold it blows. Did you believe that you had the measure of it? Did you sate yourself with greed?

Wisdom is all around you, yet as with the mariner, there is water, water everywhere, but not a drop to drink.

Are you downcast?

Click here, to read more.

Lewis made a face and clicked the link, expecting to be transferred to a website. Instead, a further e-mail appeared.

So we come to our purpose.

Our sails are fixed; our mast is of the strong-est oak. Our offering will be foolproof.

For the moment, only observe. Our terms will follow.

Your servants, sir

Lewis closed the e-mail and typed 'Farthing.com', but the screen told him that the website didn't exist. He tried a few variations, still with no success. He knew the score with mailshots; they would target one of his shareholdings with a free report to get him interested, having obtained his name from the register of a popular but beleaguered company.

The difference with this mailshot, however, was that *all* his companies had been targeted. That meant the investment house had managed to cross-reference him on five different registers; he supposed it was possible, if rather time-consuming and unnecessary.

Stranger, though, was the promise of a foolproof system on shares, although it wasn't as if he hadn't heard it before. He had received a similar boast from a racing syndicate last year, which had managed to drain the last of his precious reserves with sure things that fell at the last fence. That was before he had decided to borrow to the limit on his countless credit cards in an attempt to recoup his losses in the stock market.

An idea occurred to him and he rang BB, an old friend who had acquired his nickname on account of his passion for the legendary guitarist BB King. BB had wanted to invest at the crest of the technology boom and Lewis had given him the names of his own shares. BB had held them ever since, exactly the same companies. He had never moaned about it.

"BB, Lewis. Hi. Listen, I've received an e-mail and I'm wondering if you've received it too."

BB grumbled something into his mobile and Lewis

waited with the phone to his ear. "Okay, what are we looking for?" BB asked eventually.

"An e-mail from Farthing.com."

"From who?"

"Farthing."

"Farthing?" BB asked, with amusement.

"Yeah, they've got some Victorian gimmick going on. The e-mail's written in this fancy script."

BB didn't comment. "Nothing here," he said eventually.

"You sure?"

"Yeah. What's this about?"

Lewis sighed. "I don't know really," he conceded, "it's just a mailshot, but a really weird one. It named our five companies, that's why I thought you might have received it too."

"What's weird?"

"Oh, it's trying to pretend that it has some insider information."

There was a pause. "Could be a scam," BB said. "Remember those Mafia trials, when they were inflating stock prices with rumours and stuff?"

"Yeah, I've been thinking about that." Lewis scratched his head. "All the same, if they were trying to blindside me you'd think they'd come across as a bit more... well, plausible."

"I don't know, Lewis. You've read the e-mail, I haven't. Are we still on for squash on Wednesday?"

"Wednesday, right. See you then."

"Lewis, Lewis, before you go... are you still going ahead with everything?"

"What, quitting work? Absolutely."

BB simply sighed, tired now of attempting to talk him out of it.

"Don't worry," Lewis murmured, "I know what I'm doing."

A Sunday evening had never arrived so quickly. The film he was watching wasn't distracting him from the confrontation waiting for him tomorrow, but he was worrying about the aftermath even more. Did he really want to go abroad? What would he do?

He switched off the television. Well, he would be forty next year and he just knew that he would go insane if something didn't change. He lay back on the sofa and looked out of his window; the coffee table was directly ahead of him and he idly reached over and picked up Emily's magazine.

The crossword was at the back, he recalled. He opened it at the last page and was aware of a fusty, stale smell coming from the pages, like clothes that had been left and forgotten for years in a locked wardrobe. Strange... the black cover with the white ivy design looked and smelled brand new, as if it was just off the press, but the inside pages were worn and thumbed. Emily had clearly had the magazine a long time. Perhaps the cover had been treated with some protective coating.

The last page wasn't the crossword, it was just a blank page. On closer inspection he noticed some writing at the bottom, but the print was too small to read, probably some copyright stuff. The page opposite contained something which made him chuckle, as he recognised it instantly.

It was the original advert for the Carbolic Smoke Ball, the invention which sparked a nineteenth century court case, one of the most famous in English legal history. It was about contract law and the company's advert promised a cash payment to anyone who bought their smoke ball and caught influenza. The barristers' chambers that he used had an identical print of the monochrome advert, framed in their reception.

He smiled but frowned with his eyes. In a barristers' chambers the relevance of the old advert needed no explanation, but why would it be in a fashion magazine? Who but lawyers would recognise its significance?

He turned the page, moving backwards through the magazine. As the page was turned the same stale fabric smell wafted from the crease of the pages, which he now noticed weren't stapled or bound in any way. There must be some glue holding them together. The smell disappeared in almost a split second, as if it had escaped into the atmosphere.

There was his crossword, stretched across both the pages, with his name written in.

Who do you bring?

What did that mean? he wondered, and he had a mental flash of Emily looking down as the lift doors closed. The image in his mind, intruding into his concentration, unsettled him.

It was a strange looking crossword, not in the usual square format but stepped, like a staircase. He scanned a few more of the clues. *Swiss city*. With his name written in he now had a second letter for *Swiss city... e*. Four letters. He shook his head; he hadn't been lying to Emily, his general knowledge really was hopeless. The other clues didn't seem to be general knowledge based, but then they weren't really of the cryptic variety either. It was as if you either knew the answer or you didn't.

Holds the Weeping Wall.

Something registered in his brain, but he couldn't encode it.

As he studied the clues he noticed something else. The clues were all out of sequence, not divided into 'across' and 'down' sections in ascending numbers. He turned back another page, his nose twitching as he did so.

There were two black female models, one on each page. Or perhaps it was the same girl on both pages... no, on closer inspection he saw they were identical twins, beautiful, with short natural hair, but the young woman on the left had a slightly longer face. She also had a clear and youthful complexion, whereas her sister had a windswept appearance, as if she had worked in the fields all her life. Both women were wearing mundane, everyday clothes; long plain dresses that seemed to be made of a rough hessian. They were facing each other, their hands raised as if in prayer.

Some kind of avant-garde fashion, he supposed, turning the page and becoming accustomed to the stale smell that jumped out at him.

Two pages containing letters to the editor. He read one: a subscriber had an invention he wished to exploit and gave a PO box and a reference number. Lewis now flicked forward a few pages.

An article entitled 'Self Confidence in the Workplace', which seemed to be some sort of self-help piece for people afraid to assert themselves. There were no photographs, just a sketch drawing of a man lying in front of a desk with someone's foot on his back. The man lying on the floor was presumably the boss, the owner of the foot the newly assertive employee.

Lewis thought about his coming confrontation with *his* boss tomorrow and smiled at an idle fantasy as he turned the page, working backwards again.

There was an advert, which he had seen before in other magazines. On the left page a stylish woman in high heels looked as if she was sauntering into town for an expensive shopping trip; she was holding a leash that stretched across to the bottom corner of the right page, where it was attached to a poodle. Emily was wrong, then, about the ads. He was almost relieved to have come across one at last.

Turning the page he came across another article, entitled 'Suez: the final nail in the coffin of the British Empire'. He gave a murmur of appreciation, but became bored after reading the first few paragraphs. It was an account of the 1950s crisis where Britain failed in its gamble to hold on to some semblance of its world domination, but it was just a pedestrian recital of the facts with no analysis or literary flair. He skipped to the last few paragraphs and found that the style was the same. He couldn't imagine anything of interest in the middle of the article and decided to leave it. There weren't even any pictures.

He took a deep breath of bewilderment. He had read all sorts of magazines, but one thing was missing here, the one thing that every magazine needed, from the boring DIY weekly to the most chic European glossy. It was missing a target audience. Fashion models, history, law, inventions, self-help trivia; the content was such a bizarre mix that he couldn't imagine who would want to buy it.

Perhaps he was missing the point. Emily had said that the magazine was built for the subscribers… there must be some common link.

Again he saw Emily in his mind's eye, looking down as the lift doors closed. He cursed to himself, annoyed now that he couldn't shake the image.

He went to the centre pages and his eyes widened with surprise as he rotated the magazine lengthways.

Well, he had wanted pictures…

A naked young woman with freckled skin was splashed across the centrefold. Above her head she held a set of garden shears strained open to their limit. Perhaps it was the shears, or perhaps it was the blatant pose, but he didn't find the image erotic at all. Indeed, he was even having some trouble looking at her; his eyes would settle on her wrists, on her knees, on her belly button, but he wasn't able to fully picture the whole of her, to enjoy her nakedness.

Maybe he just felt a sense of embarrassment at such an

inappropriate interruption to the magazine. Her scornful expression was almost daring him to look and for a fleeting moment he hated himself for lingering at these pages, was repulsed by his laddish voyeurism. Then he composed himself; it must be the same avant-garde fashion house trying to make some feminist statement or something, but he didn't like it and was annoyed at having been made to feel uncomfortable.

He worked back to the front, past the articles and the poodle woman advert. He was at the beginning of the magazine and he frowned, weighing the thing in his hands and deciding that the paper must be thicker than it looked. The inside cover was blank, save for a name etched at the bottom. The name was Mary Stone. Opposite was a head and shoulders colour photograph of a woman, filling the entire page.

It was a striking face. The woman, who was possibly approaching middle age, had raven black hair tied into a bun over her left ear and the tight stretch of her hairline accentuated a high forehead. From a swanlike neck hung something on a gold chain, perhaps a pendant, which was slipped within her tunic, a low cut T-shirt or some other thin white garment.

"Mary Stone?" he asked himself, admiring her neck and then her dainty little ear. Only one ear was visible as she was facing just to his left, but her piercing green eyes were on him, had pinned him with sudden disapproval. Her scrutiny made him flush, as if she were a schoolteacher who was the object of an adolescent fantasy.

He smiled. Perhaps he was just getting older, but he found this head and shoulders portrait a thousand times more erotic than the naked flesh on the centre pages. He struggled to put his finger on what he found so appealing; even from the pose, the aloof tilt of her head, he imagined she had a presence.

Who is she? he wondered. She didn't appear to be advertising or modelling anything.

He closed the magazine and, as an afterthought, sniffed the cover. He smelled nothing but the paper. He flicked the magazine open again, and found that the stale smell had left the pages too. Perhaps it had just gathered too much dust as it hung around somewhere waiting to be read and he lobbed it back on his table and lay back.

He was taking deep breaths. It was a big day tomorrow and he was feeling sick.

He tried to sleep to music, his B&O CD changer linked up to a speaker under his bed and edited just for the instrumental tracks and repeat play. Before long he got out of bed, returned to the lounge and found the CD case to check the title of the piece that was playing.

"Track ten," he murmured, seeing the red 10 on the sound system. He studied the CD cover, as he wasn't that familiar with the names of the instrumental tracks.

"Weeping Wall," he said to himself, with a bemused smile.

It was David Bowie's album 'Low'. Lewis, to commemorate his victory, found a pen and flicked to the back of the magazine, to the crossword. He wrote in one of the answers.

"Holds the Weeping Wall... *Low*," he declared, with a satisfied shrug.

Back in bed he tried to sleep, but was finding it difficult.

Damn strange, he reflected.

He was a Bowie fan but he wouldn't have got the answer if he hadn't been listening to the album.

It was as if the clue was made for him, and this moment.

Feeling low, downcast, just as the e-mail had said.

Monday morning arrived all too quickly and he woke up feeling drained. It took the second alarm to eventually get him out of bed.

On this holy morning, the start of his new life, he broke one of his nicotine edicts and had a cigarette with his coffee. It tasted bitter in his mouth, but felt good.

He spent five minutes in the shower, gazing down at the plastic tray, then dressed slowly and carefully, turning over matters in his head. If O'Neill didn't accept his resignation gracefully, if he threw him out on the spot, without requiring notice, then this would be the last time he ever got ready for work at Harrier & O'Neill. He had chosen his dark suit with the waistcoat, the one he only wore in court and which didn't have the office-weary look of the others. He took some care in choosing his tie and as an afterthought he ran some gel through his hair and sprayed some Antaeus aftershave on his neck. Checking his watch he saw that he had fifteen minutes to spare before he had to set off.

He had rehearsed his conversation with O'Neill a thousand times in his head, had tried to anticipate every taunt and insult. He had even planned the thirty minutes he would spend in the office before he went up to see him… the essentials he needed to gather from his desk, in case he had to make a hasty exit.

He signed on to check his e-mails, to postpone the start of his day.

O'Neill would hate him for leaving… there was no getting round it. O'Neill would think he was leaving a sinking ship, would see it as a personal betrayal.

There was another e-mail from Farthing.com. He hesitated then clicked.

Lewis, welcome.

We post you the offering, but only for your observation. You are as yet unsubscribed, so it is not to be purchased.

Click to accept these terms.

He clicked, raising his eyebrows and smiling.

The company is involved in waste management. It trades on its own account but is on the brink of obtaining a five-year Government contract.

We repeat. The shares are not to be purchased.

The company is called Lowe.

Your servants, sir

Low

The offices of Harrier & O'Neill were situated between the museum and the hugely impressive city castle. Lewis had never visited either landmark, to his recollection; the museum was nothing but a direction flag for clients coming from out of town, the castle just a bus stop from his youth.

He pulled up into the raised communal car park in his MX5, his once prized sports car now showing the years. His parking space was next to a low brick wall, which after all these years he would be able to manoeuvre around in his sleep: angled in, then full turn, then straighten up; into neutral, ignition off, handbrake on. Seventeen years.

Two more of his deep breaths were required before stubbing out the cigarette. Even his most sacred edict, *never smoke in the car*, had been broken this morning.

He had never quite mastered his fear of O'Neill. Even now, when his boss could do nothing to him, when he was free, he shivered at the prospect of what was to come. He got out the car, took his briefcase out of the boot and dawdled around to the six steps that led down to the office.

Still on automatic he avoided the loose third step and walked into the reception. Helen, also on automatic this Monday morning, nodded vacantly at him from behind the small reception desk with two telephones. As with most of the buildings in this part of the city, the office was a converted townhouse, quite possibly a fashionable residence a hundred years ago before commerce invaded and occupied. The office had been refurbished but the brass chandeliers, missing screws where the yellow wallpaper had curled, attested to years of neglect. On this morning he went cold as he imagined what he believed to be the building's pain, but quickly got a grip. This wasn't in the script.

"Is Stephen in yet?" he asked Helen, meaning O'Neill. Helen shook her head and returned to her paperback.

Behind the reception was the kitchen where he now made himself a coffee. He had a soft spot for the kitchen, the first room he had been directed to when he had joined as a shy and nervous 22 year-old articled clerk. At the time he had told himself it was just a temporary job until he found something he was interested in, but O'Neill had made a special effort with him when he qualified and for a while it felt different. Then he had acquired a mortgage. And then he became scared of change and he had been here ever since.

Stuart, a newly qualified lawyer in his early twenties walked in and was surprised to see Lewis leaning against the sink and drinking his coffee. Lewis didn't like office small talk and preferred to drink his coffee alone, at his desk.

"You okay, Lew?"

Lewis smiled. "Yeah I'm fine. Just catching the rays."

The kitchen had a tiny window, which looked out onto uncollected rubbish. "Catching the rays?" Stuart asked.

"Don't worry about it. You okay?"

The perpetually cheerful Stuart offered him a resigned grimace.

"Stephen giving you a hard time?" Lewis probed.

"Yeah, I've been worrying about it all weekend. I've screwed up on a file and I've been putting off telling him."

Lewis sighed as he washed up his mug. "Anything I can do?" he murmured.

"Find me a new boss?" Stuart asked.

Lewis chortled, admiring the trainee's bravado. Lewis hadn't been nearly as brave when he was Stuart's age. He wasn't sure that he was so very brave now.

As part of his plan, his pre-meeting schedule, he went downstairs to the boardroom to collect his books. The boardroom was dominated by a long teak table, immaculately oiled and carefully arranged with coasters, glasses and two jugs of water and was sometimes used for the partners' meetings, which were opportunities for O'Neill to impose his will on the junior partners. Because Lewis hated that table, and made a point of never looking at it, he didn't see the woman seated patiently at the far end.

It was a few seconds before the woman whispered his name. He jumped and turned round from the bookcase.

"Can I help you?" he asked, putting his book down.

"Didn't the receptionist tell you I was waiting for you?"

Lewis had a violent moment in his head with Helen the receptionist. "Yes of course she did, forgive me," he muttered. "Monday morning, you know, never right until my second coffee."

She stood up and offered her hand as he walked over. Her handshake was firm but her smile was an uncertain line waiting to retreat.

"Lewis Coin," he said.

"Bernice Connor," she replied, sitting back down. He joined her and waited patiently as she took some papers out of her briefcase. He was furious with Helen for not having warned him: the last thing he needed this morning was a new client. She handed him her business card, which read 'Baron Enterprises', and he put it in the inside pocket of his jacket with a polite smile.

"You've been recommended to us, Mr Coin," she opened, in a faltering voice.

"Lewis, please. Mr Coin is my dad," he said, but the joke didn't register. "Recommended? Really? By whom?" he asked, deciding he should frown and adopt his serious lawyer air.

She briefly glanced up from her papers. "John Kravitz of Evelyn Insurance," she said. "He says you're one of the best lawyers in Cardiff."

"Well that was nice of him, but I wouldn't go that far," Lewis remarked. He remembered John, and Evelyn Insurance, both casualties of a merger. He had had a string of successes for Evelyn, the first insurance company he had managed directly, and he felt a stirring of pride in old achievements. He put such thoughts away; this job was history now. "Do you arrange insurance through Mr Kravitz?"

He was studying the woman carefully, considering her stiff upright posture and the way she was moving her papers around the desk with the index finger of her right hand. She was in her late twenties, but making an attempt to look older with her pinned back hair and lace collar.

"Oh no, we simply approached Mr Kravitz for references. Baron is a large operation and we self-insure."

"I see," he said. That was unusual: he knew of companies that carried large excesses, but had never come across an operation that shunned insurance altogether. A paraplegic claim or a mass casualty accident would close them down.

"The group's head office is in the States," she continued, "but we've just opened up a new branch in Wales. I'm the liaison for this area."

"Liaison? Sounds glamorous."

She shook her head quickly. "Not really," she said.

Even though she was not wearing make-up, except for some unflattering face powder that gave her cheeks a grainy texture, he could see that she was very attractive. Classically attractive, with strong but well carved features. Her loose blue outfit gave few clues to her figure although very much on show was a long sensuous neck. He smiled in his mind; he had a thing about necks.

"That's what the company likes to call me," she added, touching her neck self-consciously. "A liaison; in reality, I'm a purchaser."

"And today you're purchasing a lawyer?" he asked.

She was taken aback. "Well, possibly," she conceded.

For a lawyer who had lost all confidence in his profession, he was enjoying this conversation. "So, what does Baron do?" he asked.

"Oh, that would take some explaining, but suffice it to say that we're in the energy business."

"And how can I help you?"

She returned to her papers and reached instinctively for her pen, again wrong-footed by his directness. "Well, the group has a lot of litigation, claims from the employees. We have twelve plants in the UK and there's a big union presence."

"Employer liability, that's me," Lewis confirmed.

"During the last year we've been using a London firm. The solicitor there is very nice, and I think he's very capable, but he's lost all the cases he's taken to trial."

"Any particular reason for things going wrong?" he probed.

She shuffled uncomfortably. "What do you mean?" she asked.

"Well, did your solicitor fail to get some important

evidence or call the right witnesses?" He noticed that she was prickling at the implied criticism of the lawyer. "Litigation is not an exact science," he added, "I'm just curious, that's all."

She was looking at her papers. "I agreed with all his recommendations… they all seemed to make sense, we had strong cases… but we've lost five trials in a row now and the union is… well…"

"Walking all over you?" Lewis offered.

She nodded mournfully. "To tell you the truth I don't know *what* went wrong. I think… I think we've just been unlucky."

"Wasn't it Napoleon who said that the worst failing of any general is to be unlucky?" he observed.

As she sighed to acknowledge this simple truth he could almost hear the ice cracking. He suspected that she probably hadn't wanted this meeting, had wanted to stay loyal to the London lawyer, but someone had overruled her.

"You have a nice way of putting things, Mr Coin," she admitted.

"Lewis?" he persisted.

Her eyes flickered. She had doe-like and melancholy eyes. "Are *you* unlucky, Lewis?" she asked softly.

He indulged himself with a flirtatious grin. "That's something you'll have to find out for yourself," he answered, with a raise of his eyebrows.

"I hope you're lucky," she added seriously, looking him squarely in the eyes for the first time. He detected her concern, realised that this meeting was tremendously important to her.

"Don't worry about the union," he said in a grave voice. "We'll knock them into line in no time."

He was walking her to the door when a tall and heavy-set man appeared above him on the stairs.

"Lewis, my office *now*," the man muttered.

"I'll be right there, Stephen," Lewis replied without looking up.

"*Now*, young man."

Lewis stiffened but Bernice pretended to ignore the exchange; it had started to rain and as she opened her umbrella in the porch she threw a quick suspicious glance at the figure on the stairs. She smiled her farewell to Lewis.

This morning Lewis decided not to care about having his authority destroyed in front of a client, for as he made his way up the stairs and followed O'Neill into his office he thought that now was as good a time as any to drop his bombshell.

Lewis settled himself into the chair opposite the senior partner – now the only senior partner since the mild mannered Mr Harrier had retired some years ago; his departure had marked the deterioration of the firm's fortunes. O'Neill collected a court summons from the top of his post, the post he always opened himself, and shoved it across the desk. "What's this?" he asked.

Lewis glanced at the document. The court had returned the summons because one of the boxes hadn't been completed; he had asked Stuart to issue it for him last week.

"My mistake," Lewis replied quietly.

"Get it sorted," O'Neill grumbled and picked up one of his own letters, to signal that the audience was over.

"Stephen, I've just seen a new client. She is offering us employer liability work. There could be a stream of cases coming in."

O'Neill put down his letter, thought for a moment, then

straightened his colourful bow tie. "Insurance company?" he queried. Harrier & O'Neill had gradually lost all its insurance work, the guarantee of bulk instruction, over the last few years. Larger firms with greater economies of scale were cornering the market.

"Just a company... they self-insure."

"Who?"

"Baron Enterprises." Lewis reached into his jacket for the card then muttered something under his breath when he couldn't put his hand on it. Even after all these years he was still fingers and thumbs when he was with O'Neill. "They've got a union claim which they want me to deal with."

"I thought you said it was a *stream* of cases?"

"That's the deal, but I'm to do this one first."

O'Neill sniffed and returned his attention to his letter. "Sounds like bullshit to me. Where are the papers?"

"The woman didn't leave them, she's e-mailing them, but the company's going to telegraph five thousand pounds into our account. I'm going up to see the operation after I've had a chance to have a read through."

"So when's the appointment?"

"She's going to ring me."

"Why? Why didn't you make the appointment straight away?"

"That's the way she wanted it, Stephen."

O'Neill was still reading his letter. "You won't get the phone call, and you won't get the case. This is a tinpot operation looking for some free advice. How many times have I told you to look out for time wasters?"

"No, they're sending five grand to us, as I said."

"So this company doesn't possess a chequebook?"

"I... I..."

"It's a simple question."

"Well, I didn't ask."

"You didn't ask. That's helpful. How long were you with her?"

"About an hour."

"So you've just cost this firm a hundred pounds..."

"For goodness's sake, Stephen, this is a new client..."

Lewis stopped himself as O'Neill looked up. The large man's secret weapon was a stare, which fixed its victim from behind thick-rimmed spectacles; he had a long face, punctuated by a thin moustache, and the result would almost have been comical if the stare was not so emotionless and unyielding.

"In a moment you and me are going to fall out," O'Neill warned.

Lewis nodded to keep his anger under control, feeling hatred for this man. It wasn't just this meeting, but thousands before it. He took a deep breath to compose himself. "Stephen, I've got something to tell you," he murmured.

O'Neill sat back heavily in his chair. He didn't speak, just folded his arms.

Did he know already? Had he been expecting this?

A moment of silence drained the room of energy. Lewis knew his resignation notice would slip out of his mouth as a weak lament and it would end as it began, with him in fear of this man, completely subdued by the force of his personality. The confidence in the workplace article filtered through his thoughts, as he pictured the sketch drawing of the boss, prone on the floor with someone's boot pressing him down.

"I'm asking you to trust me on this," Lewis muttered, his tone containing just a careful degree of defiance. "She will ring. We *will* get the case."

He would be damned if he was going to let O'Neill win the last round. He would hand in his notice when the instruction was on his desk: Bernice had made it clear that he was the lawyer Baron wanted, that Harrier & O'Neill meant nothing to them.

The notion of being missed when he left, and of proving O'Neill wrong, appealed to him.

His revenge would be cold blooded.

Lewis had very little to do that morning as he had worked late over the past few weeks to enable him to leave with a clear desk. He searched the Internet for Lowe, which he discovered went by the full name of Lowe Waste Management.

There it was. It was a small company but seemed solid enough, the Bloomberg terminal recording several respectable transactions with the interim report making positive noises. The share price was 3p. He groaned. That meant the buy price was 4p and the sell price was 2p; 50% of your investment lost before you even started. That was why he had never bought penny shares.

But he was feeling brave and reckless this morning. He logged on to his trading account and liquidated his entire portfolio, netting around £4000 from a borrowed investment of over twenty times that amount. With the money he bought Lowe, telling himself it didn't really matter any more.

Surprisingly, he slept well that night.

Tuesday heralded a late September burst of sunshine that filled the park opposite the offices with picnickers and even a few adventurous sunbathers. The sunlight was streaming through Lewis' office window as O'Neill walked in and announced that £5000 had arrived in the firm's account, reference Baron Enterprises.

"When are you going up?" O'Neill asked.

"I'm still waiting for the call, Stephen. Don't worry, she'll ring."

O'Neill briefly considered some papers on Lewis' filing cabinet then sniffed as he put them back. "Well of course she'll ring, they've delivered the money. Tell them it's one hundred and twenty per hour, including travel time. There'll only be the one case after all, no matter what she's telling you."

Lewis nodded absentmindedly. "I'll try," he said. £120 was a fair market rate but he would be expecting them to negotiate a discount, especially if there was to be any level of ongoing instruction. £90 was nearer the rate the firm had been charging for the last few years; there were too many personal injury lawyers pitching for this type of work.

"How did this company find us?" O'Neill asked.

Lewis wasn't worried about the charging rate. He was pondering over when he should hand in his notice; he was feeling that he should at least do some work on the new case first. He owed Bernice that.

"Lewis?" O'Neill asked.

Lewis pulled his gaze away from the sunlit park. "Oh, John Kravitz of Evelyn Insurance recommended us," he said.

O'Neill thought hard to place the name, then smiled. "Kravitz… Kravitz… yes, he was always a fan of the firm. This is a good lesson for you, young man: you need to keep plugging with these people. I can't be expected to do it all myself." He walked briskly out of the office, flushed with success and Lewis nodded ironically. Kravitz had always insisted that O'Neill go nowhere near any of his cases.

When Lewis had finished dealing with his post he logged on to his computer again. He blinked as he read the terminal announcement: Lowe Waste Management had won a major government contract and the directors had hurried through a statement describing a projected ten fold increase in the workforce and the opening of six new depots. The share price had jumped and stabilised at 12p.

Lewis studied the terminal impassively, but his brain was working furiously. It was screaming: *sell now*! He switched to his account and called up the details, working swiftly and methodically. His face was without emotion as he sold all his holdings in Lowe and his account clocked up just under £12,000 in cash. He logged off quickly then looked furtively at the screen, as if he had just engineered a crime and made his getaway.

Then, his nerves settling, he felt the warm glow of success, back like an old lover. As was his habit of old, he worked out what he could do with the money, scribbling on his pad as he did his sums. £12,000 would take him a fair way in Spain while the trustee in bankruptcy was nosing through his affairs; alternatively, he could stay afloat with his credit card payments for another six months or so. Something might turn up during that time…

"What to do…" he muttered.

It was occurring to him that there was another option. He could re-invest the £12,000 and have a serious stab at solving his money problems. His mind was calculating four hundred per cent gains on his investment stake. It would only take a few trades…

His thoughts turned to Farthing.com. Was this just a lucky tip or did they really have a system?

And there was another little mystery that had been playing on his mind for the last few days, which he was determined to solve.

Baron's court papers were pumped down the Internet and Lewis was printing them out when Bernice telephoned. They arranged an appointment at Baron's Newport branch for Thursday; she had a sweet telephone voice and she gave him the name of the man he would need to meet, a Mr

Howard Raine, the manager of the Newport branch.

Her cautious tone suggested that the outcome of his meeting with Raine was important. Lewis was disheartened, concerned that O'Neill might be proved right after all. Bernice, as a 'purchaser', must have had the authority to instruct him on the one case, but he was suspecting that any ongoing instruction would be Mr Raine's decision.

The formal business concluded he said, "Bernice, you might know this because you're the jet-setting type." He heard a good-humoured huff at the compliment. "Name me a Swiss city."

"Geneva, Zurich," she answered.

"Four letters, second letter 'e'."

"Oh right, em, Bern?"

"Bern?" he asked, with a frown.

"The capital of Switzerland," she clarified.

"Bern, yeah of course," he said, clearing his throat to hide his embarrassment.

"Why do you ask?"

"Oh, it's just a stupid crossword. It's been driving me crazy."

He wrote Bern into the crossword when he got home. Somehow it seemed right that he should do so, even though his theory made it completely unnecessary. He was throwing the word *Bern* around in his head as he ate a takeaway curry and forced down two naan breads, which he knew to be the most fattening thing on an Indian menu. He could almost feel his crazy metabolism breaking the fat down even as he ate. Weighed down and clutching his stomach he had two cigarettes, one after another, eventually tasting the tobacco through the chilli.

He signed on to find another e-mail from Farthing. com.

Lewis, welcome.

So we come to our purpose.

We take it any doubts have been removed. You will be disappointed, no doubt, that we told to observe rather than joining in the enterprise. Do not be disheartened, for your patience will be rewarded.

Click to continue.

He clicked, thinking that for a smart organisation they weren't so smart.

Tomorrow we will tell you of a small company dealing in pharmaceuticals. It is an English company but the directors have been developing a new treatment for breast cancer in their Swiss clinics.

We will of course be requiring you to subscribe before we supply you with the company's name. As a professional man you will understand that the subscription price will be commensurate with the service.

Your servants, sir

Lewis' eyes wandered over to the magazine, The Shilling, languishing on his coffee table.

He had his self-satisfied smile, the one he reserved solely for himself when he was particularly pleased with his analytical skills.

BERN

The rain was beating against the glass, the water dribbling through the ill-fitting rubber inside the window frames. On the wharf, when the weather raged, the apartment was like a ship: the window would bend and creak with the stress of a mighty suspension bridge and the plastic tiles on the roof above would chatter irritably.

Lewis had The Shilling on his lap. It was closed, for he was considering the cover as he attempted to recall his dialogue with Emily.

Something of an exclusive club... my subscription's coming to an end... you wouldn't believe the good fortune coming your way.

He smiled and nodded.

Low... Lowe Waste Management... Bern... a Swiss company...

Once again he tested the theory in his head.

Emily worked for Farthing.com and she had deliberately left the magazine behind on their behalf. The subscribers to The Shilling were a network of stock market traders and relayed information to each other, but in code to avoid detection. Like ciphers.

That was why there were no adverts... apart from that lady with the poodle.

So why put it in code if it was legal?

To prevent competitors and hacks getting their hands on it, he told himself. Microsoft didn't broadcast its next software breakthrough and Harrier & O'Neill didn't publish a list of its clients. He was satisfied with the answer, even though he knew he was only arguing a case.

The Crown versus Farthing.com and subscribers.

Well, ignorance was bliss. It wasn't his fault if someone was sending him share tips.

He decided to read the article on confidence in the workplace, wondering if it might explain the network in some way; he opened the magazine, and found the right page. The fusty smell of old clothes had gone, he noted, as he settled into the article.

It was a longwinded and lazy recital of psychological techniques to build confidence and assert authority, with the use of body language and self-imaging techniques. Half way through the article he started to scan read, as he would scan read medico-legal reports on whiplash injuries. He yawned. The words were in a small print and the article seemed to go on forever.

Towards the end he frowned, then reversed a few paragraphs. He read one section again, more carefully this time.

Imagine a time, a time in the past or a time in the future, when you are happy, confident and in control. Imagine a time of personal success in the workplace when everyone admires and respects you. Look at yourself standing there. You are successful; you are smart, dedicated, experienced and capable. You deserve respect. You deserve to be admired, don't you?

Close your eyes and keep that image of yourself firmly in your mind. Remember that success is no more than your self- perception, while confidence is the outward expression of inner belief.

Now, step into your body and feel the power rushing through you. The strength becomes a second skin. Glory in the power that is generating through you. You can do anything now. Anything. And if your boss takes on so, think of him under your boot, your boot pressing down on his face, squeezing so hard his weasel eyes pop out of his fucking head.

Self-visualisation is a technique used the world over to build strength and confidence. Athletes often have it as part of their training program. The theory was first expounded...

He re-read the section, then the whole article, slowly and carefully. It took him half an hour, but he found nothing else in the same vein. Perhaps the writer had got bored towards the end and just decided to drop it in. Then again, it could be another code, a message hidden in a long boring piece of text.

He needed to offer up these explanations in his head because he didn't want to admit to himself that he felt uncomfortable, just as he had felt uncomfortable when he turned to that centre spread of the shears woman, the first time he had flicked through. The section in the article was inappropriate and crass; it interfered with his sense of ease.

He took a sneak look at Mary Stone, the beauty on the first page; he was starting to fantasise about her a little and almost believed that he could see a little more of her ample cleavage, that whatever she was wearing had slipped just a little. As before, he admired her neck and dainty ear. Her skin was almost too perfect, and it was almost a relief when he noticed for the first time a small pockmark above her left eyebrow.

He liked the way she was looking to his left, but with the face front switch of her eyes towards the camera. This wasn't an amateur photograph, he decided; there was such a sense of immediacy the cameraman must have told her to look at the camera just as he snapped his photograph, for the result was an illusion of blurred movement. On both occasions when Lewis had turned to her page he had imagined that her eyes had darted towards him.

He made his way back to the twins. He had already noticed that the right twin had a weathered appearance, but now he made out a few wrinkles round her eyes. That was odd, and not because her twin looked as youthful as ever, but because he couldn't remember seeing the wrinkles the first time. He frowned and pulled his fine hair back over his ears with three fingers. Perhaps the photographs were holograms: his grandmother used to have a picture of a Japanese lady who used to wink at him as he walked past.

A particularly aggressive gust of howling wind rocked the window frame, bending it in and lifting him from his studies. Whenever this happened he had the nightmare image of the glass shattering, but as always the crisis passed and the weather retreated.

Returning to the magazine, and taking a breath, he turned to the double page spread of the naked woman with the open garden shears. He slowly turned the magazine lengthways. Once more he found the photograph difficult to focus on, feeling conflicted by her hostility and by his own salacious curiosity. The picture arrived in his mind in snapshots: her eyes, narrowed, her mouth, scowling, her left elbow, a knee, both red as if she had carpet burns; one of her petite breasts, boasting small but angry scars that looked as if they may have been made with a serrated knife. His eyes wandered upwards to her hands and the shears. He frowned again, then shook his head and put the magazine aside.

He had set his alarm early, almost an hour before he had to go through his morning routine, although he found it torture getting out of bed even though the buzzer was going. He had cramps in his legs.

Still, this was important: the share tip for Lowe had arrived early in the morning and he spent the hour online waiting for the e-mail to arrive. He went through six cigarettes as he sat back staring blankly at the portal, putting this particular binge down to the stress and boredom of the wait, but he was aware that he had been smoking more over the past few days. He was buying packets of twenty again.

He considered his watch and sighed; it was nearly time to go to work, but perhaps he could nip home at lunchtime. When he looked up, the e-mail was there, 'Farthing.com sends its felicitations'.

Lewis,

Someone has been very opportune.

So, you purchased the company. In spite of our caveat, you took advantage of our generosity.

Nothing is for free.

Click to continue.

What the hell did you expect me to do? he fumed. He banged his mouse.

We bid you farewell. Your servants, sir

'I don't believe this,' he whispered, then clicked 'reply to e-mail' and typed out a short message. *Dear Farthing.com. Please accept my apologies for buying Lowe*

Waste Management; I'm afraid I didn't quite understand how important this was to you. I'm prepared to pay any subscription you want.

He clicked 'send' and the AOL symbol spun briefly before the computer went dead with a dull pop. Cursing, he smacked the monitor with the flat of his hand and felt a sting; he considered the palm of his hand, which was glowing and tingling. Gingerly now he touched the monitor with two fingers, then pulled them away like lightning.

"Shit!"

The monitor was red hot.

He spent most of the morning pretending to work, but really licking the blisters on his fingertips and thinking about Farthing.com.

So, Lowe must have been some sort of initiation test. Well sod them; he didn't need to join, because he only needed one more success like Lowe Waste Management. He had almost £12,000 in cash, and with the money in his current account, if he cancelled all his direct debits, he could bring it up to around £15,000. They hadn't given him the name of the company, but there couldn't be that many small pharmaceutical companies listed in the stock exchange with a Swiss connection. If he could just find it, and buy it before the cancer treatment was announced.

He logged on to Yahoo, cross-referenced the information and came up with five likely candidates, small pharmaceutical companies with under a million capitalisation. He switched to the Bloomberg terminal but the information on the companies gave no hint of anything Swiss.

One of the five, however, a company called Clear Medical, was a recent floatation. He remembered that Lowe was also recently floated, and as a recent issue the accounts of the old limited company would still be available. There was no time to order a search, so he decided to drive down to Companies House, which was only ten minutes away if he was prepared to risk the speed cameras.

Companies House, a division of the civil service long ago cast out into the sticks, was a grey and featureless complex of buildings with a guard who just waved him through the already open barrier. It was noon by the time he was at a screen sifting through Clear Medical's annual returns, his heart pounding. The last twenty minutes had been stressful for he had been walking in circles as he waited for the company microfiche, ignoring the irritated looks of the staff. He even dived ahead of someone to get to an available screen, barely muttering an apology. He scrolled greedily through the company's records.

Registered office, London. Damn. Directors' addresses? London. Shit. Directors' nationality, English. Well, that was it then.

With a resigned face he scrolled back to the previous annual return. It was the same information, as he expected. He scrolled back to the first return filed and blinked as he studied the screen. Bingo. Directors' residence, Bern, Switzerland. Nationality, Swiss. The directors must have changed their citizenship shortly after arriving in the UK.

He considered the screen awhile with his smug private smile. Then he was out of his chair and racing out of the building as fast as his legs would carry him.

Clear Medical's share price fortunately hadn't moved and there were no announcements. It was 12.45 by the time he had pumped £14,800 into Clear Medical at 6.5p and as the buy order was acknowledged he breathed a sigh of relief and sagged back into his chair. The running had taken it out of him and he was patting his forehead and his neck with his handkerchief, but to no avail. He lit a cigarette and coughed.

He forced himself to relax by thinking of something else: he needed to buy a new computer and made a mental note to go to PC World on Saturday. While he was at it, he would change his e-mail address to stop Farthing.com sending him any more viruses. Bastards. He would have sued them if he knew who they were.

He supposed that buying a new computer didn't make much sense if he was off to Spain in a couple of weeks; he admitted to a nagging doubt in his stomach over the whole Spain idea, but he didn't want to think about that now.

He carried out a task on one of his files before checking the price for Clear Medical, again. It hadn't moved but it had only been an hour.

He moved on to another task and spoke into his Dictaphone in a bored monotone. After about an hour he stopped.

If Farthing were going to send the name of the company anyway, why have the cipher 'Bern'?

He checked his portal again and considered the share price suspiciously. There was still no movement.

He lit another cigarette.

The bang of the squash ball, the sweat pouring out of him as he ran from wall to wall, was just what he needed that evening. He had been thinking too much recently.

As usual Lewis won the first game before being demolished by BB on the next three. BB kept telling him to give up smoking.

After the game they had a pint of orange juice and sparkling water in the bar. BB, a handsome man with a Roman nose and an equally prominent chin, rarely sweated after a game; he was looking composed and healthy as he talked about this new venture which planned to sell Welsh tourist information over the Internet. He wasn't sure how the nuts and bolts fitted together; the other guy who he was partnered up with was the IT whizz.

Lewis and BB had lost touch for many years; Lewis had sold his saxophone and abandoned his adolescent dream of becoming a rock star in his late twenties. BB was less fortunate: he was cursed with talent and a realistic prospect of success, which he had been duty bound to explore. Now that he was out, completely out, he had been looking for quick financial strategies to make up for the loss of a career. They had met again by chance, two years ago, and found they still had a lot in common.

Over their orange juices Lewis told him about The Shilling, Farthing.com, Lowe Waste Management and Clear Medical. He told the story slowly and carefully, pausing to drink his juice when anyone walked near the table. BB found Lewis' caution amusing. He was three years older than Lewis, and what had once been a right of seniority in their youth now existed in the form of sceptical protectiveness. He had never offered any reproach for losing his meagre savings on the stock tips; the decision made, the damage done, he had put it down to his own folly.

"Clear Medical," BB murmured. "Has it gone up?"

"Not yet."

BB shook his head and drained his glass. Lewis was starting to feel uncomfortable as he tested the facts again; things seemed less clear to him now that he had actually told the story, out-loud, rather than just throwing theories around in his head.

"It'll go up, BB, you'll see," Lewis declared. "Buy some."

BB made a grating noise in his throat and shook his head. "I've got to say it, Lew," he said, "I think you're barmy. This looks wrong to me."

"Well I agree it could be insider trading," Lewis responded, "but that can't rebound on *me*. As far as I'm concerned I'm reading stock tips. The Sunday newspapers have stock tips." Lewis offered him a reasonable smile.

"That's not what I mean. And I don't believe it's insider trading anyway. I think it's a con."

Lewis reached for a cigarette, before remembering he couldn't smoke in the bar. His hands were shaking and he put them in the pockets of his fleece.

"What do you mean?" Lewis asked casually.

BB tapped his empty glass on the table. "Have you seen *The Sting*? You know, the film with Robert Redford and Robert Shaw?"

"Yeah…"

"Well this is a classic sting, isn't it? You're given a tip, but you wouldn't have put too much money into it because you're sceptical. Then, the clever bit, they pretend to get angry with you, make you hunt out the next one. That sweeps away any remaining doubts that you had and you bet your house. You bet your house because you think it's the end of the line and that you won't get another chance."

The colour was draining from Lewis' face. "So you think they deliberately pumped up Lowe to make me put everything into Clear Medical?"

BB flicked his glass to see if it hummed. "Mind you, they probably thought you had a lot more cash than you actually have. I bet they're sick as pigs that all their time has been spent for only fifteen grand, and most of that is their own money from the first sale. That's probably why they didn't contact *me*. I haven't got a regular job, but you look good on paper: a single professional guy in his late thirties with a fashionable postcode."

"So you think Clear Medical is a sham company?"

"Waiting to fold, money to be directed to a secret Swiss bank account, perhaps? Didn't you say that the directors wanted to disguise their Swiss nationality?"

Lewis drooped in his seat and whispered the word 'fuck'.

"You've got to admire it, the setup I mean," BB mused. "Giving the image of some secret society with this magazine thing; and the crossword... well... that's a masterpiece. People are far more ready to believe something if they work it out for themselves, aren't they?"

Lewis nodded despondently. BB frowned and said, "I'm surprised you're so bothered, Lew. You're giving it all up anyway, aren't you? You're going to Spain and everything. And it's not as if you had that much to start with."

Lewis nodded again. "I know," he muttered. "But it's been a good week for me, up until now. I've even got a new client who I'm seeing tomorrow. Somehow, impossibly, I thought my luck was changing."

BB took the point and his expression showed regret at having trivialised the whole thing. "I could be wrong, Lew," he said softly.

"You're not wrong," Lewis muttered. "If you were me, what would you do?"

"Well, obviously, sell the shares first thing tomorrow morning. You might be lucky. Remember, they're not expecting you to have figured it out yet, so there may still be time. Then, I'd have a word with this Emily woman."

"Emily – of course! Hell, I'll ring the agency *now*." Lewis reached into his bag for his mobile, but BB stopped him by putting his hand on the bag.

"Sell the shares first," BB said. "It may be that she was just told to leave a magazine at your place, so she won't be any help anyway. But if she's in on it, she'll give you some bullshit and then send word straight back to the directors, won't she? They'll make sure Clear Medical goes super nova pronto. No, wait until you've got your money."

Lewis hesitated, and then leaned back in his seat. "God, you're right," he said. "BB... *you* should have been the lawyer."

BB shrugged with the attitude of things past are things past, things lost are lost forever. He got up for a refill from the bar.

As soon as he got home Lewis went straight to the crossword and studied the clues. He had the notion that he could put BB's theory to the test; if a third clue gave the name of a company, or the clue for a company, Farthing. com could be a genuine organisation.

He scanned the clues.

She says.

Stupid stupid song.

Published in a mirror out of town.

What kind of clues were they? Eventually he found one that he could do.

Made the fires... Lit *the fires.*

He wrote in *Lit* then tried 3 down again, with the benefit of the newly acquired first letter 'L'. *Do not accept it.* Some contract law point? Offer... acceptance... he was reminded of the advert at the back of the magazine for the carbolic smoke ball.

He sighed and said goodnight to Mary Stone. She didn't seem so happy tonight, as if her stately smile has lost some of its crease around her cheeks and her eyes had narrowed by just a fraction. He knew how she felt. He flicked distastefully to the woman with the garden shears, frowned, then dumped the magazine on the coffee table.

As he was drifting into sleep he was thinking of companies that could have any connection with the word *Lit*.

But he knew BB was right: the rest of the crossword was probably all gobbledegook and there *were* no answers to the clues. That made sense actually, if they only intended feeding him Low and Bern.

First thing tomorrow morning, he was selling.

He rang his broker bang on 8 a.m. as the market opened. He was told that he couldn't place a trade on Clear Medical at the moment because the shares had been suspended. They were suspended before the open. Why? Because the directors had called a creditors' meeting... no, the announcement didn't say any more than that... no, there was no other news. Place an order to sell immediately that the suspension was lifted? Certainly, to sell at best price. Yes, at best, immediately after the suspension was lifted.

Lewis was laughing ironically as he stepped into the lift, but he had a defeated expression as the doors closed.

LIT

The one bonus arising out of his misfortune was that he no longer gave a damn whether Howard Raine liked him or not. Spain was calling again. Fired up aggression had never been his style – he had always believed in reason and fair play – but he was ready to take a bite at anyone now.

Baron Enterprises was nowhere near the industrial estates and the route had required twenty minutes of country roads. As he approached he saw the smoke over the trees. He pulled up into a cleared area of uneven waste ground, which presumably served as a car park, although there were no cars, and as he turned off the ignition he looked at the building. The factory was rather quaint, old fashioned in an industrial sort of way, more like a workhouse with its drab exterior and tall stone chimneys.

He was still imagining new methods of torture and death for the proprietors of Farthing.com as he got out of the car. Bernice was already at the entrance, waiting for him.

"Hello again," he said, with a peck on her cheek. He knew he was being too forward from the way she stiffened, but he didn't care. He didn't recognise her perfume, but it was subtle and reminded him of jasmine and spring. He appreciated scent; he had always worn the best aftershave, today it was Jaipur, notwithstanding that from about 10 a.m. onwards he only smelled of stale cigarette smoke.

"Mr Raine is ready for you, Lewis," she said. "I've told

him all about you." He picked up on the hesitation in her voice, and also noticed that she was wearing a little more make-up this time, just some eyeliner and pale red lipstick. God, she looked good.

She led him through what appeared to be the clerical wing of the factory, although the furnishings were bare, almost non-existent; there was the occasional antique chair, and he saw two small framed pictures of adverts for Pears soap and cough mixture. The teak reception desk was unmanned and as he walked past he imagined he saw a layer of dust on its surface, but put the effect down to the soft lighting coming from imitation oil lamps. Behind the reception he noticed the flicker of a computer screen. The computer discreetly tucked away, together with the faint banging in the distance, were at least confirmations that this was a factory and not a museum.

"Where is everyone?" he asked. The floor was untreated stone and his voice, like their footsteps, echoed.

"The receptionists only work part time," she answered. "Actually, I've never met them."

"That can't be good for business," he remarked.

She quickly shook her head. "It makes no difference. Only a few people have our telephone number, and we deliberately chose a remote location. You'll understand why when Mr Raine has explained what we do."

They were passing through a corridor, the stone walls grey, chipped and made incongruous by imitation candles on wooden pedestals, nailed in at regular intervals.

"You're worried about this meeting, aren't you?" he asked.

"A little," she confessed.

"Why?"

He accompanied the question with a sideways glance; they were the same height with Bernice in heels.

"The lawyer in London I told you about, he was my

choice, as you know," she said. She stopped at a featureless wooden door and her plaintive sigh told Lewis this was the door to Raine's office. Some distorted messages could be heard over the tannoy, calling someone to a certain room for an immediate something or other, and the crackle of electrical voices made her shiver. "Mr Raine never liked the solicitor, to tell you the truth, and I sort of stuck my neck out, I suppose. Even though we were losing the cases I convinced Mr Raine to keep using him. Well, Mr Raine was right and he hasn't let me forget it."

No first name terms here, Lewis was thinking. O'Neill was positively cuddly compared to the sound of this Raine character.

"You can't blame yourself," Lewis said, "and I don't even think the lawyer was to blame either, if I'm being truthful. He was probably very good indeed. You shouldn't rule out using him again."

A quick frown registered her surprise at his statement as she carefully knocked the door; he smiled at her, acknowledging the riddle he had posed, the lawyer who was talking himself out of work. She cast a vulnerable figure as she waited for her knock to be acknowledged, like some abandoned urchin in need of protection, and he felt a strong compulsion to kiss her, there, in the corridor. It would be so simple; a hand on her shoulder to gently turn her towards him, a soft "don't worry… I'll look after you", then reaching over, their lips touching…

He resisted the urge, but as the door opened and he entered the room he felt as if his feet were on fire.

Howard Raine's office was in keeping with the factory. The desk where he was seated held a computer, a telephone, a fountain pen and a white unlit candle. There were four straight-backed chairs, lined neatly against a wall, a filing cabinet in one corner. These furnishings aside, the room was empty and Lewis wondered if they were waiting for their furnishing suppliers and decorators to visit; perhaps they needed the candles because there were power cuts in this remote location. Again, the stone walls were unpainted, although one small-framed picture was in place on the wall behind the desk. Lewis could see that it was a black and white photograph, but he was unable to make out its detail. It was taken at a great distance; there were some people standing outside what appeared to be a long warehouse. They were standing awkwardly, as if they had been forced to hold a formal pose.

Raine was a middle-aged man with a round yet solemn face and thinning salt and pepper hair, carefully combed from a high side parting. He had long sideburns but otherwise he was very closely shaved and dressed immaculately in a dark narrow-lapelled suit, with a white cravat. He acknowledged Lewis with a nod and slid over a confidentiality agreement with his left hand, offering his fountain pen with his right. Taking the document and the pen Lewis noticed that the man had no wristwatch; an odd imagining led him to think that he had a far more ornate timepiece secreted in his waistcoat.

The confidentiality agreement stated that all matters discussed relating to Baron's operations were secret and not to be disclosed and Lewis considered the fountain pen as he signed it; it was a normal ink pen, thankfully not a feather with a scratchy nib.

What the hell is this Dickensian thing all about? Lewis wondered, feeling as if he was in a scene from Bleak House. He resolved to question Bernice about this after the meeting, as he pulled up one of the uncomfortable chairs and sat opposite Raine with his e-mailed file on his lap. Bernice also took a chair but sat a little further away from the desk.

Raine's explanation of the business was sketchy:

Baron used a process called Articulating Resistance Energy, an inventive method of reducing, sometimes removing altogether, the need for fuel injection. It was a gravitational and stress-factored form of energy. All the products were protected under patent but the customer base – vehicle manufacturers mostly – were also under strict agreement not to disclose the process. There was a government partnership on the secrecy element too, on both sides of the Atlantic: the technology was still in its infancy and they didn't want to ring any alarm bells with the oil-producing nations.

Bernice was nodding in nervous agreement as Raine talked and Lewis could see why she was so scared of him. Raine had a cold, distant manner but also there was something rather strained about his delivery, as if he was saying lines in a play where he needed prompting from the pits. Speaking to subordinates appeared a chore for him, requiring effort. Lewis imagined that the man would be quite frightening when angered.

Baron's problem was the number of claims being spurred on by an aggressive union presence, Raine went on to explain. There were accidents on the shop floor; lots and lots of accidents.

"Because," Lewis suggested, "the employees aren't permitted to know how this process works and this makes health and safety training impossible."

Raine had been looking at the opposite wall as he talked but now came to a stop. He clearly didn't appreciate being interrupted, but he ran a finger down the wide parting of his hair as a signal that Lewis' assessment was not completely wide of its mark.

"And when plastic coils shoot out of production holes for no apparent reason," Lewis continued, "you've got no choice but to settle because you can't risk explaining the process in court." He was referring to the file on his lap, which was labelled *Mr Vernon Jones, production worker, assembly site B. Accident, 20/6/01.*

Raine took out an e-mail from his desk drawer, the short advice Lewis had sent to Bernice yesterday. "They're demanding... demanding... one hundred and fifty thousand pounds in damages," he read sourly. "You say it is worth a maximum of... ah, of eighty thousand." He set the e-mail aside. "We have to settle the claim at any cost, Mr Coin."

Lewis shrugged. "If you want to pay them what they're asking, then you don't need me. All you need is your chequebook." He sensed that Bernice was tensing.

Raine made full eye contact for the first time. "So, what do you propose?" he inquired. "We've fought claims before and we've lost." Bernice looked at the floor guiltily when he said this.

"That's because the union sees you coming," Lewis said. "They know the cases that you'll fight, the cases that don't involve the process itself. Bernice has told me that your witnesses changed their evidence in the box, so I wouldn't be surprised if the claims were rigged to trap you in court, to teach you a lesson and to stop you defending anything else." He held up the file. "But they're not expecting you to challenge this one. They're expecting you to bend over, as usual. We need to take the fight to the union for a change, trip them up, get them paying costs, increase their membership subscription fees."

Raine considered Lewis with a bemused pursing of his thin colourless lips, then sat back in his chair. He wasn't convinced, but he seemed impressed all the same.

"Let me see what I can do," Lewis offered. "I'll sound out the other side, do some digging and report back here in a few weeks."

"Don't think you'll have any success... success with the union lawyer," Raine said in a sly whisper. "The man doesn't deal."

"Really," Lewis returned.

Raine nodded slowly, his lips now finding a lizard smile. "Our last lawyer was afraid of him, I think. I know that Ms Connor… ah, Ms Connor is afraid of him."

Lewis glanced at Bernice and saw her face redden. He was starting to realise why the poor girl had no self-confidence.

"I'm sure you're right," Lewis said in an even voice. "I'm sure the union lawyer is very cocksure. Your payout history has seen to that."

Raine's expression darkened at the subtle rebuke, but only momentarily so. "Well, do what you can," he said, reaching over and offering his hand across the desk. As Lewis took it he detected the rank smell of stale clothes, but was careful to keep his eyes on Raine as he acknowledged the curt nod.

When Lewis got to his car he quickly lit a cigarette. Bernice followed him out shortly afterwards; she was carrying Vernon Jones' personnel file, which Lewis had requested.

Lewis knew that Bernice wasn't a smoker, but his craving had now overcome his desire to impress her. "Trying to give up," he murmured, as she noticed the cigarette.

"That's easy," she declared, "just stop lighting them."

He chuckled. "Just stop lighting them. Right. Now why didn't I think of that?" He took a second long drag of his cigarette then stamped it out on the floor. "You okay, Bernice?" he asked.

Her face brightened. "Lewis, I thought you were wonderful in there. Thank you." There was a measure of relief in her tone, but neither her face nor her words carried any romantic invitation. He knew he looked like a stick and he wondered at what point in their brief relationship she had noticed his physique.

"Raine isn't so bad," he said, shrugging off the compliment. "Look, I know this job's important to you, Bernice, but do yourself a favour and relax more. Everything'll be okay." He had a pang of guilt as he wondered what Raine would say to her when she announced that the new lawyer had just run off to Spain. She handed him the personnel file and he clicked his briefcase open and steadied it on his knee. Half a dozen Mars bars fell out which he quickly collected up.

"How many?" she asked, amused and putting a hand to her mouth.

"I can eat anything," he murmured.

"Lucky you," she said, patting her hips. He smiled at her; she was wearing a jacket and skirt that was a little more fitted this time and he had already noted that she was curvy, about half a stone away from being plump... his taste precisely.

"Nah, it's a curse," he said. "No matter how many I eat I still can't get a pound over 10 stone, and I'm five foot ten."

She sighed. "I can imagine worse burdens," she said quietly.

"Bernice, what's with the Victorian thing?" he asked, as he got into his car. He had been waiting for the right time to ask this question and her aside on 'burdens' went over his head.

"What do you mean?" she asked.

"The décor and everything."

She glanced back round at the building. "It's no mystery," she said. "Baron buys derelict sites. They keep them looking derelict so as not to attract attention from competitors. This was a nineteenth century building so they thought they should just keep it in character." She shrugged good-naturedly. "They don't spend a lot of money on furnishings."

Lewis nodded forlornly as he put his key in the ignition. He supposed that the furnishings were already here when they moved in and Baron was just a skinflint organisation. So much for the idea of asking for a high hourly rate. But he was still confused.

"What about Mr Raine then?" he asked.

"I don't understand."

"The way he was dressed... the cravat and..."

"And what?"

Lewis didn't continue. Just because Raine wasn't wearing a wristwatch didn't mean he used a waistcoat timepiece, and his cravat was no more eccentric than O'Neill's colourful bow ties. Lots of people used fountain pens...

"You really were wonderful in there, Lewis," she repeated.

He winked at her as he drove off, but by the time he was back on the motorway the success of the meeting was long behind him. He was back to thinking about the money he had lost and his new burden: Bernice Connor of Baron Enterprises and the certain knowledge that he was going to let her down.

Friday morning arrived like a hangover.

As he struggled out of bed his legs were wobbling. He had gone to bed after a movie, having sipped only two glasses of wine, but he felt as if he had done three laps around the city during the night. As he reached for his dressing gown he gasped with a sudden pain in his left side. He had a bruise there; he must have fallen out of bed at some point.

He put his uneven sleep pattern down to the stress of the week and resolved to keep himself busy to take his mind off the share fiasco. It was bin day and into the black bag that he pulled around the apartment went The Shilling. He dragged the bag after him into the lift and then, outside the apartment complex, he lobbed it into the stone storage room. He gave a final glance at the black bag before he pulled the door shut.

In the office he received an e-mail from Bernice, briefly telling him that Mr Raine was very impressed and would be monitoring the Vernon Jones case with interest. Lewis smiled when he read it, thinking that precious Mr Raine could go and stick his head up his arse. But he was still feeling guilty about Bernice; he had decided to at least have a stab at settling the Jones claim, to help restore Bernice's reputation, before he quit.

With this in mind he made a telephone call to the union solicitor, one Simon Marker, a partner in a small firm in Manchester that he had never heard of. The firm may be small, Lewis was thinking as he dialled, but they were doing well if they received all the litigation from the twelve plants. Even the letterhead looked aggressive, specifying interviews by appointment only, written communications only by e-mail. This was going to be a difficult conversation, for which Lewis would normally have a cigarette on stand by. His cigarettes were in his jacket, which was on a hanger on the door and he wouldn't be able to fetch them while he was on the telephone. He had decided to hang up, fetch his cigarettes then redial when his call was answered. An automated voice put him straight through to Marker. Marker muttered a quiet "yes" and Lewis quickly introduced himself.

"So, new blood," came the response.

"I'm acting on the Vernon Jones claim," Lewis clarified.

"Just that one, Mr Coin?"

"That's right."

"So, on a trial run, are we?"

Lewis was in no mood for this. He had spoken to too many arrogant claimant lawyers in his time not to know where this was going. "I'm ringing to sound you out on a settlement…" he began.

"No need to sound me out, Mr Coin," Marker rasped back. "You've seen my valuation of the claim."

"I have, and you can't support it. The…"

"What do you mean that I can't support it?"

"As I'm trying to say…"

"I take exception to the inference, Mr Coin. My Statement of Truth accompanies the schedule of loss."

"Yes, I know, but…"

"Are you suggesting the claim is fabricated?"

"I didn't say that…"

"Are you saying that I have inflated the claim?"

"No, I…"

"Good. I am gratified that you are not inferring that my client and I are liars. So, do you have an offer to make?"

"Well I would like to discuss the case…"

"I'm not interested in discussions, Mr Coin. Do you have an offer to make?"

Lewis' eyes narrowed. He didn't answer.

"MR COIN – DO YOU HAVE AN OFFER TO MAKE?" Every word in the sentence was emphasised as if he was speaking to someone who was both stupid and deaf.

Lewis frowned. "No," he said, putting the phone down.

He took some deep breaths. Oddly enough, it felt good; really disliking someone new was like a jolt of adrenalin. He was even ready for O'Neill when he strolled into the office shortly afterwards to obtain a resume of the meeting. Lewis didn't give him all the details, the confidentiality agreement forefront in his mind, but told him enough to satisfy him that it was worth the trip. O'Neill listened patiently and offered Lewis one of his full strength Benson & Hedges, which Lewis declined, tapping his chest.

"What about the hourly rate?" O'Neill asked.

"Bernice, that's the purchaser, has said that I should charge what I normally charge for the moment."

O'Neill nodded and said, "Good, charge them a hundred and twenty an hour then."

"Fine," Lewis returned, "although I don't think we'll do so well if more work comes our way."

"Why not?"

"They struck me as being a bit miserly. I think they'll squeeze us below a hundred an hour. Bernice has mentioned they have a fixed fee scale but she's not allowed to tell me what it is. Who knows? It could be as low as seventy-five if there's to be bulk instruction."

O'Neill was about to say something, but changed his mind. For a split second the two men had a moment of empathy; they both knew that the firm needed the work no matter what charging rate was on offer. "Do your best," O'Neill said eventually, getting up. "It sounds as if you've done rather well already."

Lewis nodded, as always puzzled and irritated when O'Neill showed his nice side, challenging the image of the tyrant boss.

Stuart came in to see Lewis next, anxiously seeking his help on an unfortunate landlord and tenant case that O'Neill had dumped on him, which was grossly unprepared for a trial in a few weeks' time. Lewis did his best to help, explaining how to get subpoenas issued at short notice and offering advice on how to locate the witnesses who should have been proofed a year ago. Stuart wrote it all down gratefully.

"Thanks Lewis, you're a real mate," Stuart said as they wrapped up.

Lewis waved away the thanks. "They don't warn you

about O'Neill in Law School, do they?" he murmured.

It was the middle of the afternoon by the time Lewis was alone again. He could almost smell that Friday 5.30 lager now, the best part of the week, without doubt.

As he sat back he realised that he hadn't had a single cigarette all day. It hadn't been intentional; he just hadn't had the time to smoke one. Well, there was no phone ringing now, no interruptions and he walked defiantly over to his jacket and took out his packet of Silk Cut. Back at his desk he put one in his mouth just as the phone rang. It was his bank, informing him that the suspension on Clear Medical had been lifted and his shares sold.

He groaned and put the cigarette down, unlit. It looked as if the creditors had made short work of the company if it had only taken twenty-four hours to work through the money. 'Did I get anything for them at all?' he asked in a resigned voice.

"I'm bringing up the details now," said the clerk. "Yes, Clear Medical sold at fifty-two pence per share."

Lewis nodded wearily, then frowned. "Did you say fifty-two pence *per share*?" he asked.

"Fifty-two pence per share, Mr Coin. The company was temporarily suspended because of an announcement on a breast cancer treatment: it's being taken over."

Lewis opened his mouth but no words came.

"Mr Coin?"

"Yes. Sorry."

"You have almost one hundred and twenty thousand pounds in your account. Would you like to place any trades?"

Lewis' face had drained of colour. The telephone was shaking in his hand. "Er, no. Transfer it into my bank account."

"Your current account?"

"Yes."

"Wouldn't you prefer a higher interest account?"

"No. Thank you."

He carefully replaced the telephone and stared at it blankly for a few moments, before his face creased into a wide smile.

One hundred and twenty thousand pounds... sitting in my account...

Oh my God... I'm saved...

Then his face dropped, as he remembered a certain magazine that the bin men would have collected this morning.

He had recently got into the habit of having a Friday drink with Stuart and other members of the firm, in one of the trendy pubs that caught the after work custom and which were very busy until about 7p.m.. Stuart, through his connections with the trainee associations, knew a lot of young female lawyers and Lewis needed the introductions. Today, however, he went straight home and on arrival mournfully poked his head around the door of the storage room.

So, BB was wrong, and he was right, The Shilling was a traders network. Driving home he had been trying to picture the crossword in his mind, but without success. He remembered most of the clues but he needed the boxes to give him the length of the answers. *Lit*, he suspected, was only part of a name, or perhaps a clue, to the next share tip.

All the black bags in the storage room were gone; the bin men didn't always turn up, but they did today.

But there was his magazine, The Shilling, on the damp stone floor. He picked it up and after pacing around in confusion for a few moments remembered that he hadn't tied up his bag. One of the bin men must have noticed it at the top and had a read through before casting it aside. Lewis shook his head, unhappy at the thought of a stranger's hands on his treasure.

His disdain increased in the lift as he noticed that the magazine had picked up a smell. He couldn't place the smell, but it was faintly inappropriate, most probably a combination of the remains of his Wednesday curry and the bin man's body odour.

The lift juddered to a halt and he dropped the magazine and punched the buttons. Damn it. This had happened to him twice before, and the first time it happened he nearly went crazy. The lift was small with no mirror and on the control panel there was a telephone number in case of emergencies, but no telephone. His mobile was in the car and so he cursed his mobile and cursed the lift.

Come on, come on. He punched the buttons again and the power returned and the lift moved. With a deep sigh of relief he leant down to pick up The Shilling. It had fallen open at the first page, Mary Stone's page.

The moment was fleeting, just a flash in his mind's eye to be stored as some obscure and unreliable image in his memory. When he would re-visit it he would see himself collecting the magazine from the floor, his attention on the lift doors, which had started to open.

His eyes were still on the doors as he stood up with the magazine in his hand. He closed the page and his attention switched to the portrait photograph before the front cover locked it away.

He was already walking out of the lift before his brain reported a curiosity: that Mary Stone's eyes were closed, her face contorted, as if on the point of orgasm.

He spent the evening savouring the thought of the money in his bank account, and studying the crossword. Eventually he found the answer to a clue, the answer having been in front of him all the time.

The Shilling says...

Fashion. Ambition. Temptation. *FAT.*

Was this another part of a share tip? he wondered, as he wrote in *Fat* and his restless fingers found his wine bottle. Red wine had never tasted so sweet as the revelations of the day finally sunk in. He wasn't smoking though: he had left his cigarettes in his car in his eagerness to get to the storage room, and he hadn't fancied the prospect of fetching them and using the lift again so soon. It now occurred to him that he hadn't smoked all day. In all the excitement, he had simply forgotten to smoke.

It had been so easy. What was it Bernice had said? *Just stop lighting them.*

But no one just forgot to smoke: it was in the nature of addiction that it needed to be served, whatever the circumstances. Perhaps his body had just gone through some kind of chemical reaction to nicotine; maybe that was why he was sleeping so badly, why he imagined that face in the lift.

He sipped his wine and returned to happy thoughts. His debt, his impossible crippling debt, was cleared; he had even gone off the idea of smoking. With the help of the wine he concentrated on these two little miracles, to ignore a series of uncomfortable coincidences.

Part Two:
Riding it

1	across	who do you bring?
2	down	to own
3	across	made the fires
3	down	do not accept it
4	across	no rooms
5	down	the process
6	down	she says
7	down	how many now?
8	across	weight hanger
9	down	The Shilling says

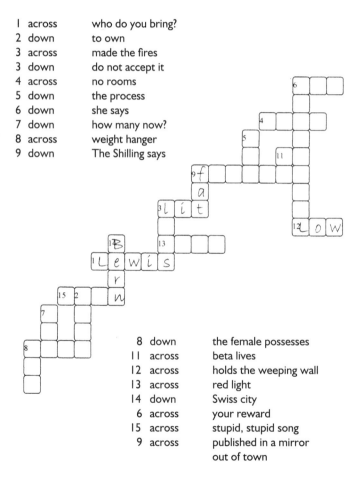

8	down	the female possesses
11	across	beta lives
12	across	holds the weeping wall
13	across	red light
14	down	Swiss city
6	across	your reward
15	across	stupid, stupid song
9	across	published in a mirror out of town

FAT

He had been waking with cramps and bruises, as if he was being mugged in his sleep. That night, for the first time, he remembered his dream.

His bedroom was cast in taupe shadows and a mist was rising from underneath the bed. The Weeping Wall, the music from the Low album, was playing somewhere in the roof, the synthesised chords just faint echoes.

He was overcome with weariness as he lay on his back, so weary he might as well have been strapped down. He knew that he was on the tail end of a long, frenzied dream for his bed sheets were soaked with his sweat.

Yet beyond the exhaustion, he felt the anticipation. He was aware that his body had been guided, checked, guided and checked through the nightlong experience and now as he lay there, he would be released. The sense of shame, the wondrous shame that comes only with forbidden lust, was overpowering.

The twins from The Shilling were on the bed with him, having stepped out of their pages to rouse him in the early hours. They were naked except for fright masks, a kitten with fangs and a blooded Alsatian, which they had pulled on when the third woman appeared. Their bodies were glistening with activity, but they were now in repose at his sides, aimlessly pulling at his chest hairs.

He groaned in his sleep, in ecstasy.

"You know what you like, don'tcha? Don'tcha, my little soldjar?"

Mary Stone was speaking in a Cockney accent and

inclined her head as she introduced her secret voice to him. Her plain white tunic was damp with her exertion but her hands and lips were cold as she moulded him like a potter, massaging him until he was bigger than he had ever been, bigger than he could possibly be.

"All spent, my love?" she asked. In the fog of the dream he met the physical as he felt his approaching orgasm, impossible, unstoppable, and as he braced himself to meet it, the woman with the garden shears marched out of the shadow and snipped.

He woke screaming.

"Fuck! Fuck! Fuck!" he shouted, before finding a semblance of recovery and lying back, exhausted. "Fuck," he whispered.

Eventually he got to sleep again, curled up in a ball, both his hands on his crotch.

It felt good to shop again as he proudly carried his boxed computer out of PC World. That morning he had ritually cut up all his credit cards – after telephoning his bank and paying every one of them off – and had sworn an oath never to have a credit card again.

With the remaining money he put £5,000 into his deposit account for emergencies and allocated £2,000 for the computer and some long- overdue clothes shopping. The rest he made payable to the mortgage company, a grand cheque for £90,000 which he posted on his way out.

After he had set up his new computer he rang AOL to restore his old e-mail address. He supposed that he was still hoping that Farthing.com would contact him again and perhaps, subconsciously, that was the reason he put aside £5000 for 'emergencies'. Remembering the virus, as a precaution he rang his bank again and took out a comprehensive insurance policy that covered his computer, software glitches and all.

All done, he made himself a coffee. It felt strange, not having any shares any more, no more hoping that *The Sunday Times* would be optimistic of a market recovery, no more bracing himself for bad news when he came home and switched on Bloomberg. He felt a sense of release, yet he also missed the excitement, the idea of having lottery tickets that just might come in.

Those days are gone, he reminded himself.

It was midday and he still hadn't smoked. That morning he had decided to build on his previous day's success and although he had given up many times in the past, this time he knew it was different. He felt completely free, for he was certain that he would never smoke again. There were no feelings of regret, of loss, or of sacrifice. No pangs at all.

He wondered if it was the shock to his body yesterday, the sudden nicotine rejection, which caused him to dream last night. Maybe it was even responsible for that odd moment in the lift, when he imagined that Mary Stone's face had changed.

He spent the afternoon on the sofa, listening to music, completely at peace with himself, but by the time he was on the third album he started to wonder whether peace was overrated. Now that his problems were gone, the crisis passed, he realised that he was still unhappy.

Perhaps that was what the dream was telling him. That he was lonely.

God, he needed a woman.

During the week he did a little research on Mr Vernon Jones, production worker in Assembly Site B.

The court papers stated that Jones was confined to his home, unable to drive. The spring coil, which shot out into his back, hadn't caused any fractures but it was a nasty injury and the medical evidence exhibited photographs showing extensive bruising. The orthopaedic consultant considered that Jones had sustained a soft tissue injury with some related nerve damage. He would never be able to work in heavy production again. Baron had agreed this as a joint report, so they were prevented from obtaining further medical evidence.

Lewis rang Bernice and gave her the name of the orthopaedic consultant. He asked her to check the other files to see whether he had been used before. She checked five files and confirmed the consultant has been used on all of them, every time at the invitation of the union. Lewis didn't explain the reason for the inquiry.

From the personnel file he saw that Jones had been a keen footballer before his accident, and had some trials in his teens. He was 23 now and lived in Blackwood, a small valley town, and Lewis rang the town hall to find out the names of the nearest football associations. There were three likely candidates. He rang them all and discovered the club that Vernon had always belonged to. Posing as a talent scout for a national team he asked whether Vernon Jones still played, but was told that Vernon didn't play any more, not since he had been injured. That was a shame, Lewis remarked, as he was coming to their next fixture. When was that? Thursday.

On Thursday evening he stood in the mud, behind a fence watching a local football game, bored out of his mind. The only football he ever watched was the World Cup and close up he was surprised at how brutal and bad amateur football was.

He had put on his oldest pair of jeans and a sweater so as not to look out of place. He looked completely out of place, however, especially when he attempted the odd groan in synch with the small crowd when shots at goal went wide.

He believed he had identified Vernon, a midfielder who

frequently stopped running to rub his lower back and shake off teammates who came up to see how he was. When the game was over, and to make sure of his identity, Lewis raised his hand from behind the fence and shouted, "Hey, Vernon." Vernon looked over, but not recognising him shook his head and dawdled off.

A man next to Lewis asked, "You here to see Vernon then?"

Lewis smiled at the elderly gentleman. "You could say that," he replied. "Do you know him?"

"Well I know his dad. His dad said that Vernon was hoping that someone would be coming along this evening." With his eyes the old man indicated a group of people standing quietly at the other end of the fence. "His Dad's over there if you want to speak to him."

Lewis nodded without looking round. "That's okay, I'm in a bit of a rush right now," he said. "But do me a favour, will you give him my card?" He handed him one of his business cards, Harrier & O'Neill, Solicitors. The man read it and glanced down at the squash bag Lewis was carrying.

"Does he know who you are?" the man asked suspiciously.

"He will."

Friday, early evening, it was Lewis' turn to get a business card, but this time with a home telephone number written across it in biro.

It belonged to a young lady called Gemma, who he had been plucking up the courage to ask out for several months. She was not particularly pretty but she was a cheerful soul and always had a smile ready for him. His suspicion that she was interested was confirmed in spades after he struck up a conversation with her; her hand was on his arm as they talked at the bar, the rest of his crowd observing from a respectable distance. Stuart would put his thumb up to him whenever he looked over and Gemma glanced round a few times, but didn't seem to mind.

As Lewis struggled through the crowd to get to the loo Stuart slapped his hand on his shoulder. "Looks like you're in," he declared. Lewis' fellow junior partners, Graham and Rhys, both married and shortly to go home, raised their pints in salute.

"Must be my lucky night," Lewis said, puzzled. "I'd hoped she liked me, but she's all over me."

"We noticed," Rhys said in his broad, valley accent.

"Stuart, did she say anything to you before, y'know, about me?" Lewis asked.

Stuart shrugged and shook his head. "Don't be so surprised," he declared generously. "You're looking good."

Lewis made a sound between his lips. "Yeah, right."

"You've put on some weight."

"Yeah, right."

In the loo Lewis studied himself in the mirror. It was true; the hollows in his cheeks were gone. He was almost looking healthy and the tightness of his shirt suggested he might even have some weight around his chest and shoulders. It must be giving up the fags, he reflected. Everyone knew that you put on weight when you quitted, although it had never worked for him before.

He took Gemma for a meal an hour later and after that they went home together. The evening was fun, but in the morning he knew that he didn't want to see her again. He found it odd that he was suddenly getting picky, either that or he just couldn't stop thinking about Bernice Connor. If that was true then he was being stupid; he had no chance with someone like Bernice. No chance at all.

He decided it was better to get the conversation over with there and then, knowing Gemma was a friend of

Stuart and he would have to see her again in the bar. He fumbled it. This was really difficult, he realised; it was much easier being on the receiving end. I really value you as a friend... one of those things... not looking for a serious relationship. Unintentionally his words come out ruthlessly in a flat and careless fashion. He was also painfully aware that he had said some things he shouldn't have, last night, to get her into bed.

She was crying when she left the apartment and he felt like a heel.

The next evening he played squash with BB and won for the first time in recent memory. BB congratulated him on giving up the fags and echoed Stuart's comment that he was looking good on it. BB was still taking long breaths in the bar, having been completely unprepared for Lewis' assault on the court.

Lewis took a plastic bag out of his holdall and carefully pulled out The Shilling; the gesture was reminiscent of a holy sword being drawn from a scabbard. He had told BB about the Clear Medical success when they had booked the game, and BB had groaned and said that was another one he had got completely wrong.

"Ah, the famous crossword network," BB, declared. "So, what do we have to go on so far?"

Lewis shook his head reflectively. "*Lit* and *Fat*. I can't make sense of either of them. I've cross referenced on the net for hours." He noticed that BB had his hand out waiting for the magazine; Lewis experienced an unhappy sensation when he passed it over to him, which turned into irritation as BB roughly flicked through it.

"Fat and Lit," BB mused. "Weird magazine. Who's she?"

Lewis lightened up a little. "Well her name is Mary Stone, but I don't know who she is. She's gorgeous, isn't she?"

"Do you think so?" BB asked as he laid her out on the table. "She's okay, I suppose. She's got bad skin."

"She's got beautiful skin," Lewis murmured, baffled. "Okay, so there's a pockmark above her eye."

"No, I don't mean that. Look, there are lumps under her make-up, and she's wearing loads of it."

Lewis glanced at the photograph again, resenting BB's criticism. But he was right. There were blemish shadows on her skin and he now saw that she was plastered with foundation. Her skin had seemed so natural before... perhaps it was the stark bar lighting. BB continued to flick through, lifting his eyebrows when he came to the photograph that required him to turn the magazine on its end. Lewis grunted, motioning to the people at the next table, and BB hurried on, now with a smile.

"I know," Lewis said.

BB stopped at the twins. "Who are they?" he asked.

"Twins," Lewis answered with a shrug.

BB frowned. "They're not twins – that one's older."

"No, they're twins," Lewis said. "The one on the left has just looked after herself better." His eye caught the pages just before they were turned. The left twin's face seemed to be a little rounder, her features smaller. The twin on the right had crows feet round her eyes. Her forehead had a very faint red tinge, as if she had rubbed in a fingertip of blood.

BB turned to the crossword and studied the clues, after a time he whistled and shook his head.

"Tough, aren't they?" Lewis said.

BB handed The Shilling back to him, screwing up his nose. "What's that smell?" he asked.

Lewis hastily returned The Shilling to his plastic bag, which he then discreetly slipped back into his holdall. "Yeah, sorry about that. It's the magazine. I threw it out with the rubbish."

BB waved his hand in front of his nose. "Smells like dog shit," he muttered. Lewis nodded in reluctant agreement. The smell had got worse and he was keeping the magazine next to an open window at home. The paper must have reacted with something.

"It's a weird magazine, you know," Lewis said quietly.

"You don't say," BB agreed.

"I mean, some of the articles. I was looking through it last night. There's this letters page, you know, letters to the editor. There's this one letter, well, you'll never guess what it's about."

"Surprise me."

"Handy tips on how to be unfaithful without your wife finding out."

"You're kidding?"

"Seriously. It's written by this guy who describes himself as a 'serial adulterer'. The golden rule: deny, deny, deny, no matter what the evidence. Mrs Wife, as he calls her, will always want to believe you. Then there are all these 'tricks of the trade'. Always shower after you've had sex and keep a squash kit with shower gel in your car. Invent imaginary friends from school who are shy and needy. That sort of thing."

"Bloody hell," BB said with a smile.

"He even lists a few discreet hotels. But that's not what's really freaky. This letter is next to a letter from a housewife giving a recipe for chicken soup. I could give you another example; an article's in there on confidence in the workplace. Stuff that looks ordinary, mundane even, then something really inappropriate pops out. It's bonkers."

"Let me have another look," BB murmured, but Lewis shook his head. "Lewis?" BB asked, perplexed, holding out his hand.

"I can't," Lewis answered, "I mean I don't want to. This

is the first time I've brought it out in public and it doesn't feel right. I feel as if everyone's looking at it."

"The smell you mean?"

Lewis shifted in his seat uncomfortably. He wanted to go home, to be alone with his magazine. "Sure. I'll show it to you again when you're round next."

They drank in silence for a time, and then BB gave him a progress update on his dot.com Welsh tourist project. He had been gathering a lot of useful information from the Post Office and had collected brochures from the obvious tourist spots. Now he was waiting on the guy he knew who was going to set up the website, again describing him as a computer whizz. Lewis wasn't really listening.

"Not boring you, am I?" BB murmured.

Lewis' eyes sprang to attention. "Sorry…" he said.

"Lewis, what's up?"

Lewis shook his head. He took a sip of his drink and said, "You're going to think I'm crazy."

"Why?"

"I'm not so sure any more that the magazine is a traders network."

BB put his drink down. "Go on," he said darkly.

Lewis hesitated, conscious of the absurdity of what he was about to say. He made a point of speaking calmly and slowly. "It's just that my life has got better in the last few weeks. A *lot* better. It started with the money, the shares. That was my serious problem then, the thing that had tipped me over the edge. But other things are happening now. I've given up smoking."

"You've always wanted to give up smoking," BB pointed out.

"I know, I know, but Bernice says 'stop lighting them,' and I do."

"Bernice?"

"Oh, this client I've got. Then I write in the crossword,

the word 'Lit'. And I stop lighting them. *Light* a cigarette, present tense. *Lit* a cigarette, past tense. My smoking is in the past. Coincidence?"

"Coincidence," BB confirmed, with the beginnings of a grin.

"Then I write in the word 'Fat', and I'm putting on weight. For the first time in my life I'm putting on weight. I've put on half a stone this week."

BB had a very open mind and was seriously mulling this over. "So you don't think 'Fat' and 'Lit' are share tips at all?" he probed.

Lewis shook his head. "I think The Shilling is making good things happen to me, sorting out all the problems in my life."

"And it even lets you beat me at squash," BB joked.

"Christ, I'm being serious!"

BB gave him the stern look he used back in the band days, when Lewis played off key. "I know you're serious, Lew, that's what I'm worried about. Get real. What are you saying, that this little band of insider traders has an interest in seeing you put on weight and give up fags? Don't you think it's more likely that because you found significance in the first two clues... what were they again?"

"Low and Bern."

"Low and Bern, then you're automatically looking for significance in the others? Farthing.com aren't speaking to you any more. There are no more clues, no more share tips. They'd have sent you a new magazine and e-mailed you if you were still in the network."

"So Lit and Fat are just coincidences?"

"Subconsciously the crossword could have affected you, I suppose... with the giving up smoking I mean. That and what this Bernice woman said. Then in your head it's meant to happen, so it happens."

"What about the weight?"

"Everyone knows you put on weight when you give up."

"But I haven't before."

"No, and you haven't been thirty-nine before. Lew, the years catch up with the most active of metabolisms, even yours."

Lewis nodded reluctantly. He had a point.

"And," BB added, touching his glass, "Lit and Fat are common words, aren't they? You know, they can mean a lot of things. What would you say if in the last week your chip pan caught fire? You'd say – Ah! The crossword! It's like daily horoscopes, where there's something for everyone. If you look hard enough."

Lewis stared at him blankly for a few moments, then laughed. "You're right, completely right," he said. "God, I'm so embarr-assed now." He looked up and smiled. "Forget this conversation ever happened."

"Anything else bothering you?" BB asked.

Lewis shook his head and finished his drink. He wasn't about to tell his friend about his dream or the experience in the lift. An active imagination needed no explanation... but anyway, they were private images, for his contemplation only.

"What did Emily say afterwards?" BB asked.

Lewis almost dropped his glass. He had completely forgotten about Emily!

On arriving home Lewis wrote in another clue. The answer had popped into his head as he was driving back, when he wasn't even thinking about the crossword.

Do not accept it. Do not accept less. Less.

It was so obvious he was amazed he hadn't got it before, especially as he had two of the letters already.

Okay, now he had the answers to three clues... Lit, Fat and Less.

Litfatless.

Lesslitfat.

No, it still didn't sound like a company, but he would think about that later. He telephoned Janet, the 'manageress' of Encounters.

Janet remembered him immediately. He was the young gentleman in Cardiff Bay, the penthouse. She sounded a little disappointed that he hadn't called since. Had everything gone well?

"Very well, thank you," Lewis answered, a little impatiently.

"Would Sir be interested in a further booking?"

He nodded. "Yes, yes I would. And as soon as possible please."

She offered him an understanding sigh. "Let me see." She put the line on hold for a few moments and he imagined that she was flicking through her diary. "This Thursday is the earliest I can arrange," she said, returning to the line.

He smiled. "That's fine," he said.

"Stephanie. Lovely girl. Tall, auburn hair."

"Oh, no, I'm sorry, I didn't explain. And I'm sure... I'm sure Stephanie *is* a lovely girl. But I'd like to book Emily again please."

The line went silent.

"Janet? Are you there?" he asked.

"I'm sorry, Mr Coin, that's impossible..." Janet's accent had slipped a little.

"No really, the money's not a problem..."

"Emily died in a car crash. Four weeks ago."

LESS

It was three weeks to the day since he was last here at Baron Enterprises and Bernice was again waiting for him at the entrance. As he approached she had a puzzled expression.

"Lewis, I wouldn't have recognised you," she whispered.

He kissed her on the cheek, proudly aware that his aftershave was still fresh. This time she didn't stiffen; she instinctively turned her head but favoured him with a shy smile.

"Well I've put on weight," he admitted.

"Must be the Mars bars," she declared cheerily.

"And I've stopped smoking."

"Really? That's wonderful! I told you just to stop lighting them, didn't I?"

His eyes darkened for a moment, as he nodded. She noticed the sudden change in his demeanour and her puzzled expression re-appeared. "So you did," he agreed, collecting himself. "Shall we go in?"

Raine was on the phone as Lewis and Bernice entered and he put up his hand to request a few seconds. Their two chairs were already in place, opposite him. "I can't speak now, the lawyer's here," he murmured and put the phone down. He paused, then looked up at Lewis. "Have you spoken to Mr Marker?" he asked.

"Oh yes," Lewis replied, putting his briefcase on the floor.

"Did you make any progress?"

"None at all."

Raine's eyes went to the opposite wall. "I see...' he said.

Lewis took his file out of his briefcase and Raine considered it suspiciously. "As I explained last time," Lewis said, "we have to move from strength; and, as you warned, Mr Marker doesn't deal. We have to make *Mr Vernon Jones* deal."

"And how do we do that?"

Lewis tapped the cardboard of his file. "Remind him of his football game, a couple of weeks ago?" he suggested.

Bernice looked up from her notepad.

"I was there, cheering him on," Lewis explained. He briefly recounted how he had pretended to be a talent scout and visited the football ground.

"So, fit as a fiddle and playing football..." Raine mused, taking this in. "That little... ah, that little fraud."

"Something like that." Lewis felt a pang of conscience as he recalled Vernon struggling around the pitch, rubbing his back.

Raine found the beginnings of a smile, but he was still looking at the far wall. "It's a shame we couldn't have filmed it," he considered.

Lewis nodded and said, "You'd need a specialist to conceal a camera in that sort of situation, but he knows I was there. And he knows about my bag," he added meaningfully.

Raine's eyes darted to him. "What was in the bag?" he whispered.

"Nothing."

"What do you mean, *nothing*?"

"Well, it had my squash gear. But it was big enough to hold a camera. If you catch my drift."

Raine sat back in his chair and thoughtfully ran

his finger down his hair parting. Lewis glanced over at Bernice, but she didn't seem impressed. He was rather put out.

"Very well," Raine decided, "we'll pay in the eighty thousand, as you… as you suggested." Bernice nodded in full agreement at the mention of Lewis' initial valuation of the claim, appearing relieved that they had returned to the fundamentals of the claim, leaving behind the tactics and tricks.

This was the instruction Lewis was prepared for and he wasn't going to be brave and talk them out of it. One thing he had learnt from bitter experience was that if a client wanted to settle, then you settled. If you didn't, then it became *your* case, not the client's. *Your* head was on the block at trial.

"Pay in… less," Lewis muttered.

He concealed his astonishment at the words that had just come out of his mouth. Bernice studied her notepad and frowned, while Raine requested a figure with his eyes.

"Fifteen thousand," Lewis suggested, stone faced.

Raine was amused. "Fifteen thousand? Well Mr Coin, we'll follow your advice, on this occasion. Fifteen thousand it is." He looked at his watch to signal that the meeting was over. As Lewis shook the man's hand he noted that the wristwatch was a Rolex. There was no cravat today either, instead a striped executive tie and no smell of old clothes. The factory was just as drab as before, but better lit and more welcoming on this, his second visit.

People visiting Harrier & O'Neill for the first time were probably thrown to find an office inside an Edwardian townhouse, Lewis reflected, realising that he had probably overreacted before when he found his client in an old Victorian setting. It was probably those e-mails from Farthing.com, written in copperplate script that had sent his imagination into overdrive.

No, Baron was just a company who wanted to save money, a big company with a massive potential workload. This could have been a superb new instruction that would have changed the fortunes of his firm, if he hadn't just screwed it all up.

Why did he tell Raine to pay in *less*?

Raine kept Bernice back for a few moments after the meeting was over. She caught Lewis up at the reception desk, which was again unmanned.

"Lewis, I've got to tell you something," she said breathlessly.

"Mr Raine wants to pay in the eighty thousand after all?" he asked hopefully.

"No, no, that's fine. If you think so."

Lewis sighed. "What, then?"

"It's your file. He doesn't like paper files."

"I know. I e-mail everything."

"No, he doesn't want any paper files at *all*. All documents to be scanned, and original documents to be returned here, by courier."

"Why for God's sake?"

Bernice had the hurt look of *I'm just the messenger*. "You know what Baron's like about confidentiality," she explained. "They're afraid of anything being left around." She gestured to the reception, which was so scrupulously tidy that there wasn't a paper in sight. "You'll have to tighten up on your computer access too. Authorised users only. Full vetting software."

He whistled. "Well, that's expensive. Let's see if Baron gives me any more cases first."

"They will. I'm sure of it."

He nodded, not so convinced. He wasn't looking forward to Marker's curt rejection of his offer, nor was he looking forward to his next meeting with Raine when he had to admit that he was right about the £80,000 after all.

How many times had he told trainees this? It's not about what you know it's about what you can *prove*.

"You weren't too impressed with my football stunt, were you?" he asked in a matter of fact voice.

She smiled nervously. "I'm sorry. Did it show? I was just surprised, that's all. You know what you're doing."

"When the union fights clean, then I'll fight clean," he offered. "That's fair, isn't it?"

"You're right, I'm sorry," she replied. "I know you're working so hard for my benefit. You want Mr Raine to be impressed for my sake." A few moments passed as they both tried to find their next sentence. A tannoy broke the silence. The message contained Bernice's name and she sighed.

"Actually, Bernice, I'd like to ask you something," he said cautiously. "A favour, actually." She smiled expectantly, but her smile faded when she heard the question. "I'm trying to locate a company in London, for... another client. Can you help me?"

"What's the company?" she asked.

"It's a fashion business, or some kind of model agency. It's called Circus, but I think it's gone bust now. Do you have any connections with that sort of thing?" He was now pondering over the faded smile. Had he detected a flicker of disappointment? Was she hoping he was going to ask her something else?

"Baron sponsors a lot of companies," she mused. "Who runs it?"

"Emily Webber and Anton something." He grimaced with embarrassment. "Sorry I can't be more specific."

She nodded. "I'll see what I can do. What do you want to know?"

"Anything," he said, with a shrug. "Anything at all."

Lewis was now on his fourth re-draft.

He was composing the e-mail that would accompany the settlement offer of £15,000. He knew from experience that when it came to settlement proposals, generally the less you said the better; parties in strong bargaining positions didn't need to press the strength of their case. Marker would know that better than anyone.

But Lewis knew that silence wouldn't do, not this time. He needed something; something which would get Vernon Jones rejecting his lawyer's advice and demanding that he take the money. Jones already had his business card and would have been told that he was carrying a bag. A hint was needed that the bag contained a camera.

Lewis had tried subtle innuendo. *The ball's in your court.* Jones wouldn't catch on. He had tried bare face aggression. *Your client should not regard this offer as a springboard to negotiation: the claim will be defended to trial.* Marker would throw it back at him.

NOW DO YOU HAVE AN OFFER TO MAKE?

His chest tightened as he remembered Marker's taunt. "Yeah, I've got an offer," he murmured. He typed: *We put you on notice that we will be relying on video surveillance evidence of your client. The videotape will be disclosed immediately prior to the trial.*

He clicked 'send' and took a deep gulp of air.

He could get struck off for this, he realised. Deliberately misleading a claimant that he had him trapped on film. Lying to another solicitor, an Officer of the Court. Putting his lie on paper.

Well, he told himself, that's what he had wanted Vernon to believe, with his 'the ball's in your court' inference. Was it *so* different, what he was doing now? It was Vernon who was playing football, after all. He was the fraud, as Raine had said.

All the same, if the offer was rejected he had better

come up with a good excuse for not disclosing the video evidence. Would Marker smell a rat and call him up before the judge *demanding* that it be disclosed?

In that moment he hated e-mails. At least with a letter you could run after the postman and get it back.

Oh God, what have I done? he thought, putting his head in his hands.

Janet of Encounters hadn't been forthcoming about Emily. She hadn't known her that well, none of the girls had: Emily had only been registered for a week and because of other commitments Lewis had been her first booking.

She had died in a car crash on the Sunday she had left his apartment, late at night on Newport Road. Lewis obtained the Police Accident Report the next day. Collision with a building... she had driven right through a protective barrier. She had been drinking; an empty bottle of Bell's whisky was in the car and she wasn't wearing a seat belt.

Emily was strictly teetotal, yet he remembered her saying something like: *don't drink, not any more.*

So she went back to it. That night. Perhaps she couldn't cope with the thought of being a prostitute, of having fallen so far from her luxurious lifestyle with her holidays in Capri. But she had been cheerful in the morning, in fact a lot more cheerful than she had been the previous evening. It didn't make sense.

He knew that he was reaching, that he didn't know Emily's heart. People did stupid things and met senseless ends. He had searched Companies House for Circus, but no such company was registered. That meant Emily and Anton were simply in partnership together, and without an address, tracking down Anton would be very difficult indeed.

He had the notion that he needed to speak to Anton,

because he needed to know more about Emily. He felt some strange bond with her. Still vivid in his memory he could see her looking down, forlornly, as the lift doors closed.

She knew something, he realised, and whatever it was had killed her.

The revelation startled him. For the first time, since The Shilling had come into his possession, he felt a twinge of fear.

Lewis was still pondering the possible reasons for Emily's suicide as he considered his half-full glass of water at the boardroom table. The boardroom was below ground level; it had originally been the cellar of the Edwardian townhouse and the room was awash with strong artificial light. If he looked up, the halogen in the ceiling would make him squint, so he kept his eyes on the water jug, which provided a reflection of his hand.

Partners' meetings were rare events, invariably precipitated by danger and change. This one was in recognition of profits continuing on their downward spiral. The meetings were also small as the practice was small, just O'Neill and Lewis and the other two junior partners, Rhys and Graham. This didn't prevent O'Neill turning it into a formal affair, however, and as he sat at the head of the long table he had the serious face of a troubled Managing Director of a large corporation.

O'Neill had one of the secretaries make them all coffee in the tiny client cups with matching saucers. Everyone made their own coffee in Harrier & O'Neill, in big worn-out mugs, but O'Neill always made the meetings an exception to reinforce the authority of the partners. The whole office whispered when these meetings took place.

The secretary was a very pretty nineteen-year-old, but famous throughout the office for being in a 'serious relationship'. She threw Lewis a smile as she put the coffee tray down and he noted that this was the second time this week that he had been so favoured. She didn't usually smile at any of the men, for she took great pride in being an unobtainable prize. O'Neill, Graham and Rhys lit cigarettes, using their saucers as ashtrays. Lewis leaned back and studied his fingernails.

O'Neill opened by saying that a concerted effort was needed to get work in, although he gave no practical suggestions on how this was to be achieved. He was certain that there were files in the office, which were waiting to be billed. He talked at some length about how much it cost to run a practice, as usual giving the wild estimates of the office overheads, which would make any observer wonder how the practice could run at any level of profitability. Finally O'Neill came to his favourite subject: postage.

"I don't know how many times I've said it," he muttered, "but Friday post is still being sent first class. First class: on a Friday. Do you know how much that costs us?"

A brief pause and a look down the table made Graham and Rhys shrug and shake their heads.

"I can't do everything myself, gentlemen," O'Neill said. "Now, I want you to check the post. Nothing is to go first class on Friday and during the week only important mail is to go first class. There'll be two trays by the franking machine." He sniffed and sat back to signal the end of the meeting. The firm's crisis solved with penny postage.

"Don't you think we should address the more fundamental problems, Stephen?" Lewis asked gently. Graham and Rhys looked round and settled back into the seats from which they had risen to leave.

O'Neill swivelled his spectacled gaze on Lewis like the turret of a tank. "Fundamental problems, young man?"

Lewis swallowed. He had been here before and he knew that his voice was going to emerge shaking. He wasn't wrong, but nevertheless he managed to get his sentence out in one breath. "The fact that we haven't got a client base any more and that no matter how much effort we put into it and how many overheads we cut, our profits are going to keep going down if we don't do something drastic and do it quickly." He looked down breathlessly.

If O'Neill was surprised at this challenge then he didn't show it. He said, "Running a law practice is all about economies and management..."

"No, it's not," Lewis muttered. "We need work. It's as simple as that."

"What are you saying?"

"I'm saying that we're in trouble," Lewis responded, his voice a little stronger. "We need to face up to it, we're a high-street practice again, not an insurance practice. A high-street practice can't feed more than three litigators, there just isn't enough work to go around." He paused. "We have to cut our staff, and we have to start advertising. Get back into the Citizens Advice Bureau. Put flyers in hospitals, that sort of thing."

"Do you know how much hospitals charge to let you put flyers up?" O'Neill remarked coldly.

"For God's sake, Stephen, can't you see? We haven't got any choice. The work isn't coming through the post any more. We have to go out and get it like everyone else does." Lewis paused again, hoping at this point for some input from Graham and Rhys. He was disappointed. "And, another thing..."

"Another thing?"

"We *all* have to work now. We're not big enough to support an administrative partner."

Lewis could almost hear Graham and Rhys' inward groans of astonishment. He was referring to the fact that O'Neill hadn't had a full caseload in about five years. On the odd occasion he took on a case he hauled it around the office boasting a complexity that wasn't there. It was a sensitive subject; when the legal reforms took place a few years ago O'Neill hadn't bothered to make himself familiar with them and the junior partners also suspected he was scared of litigation now, after so many years of delegating.

O'Neill took a considered breath. "My efforts, young man, saved this firm. My efforts made this firm what it is. I was litigating before you even knew what the word meant. I brought the insurance work in, remember, and all of you managed to fuck it up. Now, in a moment you and me are going to fall out in a big way. You know where the door is, and you can hand in your partnership papers as you go. If you don't, I suggest you have a long think about your attitude. Alright?" O'Neill got up and stalked out of the boardroom, gently closing the door behind him. His voice had been completely calm throughout the entire exchange; Lewis had always wondered how he managed to do that.

"You're right, Lewis," Rhys whispered, after O'Neill had gone. Graham nodded.

"Yeah, cheers guys," Lewis muttered.

Thanks for the support, he thought.

Back at his desk Lewis was wondering whether he had done the right thing, taking O'Neill on in that way. There would be a couple of weeks with the two of them avoiding each other and O'Neill always won that battle with Lewis' eventual apology. Furthermore, he might be in need of O'Neill's help soon: if Marker called his bluff on the video evidence he was going to need all the friends he could get.

He checked his e-mails and there was one from Marker. He opened it with his stomach churning, but it was just an acknowledgement of his offer. Well, he would know soon enough because under the court rules the payment had to be accepted or rejected within 21 days. Marker didn't say anything of note in his e-mail; there wasn't even a sarcastic remark over the level of the payment. Lewis couldn't decide whether that was a good or a bad sign.

At home he wandered round the apartment at a loose end. He had made an effort to ignore The Shilling, which was on his mahogany table near an open window. As it happened the fresh air wasn't necessary because the magazine only smelled close up. He was deliberately ignoring it because he was thinking of the article on Suez, the first thing he had read, where he just managed the first and last few paragraphs because it was so dull. As with the piece about confidence in the workplace, he had a suspicion that there was something nasty buried in the middle somewhere.

Well, he wasn't going to read it. Whatever was buried could stay in there. He had noticed over the past few days that he was getting a little compulsive about the magazine... that he was fighting a constant urge to look at it. He recognised this compulsion and it troubled him: it was as if his nicotine habit has been replaced with a new addiction.

He knew BB was right: this was all a product of his imagination. After all, he couldn't blame The Shilling for that £15,000 settlement offer; the crossword simply said 'less', which could mean anything. *Anything*. He had decided, in front of Raine and Bernice, to translate it into his life, to get meaning from it. Then he took it a step further and unethically tried to justify his decision.

And that was probably going to get him struck off, he. thought ruefully. At the very least he would lose Baron as a client when Marker threw his bluff back in his face.

Eventually he got tired of pacing and worrying and sat down in his armchair. The magazine was in his hands.

He opened it carefully, turning the pages by reference to their corners, trying to ignore the whiff of dog excrement as each page was identified without it being opened. He wanted to avoid the models; BB's observations had disturbed him, although he believed it was just a trick of the light. He would look at them again in natural light, Saturday perhaps.

Look at them *now*, Lewis. *Look at them.*

But he wouldn't. He opened the magazine at the double page advert of the smartly dressed woman with the poodle trailing behind her on a long leash. He winced and sprayed air freshener on the pages.

Well, the woman was as happy as she was before, and seemed to have lost none of her looks. One hand was on her summer hat, one hand holding the leash, and she was tripping along nicely. Nice short outfit, light blue, perfect for shopping in Harvey Nicks and complementing most accessories. No change there.

The spray evaporated and made the pages glisten, but it was definitely an improvement. He smelled his fingers and they were fine, the smell wasn't rubbing off. He gingerly put his nose to the pages but couldn't detect any point of origin: something must have stained one of the pages somewhere, or something was in the crease, something that was rotting. If so then it was little wonder that it was getting worse by the day. Maybe he should take it to someone, get it fumigated.

Perhaps you should just throw it out, Lewis, he told himself. It's just a bloody magazine.

He turned to the crossword and he found an answer to one of the clues.

No rooms.
No room at the inn.
No rooms at the inns.
Inns.

He wrote in 'Inns'. He shouldn't be too surprised, he reflected; the crossword had been in his head for over four weeks now and he probably knew the answers to all the clues, if he were to concentrate as if his life depended on it.

No room at the inn – where did that come from? Ah, Joseph and the Virgin Mary, Christmas Eve. So The Shilling had religion. Well, that was cute.

This time he didn't even attempt a guess at a share tip. He knew deep down that there were no more solid gold investments; he had to make it as a lawyer. Another twenty-five years in this beaten down industry to reach a lonely retirement that he would be too tired to enjoy.

Well, at least he had given up smoking so he could enjoy a few more years of that lonely retirement.

He flicked back through the pages, stopping again at the advert with the lady and the poodle. The air freshener had left a grey blotch which half covered the poodle's head. It was the first time he had had a good hard look at the animal but it was okay, it was just a little doggy. No fangs, no bald patches.

It was just a little ball of fluff tugging impatiently at its leash, with a tiny spiral of excrement, which the dog had parked discreetly by its back leg.

INNS

The sunlight was streaming through the balcony windows as Lewis was gently delivered up from his dreams. He didn't want to wake up.

His arm was draped around the shoulders of the woman dozing next to him; her head snuggled into his chest. His other arm hung lifelessly out of the bed, a casualty to the exertion of the night. He was exhausted again, unable to move.

His eyelids flickered as he resisted the inevitable. He squeezed the woman's shoulder bone and she moaned peacefully.

With the intruding sunlight came the noise. The Bay brought seagulls at this time of the year, which were squawking as they flew past his little terrace. His eyes opened remorselessly.

The Weeping Wall was playing, the little bells chiming under the bed. Then came the voices in harmony, the treated guitar, the wailing over the bells. The voices came again.

"All spent, ain'tcha? Ain'tcha, my little soldjar?"

His bed smelled of death, of decay. The woman's green eyes glinted with pleasure, but her face was sallow and pitted with holes. She pressed her breasts into his chest and he was aroused, wanting her again.

"All spent, my love?" she whispered, then licked his ear.

He woke with a start, sweating.

That was his third erotic dream this week. He groaned,

realising that his libido was going crazy.

"Bernice..." he whispered.

Lewis' diary flagged day twenty since making the settlement offer on Vernon Jones. There was still no response from Marker.

During those three weeks Lewis' weight had plateaued at around eleven and a half stone. He was almost relieved when he weighed himself on the weekend to see that he hadn't put any more on, and to be on the safe side he had stopped eating Mars bars. This was probably his perfect weight, he decided: shaped, but slim. His face in the mirror was different. The flesh in his cheeks and neck now softened what had previously been a gaunt, hunted reflection and he had a rascally squeeze around his eyes when he smiled.

Bernice had telephoned to offer her report on Circus; her contacts had confirmed that it was a legitimate model agency in London, which had been very prominent for a short time. She didn't have any details for Anton or Emily Webber, but she had an address for one of the models that used to work for the agency. The young woman had left the fashion industry.

Lewis was thoughtfully tapping the name and address of this ex-model with his pen when the phone rang. It was Marker.

"So, what's this video evidence you've got?" he rasped.

Lewis smiled. He didn't answer.

"My man's prepared to admit that he walks to the shops sometimes, carries a few bags occasionally," Marker continued. "Is that what you've got?"

Lewis still didn't answer.

"Mr Coin, are you there?"

"Ball's in your court," Lewis murmured.

"What the *fuck* does that mean?" Marker snarled back.

Ah, lovely. So, Vernon had told him about the football. "Mr Marker, can I ask you to moderate your language?" Lewis answered politely. "May I remind you that we are both Officers of the Court."

There was a sound on the other line made deep in the man's throat. "Okay, alright, cards on the table." Marker softened his tone a little and Lewis sensed the effort that was needed. "Now you've made your point, you've lowered my man's expectations. So, he's thinking that perhaps the orthopaedic consultant saw him on a bad day." He grunted out a laugh. "You know how it is. But are you going to make a sensible offer now?"

"I have made a sensible offer."

"Fifteen thousand? Now come on, that's ridiculous."

"Is it rejected?"

"It doesn't even begin to address the value of the claim."

"Is it rejected?"

"It will be."

This was a standard ploy and Lewis was surprised that Marker could be so obvious. If Jones' instructions to Marker were to accept the £15,000, then Marker couldn't formally reject it.

"So it's not rejected?" Lewis asked.

"I'm advising my client to reject it."

"I see. Well, once it's rejected we'll go from there."

"As I said, Mr Coin, cards on the table. My man's prepared to take eighty thousand to bring matters to a close, here and now."

"I'm sure he is," Lewis responded in a flat voice.

"Well, what's your figure?"

Lewis twisted the knife, joyfully. "My figure, Mr Marker, is the one in front of you. And I didn't think you cared for discussions on negotiated settlements."

Marker mumbled something obscene under his breath and put the phone down. The next day Lewis received the notice of acceptance for the offer: the claim had settled for £15,000. He copied the e-mail to Baron and Baron telephoned half an hour later.

"Bernice?" Lewis asked. There was a pause on the other line.

"No, it's Howard Raine."

Lewis stiffened in his chair. "Oh, hello Mr Raine."

There was another pause.

"Mr Raine?" Lewis whispered.

Raine was formal and awkward, as if he didn't care for telephones. "Can you come to my office next week? Monday, midday?" he asked.

"Certainly. I'll look forward to it."

The line went dead without a goodbye. Lewis breathed out and sighed, then brought his hands together with satisfaction. He decided it was time to go and see O'Neill.

"How many cases do you think they have?" O'Neill asked, after Lewis had told him about the settlement and the meeting set for next week.

"I don't know," Lewis answered truthfully. "But they have a lot of accidents."

"Why?"

Lewis was still mindful of the confidentiality agreement he had signed. "It's a big factory," he said.

O'Neill was pretending to read some papers in front of him. "I wouldn't get too excited, if I were you," he said. "They're not an insurance company. How much are you billing them for this?"

"They said to bill normally on this one so I'll charge a hundred and twenty. You'll remember that I said they have a policy on fees."

"What policy?"

"I don't know yet."

O'Neill nodded and touched his dicky bow. "Try and keep it at a hundred and twenty. We can't operate profitably below that."

Lewis forced back a look of irritation. They had talked about this and O'Neill had appeared to accept that they would have to take whatever was offered. "I'll try, Stephen. But if it's bulk instruction I can see them wanting a discount."

O'Neill didn't seem to hear the statement, for his mind was now on something else. He sniffed, leaned back and made eye contact. "About our disagreement in the boardroom..." he said. Lewis went cold; in his excitement he had completely forgotten that they weren't speaking.

"No hard feelings?" Lewis offered.

"It depends on whether you believe what you said."

"We're all under pressure, Stephen. I'm just trying to do the best for the firm, that's all. But you're right, I shouldn't have said what I did."

O'Neill took off his spectacles and wiped them carefully with his handkerchief, accepting the terms of the peace treaty. He was very shortsighted and his eyes were squinting. "Fifteen thousand eh?" he said.

"Fifteen," Lewis confirmed with a grin.

"He'd have probably have accepted less, if he'd been pressed," O'Neill remarked.

Lewis didn't believe in fate. He knew The Shilling was bringing him luck, but it was *his* luck. Prophecies could be made to come true.

It was like Macbeth: if Glamis believed he would be become king, then he would see to it that he became king; but it was Glamis that wielded the knife.

Or like the Oracles in Ancient Greece. They would give

a prediction to a Greek king, and the king, encouraged and directed, would see that it came to pass.

Lewis was only vaguely aware that his thoughts were floating in a mist. He was no longer looking for share tips; the crossword had taken on wider dimensions.

Inns.

He shook his head as he wondered what *Inns* could signify. A thought occurred and he turned to the centre pages with the shears woman. He nodded as he ran his three fingers through his hair; yes, the shears had come in, they were almost shut. He was trying to work something out in his head, and he dared to move his eyes downwards, finding the resistance, which he couldn't understand. She had a firm, healthy body, even if her skin was so pale it appeared as if she had never seen the sun. She had a nubile figure, small breasts and hips, but her expression, the hostile face that said *I hate you and dare you to look*, had the weariness of years.

The smell of dog excrement was wafting from the pages, but it was what he saw crawling up the inside of one of the shears woman's legs that made him wince.

He turned back quickly to the crossword, annoyed that the picture had disturbed him again.

Perhaps he should pull the pages of the shears woman out. He considered this seriously for a few moments, but decided against it; to pull any of the pages out seemed wrong, as if he were performing a mutilation. His eyes darted to something that was scurrying near his feet. Instinctively he crushed it with his shoe.

He considered the squashed black mess on his laminate floor. It was a cockroach, and he felt a sense of panic at the notion that his apartment might be infested. It was the first one he had seen; it was probably just a refugee from the pesky terrier next door.

He frowned as an uncomfortable idea took root in the

back of his mind. Should he go back to the shears woman, just to make sure that the cockroach, the one that had been crawling up the inside of her leg, was still there?

The idea frightened him.

I'm going crazy, he thought. He took a breath and returned to his crossword, eventually losing his frown in the solace of concentration and analysis.

"Inns…" he murmured to himself. "Inns…?"

Drum and bass was pounding through the bar and Lewis felt the vibration even inside his bottle of Budweiser. The legion of voices formed a constant murmur behind the beat. Lewis had forgotten how loud town pubs could be.

He barely recognised the city centre after dark. His old watering holes, the ones he frequented unsuccessfully in his twenties, had long gone to be replaced by franchised theme pubs that were licensed until midnight. They found themselves in an Australian bar with boomerangs, kangaroo models and photographs of Neighbours stars as décor, yet Lewis felt oddly at home as he planted himself next to a pillar with BB.

"What the hell did you want to come into town for?" BB asked in a loud voice as he competed with the noise.

"I just fancied going to a few pubs for a change," Lewis replied, but slowly mouthing the words so BB could read his lips. Lewis' slacks and shirt were new and he had a thin linen jumper draped carefully over his shoulders. He had applied some wax to his sandy brown hair, which made a few strands glisten as if they were sun-bleached blond. His hair was shorter now, and his face, fully on show, had a sculpted confidence.

BB had mentioned that his Welsh tourist project had hit a snag. His computer whizz friend had said they needed more money to finish the website. "Have you had any more share tips?" BB asked.

Lewis' attention flickered to two girls at the bar, who looked away when he saw them watching. Another girl smiled at him as she collected her drink and turned away from the bar. He glanced around the bar again, closing down female eyes as he located them. He smiled to himself and felt the spring in the back of his clipped hair.

"Lewis?" BB asked, frowning now.

"Nah, no more share tips," Lewis replied.

Someone bumped into Lewis. Both men looked round at a girl with big hair and an embarrassed smile. From the way she recovered herself it seemed as if she had been pushed by a group of girls, who were giggling a few feet away.

"Oh sorry," the girl said, fixing her hair that had so much hairspray it would have stayed put in a storm.

"No problem," Lewis said. "You can bump into me anytime."

She raised her eyebrows as she sidled off. Lewis knew that BB was considering him curiously.

"Well she didn't stay, did she?" Lewis said. "She was probably just on the way to the loo."

"Yeah, to wring out her knickers."

Lewis laughed and shook his head. When they had finished their Buds they made for the door and Lewis scratched his nose with embarrassment as more female eyes followed his progress.

In the second bar a girl came up to him and asked him for a light, but continued to hover when he said he didn't smoke. After a while Lewis made an excuse and he led BB to a table in a quiet section of the upstairs gallery.

"It must be the extra weight," Lewis remarked with a confused grin as they sat down. This night was turning into a revelation, yet if he was truthful with himself he wasn't too surprised. The tasty nineteen-year old in the office, the one who never smiled at anyone but who now smiled at him all the time, had given him the first inkling. No, it was even *before* that: he had detected it with Gemma, Stuart's friend, a few weeks back. Gemma wasn't a babe, she was in his range, but she had been all over him.

He gave BB an update on The Shilling, describing how the shears had come in, and the dog excrement had appeared next to the poodle.

"I've got a theory," Lewis announced.

"Throw the thing out," was BB's response.

Lewis didn't hear him. "It's not the same magazine," he said. "I picked up a different magazine from the rubbish."

BB tapped his Bud. "A different one...?" he murmured.

"Right." Lewis had a big grin. "I throw the magazine out, and the organisation who are watching me, Farthing. com or whoever, get into the storage room. They study my handwriting on the crossword, perhaps take a photograph of it, and then copy my writing on a new edition. They leave the new edition on the floor of the storage room but with new pictures and a smell of dog shit. I'm telling you, BB, those shears have come in. There's a cockroach too, and I didn't see that the first time. Okay, I didn't look too hard, but I would have seen it. It's not the sort of thing you miss. It's a new picture."

BB stared at him blankly for a few moments. "You're crazy," he said after a time.

"Why?"

"First of all, you noticed the changes in the magazine before you threw it out, remember?"

Lewis shook his head. "Just small changes," he said. "I think there's some trick photography going on, sort of like hologram tricks; but the shears woman and the poodle with the dog shit, they're new."

BB was unconvinced. "Okay," he said, "let's assume that

you're right. Why would Farthing go to all this trouble?"

Lewis was taken aback; he hadn't even considered the question of motive. "Perhaps they're trying to wind me up," he suggested, "as a punishment for taking their share tip. Or perhaps it's still some sort of initiation thing. They're probably some sort of secret society."

"Oh for God's sake, Lewis, can you hear yourself?" BB said, shaking his head. "Throw it out. This is crazy."

Lewis winked at a girl walking by.

"What's the latest clue?" BB asked, ignoring Lewis' eye contact with the girl.

Lewis didn't reply. He had the notion that perhaps BB was jealous that he was getting all this attention.

"Lewis?" BB pressed.

"Inns," Lewis admitted.

BB looked at his Bud, then smiled. "So is *that* why you wanted to come to town?" he asked.

Lewis shrugged.

"It is, isn't it?"

"Don't try and pretend you haven't noticed all the girls looking at me," Lewis protested. He was enjoying his night of triumph; BB usually had all the success with women.

"I've noticed," BB confirmed.

"Well then," Lewis muttered.

"Well what?"

Lewis put up a finger to answer, but frowned and didn't say anything.

"Exactly," BB said. "You're talking nonsense. You must either be saying that all these girls are employed by Farthing, or that the magazine has sprayed you with some sort of pheromone. Perhaps it's been dipped in pig sweat."

Lewis' expression contained some apprehension. "I'm just saying that the answer to the clue has improved my life again," he muttered, now identifying the countless holes in his theory.

"But I thought they were punishing you?" BB returned with a grin.

Lewis didn't reply.

"There's no mystery, Lew," BB said gently. "You've put on weight and you're confident, that's all. Girls can smell confidence: sex appeal is all in the mind."

Lewis nodded reluctantly. "All the same, if it wasn't for the crossword I wouldn't be here," he muttered.

BB let out a long sigh. "Throw the bloody thing out," he repeated wearily. "I'm starting to worry about you." He checked his watch and announced that he was going home.

Lewis decided to hang around and get another drink from the bar. He didn't find his way back to the table, though, but hooked up with the girl who had followed him in from the Australian bar. They went home together and in the morning he promised to ring her. He didn't ring, but instead went out alone on Friday night and met a professional dancer. Then, on Saturday night, he met another girl, the prettiest of the three.

On Sunday all three girls called him, so he booked them for dinner, a drink and a movie interspersed during the week. He would have to be careful to remember their names. Big Hair – Jenny; Leggy Dancer – Lorraine; Button Nose – Kimberley, or Kim.

He spent most of Sunday watching the movement of his B&O CD changer, selected to random play, with distant fascination. The girls' names with his nicknames were written on a piece of paper on his lap. Three nights of sex with different women had left him with a feeling of numbed exhilaration, yet still he felt uncertain and unfulfilled. The sex, great as it was, wasn't enough. He knew that when he was with the girls he would be thinking about Bernice.

He groaned. Of all the times to start falling in love with someone: just as he had learned how to get his kicks and thrills, but before he had had the opportunity to enjoy them.

On Sunday night he summoned up the courage to read the Suez article, in full. He had been putting it off. As he moved through the magazine he made a careful point of avoiding the shears woman. An alarm bell was waiting to ring in his brain if he turned to those pages, although his rational mind reassured him: the photograph was unpleasant, that's all, and so there was no purpose in his looking at it again. He knew the cockroach was still there. It had to be.

He read the Suez article quickly and was relieved; as he had hoped, it was dull from beginning to end. There were no sudden tricks in pace and style. No nasty surprises.

He turned to the crossword and studied another clue.

The female possesses.

He smiled and wrote in the answer.

Her. Her eyes, her hair, her neck, her sex appeal.

Her breasts, he considered dreamily, thinking of Bernice. He was starting to get the measure of this crossword.

He read the Suez article again, but slowly this time to make sure he hadn't missed anything. He stopped at a section, about two thirds of the way through, and frowned.

Suez marked the end of Britain's aspirations of Empire, with the realisation that all future foreign policy must doff its hat to the wishes and whims of the two superpowers. Eden was to retire in disgrace and the Nation was to feel the prick of its imperialist pretensions. It was all spent.

All spent.

The phrase was somewhat inappropriate to the text, but that wasn't what was bothering him. Mary Stone had said something similar in his dreams... *all spent, my love?*

He had an idea and collected a notepad and a magnifying glass, which had been sent to him years ago by a grateful forensic expert. He turned to the front of the magazine to find Mary Stone and her eyes flashed at him as he opened her page.

He had remembered that the page opposite Mary Stone contained some writing that was so small it was illegible. With the benefit of his magnifying glass he saw that it read: *By subscription only. All contributions to the publication to be delivered via our standard terms of trading. Published by Rever of London.*

Lewis wrote *Rever of London* on his notepad. His magnifying glass wandered over to Mary Stone and he clearly saw the blemishes under her skin, the shadows made by tightly packed foundation cream. BB was right. In one of her large green eyes he believed he could see his own reflection, but it was just a reverse reflection in the glass. He moved the magnifying glass down. He was sure her cleavage was getting lower. He examined the ultra thin gold chain around her neck, which connected to a round flat object tucked into the neck of her tunic.

He breathed out thoughtfully and turned to the letters page, to find the subscriber who was advertising a patent. It occurred to him that if he examined the patent application he would be given the address of a subscriber. He wrote down the patent application number on his notepad and put the magazine back onto his coffee table, pleased with his detective skills.

All spent... it was a coincidence. Either that, or he must have seen the phrase in the Suez article, even though he had only read the beginning.

He slept peacefully that night, so worn out by the last three days that Mary Stone didn't need to visit his dreams. In the morning, as he lay in bed listening to the radio, he wondered whether he was being ungrateful by being so suspicious. He had never been so happy, so looking forward to his week: happy clients, happy boss, no money problems and plenty of sex.

Her.

What could that mean? What was the crossword telling him?

Perhaps 'Her' signified Bernice: perhaps it signified that she was his next prize, his next reward.

He hoped so, from the lowest reaches of his stomach he hoped so, but still he was troubled. There were three uncomfortable coincidences that made him wary of Bernice.

One: she had said *Just stop lighting them*, and he had.

Two: she was the spokeswoman for a company that appeared to live in the nineteenth century, just like Farthing.com.

Three: the crossword answer 'Bern' was the first half of her name.

HER

As he pulled into the car park of Baron Enterprises Lewis was surprised to see that Bernice wasn't waiting for him. His mind was turning this over as he parked and went through into reception, where Howard Raine met him, offered his hand and led him to his office. The journey was uncomfortable, for Raine offered no conversation during their walk.

In the office he was introduced to Mr Booker, the branch's Health and Safety Manager; Booker appeared near retirement age and had the harassed look of a man with an impossible job to do. Raine rattled off some monotone congratulations on the Vernon Jones claim. Booker nodded along, then remarked that the union was loosening up on him in the committee meetings, although they had lodged an official protest over the covert surveillance.

"How did you respond to that?" Lewis asked.

Booker coughed, a smoker's cough many years in the making, and Lewis experienced a sense of relief at being free of the nicotine. "We told them that if their members are honest then they've got nothing to worry about," Booker replied in a thick Yorkshire accent.

"Good answer," Lewis confirmed, wondering how a Yorkshireman had found his way here.

"We've told Head Office about you too," Raine declared. "But Mr Marker is, ah, not impressed with you."

"I'd be worried if he was," Lewis replied amiably.

"Indeed," Raine agreed.

There was a pause, no one offering to speak.

"So what happens now?" Lewis asked eventually, aware that he had lost a little mind game by being the first to get down to business. Raine sat back with a thin smile.

"We have terminated our retainer with... with the London lawyer," Raine announced. "We are giving you the Newport account. You will be working directly with Mr Booker: you'll refer to him on every case that's transferred."

Lewis nodded and said, "Marvellous, thank you. How many cases are being transferred?"

Raine glanced at Booker. "About forty," Booker mumbled. "We have on average about two accidents a week. As they're notified, we'll pass them on to you." He scratched his ear and avoided eye contact with either man. Lewis suspected that he was more comfortable on the factory floor then here in a meeting with his boss and a lawyer.

"Think you can handle that?" Raine asked.

"No problem," Lewis replied. His stomach was jumping up and down with excitement. "By the way, who handles your other branches?" he asked. Bernice had told him that Baron had twelve UK factories. Where was Bernice? She should have been here.

"Other lawyers, local firms, control the English accounts," Raine answered cautiously.

"Are you happy with them?"

"I'm only responsible for Newport," Raine said, clearly reluctant at having to admit to a limit to his authority. "Head Office in the States has the final say, but... ah, they'll be watching your progress carefully now."

Lewis nodded, not taking it any further.

"But there are two things you need to know if you have your eye on the entire UK account," Raine added, his eyes gleaming.

"I didn't say…"

"First of all, one swallow doesn't make a summer. Let's see how you get on with the Newport work."

"Of course," Lewis said.

"Secondly, you will need to delegate if we're going to increase your instruction twelve fold. That means Baron must have… have full confidence in your practice."

"I understand," Lewis said. He wasn't even thinking about the UK account – Newport was enough for him. Forty new cases! Two new cases a week! He would have to clear his filing cabinets and give all the old cases to Graham and Rhys, perhaps give a few of the smaller ones to Stuart. Well that was fine: Graham and Rhys were moaning that they didn't have enough work. On second thoughts, he would free up Stuart completely, to help him on the Baron cases.

It occurred to him that he could even go on his own now, with a little office somewhere and a secretary. But it was too early days to think about that; Raine had warned him that he was still on probation.

"Ms Connor has told you about our strict policy on paper files?" Raine asked casually.

Lewis nodded. "Understood. I'll have an IT specialist come in this week to set up the secure portal."

"Use ours," Raine murmured. "I'll arrange for him to contact you. Baron will pay for everything."

Lewis smiled his thanks at having been spared a difficult conversation with O'Neill. He supposed that now was the time to raise the question of the hourly rate; he was still pessimistic about meeting O'Neill's hopes of one hundred and twenty pounds an hour.

"As you know, we have a policy on solicitors' rates," Raine said.

Lewis managed an expression of mild indifference, as if the rates policy was the furthest thing from his mind.

"The policy is non-negotiable," Raine added.

Lewis nodded, disheartened.

"The rate is two hundred and fifty pounds an hour," Raine announced.

Lewis' stomach didn't leap this time; it froze, in shock. "Two hundred and fifty?" he repeated quietly.

Raine nodded. "Plus expenses," he confirmed. "The company has always paid well above the market rate, but there are two... ah, two catches. First, it is no joke, our policy on confidentiality. If you breach it we will close you down. Second, you are our lawyer twenty-four hours a day... every day. We can call you anytime and you always leave a contact number. Is that agreed?"

"Agreed," Lewis said.

For two hundred and fifty pounds an hour he would happily hoover Raine's house and give birth to his children.

As the meeting closed Lewis attempted to make some light conversation, feeling that it was the least he could do given that they had been so generous. All his questions on how the factory was doing were deflected politely. Lewis made one last stab. "Now that the case has settled, has Vernon Jones returned to work?"

Booker had been looking at his lap throughout the entire meeting with a depressed face. "No, he's not coming back," he muttered, without looking up.

"You've sacked him?"

Booker shook his head and cleared his throat. "No no, we'd have happily had him back. He was a good lad. But he's in hospital, having a back operation."

"Back operation?"

Raine's eyes glinted with satisfaction as his thin lips found a smirk. "Ironic, isn't it?" he said. "That football game really *did* put his back out. We had a call from the hospital yesterday, they say that he has neural damage, or some such thing… caused by extreme exertion before his work injury had been allowed to heal."

Lewis didn't say anything. He was replaying his call to the football club when he had posed himself as a talent scout.

"His fault for deciding to play," Booker remarked acidly.

"Greedy, foolish young man," Raine agreed.

Lewis sat silently for a few moments, then nodded, shook hands with both men and left. In spite of his triumph he was feeling downcast as he wandered back to his car. He knew that any feelings of guilt over Vernon Jones were misplaced, but Raine and Booker's closing remarks almost seemed like taunts to his subconscious, as if they carried some double meaning.

His fault for deciding to play.

Greedy, foolish young man.

On the drive back Lewis had stopped off at the Patent Office to collect a copy of the specification from The Shilling subscriber, then parked in a lay-by to read it. He studied it only briefly before he slipped it back into his briefcase; it was a pulley device, an invention called *The Hour*, filed by one Mr S. Dove with an address care of a firm of solicitors on the south coast. Lewis called the solicitors on his mobile, but the number given on the specification wasn't recognised. Well, he would look up the number when he got back to the office.

By the time he had returned to the office he had decided that he wouldn't bother. The solicitors wouldn't release Mr Dove's address, they *couldn't* release it. Better to follow up Bernice's lead on the ex-model, when he had the time.

Bernice… why hadn't she been at the meeting? He felt aggrieved – after all, he had gone to all the trouble with Vernon Jones to save her job.

As he parked, automatically avoiding the low wall, he knew he was kidding himself. He had pulled the stunt on Vernon Jones to impress her. He wandered despondently down the six steps to the office door.

Bernice was sitting uncomfortably in the reception area. O'Neill was also there, shouting at Helen over a letter with a first class stamp, which had been returned in the post. Bernice was trying to pretend she wasn't hearing the exchange and she stood up quickly when Lewis entered. His eyes registered his surprise but he quickly gestured her downstairs to the boardroom. O'Neill barely seemed to notice her as she sidled past his flailing arms.

"Sorry about that," Lewis said as he closed the boardroom door firmly behind him.

"Not your fault, surprise visit," she said. She opened her briefcase with an efficient click. "I've brought you some brochures on internet security. It's company policy I'm afraid."

He looked at her and blinked. "You've got your hair down," he said. She had thick wavy hair and he found it hard to imagine that she was able to get it into such a tight knot.

"I know," she said, smiling.

"It suits you."

"Thank you. Oh, and congratulations on the case."

She was wearing her prim blue suit, but the jacket was open today to reveal a Mondi top that was not as discreet as he would have expected. She had a slim waist given the generous dimensions of her breasts. Lewis felt his pulse quicken.

"I was hoping to see you at Baron today," he said.

She smiled and considered her brochures, then looked up, suddenly uneasy. "You've been there?" she asked.

"Of course," Lewis replied. "Mr Raine made the appointment last week."

Bernice stared at him with a blank expression.

"What's the matter?" he asked.

She shook her head and put a crooked finger to her lips.

"Bernice?"

"Oh dear," she murmured, shaking her head again.

"Bernice – what's the problem?"

"Mr Raine didn't tell me," she said. Her eyes were filling up. "I mean I knew you were getting the account, when you got the settlement and everything, but Mr Raine said he wanted to tell you himself."

"Well, I can understand that."

"No, but he didn't tell *me* about the appointment."

"I wouldn't read too much into that."

"No, no, it isn't right. It isn't right at all. He should have told me." A tear started in the corner of her eye that she spotted away with a finger, and Lewis fought back a fierce compulsion to hug her. "He must be displeased with me. I know it. I just know it."

Lewis' hand settled on hers. Her hand was cold. "That's ridiculous," he said gently. "How could he be displeased with you? You found him a new lawyer and on the first case the new lawyer has saved the company – well what is it? – one hundred and thirty five thousand pounds?"

"You think so?" she asked, brightening up.

"Of course! Besides, there was someone else at the meeting."

"Who?"

"The Health and Safety Manager, Mr Booker."

Bernice nodded, a little reassured. "That could explain it," she conceded. "Mr Booker and I don't really get on. I keep complaining to Mr Raine about the number of accidents, you see. Mr Raine wouldn't want us both there at the same time."

"You can't really blame Booker for the accidents," Lewis commented. "After all, he's not allowed to explain to the workers how the process works. In fact, I bet he's got a difficult job. He looked a bit harassed. I don't know how he gets round the HSE."

"HSE?" Bernice asked.

"The Health and Safety Executive."

Bernice nodded. "Who are they?" she asked, a little shyly.

Lewis smiled at the joke. Then he realised that she wasn't joking. "Eh, national body that has to be notified whenever there's a serious accident in the workplace. When they're notified sometimes they visit and put changes in place, sometimes even put up prohibition notices."

Bernice was looking thoughtfully at her papers. "How would they know if there was an accident?" she inquired.

Lewis shrugged and said, "Well the employer has to notify them, by law."

"Oh I see." Bernice was still looking at her papers, her lips pursed.

"You'll have to give me the HSE notification if there's a case to defend on liability."

She didn't answer.

"Bernice?"

"Baron won't defend them," she answered. "The cases will just be about the amount of damages, like with Mr Jones."

"You're worried about all the accidents, aren't you?" he asked.

She nodded despondently.

"But I've got a feeling that you aren't about to risk your job over it," he added. "Baron are a lot more generous than I believed. I'm betting that you're on a pretty respectable package."

"Trust and confidence are very important to them," she confirmed, in a deeply serious tone. "They *are* generous.

And I need this job, Lewis. I need it desperately. I've got… got commitments back home."

"Come out with me one night, we'll talk about it," he suggested. She was taken aback at this sudden change in the dynamic of the conversation, then she smiled sadly.

"Lewis, I think you're wonderful, I really do. But I can't."

Lewis' heart sank. "Boyfriend?" he asked.

"No, nothing like that." She shook her head firmly.

"What then?"

"I'd be sacked if Baron knew we were seeing each other because they'd think my position was being compromised. They've got strict rules on relationships. They're afraid of information leaks."

"Oh, right." His spirits lifted; at least he was in with a fighting chance. "Okay, so we don't tell them."

"No, it's too risky."

"We won't even go out. Come to my place, we'll eat, we'll talk, no one will know," he argued. She shook her head again, unconvinced. Then, without warning, he reached across the table and brushed his lips against hers. Instinctively she leaned away. She left the brochures on the boardroom table and collected up her briefcase.

"I have to go," she said, as she hurried out.

"Ring me," he called to her back as she made her way up the stairs. At the top of the stairs she paused, then threw him a quick smile before she left. He was slumped against the boardroom door when the nineteen-year old, Tracy, came out of the typing room and favoured him with a big smile.

"Who was that you were talking to?" she asked.

"Just a client," he answered smugly. Her eyebrows were raised as she walked past him.

Tracy, Tracy, he thought. First you can't take your eyes off me and now you're getting all jealous on me. I have to admit to myself: I'm just a sex machine.

The sex machine didn't manage his Thursday rendezvous with Big Hair; Monday night with Button Nose and Tuesday night with Leggy Dancer were more than enough for him. Wednesday he squashed with BB and when Thursday came around he couldn't face the thought of sitting through more hours of small talk with an immature town girl. He was relieved when he freed up his time to enable him to watch a film with a takeaway curry. Godfather II, vindaloo and red wine. It felt like paradise.

But that night Mary Stone visited him again. She crawled into his bed and whispered something in his ear that acted like adrenalin and he ran around the apartment, naked, trying to find her. He seemed to run for hours, for days, until eventually he found her in one of the wardrobes, where she dragged him inside and closed the door. The rotting aroma in the tiny space was oppressive and his sense of smell took on a blind man's acuity in the pitch darkness. His chest was pounding with the exertion, yet he couldn't escape his desire for her. His hands were lovingly on her shoulders, his legs going weak as she brought him to climax to the music of The Weeping Wall. She had begun with her lips and her tongue, but then she started to bite.

This time he didn't wake up.

"Please, please stop," he whispered.

"Don't make me laugh, you know what you like. Don'tcha, my little soldjar?"

"Just be gentle, please, please be gentle."

She chortled as she began a fresh assault with her teeth. His hand reached over helplessly to her thick and lustrous hair, and he stroked it awhile, until her hair slid off her head. Her head was as smooth as an eggshell.

He woke at last and reached down to check that he was

all there, still intact. His sweat had soaked the bed, as if he really had been running for hours.

It's my bloody libido, he thought, perhaps a side effect from giving up the fags and having all this extra energy. Either way, I only have these dreams when I don't have sex.

He made a decision to ring Big Hair and fix her up for next week, even though he had already arranged to see Button Nose and Leggy Dancer again. He would go into town tomorrow too, with or without BB.

He felt his eyes closing again. Well, he had had worse problems to solve.

The next afternoon, about the time he was hearing the 5.30 lager call, O'Neill stormed into his office.

"What's this Stuart tells me, that he's working for *you*?"

"That's right," Lewis replied, without taking his eyes of the computer screen. For the last few days O'Neill had been floating on air in the knowledge of forty new cases and a stratospheric charging rate, but now another one of his landlord and tenant cases had hit crisis point. Lewis had given Stuart strict instructions not to take work from anybody, not even O'Neill. Lewis had already had a minor run-in with Graham and Rhys over his appropriation of the trainee, but this dissolved when he had explained that he desperately needed help to meet the new volume of work.

O'Neill's eyes were malevolent from behind his spectacles. "You can forget it, young man," he declared. "I've got an urgent case that needs to be worked on."

"Well I've got forty of them, Stephen."

"Stuart is my assistant, not yours. You'll manage." He turned to leave.

"Stephen."

Lewis' voice was sharp but measured, just like O'Neill's. He smiled at the computer screen as he noticed its effect, as he saw O'Neill stop in his tracks.

"Stuart is busy, very busy. So are Graham and Rhys, and David and Paul. They've had to take my entire caseload over. Be thankful that they're busy. I've got forty new cases, some of which need investigating urgently. All need reports and valuations. They're all going a hundred miles an hour with me in the driving seat, clocking up at two hundred and fifty. I can expect another two in next week, and two more the week after that. Now, do you really want to lose this account?"

O'Neill softened at the mention of money. Lewis could sense that he was doing the calculations in his head, all over again.

"I don't like my authority being challenged," he returned guardedly.

"Fine. Tell Stuart that it's *your* decision."

O'Neill shrugged and held up his file. "Who's going to help me with this?"

Lewis smiled at him and then returned to his computer screen. He didn't answer.

Lewis didn't go home that night. He met a girl in the 5.30 bar and she left with him at 6.30. He had needed no introduction from Stuart; no one even knew who she was.

Rhys and Graham watched him as they left, mystified. Stuart said, a little too loudly, "You're the man."

"Just on a roll," Lewis replied, insensitive to the feelings of the girl on his arm.

He insisted that they go back to her place. He had become uncomfortable with having sex in his own bed, because that was where Mary Stone always found him.

Well, she wouldn't find him tonight.

When he wandered in on Saturday morning he slumped on his settee with his post, thankful for a few hours to himself. He put on some music and as he placed his remote control back on the floor he noticed the patent application that he hadn't had the time to read.

He put his post aside and flicked through the document, trying to make sense of the diagrams. It was a machine that seemed to be operated through a complex system of weights and pulleys. There was no fuel or electricity needed, the movement of the operator gave it a kinetic energy. No, the user wasn't called the operator, he discovered, but the *subject*.

The subject is placed here... he read, turning the diagram upside down to study a rudimentary drawing of a man with his arms pulled out on levers, with his legs spread-eagled on two turning wheels.

The moving body of the subject activates the levers, here, and here, so keeping the machine in motion.

In a second diagram heavy weights were depicted crushing the spine over a number of complex processes, while the arms remained pinned. It was a sort of mechanical crucifixion.

The invention is called The Hour because it takes, on average, an hour for the subject to die.

It was an instrument of torture, Lewis realised, hardly able to comprehend that this thing was in his hands. He read the registrar's grounds for refusal. Refused on moral grounds. No shit. Police investigation recommended against the applicant and his appointed representatives. Damn right.

He decided that Mr S. Dove needed some serious help. He reached for The Shilling and held it up, considering the black cover with its creeping white ivy and inscription: Fashion. Ambition. Temptation.

"You are out of here," he murmured. All the same, he found his pen and wrote in another answer to the crossword.

Weight hanger.

The Hour.

Hour.

And then he threw the magazine down in disgust.

Later that day Bernice called. She spoke nervously and quickly. He spoke quickly too, as he gave her his address. They both put the phone down without saying goodbye.

He spent the rest of the afternoon on the settee, curled up in a ball, smiling.

HOUR

Bernice allowed him no more than a peck on the cheek as he let her into the apartment. Throughout the evening she would smile only occasionally, but he knew it was a persona she brought out for situations such as this, if indeed she had ever been in such a situation: in a man's apartment, on the first date.

After dinner they sat on the sofa, and she ensured that there was a safe distance between them. She had, however, gradually relaxed during two hours of table talk and had eventually told him about herself.

She lived with her brother, Jamey, in London. Jamey was five years younger than her and had a rare form of leukaemia; their mother died when she was only nineteen – they had never known their father – and she had dropped out of university to look after Jamey rather than see him institutionalised. She commuted during the week, and the only time that was her own was on the weekend, when Jamey was hospitalised for treatment. During the weekdays he had a professional carer and support equipment, which used up most of the money, but she had built up a savings account for him, to fulfil his lifelong ambition of going to Florida. When Lewis asked whether that would be possible she nodded her head vigorously and insisted that it would be so. Her eyes told a different story, of a tower of hope that she and Jamey constructed long ago, which crumbled a little with every month that passed.

Lewis was humbled by her story. Not too long ago he had thought himself the world's unluckiest man because he had lost some money on shares. He had been on the point of throwing in the towel and escaping to Spain, flying away on his own pathos. Here was Bernice spending half her life on trains to earn money for a dependent brother. He understood now why she was so careful with her job, why everything about her, her reserved demeanour, her attempts to make herself look older, were all carefully laid precautions for keeping it. She was wearing her hair up tonight and perhaps it was part of her persona now, although she looked great in her jeans and loose shirt.

"You had your hair down when I last saw you," he said. His words were slurring a little; in his nervousness he had drunk too much wine. She was sitting up correctly, occasionally running her finger around the rim of her wine glass. It was only her second glass of the evening.

"Is that why you asked me out?" she asked.

"Yeah, guess so."

She smiled. "So you only find me attractive with my hair undone?"

"No, no. It's just that I glimpsed a different side of you, a less defensive side, I suppose. It gave me courage."

"You were very forward, if I remember," she remarked with mock severity.

"Sorry."

"That's alright."

"I like you, Bernice."

"I think you'd better call me *Bernie*. I'm only known as Bernice in work."

"Yeah, I like that. Bernie?"

"Hm mm?"

"I like you."

She sipped her wine and reflected on the view. "Well, I like you too," she said.

He sighed inside, rejoicing at these words, but he felt at a loss. These days he was used to being in control of such situations, but he was struggling to find the right words.

She seemed to sense his anxiety as she carefully placed her wine glass on the coffee table. "Oh, did you speak to that model?" she inquired, to casually change the subject.

"Model?" he asked despondently.

"You know, the ex-model. The one that used to work for that agency you were trying to find."

"Circus," he confirmed. He shook his head. "Actually, Bernie, there's another favour I'd like to ask of you." He had scribbled a name on a piece of paper, which he now passed to her.

"Rever of London," she read. "Publishing house."

"It's not listed," he said.

"You want me to ask around?"

"Would you?"

She shrugged and sighed, but he suspected that she was glad to be of help, a reconfirmation of her executive prowess. He had the impression from her occasional asides throughout the evening that she wasn't too confident of her skills, that she couldn't quite understand why Baron had hired her, let alone why they paid her what they did. She wouldn't declare what her salary was, nor would she describe the circumstances in which she landed the job; he supposed this was another wall of Baron confidentiality, which no amount of red wine was going to break down. She had nimbly parried all of his questions about Baron and Howard Raine until he had got tired of asking and gave up. However, she must have mentioned a dozen times how important it was that no one should know she was here.

He smiled his thanks as she neatly folded up the paper and placed it in her bag. "I don't know what I'd do without you," he said.

"You have a lot of clients who seem to be lost," she said ruefully. "I think you need a full-time private investigator. Still, I know a lot of people through my position in Baron. I'll call in a few favours."

"What exactly is your position?" he asked casually.

"I told you. I'm the Newport liaison."

"Yeah, but what exactly does that involve?"

"Hiring and firing!" she said suddenly, pointing two fingers at him like guns. His mind was turning as he laughed. When they had first met he assumed that she would be preparing all the claims materials, but he now knew that Mr Booker handled all that apparatus. Bernice didn't even know what the Health and Safety Executive was, so she clearly had little knowledge of litigation. He couldn't see her having a role on the factory floor either. He thought about the distant banging from the old warehouse and couldn't imagine her as part of that with her neat hair and suit. And from the potted history of her life he knew she hadn't obtained any academic qualifications. In fact, he didn't think she hired or fired *anyone*: even *his* hiring all came down to that crucial first meeting with Raine. So, what did she do? Really?

For God's sake, Lewis, stop being so suspicious, he thought. Here you are with a beautiful date and you're being Sherlock Holmes.

The CD that had been playing came to an end; there was a pause as the disc of the B&O CD changer disconnected and the silence prompted her to look at her watch. He suspected she had been waiting for such an opportunity.

"You want a taxi, don't you?" he asked. She considered him with a resigned face and nodded. "Did I do something wrong, Bernie? Did I say something?"

She had that sad smile again: the smile that pictured an impossible fantasy. "Lewis, I've had a wonderful night," she said. "Really wonderful." She reached over to him, kissed him and her lips parted for a fraction of a second. He put a hand on her back and felt her breasts briefly press against his chest before she pulled away. His heart skipped a beat: he knew he wasn't going to sleep well tonight.

"Bernie, can I ask you something?" he murmured. She threw him a cautious glance as she collected up her handbag and took out her mobile. He swallowed and asked, "What would you say if I was to tell you that I get bad dreams, I mean really bad dreams, if I sleep alone?"

She got through to the taxi company and politely gave the address, telling them, on Lewis' direction, to ring the buzzer. She gave a false name and put the mobile back in her handbag, then turned to him with her arms crossed. "Lewis Coin," she said, "I'd say that that was probably the most feeble pick-up line I've ever heard in my entire life."

"Right," he agreed as he finished his wine. He managed a smile.

After Bernie had left he decided to get steaming drunk and knocked back two bottles of wine. He threw up on the way to bed and barely felt himself touch the sheets.

Sunday he nursed a hangover and was still feeling delicate over his Sunday bar meal in the Bay Hotel. He hadn't dreamed, but that could have been because of the booze, he wasn't sure. Then again, maybe it was that kiss, just that one kiss, which was enough to keep Mary Stone away.

Mary Stone! What was he saying? Keeping his libido at bay – that's what this was all about. He knew he was crazy about Bernie, that he must have been thinking of her all along. And in a way, perhaps Mary Stone reminded him of her; they both had the figures he dreamed of, and the swanlike neck. They both wore their hair up, with sensuous modesty. That could be it.

That and all the crazy things that were going on with his body right now. Good things though, he reflected as he sipped his Guinness. He smiled at two members of the bar staff.

They think I'm lonely, he realised. Well, about a month ago they'd have been right.

He enjoyed his private joke. He couldn't stop thinking about Bernie, and he suspected that he was entering that irrational phase when all he did was think of Beatles songs. *Got to get you into my life.* That was a good one. He hummed it a little. *Here, there and everywhere.* It was perhaps a little sentimental, but why not?

Bowie never seemed to work for him when he was in this type of mood.

The Guinness felt good in his stomach; he imagined his metabolism absorbing it, instead of destroying it. There were still no cravings for nicotine; a few weeks ago he couldn't have imagined enjoying a Guinness without a cigarette in his hand.

Nothing wrong with being happy, he decided, taking another glug.

Sunday night creaked.

He smelled WD 40.

He was walking, at least he had the sensation of his legs moving, although they were going in awkward directions, and floating on air. He was moving in a circle... no, in an orbit, as the framed picture in the bare room was occasionally passing his eyes on a vertical trajectory. The picture was the one in Raine's office: the buildings and three people in the far distance. His head was spinning and the arid taste in his mouth told him he had been sick some time ago.

The creak of the machine, of hydraulic joints finding

points of resistance and release, sounded in time with his legs. He felt the distant presence of pain, distant because he was dreaming, but if he concentrated the agony became part of his experience.

His legs, he realised, were disjointed, as only through the fracture of his ankles and femurs could he follow the direction of the machine. It had been a blessing when his bones had finally cracked. His arms were spread-eagled and something was pressing into his back, pushing out his stomach as his spine fought against the pressure.

The chiming bells of the Weeping Wall were sounding somewhere in the distance. A voice in his head, the real him sleeping in bed, cursed with anger and frustration.

He was rotating on the invention called The Hour. The fresh-faced twin was kneeling on the floor, painting his face with a thin artist's brush, as his head passed by like the hand of a clock. Her older looking sister was sticking hatpins into his chest. She was taking special care to synchronise the coloured heads of the pins, to make a rainbow. He sensed that Mary Stone was here, watching him, waiting for her entrance.

"Fuck this!" he shouted, and woke up.

Shortly he started to laugh.

He was awake and he wasn't even sweating. He had beaten it... he had actually beaten it.

It was just before midday when Helen put through a call, saying that the man had withheld his name. The caller had heavy breath and was wheezing down the phone as the call was connected.

"Lewis Coin, can I help you?" Lewis said.

"Yes, I'm looking for the solicitor who visited the Patent Office yesterday."

"Yes, that's me. Who is this?" Lewis guessed that it was someone from the Patent Office saying that the copies had to be returned, that access was restricted on moral grounds. But he was wrong.

"This is Mr S. Dove," the caller wheezed.

Lewis struggled to get up to speed in his head. His instinctive urge was to put the phone down in disgust, but this was a real subscriber to The Shilling, someone like Emily who carried crucial knowledge. He was also the inventor of a torture machine, however, so there was no question of meeting this man in his apartment. It had to be a public place.

"You requested the application, so I assume that you're interested. Are you?" Dove asked.

"Very interested," Lewis confirmed. "Can we meet for lunch to discuss it?"

"I don't like busy restaurants."

"Neither do I, but I know a good Chinese and there's a table I always take near the kitchen where no one bothers you."

There was a pause. "Very well, tomorrow?" came the voice.

"No, I'm only free today. I can be there in half an hour." Lewis was thinking quickly; Mr Dove would probably check up to see if he was a subscriber, but this way he wouldn't have time. He wouldn't have checked yet, because the patent copies were signed for in the name of the firm.

"It's short notice," Dove grumbled.

"I'm on a trial tomorrow which is going to last the week," Lewis explained. "It will be a shame if we don't get a chance to discuss your... your *work*."

"That's true. Yes, that's very true. We must leap on the moment. I'll leave now. Where is this place?"

"You're in Cardiff?"

"I'm outside the Patent Office. Where's the restaurant?"

Dove was out of breath and sweating when the Chinese waiter showed him to Lewis' table; he was a large, heavy man with an upright posture but who clearly didn't care for exertion of any kind. He was trying to regain his breath as he took off his jacket before sitting down; he was wearing a short- sleeved shirt and even though it was a cold April day his sweat had stuck the polyester cotton to his chest and arms.

"Let me take your jacket, I'll hang it up for you," Lewis offered, while passing him a glass of wine that had already been poured. Dove took the glass uncertainly and sat down. "Nothing worse than leaning against your jacket when you're having a meal, with car keys sticking in your back," Lewis added. Dove was about to say something but Lewis was already walking to the coat stand at the entrance, where he hung the jacket up next to his. He returned quickly and settled back into his chair in a relaxed fashion.

"Thank you," Dove said, with a shrug and a sip of his wine. He frowned appreciatively and took a longer draught. There seemed to be no sign of his perspiration coming to an end. Lewis gingerly managed a finger spring roll with some satay sauce, which the waiter now brought without the need for an order.

"So, you approved of my invention?" Dove asked, already having cleared the spring rolls and moving on to the dim sum. Lewis caught the waiter's eye and mouthed the word 'duck'. The waiter nodded and made for the kitchen.

"Certainly, absolutely," Lewis replied, floundering a little.

"What in particular interested you?"

"Oh, many things... no electricity... it just keeps going by itself, doesn't it?" In his head, Lewis saw a big exclamation mark next to an even bigger question mark.

He had been hoping that the dialogue would slip towards The Shilling without any prompting.

Dove nodded enthusiastically as he ate. "Self-propulsion is a wonderful concept," he agreed. "I'm fascinated by pedal cycles, for example, and all the different forms that manifest energy." He sighed then said, "Gravity...' as if he were naming his favourite film actress.

Lewis nodded, turning the word *gravity* round in his head as he regarded Dove's huge frame. Then he was reminded of Baron's 'process', the Articulating... something... something, the components that created their own energy without the need for fuel. He went cold as he wondered whether there was a link.

"Have you heard of Baron Enterprises?" Lewis asked.

"Who are they?" Dove responded, offering Lewis a full view of the dumplings in his mouth.

"Never mind," Lewis said, relieved.

The duck arrived. Lewis had already had a long word with the waiter before Dove had arrived and when he had slipped a twenty into his pocket. Keep the food coming as quickly as possible, he had said. He didn't want Dove to have a moment to sit back and think. There was another bottle of wine, already opened, on standby.

"So how long have you been a subscriber?" Lewis asked, refilling Dove's glass. The glass had prints from the man's wet palms.

"Oh, about two years now," Dove replied, nodding with approval as his glass was re-filled.

"Are you rich yet?" Lewis asked jovially.

"What do you mean?" Dove mumbled, forking the shredded duck onto his plate.

"Well, it only takes a few of those share tips, doesn't it?"

"Yes, but Farthing only allows you to invest modest amounts at a time," he remarked as he rolled a duck pancake which had too much filling and which was falling out of the wrapper as he lifted it to his mouth. The pancake stopped short of his mouth, however, and was returned to the plate. "As you *know*," he said slowly.

"Yes of course," Lewis smiled, and made to top up his glass. Dove waved the wine bottle away.

"How did you get the application number of the patent?" Dove asked.

"Through The Shilling of course, in the letters page," Lewis responded, looking hurt.

Dove nodded. "Do you pay your subscription annually or monthly?" he asked.

"Oh, monthly," Lewis replied casually, his heart pounding. Dove stood up quickly, like a badly launched rocket, knocking his chair over in the process.

"Where's my jacket?" he growled, looking around. Lewis gestured to the waiter again, who promptly trotted to the cloakroom at the entrance. He collected Dove's jacket and waited by the door.

"I'm sorry, there must have been some misunderstanding here," Lewis said. "Don't worry, I'll pay for the meal."

"I know you will," Dove said and stalked out of the restaurant snatching his jacket from the waiter on route. Lewis placed some money on the table, then allowed a few seconds to pass, his hands on the table, before he also jumped up and left.

He had Dove's wallet in his hand during his telephone conversation with BB and he was scrunching the worn leather in his palm as he talked.

The credit cards had revealed that Dove wasn't his real name, which hadn't surprised him in the slightest. The police were probably still looking for an S. Dove and a fictitious firm of solicitors. There was nothing in the wallet with an address, although there was a printout of an e-mail from Farthing.com. Dove had already let it slip that Farthing was connected to the magazine, but this was concrete proof and Lewis was basking in the knowledge that his original theory – that The Shilling was a cipher for share tips – was correct. And the e-mail was gold dust. It read:

Eight across.

Riches can be torture.

Look in the edition of The Independent this Thursday.

Your servants, sir

Lewis had the financial section of *The Independent* on his knee as he talked to BB. He explained that a company called Hour Glass was tipped and which cross-referenced to the clue in the crossword. He asked BB to buy the stock on his behalf so Farthing.com wouldn't trace the purchase back to him.

"I don't know," BB muttered, "I don't want to get involved."

"They can't find out. This is a share tip. If you buy it, all it means is that you bought *The Independent* on Thursday."

"What if Dove goes back to Farthing and tells them you've got his wallet? Maybe they'll pull the stock."

Lewis nodded and said, "I know, I thought about that. But I don't think he will. He'll be afraid of being expelled. Remember how quickly they expelled *me*? I bet he's broken the rules by printing off the e-mail, too. No, he'll cancel his credit cards, which are probably in an assumed name anyway, let me have the tip and put it down to experience."

"How can you be so sure?"

"Simple. He hasn't contacted me, even though he knows I stole his wallet. He's putting as much distance between us as he can."

"Okay, but I still don't want to rush into anything."

Lewis sighed irritably. "The way Farthing works is that the subscribers have a limit they can invest. That way they stay hungry. The share profits are more like wages, I suppose. That's why they threw me out when I went out and bought Lowe Waste Management. But we've got a chance to make a killing here."

"Wages for what?" BB asked. Lewis had told him that the Hour was an invention, but nothing more.

"Well it's a network, isn't it? They all make whatever contributions they can. This guy invents things. Perhaps they wanted me for some legal advice. The share profits mean that the subscribers don't have to work, which frees up their time. There certainly isn't a subscription fee, anyway; that's how he twigged me, so the subscribers must be doing *something*. Look, we'll split the profits."

"Split the profits?"

"Yeah, I've raised thirty grand on my flat. Buy thirty grand tomorrow in your name. Then we'll split the profits, two thirds me, one third you. Call it a payment for being my broker! How does that sound?"

"You seem pretty confident they're going to go up," BB murmured. "Be careful Lew."

"I am being careful." Lewis' tone showed his irritation. "BB, we'll never get lucky like this again. It was quite a coup, wasn't it, getting that wallet? I told you I was right about not throwing the magazine out, didn't I?"

Lewis spent another fifteen minutes reassuring BB, confident in the knowledge that he was going to go for it. It was the same old story… make them do the sums in their head. Eventually he smiled and sat back, thinking that he would have made a good con man.

BB bought the shares first thing the next morning and then they both had a nervous weekend. A takeover deal was announced on Monday, and the shares tripled in price. BB rang him, elated, wondering whether they should invest more. Lewis told him, in no uncertain terms, to sell the stock immediately. He had been following the progress of Lowe Waste Management and the Swiss company Clear Medical and both their fortunes had soured. Farthing. com's recommendations were clearly not for long-term investors.

The following Saturday Bernie came round again and Lewis presented her with a necklace, a fine chain with a diamond pendant. She hadn't been able to make the previous weekend because Jamey had relapsed, but he was stable again now. She had telephoned Lewis from the hospital a few times, giving him whispered progress updates. He had wondered whether Baron owned the hospital or had spies posted.

Her caution was rapidly disintegrating as she looked at herself in his hall mirror, her fingers on the diamond. "Oh Lewis, it's wonderful, just wonderful."

"You're wonderful," he said. "And it's nothing. I've had a good week, that's all." He took her hand and led her to the sofa. "And don't worry," he said, "there's no strings, and no more stupid get-you-into-bed lines. I've got all that under control." He smiled. "I'll wait as long as you want to wait."

"I don't want to wait," she said, and then looked down in disbelief at her own temerity. Lewis melted.

"It's okay, Bernie, I don't want to you to do anything you don't want to do. I... I love you."

It had only been two weeks since that first awkward date, but they both knew that things have changed. He had missed her desperately, and he saw in her eyes the shared experience.

She whispered, inaudibly, the words "I love you too." They reached for each other.

In the morning Lewis was relieved to find that he was still in love, that it wasn't all a mirage built on lust and fantasy. They had a cosy breakfast on his small balcony, both wearing their sweaters as they ate their croissants to the sound of the seagulls.

He had chosen this moment to show Bernie The Shilling, explaining that it was better to read it in the fresh air because it had picked up something bad in the rubbish. He gave her a brief history of the companies he had bought on the strength of the clues, and told her about Farthing.com. He didn't take the explanations any further. Bernie began with the crossword then methodically turned to the beginning of the magazine. She remarked on the six noticeable pockmarks on Mary Stone's forehead and turned the pages suspiciously. She winced as she turned to the pages Lewis knew contained the shears woman.

Lewis was looking away now, playing with his shoelaces. He hadn't looked at the photograph of the shears woman since he had stamped on the cockroach. The pages frightened him.

She winced. That means she's seen the cockroach.
The cockroach is still there...

He frowned at these intrusive thoughts, not knowing where they came from.

Bernie had come to the photographs of the twins and now took the opportunity of laying the magazine out on the balcony table.

"I don't wish to be unkind," she said, "but this woman on the right really shouldn't be a model."

Lewis glanced at the photographs and nodded, noting the streaks of grey in her hair. The twin on the left looked pubescent, barely into her teens. The older twin seemed slightly taller now and their hands, still in prayer mode, were no longer parallel.

"What's that smell?" Bernie asked.

"As I said, it picked up something in the bin," he replied.

Her nose twitched with distaste as she turned the page.

"*Mrs Wife*," she murmured eventually, having found the letter from the 'serial adulterer'.

"I know," he said.

She read another letter. "Now that's odd..." she muttered.

"Everything about this rag is odd," he remarked.

She pointed to a letter in the top corner. "No, I mean there's a letter from a reader, commenting on the letter from that awful misogynist."

Her finger was on a small letter in the top left hand corner, which he hadn't noticed before, probably because it was so short.

Sir,

I was interested in the letter from the serial adulterer.

I have had three husbands in my time, and they may or may not have been unfaithful. I cared not.

I have always thought that adultery must be a lonely craft. Your subscriber may find the experience more thrilling if he were to tell his wife of his infidelities, preferably while administering a sound beating.

Respectfully yours,

A widow.

"The adulterer must have written in before," Lewis decided, frowning. He had the vague notion that another letter used to sit in that far corner, some letter that was so bland he couldn't remember what it said.

Bernie glanced at him and shrugged. "Well, I just hope the Widow was being sarcastic about the beatings," she said, then closed the magazine and smelled her fingers. She took a perfume spray out of her handbag and squirted it into the cold morning air. "I think your friend BB is right," she said. "I think you should throw it out."

"I will."

"When?"

"I was going to throw it out a few weeks ago, when I came across... well, something bad."

"So why didn't you throw it out?"

"I have to keep it. For the moment at least."

She shook her head in confusion. "You really think it's about share trading, or whatever you call it?"

"I know it is."

She put a crooked finger to her mouth as she remembered something. "Rever of London," she murmured. "Is that why you asked me to search the name? Do they publish this thing?"

"Yeah. Did you find anything?"

She shook her head slowly. "Nothing at all. Believe me, Rever of London doesn't exist."

"You're sure?"

"If I couldn't find them, with all the contacts I've got in Baron, then they don't exist."

"What contacts are these?"

"Ah, that's trade."

He sighed. Even now, she wasn't prepared to be open about Baron, and he was again wondering whether her contacts were as extensive as she was making out. "You're not still worried about losing your job, are you Bernie?" he asked, thinking about the false name she had given when she had called the taxi before.

"Always," she admitted.

"Don't worry, no one's going to find out."

"You need to be very careful... Lewis, *please* be careful," she implored. He could see that she was shaking.

"Of course I will be. Look, if it's the weekends here, not going out at all, well that's fine... but I'd like to think that at some point in the future we can lead a normal life."

"But what's wrong with this, Lewis? We're happy here, aren't we?"

"Never been happier," he agreed, "but I want to take you out, Bernie, you know, restaurants and weekend trips. Normal stuff."

"Lewis..."

"I want to send you flowers. I don't want to have to lie."

"Lewis, please..."

"*I'll* help you to look after Jamey."

She stiffened and turned away. He decided not to press it any further; in fact he may have already gone too far and he realised he had better retrieve the situation quickly.

"Last night was the best night of my life," he said, truthfully. She was still looking away but her hand found his. She gripped it tightly.

"It was wonderful," she whispered. *"You're* wonderful."

After Bernie had gone he came back out onto the balcony to collect The Shilling, which had been left on the freezing cold patio table. The wind had blown the magazine open to the page of the crossword, and there was a long box answer running down which caught his eye. It had the letter N planted as the third letter, and the last letter L. He knew the clue.

She says.

He supposed that he knew the whole crossword, inside out, if he were to really test himself, but only now did the answer to this particular clue come to him. He wrote it in with the pen that always seemed to find its way into the crease of the magazine. The answer fitted. He took the magazine inside and left it near an open window.

Wonderful.

He supposed that it was all too good to be true, his theory that this was just an insider trading magazine. Just a little too neat. Someone, somewhere, had the lowdown on him and was manipulating him. Someone knew that he wanted Bernice Connor, knew that she said 'wonderful' all the time.

He hated thinking this way, turning the people in his life into suspects. In fact he wasn't going to think like this; he was prepared to believe that it was coincidence.

Happiness was fleeting, and he was going to hang onto it with his teeth if he had to.

Part Three:
Suspicion

1 across   who do you bring?
2 down   to own
3 across   made the fires
3 down   do not accept it
4 across   no rooms
5 down   the process
6 down   she says
7 down   how many now?
8 across   weight hanger
9 down   The Shilling says

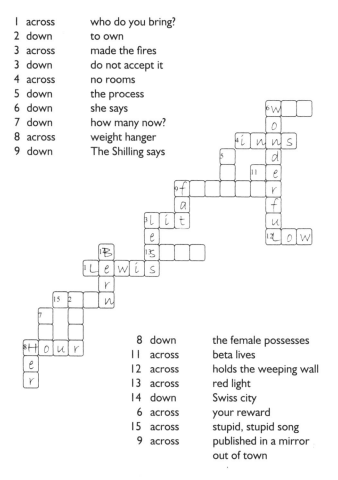

8 down   the female possesses
11 across   beta lives
12 across   holds the weeping wall
13 across   red light
14 down   Swiss city
6 across   your reward
15 across   stupid, stupid song
9 across   published in a mirror
        out of town

WONDERFUL

A congenial partners' meeting at the beginning of summer 2002 had O'Neill announcing an increase in the partners' drawings. Baron's £250 charging rate was starting to impact, although O'Neill attributed the increase, at least in part, to his domestic economies.

"Perhaps we should introduce ourselves to Baron," Graham suggested to Lewis, after congratulating O'Neill upon the innovation of second-class Friday postage.

"Take some of the pressure off you," Rhys agreed, equally anxious to bill at this astronomical charging rate so as to help him meet his costs target.

Lewis said nothing, just cleared his throat as some cigarette smoke wafted across the boardroom table. Out of the corner of his eye he noticed that O'Neill was staring at him.

"What do you think?" Graham asked.

"Thanks, but I can manage," Lewis answered. "I'm busy, but I'm not overburdened by any stretch."

"Yes, but it would be good if Baron could meet all the partners," Graham remarked. With a glance at O'Neill he said, "Perhaps we can organise a drinks thing at the office."

O'Neill's eyes were still on Lewis, but he said nothing.

"No, I don't think so," Lewis murmured.

"Well what would you suggest?" Graham asked. "Should I book a restaurant or something?"

Lewis shook his head firmly. "Baron only wants the

one contact point."

O'Neill now sniffed and leaned back in his chair. "Baron is a client of this practice, young man," he said.

Lewis studied his fingers. "Sure, but that's the way they want it." He looked at O'Neill with a shrug that said that all further suggestions and questions were pointless.

Lewis didn't mind the fact that the pay rise was being spread evenly between the four of them, but he felt a vague sense of injustice that his efforts hadn't been fully acknowledged at this meeting. Well, he could at least make it clear that Baron was his client, and his alone, then let them sweat about it.

The pay rise came at the right time, for Lewis had been eyeing the duplex penthouse of a new development in Cardiff Bay and with his Hour Glass profits, and a part exchange on his apartment, he was just able to secure it. Cardiff Bay was booming and the duplex non-negotiable at £450,000, but all Lewis saw was the magnificent floor to ceiling window, the water view and the 2500 square feet. On the day he exchanged he was elated. The next day, he was stressed and fearful.

With a colossal mortgage hanging over him, Baron's good favour was more important than ever and in late June an important case came to a head. This was a test case for the union overtime rate, which would affect future claims from all the UK factories and Marker had the bit between his teeth. Lewis was insisting that the claim be defended, he matched Marker with case authority for case authority and aggressive e-mail for aggressive e-mail, and on the last day of Marker's deadline the union threw in the towel and paid costs. Lewis danced around the office for a full hour, but there was no call from Mr Booker in response to Lewis' triumphant e-mail, or from anyone else at Baron.

That weekend Lewis asked Bernie if Mr Raine was

pleased with the progress being made, to which she smiled and said "I'm sure he is." To Lewis this simply signified that she didn't know.

He had been expecting some sort of acknowledgement for his efforts. Was Baron expecting him to work wonders, similar to the Vernon Jones business, on every case? Surely, they had to understand that the claims needed to be settled at reasonable levels. He couldn't keep pulling rabbits out of hats…

"I think you're doing a wonderful job," Bernie insisted.

It was their last weekend in the Atlantic Wharf apartment, and he was experiencing pangs of regret at leaving. The walls were paper-thin but at least they were his: how could he have been so stupid as to get into debt again? The Baron instruction could be history at any time, and for any number of reasons.

As if Baron had a blueprint of his fears, his heart twitched and his stomach turned when Raine telephoned at one minute past nine on Monday morning. With an abrupt and miserly use of words he summoned Lewis to Newport.

Lewis swallowed and tasted something unpleasant as he parked and looked up at the brick chimneys of the warehouse. They were still smoking he thought, which had to be a good sign. In his head he composed a few pleasantries, just in case Raine was in the mood to chat.

"I've brought some notes on some of the cases, if there's any you want to talk about," Lewis opened uncomfortably. Was Baron going out of business? Re-locating perhaps? Had they found another lawyer, God forbid?

"I don't discuss individual cases," Raine answered, shaking hands without making eye contact. He settled back into his chair with a long, exhausted sigh. "That is Mr Booker's job," he added.

"How is Mr Booker?" Lewis asked pleasantly.

Raine threw him a questioning glance, as if the inquiry was highly personal.

"I mean, how is he getting on with the union?" Lewis said quickly. He had been unable to breach the wall of formality and Mr Booker, when he telephoned, always insisted on calling him Mr Coin.

"He says the atmosphere is far more accommodating," Raine acknowledged, then carefully picked up his fountain pen and raised it parallel to his ear in contemplative repose. He then touched the nib with his forefinger, to test the ink, and with a gentle murmur in his throat he signed his name on the cover page of a thick document in front of him. "Can you guess why I have invited you here?" Raine asked after he had put down his pen.

"I have no idea," Lewis replied truthfully. He had been mesmerised by the movements of the pen, the scratch of the nib on the paper, and now blinked to break the spell.

A thin smile crept across Raine's face as he ran his forefinger down his high side parting and Lewis wondered if the ink would rub off in his scalp.

"I'm assuming you're not displeased with me," Lewis said, when Raine declined to say anything further.

"Quite the opposite," Raine said immediately, as if Lewis' show of self-doubt was his cue. He passed the document across the desk and Lewis saw that it was a service contract. "Head Office has instructed me... to offer *you*... the entire UK contract."

Lewis' brain failed to fully register the news; instead, he glanced up at the framed picture on the wall as his mind wandered. He still couldn't make out the three figures in the distance of the old and faded photograph.

"The picture on my wall interests you?" Raine asked. Lewis snapped his attention back to Raine and shook his head.

"I'm sorry, I was just thinking," he said. "Of course, I'd be delighted."

Raine gestured to the document. "You should read the agreement before deciding," he said. "There are... ah, there are some conditions."

Lewis drove back down the motorway in a daze then took a detour to his favourite Chinese restaurant. He spent an hour there mulling things over, sipping wine and fiddling with his chopsticks.

When he returned to the office he went up to see O'Neill and reluctantly handed in his notice. On being questioned Lewis told him about the new account and the conditions required to keep it. O'Neill inquired about the conditions. Lewis explained that firstly he would require a completely new bonus structure, a structure that would make him the highest earning partner in the practice, by far; secondly, there would have to be some radical changes to the firm. He listed them.

O'Neill listened patiently, and when Lewis was finished he remarked in a deadpan voice that these demands were indeed unacceptable. Lewis should be out of the office by Friday. Lewis nodded, saying he understood, but O'Neill declined to shake his hand.

The following day O'Neill walked into his office and said that he was prepared to reconsider. Lewis wasn't too surprised, guessing that his boss had being doing his sums overnight, and he set out his agenda quickly and efficiently: he wanted a meeting of the entire practice, secretaries, everyone, to be followed by a meeting of the litigation department. He was to be given a free rein at both meetings; if O'Neill overruled him on anything then all bets were off.

The entire firm squeezed into the boardroom the next morning in an atmosphere of worried anticipation, for everyone knew that no new work was coming through the post or through the door and that the firm had lost its insurance companies. The staff didn't know about Baron and weren't aware of the onslaught of instruction coming to Lewis via e-mail. Lewis was leaning against the bookcase as he called everyone to order. The clerical staff and assistant solicitors looked at him in surprise, a few turning to O'Neill, expecting him to tell Lewis to shut up and sit down. O'Neill, however, was playing with his pen, seemingly in a world of his own.

"Good news and bad news, ladies and gentlemen," Lewis announced. "First the good news. Harrier & O'Neill is in the best shape it's been in for years and everyone's job is secure. I know some of you have had your concerns and just so you can be sure that what I'm telling you is the truth, I've got an announcement. Everyone, and I mean everyone, is getting a twenty five per cent pay rise, effective immediately."

There was a group murmur of surprise, which floated like a balloon for a few seconds before it burst into many whispered conversations. Some of the secretaries were asking why Lewis, the quiet one upstairs, was announcing all of this. Everyone settled down as he cleared his throat to speak again.

"There are going to be other changes too." He glanced up at the cheap strobe lighting above the boardroom table. "You're all being given a long weekend so that the office can be extensively refurbished. Next week you won't recognise the place, you'll all have new computers on your desks."

Another group murmur and now there was some chatter amongst the girls.

"Quiet please," Lewis said coldly. He fixed his eyes upon the culprits and the boardroom went silent. "Now the bad news. The pay rises come at a price, I'm afraid. There are going to be other changes. Harrier & O'Neill is going to be a well-run, well-oiled machine. This office now closes at five p.m.. I don't want to see people putting on their coats at a quarter to. I don't want to see late lunches. That's all over. Everyone works… and works hard."

He turned to the firm's receptionist, and said, "Helen, I want you to read your paperbacks somewhere else. If someone is waiting for me in the boardroom I expect to be told. If someone is waiting for me in reception and I'm out, I expect a call on my mobile." She opened her mouth to speak but he raised a finger to silence her. He was still annoyed over those two incidents when Bernie had surprised him in the office, when no one seemed to be looking after her. "Secretaries, I expect no less than fifty pages of type each day. Some of you have always done it, others haven't. There are no more excuses. I expect computers to be on at one minute past nine in the morning and there are no more cigarette meetings in the kitchen. No private calls. You speak to the solicitors with respect and you don't answer back. If you don't do what you're paid to do, you'll be out. That's the deal."

One of the secretaries muttered, "I don't believe I'm hearing this." She was a middle-aged woman who remembered Lewis as an articled clerk.

"Do you have something to say?" Lewis asked, turning on her. She blanched with anger.

"I don't know who the hell you think you are, my laddo, but…"

"I'll tell you who the hell I think I am," Lewis broke in. "I'm the partner who says how things are going to be. It shouldn't be a hardship to expect a full day's work for a full day's pay."

"If I want a coffee break, I'll have a coffee break," she answered without meeting his gaze, but smiling and nodding to some of her younger counterparts.

Lewis' face was impassive. "Really?" he asked.

"Oh yes."

"Well you can have it on your own time," he said. "And you can have your P45 too." He had been hoping that this particular secretary would pipe up, the mother hen in the growing centre of discontentment in the basement typing pool, which the solicitors called Red Square. Baron had promised him that they would settle any unfair dismissal claims resulting from staff walkouts brought on by the changes he had to implement.

Mother Hen almost smiled before she realised that Lewis was serious. "You know where you can stick your P45," she hissed, barging past him and stamping up the stairs. Some of the staff looked at O'Neill incredulously: O'Neill had always been a tartar, but he had never sacked anyone. O'Neill was still fiddling with his pen, seemingly oblivious to events.

"Anyone else?" Lewis asked, considering the faces in the room. "To be honest I'll recruit a whole new typing pool if I have to." No one spoke. If he could sack Mother Hen on the spot just for answering back, then he could do anything. All the clerical staff filed out in confusion, leaving only the lawyers.

The solicitors were now fully briefed on the pyramid structure that was to be introduced. On Baron's insistence, only Lewis could talk to Mr Booker, the Health and Safety Manager, and only Lewis could speak to Mr Marker, the union solicitor. All e-mails from the twenty-five or so new cases to be delivered each week would only go to and from Lewis' computer. That meant that everyone involved with the Baron account worked directly for him, preparing case summaries and damages calculations, which he would then approve and use as his own. Installed software would hide names and essential facts when printed off his computer in order to maintain complete confidentiality. O'Neill had already explained all this to Graham and

Rhys; the three men were having their own meetings now, without Lewis.

Lewis closed by emphasising a few fundamental points.

"Stephen remains as administrative partner. Rhys handles all the rest of the firm's cases. There aren't that many, after all. The rest of you work exclusively on the Baron claims, reporting to me on everything. As you'll have noticed, Stephen has given me the authority to dismiss anyone summarily. If that authority is withdrawn I leave, immediately, taking the work with me. If anyone speaks, or attempts to speak, to anyone at Baron then they're fired. If anyone attempts to access my computer, they're fired. If anyone communicates with the union solicitors, they're fired."

"How do we know this work is going to continue to come in?" Graham asked, deeply depressed. He had drawn lots with Rhys to see which of them would handle the other work, and he had lost.

"I can't explain because I'm not allowed to," Lewis replied. "What I can tell you is that the process that Baron uses is revolutionary, their client base in the States is phenomenal. If anything, the work will only increase as the plants expand. Trust me on this."

"Yes, but miracle process or not, they can still decide to stop instructing us. Where would that leave us?"

Lewis shook his head. "We've agreed a six-month break clause. We're to be given six months notice if they're going to withdraw the work. They agree that this is only fair, given the unique structure we have to put in place."

"But why is secrecy so important to them?" Graham persisted.

"It's not secrecy, it's confidentiality. Hopefully in about a year's time the process will be in the public domain and then we can all get back to business as usual. I don't like having to lay down the law like this. I'm speaking for Baron, that's all."

"But can't *you* trust us?" Graham asked. O'Neill stopped fiddling with his pen and looked up.

Lewis sighed and said, "Believe it or not, it's for your own good. I literally had to beg Baron to use the firm. I won't lie to you, they wanted me to leave, to set up in Newport somewhere outside the reach of the restrictive covenant and recruit a completely new practice." He smiled. "Have some sympathy with my position. That would have been easier for me, wouldn't it? I wouldn't have had to go to Stephen and suggest the new pay structure – that was embarrassing for me." He made a gesture with his hands. "I wouldn't have to go through all this."

Rhys and a few others shrugged and nodded at this reasonable explanation, but Graham was thinking that Lewis should look up the definition of *partnership* in the dictionary. Stuart appeared distinctly uncomfortable; he had already been at Lewis' sharp end over the Baron cases and was getting used to running up the stairs now when Lewis shouted down to him.

"Two hundred and fifty pounds an hour, gentlemen," Lewis remarked in closing, "and as much work as we can handle. That's got to be worth a few sacrifices, hasn't it?"

Harrier & O'Neill trembled during the month of July as the staff came to understand the meaning of Lewis' deadlines. One of the assistant solicitors, a smart but plodding lawyer, was sacked and replaced. Two members of Red Square were early casualties for making sarcastic comments in front of Lewis, but were replaced immediately from a hoard of applicants bidding for the salary on offer. Gradually things started to improve as everyone evolved into their new roles; Graham adapted to taking orders from Lewis then cursing him behind his back, while Stuart replaced his fear of Stephen O'Neill with fear of Lewis Coin, finding that one fear was no worse than another. And the sombre mood lifted somewhat when the newly-enhanced salary cheques were received as the office account flooded with money.

Lewis was able to shave £15,000 off the mortgage just with his summer drawings. He estimated that he just needed eighteen months, at the outside, to have his place paid for and so he decided to replace his burnt-out Mazda with a Mercedes SLK, but his requests that Bernie should join him on some romantic country lane were turned down. She was still sticking tightly to her security precautions, as before, even refusing to meet his neighbours. She continued to slip in and out after dark and order her taxis under assumed names.

Lewis was jealous of the devotion that he knew would move her to make any sacrifice. She would sacrifice their love affair, if he made her choose. Sometimes he wished that Jamey would just hurry up and die, and he hated himself.

The only person Bernie did allow into their secret relationship was BB, for she had expressed interest in meeting the one friend Lewis often talked about, and sometimes in connection with The Shilling, which kept finding new places to lurk, like a dirty pet.

She had agreed entirely with BB's assessment, that Lewis was drawing emotional support from the crossword. She had tactfully suggested that he go and see someone... someone *qualified*... and talk it through. Lewis hadn't even dignified this suggestion with a response. He simply bit his lip, in doing so, aware that he had probably just managed to avoid their first argument.

Someone qualified indeed...

When BB visited the duplex for the first time his jaw

dropped as he considered the domed thirty-foot high window set into the front elevation, which overlooked the bay. The duplex was like a cathedral on the water.

"It took my breath away too, the first time I saw it," Bernie said as she shyly offered her hand.

BB considered her for just a little too long, before taking her hand. "Right," he said.

She didn't lose her smile as BB turned away and looked up at the staged platform that led back into the bedrooms.

"Lewis said you used to be in the music business," she said.

"My tourist site's doing just fine," BB answered, his gaze still upwards.

Lewis was smiling too but his eyes now took on a puzzled aspect.

"Oh, I'm sure it is," Bernie said, nodding. "Lewis says you have a computer person working with you. Computer person... oh dear, is that the right description?"

"He's got a degree, for your information," BB murmured.

"Oh I'm sure he has. I wasn't suggesting..."

"Come and see the view," Lewis offered uncertainly. As they walked out onto the balcony BB caught Lewis' eye, but with no more than a momentary raising of his eyebrows. BB reluctantly agreed to take a photograph of Lewis and Bernie, arm in arm at the rails.

"Our first photograph," Lewis explained. "You're the only one who can take it."

"I still don't like this," Bernie muttered uncomfortably, a closing shot on a long and heated discussion earlier.

"I'll keep it in the bedroom," Lewis reminded her. "Who on earth is going to see it?"

BB snapped, then shrugged with indifference when Lewis asked him whether he wanted a coffee. Lewis wanted to say something, but instead held his breath as he went into the kitchen. He barely noticed that he was making the coffee, his hands on automatic as he listened intently for conversation on the balcony.

"Do you ever think about taking up music again, BB? I can call you BB, can't I?" Bernie asked.

"Whatever."

"So... do you intend to play again?"

"Why do you need to know?"

"I'm... I'm just interested."

"I'm doing okay. I've got irons in the fire. I may not have the big apartment yet, but I'll get there."

"Oh I'm sure you will, I'm sure."

"Well let's leave it at that."

BB only sipped his coffee before he announced that he had to leave, that he was meeting his computer friend for a drink. He merely nodded a goodbye to Bernie and said nothing to Lewis as he was shown to the door.

Lewis re-joined Bernie on the balcony, confused. He hadn't caught all of the conversation from the kitchen, but he had sensed that BB was on the verge of shouting at her.

"I'm sorry about that," he said, "I don't know what got into him. I know his tourist site isn't going as well as he hoped, and he's stressed. That guy who he thinks is a computer whizz has let him down..."

"It doesn't matter," she said, taking his hand, then she turned to look out over the bay. "Anyway, he's your friend and I thought he was perfectly charming."

BB appeared reflective when they meet up for squash a few days later and was reminiscing over the old songs and the record deals he had almost secured. Lewis sympathised to a degree, for an investment success, a really big one, always made you think you could conquer the world, but he had become angry in the intervening days. He had been considering the effort Bernie had made with BB, the effort of a woman in love, desperately wanting to be friends with her man's friend. Far more significantly, she had taken a great risk in meeting one of his friends, risking her job and her brother's welfare. When Lewis allowed himself to think of it, he fumed.

"What did you think of Bernie?" Lewis asked eventually, even more annoyed now that he had been forced to raise the subject himself.

BB shrugged. "She's okay. She seems to like you."

Lewis smiled but his eyes frowned. "You didn't think she was attractive?" BB shrugged again and didn't answer. After an uncomfortable silence BB changed the subject and Lewis smiled and nodded, going along with the conversation. Privately he was thinking that he was going to see a little less of this man now.

A full month had passed. Lewis and Bernie were standing on the balcony, when Lewis mentioned that he hadn't seen BB for some time. Bernie said that he should make an effort to keep his friends, that he should find time for them.

"For God's sake, Bernie, how can you be so nice? BB was pretty crappy to you when you met him."

"He was very pleasant, as I recall," she answered quietly. She appeared troubled. "I'm worried about you, Lewis. It's not like you to turn your back on a friend like this. It's that magazine isn't it? You still haven't thrown it out, have you?"

He shook his head. "It's not The Shilling," he said. "And anyway, I haven't written a new clue into the crossword for months."

"That's good," she remarked. "Very good," she added, after a time.

"Strange thing is," he said, "I know the answer to another clue. *Red light.* The answer is *Stop*, but I haven't written it in."

"Red light, stop. That's an easy one."

"I know. It's strange, but I didn't get it at first because I thought it might be something to do with prostitutes..." His voice trailed off; he hadn't told Bernie what Emily had been doing in his apartment that night. He cursed in his head as the mental image intruded once more.

Emily looking down, the lift doors closing.

"Funny thing is," he murmured, "that it's all been wonderful, the whole summer has been wonderful."

"That's what I always say," she giggled.

"*Wonderful*," he repeated. "Just like the last answer in the crossword."

"If you say so," she giggled again.

"This place, my car, the UK account. You. I don't want it to end." He turned to her, his eyes fearful. "I don't want it to *stop*."

She met his gaze dreamily then frowned, as she understood his meaning. "Oh come on, you can't believe that," she said incredulously.

"I know it," he said.

"No one can take this away from you," she whispered. "And I'm not going anywhere. I love you, you fool." She shook her head. "It's all in your mind, all of it. Just like BB said."

"Maybe it is," he said, "but if it's still true for me, what does it matter that it's only in my imagination?"

She opened her mouth to answer then reluctantly accepted this backward logic with a resigned sigh. "Well, in that case, don't write in the answer. Leave the magazine safely where it is, the crossword incomplete. That means it's wonderful for the rest of your life. The rest of *our* lives, okay?" She put her arm round him and gave him a playful squeeze.

He cheered up.

"It is a fantastic view, isn't it?" he said, taking her hand. It was Cardiff Bay: no obsolete dock, but the tranquil sea, framed by a huge barrage, with glass buildings on the landscape, emblems of the wealth and prosperity of the new rich. This was no night-time-only view, but a view for sunny days, where nothing needed to be hidden.

He was so contented that he felt he could almost smoke a cigarette, as if a cigarette would make it all perfect. He put aside the compulsion with a sense of alarm, put it down to the excitement.

After Bernie had left to catch her train he studied the crossword once more. "*Red light… Stop…* no, I won't write you in," he declared, leaving the magazine on the table, out of its plastic bag, as if to test his strength of purpose. He closed the windows, checking each inside lock, then fell asleep with the framed photo enlargement, the one he kept on his bedside cabinet, in his mind's eye. The picture showed the two of them on the balcony, Bernie wearing a reluctant smile.

Monday and Tuesday passed as normal days. The work was coming in at such a furious pace that the days were whizzing by, each day beginning with his barked instructions as he was given his first mug of coffee. He had arranged a timetable so that individual solicitors could come and see him to offer their progress updates and drafted correspondence, which they presented on floppy disc. Stuart dreaded his 10.45 appointment, which was becoming notorious as a time when the shouting started.

Lewis was more aggressive than normal during those two days. Somehow he knew that what he feared would come to pass. Every night and every morning he went through the ritual of checking his locks.

On Wednesday morning the magazine was on the floor of his duplex, open at the crossword. There, at 13 across, was the word *stop* in handwriting identical to his own.

Something deep inside him went cold as he walked out onto his balcony, leaving the magazine where it was. On Sunday night he had made a point of removing every pen, every pencil, from the duplex; there was nothing that could make him think that he had written in the crossword in his sleep.

The September clouds had daubed the sky with grey blotches and a chilling sea breeze made him wince, forcing him back into his apartment. He took a deep breath, then with mechanical resignation wandered around, again checking every lock, every bolt on the door and windows. Everything was in place.

"Bernie… how could you?" he murmured, when the tears eventually came.

STOP

He supposed he had been suspicious of Bernie all along. She was linked too closely with the crossword clues, but only when she had suggested that he see someone... *someone qualified...* had it dawned on him that Farthing.com wanted him to believe that he was losing his mind.

Perhaps it was some sort of initiation test, or maybe it was revenge for stealing the share tips. In the final analysis it didn't really matter.

Bernie had been caught out like a real amateur, though, because even madmen needed something to write with. She had the second key to his place and must have sneaked in on Tuesday night, or perhaps given the key to someone else, some professional. Again, the actual mechanics didn't really matter.

Logic was his enemy now, for there was no explanation other than Bernie's complicity. To put the matter beyond doubt he spent Wednesday morning checking out her heart-warming story of the sick younger brother; he rang every hospital in London that had a cancer ward, posing as a concerned relative, and sure enough there was no James or Jamey Connor.

BB hadn't liked her... he must have seen through her...

So, Bernie worked for Farthing. What sort of freaks were these people? She had prostituted herself simply for a crossword, to make some of the answers fit.

A thought crawled uneasily through his mind. Was Baron involved in all this too? Bernie had introduced him to Baron, and he worked so hard on the Vernon Jones claim for her sake, but he decided that it was impossible. There were too many claims, too much money going through the account for it to be a bluff. No, Baron couldn't be involved, because whatever else was unclear, at least the money was real.

He suspected that Baron had played some part in all this, albeit unwittingly. Perhaps Farthing had some contacts in there somewhere and were able to swing Bernie the job. That was reasonable, because he hadn't believed that she did that much in her role as 'liaison' or 'purchaser', or whatever she called herself. That was a joke – she didn't even know what the Health and Safety Executive was. No, Farthing had 'greased' her in.

With this deduction made, a grave danger loomed. What would she say to Raine when she knew that he had caught on? What lies would she tell? He had to get in the first blow, and so he rang the Newport depot manager.

"Yes, well?" Raine grumbled, as he was put through, clearly unhappy over this unsolicited phone call.

"It's Lewis Coin, Mr Raine," Lewis said. "Actually, this is a social call. I'm holding a house-warming party and I'd very much like to invite you and Mr Booker. I hope you can make it. I make a good punch..."

"Out of the question," Raine broke in.

"It's just a social evening," Lewis explained, "no one's going to talk shop..."

"It's out of the question, Mr Coin," Raine repeated.

"Right," Lewis said uncertainly.

"It's company policy," Raine added. "Things will become a little less... less sensitive when we have the official line from the US government."

"Fine. No problem. I'll tell Bernie that the evening's off."

"Who?" Raine asked.

"Sorry, Miss Connor," Lewis clarified.

There was a silence.

"Miss Connor was going to help me organise the party," Lewis remarked matter of factly.

"What?"

"Well, she helped me move in, so she offered to help with the house-warming party too. She thought it was only going to be my friends, but I thought I'd surprise her and ask her friends and colleagues from Baron as well."

"Miss Connor has been to your home?" Raine asked slowly.

"Well, yeah."

There was a further silence.

"Mr Raine, are you there?" Lewis asked. He was shaking but keeping his voice steady.

"Yes I'm here."

"Is something…"

"Do you have any proof of this?" Raine asked.

"Proof? Is something wrong?"

"Mr Coin, do you have any proof that Miss Connor has been to your home?"

"Just ask her," Lewis laughed back.

"I think you will find that she will deny it. I ask again: do you have any proof?"

"Well, okay, let me think. There's a photograph…"

"A photograph?"

"Yeah, a photograph of the two of us on the balcony."

Raine made a sound in his throat. "Will you let me see it, if it proves… ah, if it proves necessary?"

"Well of course, but you've got me worried. Have I done something wrong? I wouldn't do anything to jeopardise our relationship."

Raine grunted. "You weren't to know. You wouldn't have told me any of this if you knew, that's obvious. But you know now. Understood?"

"Absolutely."

"No socialising, of any description, with any employee of Baron. Clear?"

"Crystal."

An hour later Lewis received a call from Bernie. She was crying.

"Lewis, what did you say to Mr Raine? You told him about the photograph, didn't you?"

"Yes," Lewis answered coldly.

"How could you? How many times did I say?"

"What's he done about it?"

"He's sacked me," Bernie sobbed. She couldn't stop sobbing now and was unable to get her next sentence out.

"Good. Go back to London, go back to your fictitious brother."

"What?" she managed.

"And stay out of my life."

He put the phone down, and then went home. The locksmith was waiting for him as pre-arranged and Lewis stood over him as he changed the locks. When he had finished he made sure that all the new keys were handed over.

Lewis didn't go out for a few weeks, spending his time on his balcony, brooding. He became so depressed that eventually he decided to have a cigarette. He didn't really want one, but he was feeling mightily sorry for himself and he lit it with an air of tragedy.

The first drag tasted bitter, as it always did after a long period of abstinence, but the second drag tasted worse.

He considered the white stick resting awkwardly between his two fingers then screwed his face up. There was something vaguely inappropriate, something rancid about the taste. He threw down the cigarette and stamped on it with distaste. The packet went over the balcony rails.

The next day he re-assessed his life and cheered up. In a way, his experience with the cigarette had helped him, for at least his smoking addiction was cured. Things were still good, the money was rolling in and he would forget Bernie in time. Over the next few weeks he went into town again, but didn't meet anyone new. He supposed that he was still depressed, that it showed, and whether he liked it or not, he still wasn't over Bernie.

Bernie wrote him an official letter at Harrier & O'Neill, formally requesting a reference for a job application with a bookstore in London. He responded in an equally official manner then filed the reference request.

So, Baron weren't prepared to give her a reference and he was her last chance, he mused. It must have pained her to write to him: it was almost as if the story about the sick brother was true, that she would swallow her pride for his sake. He gave her a reasonable testimonial. If she was comfortably settled somewhere else, he reasoned, she was less likely to bother him.

The reference request arrived on the same day as an e-mail from Farthing.com. The e-mail was a further proof of Bernie's complicity, for he had changed his e-mail address and only she knew his new screen name. Perhaps he had been laying a trap for her even back then, subconsciously.

How could she have done the things that she did, just as a game? Not only the sex, but also the intimacy, the long evenings snuggled up on the sofa. What sort of hold did the network have over her to make her do that? He was pondering over this as he opened the e-mail.

The page was blank and he sat back, perplexed. Then the words appeared, one by one, slowly and awkwardly, letter by letter, as if typed by someone non-proficient with a keyboard.

Lewis,

Greetings

He had never seen an e-mail like this before, being typed before his eyes. He smiled and shook his head. These guys were crazy – they could make a fortune, what with their share research, their wonder nicotine drugs, their software and viruses, if they simply crawled out of their holes. Emily had said that the network was old and he hadn't believed her at the time, but now he wasn't so sure. Perhaps there were rules, old rules, by which they had to play.

So you jumped on the Hour.

Someone must be punished.

Who do you suggest?

He waited, but there was no more of the message. So, he was wrong about Mr Dove, the inventor of The Hour. Dove *had* gone back to the network to say that he had swiped his wallet. That was the only explanation for there was no way they could have traced the sale to BB otherwise. Hardly anyone even knew BB's real name, he had lived by his nickname for so long.

His mouse hovered uncertainly over the 'reply' icon. He clicked and typed a short response: *Punish that bitch you sent me. Keep it all coming: I'm enjoying myself.* He took a deep breath, clicked 'send', and the computer shut down with a low drone.

He picked up a piece of paper and placed it against the monitor. The paper immediately burst into flames and he shook it out with a muttered curse, discarding the embers in a clean ashtray.

That's some mean virus they've got, he thought, as he

rang his insurers. In his head he congratulated himself on having taken the precaution of taking out comprehensive cover on his new computer and for avoiding further blisters.

He was still one step ahead of them.

Lewis liked to make plans.

He would ride the gravy train for as long as it lasted and when it came to an end, as it inevitably would, then he would revert to his original idea of going to Spain, although this time he would go as a wealthy playboy. Hopefully by then Farthing.com would have grown tired of playing trick or treat, and if they hadn't he would be rich enough to take it in good heart.

He had decided to throw The Shilling away and he looked through it for the last time. With a resigned sigh he saw that Mary Stone's pockmarks had spread right across her forehead and the twins were as middle-aged mother and teenage daughter.

He turned to the shears woman and forced himself to look at the inside of her right leg, where the cockroach had been crawling. He took a deep breath and swallowed.

He had a theory about the pictures. It wasn't trick photography... it was the pages. They were specially treated so that individual films of the page dissolved to reveal a different picture underneath. That was why the pages seemed thick. They *were* thick. In fact, maybe it was the film of the pages slowly dissolving that was giving off the smell. He was tempted to have it analysed but he decided just to have done with it and throw it out. He had solved the mystery, and that was enough for him.

Friday came and The Shilling was the first thing into the black bag. This time he handed the bin man the bag and watched him lob it into the back of the truck.

He watched the truck for a time as it did its rounds.

The dissolving paper explained the disappearance of the cockroach on the inside of shears woman's leg. It was just a coincidence that he had stamped on a cockroach as he had been reading the magazine, for if he had looked at the page, when he had stamped on the thing, the cockroach would have still been there.

"It would have been there," he told himself.

Lewis was still thinking about imaginary cockroaches falling out of pages when O'Neill came into his office. O'Neill announced that Stuart had handed in his notice but he had talked him into staying and given him a pay rise. Lewis kept typing as his senior partner talked. O'Neill went on to suggest that perhaps he was being a little hard on Stuart, so Lewis listed five mistakes that Stuart had made in as many days. The last one, on file 'Jones 32', involved a missed deadline.

"They're small matters, really," O'Neill remarked as Lewis described the procedural errors.

"Nothing is small with this account," Lewis grumbled.

"But he's under a lot of pressure," O'Neill murmured. "Everyone is. You can only push people so far before something gives." O'Neill's voice was uncharacteristically gentle, but Lewis was unmoved.

"There's no choice in the matter, we have to work this way," he said. "If I let one thing pass, the floodgates open. And then say *bye bye* to the Baron account. Jones 32 could have been serious."

"Yes, but... Jones *32*?"

"Loads of employees called Jones," Lewis muttered in explanation. "I'm not given their full names or their addresses." He mumbled a silent curse as he made a typing error. "Confidentiality..."

O'Neill frowned then continued. "Stuart is doing his

best. It must be difficult for him to know exactly what you want from him all the time."

"Well he's got to learn then. I've got no problem with the pay rise, but he's got to learn."

"He says that you issue the instructions too quickly."

"Everything I say is perfectly clear. If it isn't, he only has to ask."

"I think he's afraid to."

"Well that's his look out. He should toughen up."

O'Neill straightened in his seat, but then thought better of what he was about to say. He smiled again and said, "Is it strictly necessary that everyone follows this timetable you've set up? When they can only see you at certain times of the day?"

"Absolutely. I'd be lost otherwise. My day is plotted by the minute from the moment I get in."

"I appreciate you're working hard too," O'Neill conceded.

"Harder than anybody," Lewis responded. He paused and scrolled back over the section he had just typed, nodding to himself as he read his text.

O'Neill sniffed and reflected a while. "Perhaps we should consider giving up some of the work, say a third of it," he suggested. "Let Baron find another firm to handle the London work. What do you think?"

"No way," Lewis replied, thinking of his bonuses. O'Neill nodded, expecting this to have been his answer. He considered Lewis for a few moments from behind his spectacles, masking his thoughts.

"How sure are you of these people, young man?" he asked eventually. "It worries me that they won't let us meet them, that they won't let us keep any records."

"Now we've been through all of that. Look, Stephen..."

O'Neill didn't let him finish, but stood up and stalked out.

Lewis tended to sleep late on Saturdays, to recover from his exhausting week, and on Friday evenings he was content to watch a few films with a bottle of wine while he did the weekly accounts to calculate his end of month bonus. He didn't go into town any more; there would be plenty of time for fun when he was a retired millionaire on the Costa Brava. There were no more Friday drinks with the rest of the crew either. He had tried it once but it felt uncomfortable; no one was relaxed around him now, not even after work with a pint.

It was a beautiful Saturday morning and the duplex was awash with an invigorating, almost purifying white light. In his heavy cotton bathrobe he imagined himself as some Benedictine monk waking to redemption.

He stepped out on to the staged platform on the first floor and stretched before making his way down the metal spiral staircase. He picked up his post and yawned. They were all circulars, except for the Law Society Gazette wrapped in cellophane, which he ripped apart lazily. The Shilling fell out from inside the Gazette and tumbled onto the beech wood floor. He considered the magazine as it lay there, then he heard a noise in the kitchen.

"Bernie?" he whispered.

"In here," came Bernie's voice. From the odd clunk she appeared to be loading the dishwasher or something.

"How did you get in?" he asked, his voice louder.

"With a key. You gave me a key, remember?"

"I've changed the locks. Get the hell out of here!" he shouted.

"Why are you being so horrible to me, what have I done to you?" came the muted response.

Lewis marched angrily into the kitchen knocking open the double doors. The kitchen was in pitch darkness, the only light coming from inside the dishwasher. Its door was clunking open and closed, lighting up the kitchen intermittently and somewhere, deep down in the machine, the Weeping Wall was playing.

"Bernie, where are you?" he whispered.

Mary Stone was now illuminated at the sink unit and he saw her naked for the first time, her body covered with sores. There were hands at his shoulders and the twins were behind him, forcing him to the floor. They ripped off his clothes and held his head as Mary Stone climbed on top of him. Her face was pitted with holes and shone like the moon in eclipse.

"Well now… ain't I a picture?"

A diamond pendant was dangling from the gold chain around her neck. He was cursing to himself but he wasn't waking up.

"Ah, my little soldjar," Mary Stone hissed, "you can do better than that. I'll warrant you can do better."

Her hair had been falling out as she straddled him. The last few thick strands now came away, leaving just the bun of hair over her left ear. The twins giggled.

"Who are you?" he moaned.

"Someone who deserves a bit more civility," she answered. "Throw me out, would you? Would you?"

A light flashed, way inside the dishwasher, as if a distant beacon had been lit. A crackling sound was all around him as something black, resembling solid oil, poured out of the dishwasher and washed along the floor. The crackling became a scratching. The floor was moving, and he saw that the black tide was a swarm of cockroaches. They were running onto his hands, up his arms and up the body of Mary Stone. The entire kitchen was crawling and scratching as he and Mary Stone came to orgasm.

He woke, soaking and breathless, but he wasn't in bed, he was on the kitchen floor. He had no idea how he had got down here, although there were some empty wine bottles lying around. Maybe he had got drunk and collapsed here last night. He didn't remember.

The post was there, unopened, and the Gazette was amongst it. He considered his sealed copy of the Gazette awhile, then walked over to it, picked it up and weighed it in his hands. He ripped off the cellophane and The Shilling fell out and onto the floor, open at the crossword.

A new answer had been written in.

The clue was: *To own.* The answer was: *Your.*

So it's mine, he thought. I can't throw it away.

That's what the clue was saying; *it's yours, Lewis, to own.* Or rather, that's what the network was telling him, in returning the magazine in the post. But as he turned the pages he realised that he was wrong, for this was a different magazine. The articles and the crossword were the same but the pictures of the models were new. The twins were in the same poses in prayer mode but they had been mirror reversed and were facing away from each other. Mary Stone was beautiful again, her complexion flawless, but her eyes now flashed to his right. The article on confidence in the workplace was now entitled 'workplace the in confidence'. The entire article was written backwards, and checking the Suez article he saw that it had the same treatment, the words running in reverse. The shears woman seemed the same as before, except that her shears were completely closed and there were no cockroaches.

This must have taken them a long time, he reflected. The back pages containing the crossword and the advert with the lady and the poodle were connected to new pages: there were no rips, so when they had put the new magazine together they would have had to have recreated the crossword by copying his handwriting letter by letter. The writing looked identical, it was true craftsmanship.

He turned back to Mary Stone and saw that the round

object previously tucked into her cleavage was now released. This object, which he had initially believed to be a shilling, was in fact a diamond pendant. Bernie's pendant, to be precise.

"Bitch," Lewis murmured, surprising himself that he was so upset whenever he had a further proof of Bernie's complicity. Had he not been sure from the beginning? Was he still hoping that somehow there was another explanation?

He flicked through. The advert for the Carbolic Smoke Ball was the same as before, as were the subscribers' letters. No... the short letter from *the Widow* in the top corner was different. This letter now read:

Sir,

Husbands were a distraction for a time, before I tired of them.

My first husband could be described as an individualist. He deliberated with a silver-topped cane, he called it his ferule, when expressing himself. He had it beside him on our wedding night.

It took him a full three days to die and during this interval I arranged for his portrait to be taken. He was unable to speak so I know not whether he objected, yet it was a good likeness.

Respectfully yours,

A widow.

Finally, Lewis turned to the advert of the city woman and the poodle. It was the same, except that the pile of dog excrement was much bigger. He shrugged and nodded, for the magazine was smelling worse than ever.

Well at least it's logical, he thought, as he studied

the advert. He made out the discolouration around the poodle's head from where he had first sprayed the page with air freshener.

He carefully examined the spray mark, which had turned the paper grey and crinkly.

He frowned, refusing to believe that he could remember precisely how that spray mark had appeared on the old page, because his memory told him it was identical to the mark on the new page.

No one, no matter how skilled, could identically copy a wet mark.

YOUR

Lewis now knew that if he couldn't throw The Shilling away, then he had to find out what it was. Assistance came in the unexpected guise of Mr Marker, the union solicitor.

He and Lewis had lately had a few civilised conversations and Marker had hinted that it was the union that had insisted he deal so ruthlessly with the claims. Now they had come to realise that this was counterproductive. Significantly, Lewis realised that Marker was in the same predicament as him as Marker lamented that he hadn't had a holiday for a long while and couldn't see when he would ever be able to take one. Marker, like Lewis, was the spearhead of every claim and everyone else in his firm worked in a support capacity. Lewis had a good idea.

They agreed a two-week cessation of hostilities so that they could both take a vacation and as they struck the deal Lewis made a joke about the Christmas football game between the trenches during World War One. Marker didn't comment and Lewis gathered that humorous irony was not to the union solicitor's taste.

Lewis' first port of call was the ex-model of Circus, one Jasmine Stimple, a woman barely nineteen years of age. At first he feared the name and address that Bernie had supplied were fictitious, but the girl was listed under her parents' address in Ealing Broadway, London; he made an appointment to see her at her home, under the pretext that he was acting for some of Circus' creditors.

He didn't care to drive through London, so he took the

train to Paddington and then the central line to Ealing Broadway. He was travelling with two briefcases. The first, a heavy holdall designed for large trials, contained a few changes of clothes and toiletries, for he didn't want to appear as a tourist when he eventually met up with Anton, the final quarry in his paper chase. The second was a thin attaché case, with a combination lock. To open this case required either the combination in his head or an electric drill. It contained The Shilling, wrapped up in a few plastic bags.

Miss Stimple wasn't at all what he was expecting from a fashion model. She was tall, nearly six feet, but a long face gave her a rather bovine appearance. She was also very overweight and had a distinct double chin with a third one on its way.

They sat in the front room of a pleasant semi-detached house, but the road badly needed speed ramps for there was a constant roar of cars breaking the speed limit and at first Lewis found it hard to concentrate. Jasmine insisted on having all the windows open and there were air fresheners dotted around the room. He spent some time talking to Jasmine's mother after coffee was brought, and when Mrs Stimple had examined his business card and appeared satisfied with his credentials and his character she left the two of them alone. She gave her daughter a reluctant nod as she went out of the door, an acknowledgement of an agreement not to interfere.

"Can I call you Jasmine?" he asked. The girl nodded, her mouth full of popcorn and he waited politely for her to finish and put the empty packet aside. He noticed two bars of chocolate close by on a sideboard, one already opened.

"I've got an eating disorder," she said, following his eyes.

He smiled. "Better than anorexia," he remarked.

"Nothing wrong with a good appetite. I've always had a thing about Mars bars."

She regarded him cautiously for a few moments, then got up and walked over to the sideboard. She wasn't making for the chocolate, but for a photograph, which was secreted within an ornate jewellery box. As she sat down she handed him the photograph, saying, "That's me, in case you have trouble in recognising me... about eighteen months ago."

In the photograph Jasmine was walking towards the camera in silver underwear and a lace shawl. He wouldn't have known her if he hadn't been told, for grey hollows in her cheeks and powerful brown eye make-up combined to give her an alien appearance. Her hair was intricately pleated in a fringe, far away from the thick careless bob she was wearing now. The girl in the photograph had virtually every bone in her body poking through her skin.

"They called us walking corpses," she whispered, "the Circus girls, I mean."

He carefully controlled his reaction, one of polite curiosity, as he put the photograph face down next to his coffee. He inwardly felt disgust, but it was self-disgust for he had found the picture erotic. Somehow, the way Jasmine's face and hair had been put together had complemented the emaciated and angular appearance. As he considered the plump girl sitting opposite him he found the leap of perception extraordinary, and she nodded, acknowledging the riddle.

"You're not really acting for the creditors, are you?" she asked.

He opened his mouth to speak, then hearing the approach of a car waited for the roar of engine and tyres to pass by. "I am a lawyer," he said, "but you're right, it is more complicated than that. I knew Emily for a short time, and there are some matters I want to clear up. Emily's dead you see, and I need to track down her partner Anton."

"Emily's dead?" she murmured, then nodded to herself thoughtfully. He couldn't assess her reaction to the news.

"Do you know Anton's surname?" he asked

"They both had the same surname, they were married," she replied.

"I didn't know that. So it's Anton Webber?"

"No, Lewinski."

The Police Accident Report had given him Emily's surname. She must have reverted to her maiden name when she returned to Wales.

"Lewinski," he repeated to himself, as two cars roared past.

"That won't help you find him," Jasmine remarked. "He went to a lot of trouble not to be traced after Circus folded and all the property was sold. He's probably living in their house in Kent."

"Where is this house?"

"No idea. No one's got any idea. When Circus was riding high he and Emily would go there on the weekends and there were no telephones or anything. None of us were told where it was, in case we let it slip to the Press."

"So they were hot property with the Press then?"

"For a time, but they weren't up at the top for very long. I was the last model they recruited… or Emily recruited, I should say. Anton was really out of the picture by then."

"Tell me about Emily."

"What do you want to know?"

"Anything, really. How did you meet?" He grimaced and glanced at the open window, but she ignored his appeal.

"Oh, in a nightclub. I was with some of my friends and she came over and asked if she could buy me a drink. She showed me her card and some of the Circus press reviews that she kept in this fancy brochure. She kept saying how beautiful I was. I thought she was taking the piss and my mates started laughing. She looked at my mates,
188

then looked back at me and shook her head with this expression that said how ignorant they were. I remember that moment so well. They all shut up. She silenced them with that look, and it was as if a spotlight came down from the ceiling and made me the most important person in the place, in the whole world. I never lost that feeling, all the time that I knew her."

Lewis was smiling by the time she finished. He found the story heart-warming as he imagined Emily putting the vain teenage friends in their place. "So you were fond of her?" he remarked.

Jasmine's eyes darkened. "I hated her," she replied. "I'm glad she's dead."

This was said in time with a heavy truck hurtling past, and although he almost had to lip-read the words the declaration awakened a memory in him. He remembered that edge in Emily's voice, the command on that Sunday morning which made him write in the first answer to the crossword. "Can you be more specific?" he asked.

"Well I don't know what she was like at the beginning. Some of the girls who had been there from the start had different ideas about her. I know that Anton was just another struggling designer when she met him and she convinced him to give up the designing and set up the model agency instead. But by the time I got to know her she was drunk most of the time. Anton too. That's why Circus went down, neither of them could stop drinking. The booze didn't make her act stupidly or anything, it just made her angry. She'd storm into the office at ten a.m. and spend the morning shouting insults over the telephone at people who were ringing up to complain about missed engagements and stuff like that. She was always tight on Bell's whisky. She kept bottles in her drawer."

"So why'd you work for her?"

"She wasn't like that at first. She was great at first.

When I came to see her for that first appointment she made me stand in front of a full-length mirror and she stood behind me, explaining every part of my body and why it was special and how it could be improved. I believed her. She was great with make-up too... I don't know *how* she did it. You've seen the photograph." She paused, daring Lewis to say that Emily could make a rather plain girl look beautiful, but he simply nodded and urged her to continue. "And at that time, Circus had a good reputation, you understand. The Circus girls were respected on the circuit: the thin thing was part of the chic at first, but the problem was that we all kept getting thinner. It wasn't long before they started calling us the *Circus freaks*. Anton hated the criticism, took it all personally. He was suing anyone who gave us a bad review and spent most of his time with the lawyers."

"This Anton, did you know him?"

"Yeah, he was really sweet. All the girls liked him. He was a lot older than Emily and he seemed ancient to us. Emily liked older men, I think. She didn't have any parents... we all reckoned she had a father thing going on with Anton."

Lewis frowned. "I'm not sure you're right about the parents. When I knew her she said her family was in the Vale, South Wales."

Jasmine shrugged. "If she had a family she kept it secret from us."

He thought about this. Maybe Emily was lying when she told him she came back to Wales to live with her family. "Were they happy?" he asked. "Emily and Anton I mean."

"Sure. I think Anton was afraid of her though."

"Afraid of her?"

"Towards the end. He took a lot of interest in us in the early days, but as we got thinner he withdrew. They had a blazing row one day. Anton had this Polish accent, which sounded really comical when he shouted. I remember all of us listening to them in the office with the door closed. We couldn't hear Emily, she was speaking really quietly, but Anton was shouting, mostly in Polish, and we couldn't make out what he was saying. We did hear him shout out a reference to Auschwitz before he stormed off."

"Auschwitz?" Lewis murmured. "Forgive me for saying so, but do you think he was referring to how thin you all were?"

Jasmine didn't take offence. "Maybe. But his grandparents were in a concentration camp. He was really touchy about being Jewish, he kept saying that the backers hated him and looked down on him because of it. He was paranoid."

"Did he come back, after this row I mean?"

"Yeah, he did. Emily knew he would. And we didn't hear him complain again, but his drinking got worse."

He nodded. On his notepad so far he had only scribbled three words: *Lewinski. House, Kent*. "So, Emily made you starve yourself," he said. "Is that why you hated her?"

She shook her head with a hint of irritation. "She didn't starve us. We all ate fine, all of us. Yummy food and loads of it. We shared a house together, Circus paid for it, and Emily was there most of the time and organised the cooking."

"So how...?"

"I don't know. We just kept losing weight. And we all ate different stuff, too. Emily was like this dietician, she knew all about Oriental medicine, how to read skin colour to see what your body would accept and what it wouldn't. And she was really hot on vitamins and stuff too. I never felt hungry, none of us did. And believe it or not we were all healthy, full of zip. One day this doctor came along and examined us, I think because one of the competitors had made a complaint, but he said that we were all in the peak of health."

"Did it bother you though, the weight loss I mean?"

Her head sank into her chins as a smile crept across her face. "Sometimes, at first perhaps, but we got used to it. We'd joke about our hipbones at breakfast. We used to do *knock knock* jokes with them." She paused and her smile widened with satisfaction as she noticed him turn a little green at the thought of the breakfast bone knocking. He was remembering what Emily said to him at his apartment, that she used to 'nurture' her girls. "No, that's not why I hated her," she added.

"So where did Emily acquire all these skills? Make-up, diet and the rest? Did she have any professional help?" he asked.

"No, no, she did it all herself. There was this magazine that she used."

He glanced up from the notepad, desperately attempting to conceal his excitement. "Magazine?" he asked casually.

"Yeah, this grotty old thing she kept hidden away in her room. She must have cooked with it because it reeked to high heaven."

He pretended to write something on his notepad. "What did it smell of?" he asked.

She was puzzled by the question, but he waited patiently, looking at his notepad. "I don't know, it was just a bad smell," she answered eventually.

He looked up. "Can you describe the smell to me, Jasmine? Believe me, this is important."

She made a face and threw him a curious twitch of her nose. "You're the oddest lawyer I've ever met," she said. "Why do you need to know?"

He quickly searched for a plausible explanation. "The people I represent believe that Emily was using some illegal substances in her work. The smell in the magazine may give us a clue to what she was using."

She seemed unconvinced. "Well… what smell are you looking for?" she inquired slyly.

"Dog faeces?" he offered.

She laughed and shook her head. "No, definitely not," she replied. "It was more like bad milk, really bad soured milk. Emily hit me; she actually punched me… you know, with her fist… when I sneaked into her room and flicked through it. I'd never seen her so angry. That's why I hated her, why I decided to leave. There was this advert in the magazine, with some spilt milk and these kittens licking it up. I remember that because I thought to myself – you know, as a joke – that it was the picture that was making it smell."

Lewis' eyes twitched as he pulled three fingers through his hair, for his thoughts weren't gelling with this information. "What else was in the magazine?" he asked.

"Oh, just articles, really long, boring articles which I couldn't be bothered to read."

"What were the articles on? History? Meditation? Inventions?"

She frowned. "No, just diet stuff and make-up formulas. Some medical stuff too. I didn't get a chance to have a proper look at it. Emily found me reading it and she locked it away after that. God she was angry." He saw that Jasmine was disturbed by the memory. She picked up the empty popcorn bag and her finger scooped up some sugar that she put in her mouth.

"Any pictures in the magazine? Any models?" he persisted.

"Sure."

"What were they like?"

"I don't know. They were skinny, like us. Didn't really

look at them, I was too interested in finding out about the diet articles. I wanted to know Emily's secret."

"What was the magazine called?"

Jasmine shook her head. "I don't remember," she murmured, wearying of the subject.

He sighed and carefully assembled his next line of questioning, drawing upon his skill and experience for getting information out of witnesses with lazy memories. "But you looked at the cover?" he asked.

"Not really."

"You must have, when you found it in Emily's room."

"I suppose so."

"Okay, keep that image in your mind. Freeze-frame it."

"Okay."

"Good. Is it black with just some white decoration, like ivy?"

She screwed up her eyes as she concentrated.

"And it has a few words on the cover?" he asked.

"Yes," she agreed after a time, as her memory was activated.

"Three words at the bottom."

"I think so."

"Are those words: *Fashion, Ambition, Temptation*?"

"Yes!" she declared, smiling and nodding.

"And it's called *The Shilling*?"

She kept nodding.

Lewis continued to question her over the magazine, but Jasmine couldn't remember anything further. Eventually he tried a different approach.

"Did you ever come across anyone else in the course of your work, sponsors for example? You mentioned backers earlier on, the backers that Anton didn't get on with."

"Well there were lots of people, you know."

"But any specific names?"

"Such as?"

He took a deep breath. "Does the name *Baron Enterprises* mean anything to you?"

"Look, who do you represent?" she asked, tired of the questioning now and getting up to fetch her chocolate.

"Just trust me when I say it's important."

"You're with the police aren't you?" she muttered, breaking off four squares of Bourneville and popping them in her mouth. She crossed her long chubby legs as she sat down. He didn't answer, but waited for the chocolate to go down. If she wanted to believe he was with the police he wasn't going to correct her. "Who did you say?" she asked eventually.

"Baron. Baron Enterprises."

She broke off another few squares. "There was a Baron Finance. They were big sponsors, right at the beginning. One of the girls said that they gave Circus the start-up cash."

Lewis went cold. "Did you ever meet anyone who represented them?"

Jasmine thought about this. "There was a woman," she said at last. "A friend of Emily's, connected with the finance, though she kept very much to herself." She frowned. "I only met her a few times and I don't think the other girls met her at all."

He nodded sadly and gave her a description of Bernie, down to her height and the colour of her eyes.

"No, that's not her," came the firm response. "This woman was middle-aged, easily the other side of fifty. In fact, she acted more like Emily's mum than her mate. Emily did everything she said."

He was thrown by this information. "Did the name *Bernice Connor* ever crop up in conversation?" he asked. She shook her head, but was now preoccupied with the second chocolate bar. "Are you sure? No one of that description ever came to the house, perhaps under a different name?"

"Not that I can remember. Baron had a few people involved in some of the events, but apart from the middle-aged woman the other people were men."

He was starting to feel uncomfortable. The gnawing possibility that he might have been wrong about both Bernie and Baron was too horrible to contemplate. "Okay, let me describe someone else to you," he said.

He gave her a physical description of Howard Raine, from the thin lizard lips to the carefully manicured grey hair. She frowned and muttered that it rung a bell but she wasn't sure.

Lewis swallowed and said, "This man has a habit of running his finger down the parting of his hair."

Jasmine glanced at him, then looked up and nodded. "Yeah... I've definitely met that guy."

Lewis spent two nights in a London hotel before catching a plane to Naples and then from Sorrento he took a tourist boat to Capri. Since his meeting with Jasmine he had been calling the firm regularly to make sure everything was okay, and Graham had kept reassuring him with monotonous regularity that it was.

Travelling alone had given him too much time to think and he wondered whether he was overreacting. Just because Baron funded Circus didn't mean they were involved with The Shilling, he rationalised as he hung on to the rail of the shuttle that transported him up the mountain to Ana Capri. And just because Bernie wasn't involved with Circus didn't mean that she wasn't involved with The Shilling.

Fact: Bernie was the only person who had a key to his duplex. Apart from BB no one else had been in his home, up until the time the 'stop' clue was written in.

He put his musings aside as he stepped out onto the beautiful mountain retreat and took in the air. It was clean and fragrant. Ana Capri was everything Emily said it was, he reflected, as he stopped to buy an ice cream from a vendor at the top of the lift and then wandered into the town square. He walked down a side street with quaint cobbled stones and which was framed with trees and smelled in stages of the home-made confectionery and bakery stores that lined its route. The street took him to the Gardens of Augustus, where he smelled the mixed perfume of the flowers, as Emily had described over dinner.

Yes, she's certainly been here, he decided. No doubt of it.

This place would make anyone ambitious. He considered the stringent financial entry points that were required to retain its exclusivity, the Cartier stores and other trademarks of the rich, and for a while he forgot his mission and just strolled. He had already walked past the Quisisana hotel, a sumptuous salmon pink mansion with the flags of the world adorning its terrace; outside two guards in black uniforms with white sashes were allowing their photographs to be taken by tourists.

He took in the view from the cliff. This is the view that the Emperor Tiberius would have seen every morning when he hid away in the debauched twilight of his reign. The gardens were an ancient playground, where no doubt the Emperor as an old man hobbled lustfully after his young playmates. To the right was the coastal inlet where the myth of the Sirens originated, now the famous home of Gracie Fields. On the heights above lay the residence of Krupp, the German steel manufacturers, long abandoned now.

So much dark history here, Lewis thought. Yes, he could live here.

He swung round to look at the small fountain with the weathered Roman statues. There had been a crawling feeling on the back of his neck, as he imagined someone had been watching him from the fountain.

He pulled himself together and got into role. He was wearing his suit and carrying his attaché case: he hadn't wanted to bring The Shilling with him, but he needed the attaché case for appearance's sake and nothing was going to make him take the magazine out. It was going to stay under combination lock because he knew the answer to another clue, 5 *down*, *the process*, and he wasn't going to let anyone write in the answer. Even here in Italy he didn't trust anyone, not even the helpful and friendly concierge back at his Naples hotel.

Raine had only mentioned the name of the process once, at their first meeting. It was a complicated name and Lewis hadn't remembered it, but he remembered it now. He had woken up on the flight over with the name in his head. *Articulating Resistance Energy: ARE.* The process that Baron used to energise inert matter, which required all the banging and thumping he heard from the factory, the reason for all the accidents. He wasn't going to write the answer in as he sensed it would be a bad omen, just as the word 'stop' had been luckless. Perhaps it was the money that he could smell, here in Capri, which was affecting his judgment, but without Baron he was just another lawyer. It bothered him a little that he wasn't prepared to twist his perceptions for Bernie's sake. No, Bernie was different… that had been a personal betrayal.

And besides, who cared if Baron were involved? The claims and the money they generated were facts. If they were playing a trick on him through the instruction, well, the joke was on them.

He walked back to the Quisisana and now had an attack of self-doubt, for he had come an awful long way on what was very much a long shot. In his nervousness a rusty old trigger in his brain told him he wanted a cigarette but he quickly put it out of his mind.

Inside the reception area he began his rehearsed speech in appalling Italian from a piece of paper, which contained the Naples concierge's translation. To his relief the reception manager stopped him and spoke to him in perfect English. Lewis explained that he was acting in the estate of Emily Lewinski, and he produced a copy of a marriage certificate that he had picked up in London after his meeting with Jasmine, which recorded Emily's maiden name of Webber. Then he produced the Police Accident Report recording Emily's death. The manager studied the report gloomily and said that he remembered the Lewinskis well; he passed his sympathies on to Mr Lewinski.

"That's the problem," Lewis explained, "Mr Lewinski doesn't know, and I'm trying to locate him for the purposes of the will. Do you have an address?"

The manager nodded and walked off into an office. Shortly he returned with the Montevetro address.

"No, that's no good," Lewis said. "They moved from there." The manager shrugged. "I know that they used to buy things in Italy and send them home," Lewis went on. "I know they have a home in Kent, which maybe was used as a forwarding address." This had been Lewis' little spark of genius: if the Kent address was their private retreat then it may have been the destination for some of their many purchases.

"Kent, Kent," the manager said under his breath and disappeared again. After a long while he came back with a dispatch note from La Parisienne, a quaint clothing store in the town square. The dispatch note had a Kent address that Lewis hungrily copied into his notebook.

Back in the town square he seated himself near La

Parisienne and sneaked a look through the shop window. There was a rather old-fashioned clothes dummy, just the torso of a woman, in the front window. A woman half in shadow came up to dress it, and for a split second while he was sipping his cappuccino their eyes met. She stepped back into the shadow of the store.

When he finished his coffee he strolled up to the window and peered through. A man was behind the counter waiting upon tourists. Lewis loitered for a time, wishing he had a cigarette to give him an activity, but the woman he had glimpsed didn't re-appear so eventually he went back to his table and ordered some lunch. He kept an eye on the window, extending his lunch through three courses, but the clothes dummy remained unattended.

The shuttle was packed tight on the way back down the mountain and the trip had tired him out. He also felt uncomfortable because his suit trousers were tight round his waist and he decided to get some cool Italian suits when he was back in Naples, although the suit he was wearing was fairly new. A couple of the people in the firm had remarked that he was putting on a few pounds but as always he had taken it as a compliment; he felt the bulge of his stomach and pondered on the possibility of venturing into the complete unknown – onto a diet. Perhaps that was why his success with women had started to wane. Maybe he had some kind of ideal weight, which he needed to find again.

He looked at his paunch with a depressed face. When he looked up he caught the eye of a woman who had been observing him from the other end of the shuttle and he fancied it was the same woman in the window of La Parisienne. The woman quickly turned around and she didn't come into view again. He hadn't seen her face properly in the crush of people, just her eyes which flashed malevolently when he realised he was being observed, but as he tried to edge closer he came up against a fat American who regarded his failed attempt to squeeze past with amusement. When the shuttle came to a stop and started to unload he was still pinned to the American, but he traced the moving outline of the woman's head in the crowd. When he finally made it outside she was nowhere to be seen.

He sighed and looked back up the mountain to Ana Capri, sorrowfully. Already it felt like a distant memory, a dream place that he would never re-visit.

The tourists were dispersing to their boats and there was still no sign of the woman. He had that crawling feeling against the back of his neck again, the same as when he had looked over the cliff and imagined that someone was watching him from the fountain.

That woman... she looked like...

No, that was impossible.

Back in Naples he paid a visit to a fairly safe red-light zone, which had been brought to his knowledge by the same friendly concierge who had given him the translation. Lewis didn't allow himself to go more than three days without sex, because otherwise he dreamed of Mary Stone.

He supposed the Mary Stone dreams were a kind of love thermometer. He knew he was still heartbroken over Bernie, and when the pain ended, the dreams would end. Just as they ended when they first got together.

The prostitute he found took his euros with a rehearsed "Thank you my good friend" and showed him to the door of her side-street terrace after barely fifteen minutes. He mumbled a goodbye and wondered what he should do with the rest of his evening, whether he should have a look around the neighbourhood. He decided against it and found a taxi. He hadn't felt like sightseeing, hadn't even planned a visit to Pompeii, in spite of his interest in the ruins. Capri was different though, for he felt at home there. He wandered despondently back into the foyer of the hotel, nodding at the concierge who glanced at his watch and offered him a wide, knowing smile.

Lewis didn't like going with prostitutes and liked even less other people knowing about it. He had started to use them back home too because Button Nose, Leggy Dancer and even Big Hair had one by one broken things off with him and he hadn't managed to replace them. He was one of Janet's best customers now, and he was getting a few odd looks from his neighbours because the Encounters girls were booked for the shortest sessions possible. He hadn't really enjoyed sex with anyone since he broke up with Bernie; the Encounters girls were simply a necessity like sleep or oxygen, nothing more.

A cold dread wrapped around his body as he was taken up in the shuddering metal-barred lift of the hotel. What if The Shilling had intended for him to fall in love, only to make him throw away that happiness through his own stupidity? What if The Shilling had deliberately planted his suspicions?

At the time he thought he could have any woman that he wanted, but he was just on a lucky roll fuelled by an excess of confidence. Did Bernie really love him, for who he was?

The lift door opened and he shook his head. Bernie was the only person with a key to his place, the only person who could have written in the crossword. And she had a fictitious brother. He wasn't wrong, no matter how much he wanted to be wrong.

Reception rang him at 6 a.m. with his wake up call for his mid-morning flight back to London. His next stop was Anton Lewinski in Kent. Anton could tell him more about

The Shilling than Jasmine Stimple could, but he had to think of a way into his confidence. He'd think about it on the plane.

How will he react when he knows Emily's dead? Lewis wondered as he packed.

He remembered feeling sorry for Emily at the dinner table, as he considered her fall from the heights of Capri and the Montevetro. For the first time he recognised a parallel: she had built up her business from nothing, and then it folded; she began with innovation and talent and ended up a drunk, ultimately a corpse in a car wreck. Baron funded her start-up, just as Baron was funding him. She lost her man, Anton. The one person he had met so far who remembered her from her London days hated her.

Is that what was going to happen to him? Or rather, was it happening to him already? Maybe that's what The Shilling meant when it said *'I'm yours: I belong to you'*. Was everything that had been given to him in the last year going to be taken away?

It was this superstitious fear that made him reach for the attaché case, zip through his memorised combination and click it open. He opened The Shilling at the first page and the eyes flashed at him: Mary Stone had her first pockmark, the one over her left eyebrow. Her smile was a little wider.

"Dissolving paper," he said to himself, refusing to be alarmed.

It had to be that, or holograms. He still wasn't really sure.

He turned to the crossword and went cold. At 5 down, *ARE* had been written in, again in a handwriting identical his own.

The process.

What was The Shilling telling him?

Baron Enterprises, he realised. I'm going to lose the

Baron instruction.

He picked up his mobile but realised it was too early to call the firm. He broke out into a sweat and packed frantically.

Then he stopped, as something hit his brain with the force of an express train. He slumped on the bed and his jaw dropped.

The clue had written itself. *It had written itself*.

"Bernie..." he moaned.

ARE

Lewis knew that it wasn't simple good fortune that had made him safely file Bernie's job reference, the reference that contained the precious information of where he could find her in the expanse of London. He had kept the reference for the same reason he had kept the photograph of the two of them on the balcony: something deep in his heart, defying logic, had protested. Bernie hadn't betrayed him and wasn't working for the network. He should have trusted his heart, not his third- rate detective brain with its suspicions and smug deductions.

At midday Lewis was sitting in a café opposite the Holborn bookstore and as he turned his coffee cup in his hands he considered what a fool he had been. If the pictures could change to give Mary Stone a new face, or make cockroaches disappear, why couldn't the crossword write itself? No one had broken into his apartment.

His eyes were on the revolving door of the bookstore and the steps that led down to the street. People were trickling out in search of sandwiches and coffee, but Bernie wasn't among them. How was he to know she had even got the job? Even if she worked here there was no guarantee that she went out for lunch. Well, he would stay here until closing time if necessary. He had decided that he wouldn't go into the store, for he had an image of her calling security, or her just retreating into a back office when she saw him. No, he had to approach her unexpectedly.

He turned his cup feverishly in his hand. It wasn't like him to fiddle with things and he was reminded of the odd occasions in the past when he had unsuccessfully tried to kick his smoking habit.

He sighed. No Bernie.

Eventually he turned around to find a waitress and order some food. When he turned back to the window he saw Bernie walking along the front of the office building, wearing the blue suit she had worn at their first meeting in the boardroom. He was out of his seat in an instant and running across the road, calling to her.

She looked back, but when she saw him her face dropped and she quickened her pace. He ran in front of her and had to physically stop her with raised hands as she attempted to move past him.

"I'll call a policeman, Lewis," she said with as much menace as she could muster. Her voice was timorous, however, and she looked broken and unhappy.

"Bernie, just listen to me. I was wrong. I'm really, really sorry." A passer-by gave him a strange look, which Lewis met with a nasty glare. The passer-by hurried along.

She shook her head. "It's too late for sorry."

"I'm so sorry about your job, Bernie, I'll make it up to you. I promise I will."

Her eyes narrowed. "My job? My *job*? You broke my heart, Lewis. You broke it."

He opened his mouth to speak, but was thrown.

"How could you?" she asked, her voice welling up.

"It was The Shilling," he blurted out. "You were right, I should have thrown it away. It made me do those things. It made me think these terrible things."

This seemed to disarm her. Perhaps she had rehearsed this moment, expecting Lewis to find her and plead with her, but she hadn't figured on his saying that it was the magazine's fault. "What are you talking about?" she said after a moment's hesitation, exasperation in her tone.

"Someone wrote the answer into the crossword. Or perhaps I did it or perhaps the magazine did it. I don't know. But I thought it was you. You see, only you had a key to the duplex."

She looked up at the sky. "I kept telling you to throw the thing away," she muttered. "How could you think that I'd do something like that?"

"Well you lied about your brother," he murmured, looking at the pavement. He felt uneasy at bringing this into the equation and his hands were restless at his sides, but the business with Jamey was troubling him. Perhaps Bernie was married or something and she had invented the sick brother as a front for her other life.

She glanced around, embarrassed now that the people walking past were giving them odd looks. Holborn was not the place for an argument in the street. "What?" she said simply.

"There's no James Connor in any cancer ward in London, Bernie."

"Well of course there isn't! My real name's Tate. My brother is Jamey Tate."

He gave her a blank look. "Tate? Now *I* don't understand," he said.

She shook her head and looked skywards again. "I can't believe you checked up on Jamey..."

"I'm sorry Bernie, but..."

"Baron has strict policies on who they employ. Connor is my father's name."

He shook his head in complete confusion.

"Oh for goodness's sake... my parents weren't married!"

"So...?"

Bernie waved him away, as if summoning the effort to be angry again, for in her rehearsal she would have been angry from beginning to end. "Why am I explaining anything? After what you've done to me…"

"Bernie, please…"

"It's over, Lewis, leave me alone. Stay out of my life. Just like you told me to stay out of yours." That was definitely out of the script, and delivered well.

"This was meant to happen," he implored her, and she hesitated, in spite of herself. "We've both been set up. You must give me a chance to explain. I can explain everything."

She looked hard into his eyes then said, "I have to go home. My brother is waiting for me, because I can't afford a full-time carer any more."

"Let me come."

"No."

"Please, let me come with you."

"Lewis, I never want to see you again. Do you understand?"

She didn't wait for an answer but brushed past him. He called after her, but she didn't stop.

In spite of his failure, Lewis was encouraged. The worst reception he had feared was some kind of venomous indifference, as if after losing her job nothing mattered to her any more.

You broke my heart.

Those were wonderful words to hear.

And importantly, she thought he was making it up about The Shilling. This gave him hope because he had an idea.

At a library he made two photocopies of Mary Stone and the twins and placed each copy in a brown envelope. The first envelope he secured in a strong box at Paddington station with a recorded delivery stamp on the envelope to establish the date, then attached the key of the strongbox to his key ring. The second envelope he left at Bernie's bookshop, with a letter written on his hotel's letterhead:

Bernie, it was wonderful to see you again. I know you don't believe me about the magazine. I don't blame you, but I've photocopied three women from the magazine. You may notice that they're different from when you last saw them. In a few weeks I'll send you more copies, and you'll see how they've changed. I've got the idea that the magazine's printed on some special paper, paper that dissolves to reveal a new picture underneath. I think that's how the answers to the crossword are writing themselves. The photocopies won't change though, will they? So, in a few weeks time you'll be able to compare the photocopies and you'll understand that this isn't all in my head.

I haven't really figured this all out yet. What I do know is that I was meant to lose you. If it goes to plan, their plan, you'll never forgive me for what I did.

Try not to think too unkindly of me. The person you knew, on the balcony in the Bay, was the real me. I love you. Please forgive me. Lewis.

P.S. I'm taking my holiday in London. I'm doing some sightseeing and I'm staying at the hotel on this letterhead if you want to meet for lunch. Room 301.

He spent the rest of his fortnight in London, hoping that Bernie would call, but stayed in regular contact with the firm, to be repeatedly told by Graham that there was nothing to worry about. Lewis got the impression that everyone in the firm was happy that he was on holiday and would be even happier if he never came back.

He was true to his letter and spent his days sightseeing. At nights he returned to the hotel, hoping for a message from Bernie but always being disappointed. Nothing had happened with Baron yet either, nothing had happened with the 'process', and the waiting was torture. If he was interpreting the pattern correctly, each answer in the crossword had to be acted out before the next one could begin.

He therefore supposed that if he could write in a new answer, the significance of the previous answer would come to an end. Specifically, Baron's 'process' would no longer be in danger.

So, for the first time he thought really hard about the clues as he attempted to extract just one answer. He couldn't do it. The closest he came was '11 across', a two letter word to which the clue was *Beta lives* and where he had the second letter 'e'.

Surely, the answer was 'be'. To be or not to be… to live or to die. Beta was the Greek word for the letter 'B'. It was an easy clue, one that he supposed he had known all along. But now he wasn't so sure, now that he was aware that Bernie's second name was Tate. Bernie Tate. BeTa.

He had a sneaking suspicion that the answer wasn't 'Be', but 'i.e.'.

'I.e.' was an abbreviation for *that is to say*. BeTa: that is to say, *Be*rnie *Ta*te? But the clue was *Beta lives*. Where did the *'lives'* come in?

He realised that if he added *i.e.* to *Bern*, then he got *Bernie*. He had previously been looking for a clue that gave the answer *ice*, to make *Bernice*, but he knew her now as Bernie. Did it mean that Bernie would stop living if he wrote the clue in? He shuddered at the prospect, not even daring to write in the answer in pencil.

And he could be wrong anyway… the right answer could still be the most obvious one: *Be*.

Seeing Bernie again had put him off the idea of visiting prostitutes and with the punctuality of a credit card statement Mary Stone visited him after a few nights' abstinence. He met her in the place where he had been sightseeing that day, the Natural History Museum, and she took him by the hand and led him through the exhibits. All the lights were down and the Weeping Wall was playing through the tannoy, loud enough for it to be a rock concert although in the bubble in which they walked he sensed there was no sound and no air.

She led him past a collection of fossilised reptiles, marine dinosaurs, with plaques recording the circumstances of their discovery. He heard her remark that they were pretty... pretty, pretty, pretty. On one of the trophies was O'Neill's head, with a plaque, which read: *Made extinct by the better man*. O'Neill winked at him as they strolled past. BB's head was on the next trophy, the plaque stating: *Abandoned by evolution*. Bernie's head followed shortly; there was no plaque for Bernie, no inscription, but her eyes followed him frantically as Mary Stone took his hand and located a trap door that led into the heart of the museum, under the earth. In a cold stone room she danced for him, with a cold and distant allure, and when the dance was over she departed with a promise that she would return. He waited on the floor for what seemed an eternity: in his head the days, months, years and centuries turned like an old clock.

When he woke he was exhausted, for it seemed as if the dream had taken him through the entire night, waiting in that dark place in the belly of the museum. Alone. Hoping against hope that she would return.

He groaned, deciding that he had preferred it when Mary Stone and the twins used to gang rape him. At least he would wake up.

Perhaps he should be encouraged though that there was nothing erotic about the museum dream. Just seeing Bernie again may have been the reason: before, he had only needed to kiss Bernie to kick the dreams. Yet he was troubled by the museum plaques and by the solitude of the dream.

Did it mean he had lost Bernie for good?

Bernie didn't call. On the last day of his holiday he used the library photocopier again to make further copies of the two pictures. He was surprised that The Shilling was changing so quickly, far quicker than before; this time, in addition to the pockmarks emerging from under thick make-up, Mary Stone was starting to lose her hair. He could make out her scalp in places; it was grey and full of sores.

The twins were also changing more quickly. The weatherworn woman on the right already looked middle-aged, her sister in her early teens.

Although it was hardly necessary Lewis marked the changes with a red pen and in a short note to Bernie also made reference to the fact that Mary Stone was wearing her diamond pendant. In a rather desperate appeal he said that they were both in this together. He boarded his train, uncertain of his note, wondering whether he had gone too far and really scared her off now.

Lewis' brain rocked and juddered with the train as he journeyed home, the experience made no less uncomfortable by a first class ticket and a table cubicle to himself.

What had gone wrong?

He had gone to London as a cocky, amateur sleuth, and obtained more information than he could possibly have hoped for. Instead of finding out about Emily, however, he had discovered the beginnings of his own ruin. In establishing that Bernie hadn't betrayed him, he had sunk into an even deeper despair than when he had lost her. It was not apathy that had made him spend the rest of the holiday sightseeing, instead of seeking out Anton. Knowledge was dangerous in this game being played and he was afraid of what Anton would tell him.

Curiosity killed the cat, and he had a mental image of

the page in the magazine Jasmine had described to him, with the cats licking up the milk.

His mind now found an imagined picture of Emily, dead at the wheel, the empty bottle of Bell's whisky rattling at her feet. Why did she come to his house that night? Why did she leave the magazine?

Who do you bring?

Lewis...

He shuddered. She made him write it in. Thinking about it now, it was significant to her that the writing had to be his. She had insisted on it. He signed his name as he would sign some credit agreement or any other contract.

A contract...

The Carbolic Smoke Ball... that advert for that nineteenth century contract law case. The offer to the entire world.

Other things about his short time with Emily seemed to be making sense now, such as when she hung around on the Sunday morning without taking the hint to leave. She was at his place solely for that purpose... to sign him up.

He was also coming to suspect that she had played him, that there were questions that she would have answered, that she would have been obliged to answer, if she had been pressed.

If you want to know then I will tell you... but it will take a long time...

Were there rules she had to follow?

He shook his head and again saw her in his apartment in his mind's eye, turning the pages of the magazine with irritation as she fielded his questions. Then, as always, that image of her, looking down with resignation as the lift doors closed.

He had the vaguest of suspicions that he had to sign

someone up too, before this was over.

Bern...

That clue means more than just a Swiss city...

Well, it wasn't going to happen.

He clipped open his attaché case and turned to the crossword. *Who do you bring?* That was the first clue. The clues were out of order, not arranged in numerical format. Why was that? He had thought it strange the first time he studied it: why not have all the 'down' clues together in a column, in numerical order, and then all the 'across' clues together in a separate column, as with any other crossword? Logic told him that the sequence must be significant, so he took out his pen and wrote out the answers to the first seven clues, which were the most answers that he had been given in uninterrupted sequence. On the bottom of the crossword he wrote:

Lewis your lit less inns ARE wonderful

He shook his head. It wasn't complete gibberish but it didn't mean anything. With a shrug that admitted he might be wrong he clipped the attaché case shut, spun the combination lock and tried to sleep.

He opened his eyes at Bristol Parkway with the heave and hiss of the train leaving the station, and as he yawned himself awake he was immediately aware of his stomach rumbling. He had already had a couple of sandwiches but he was feeling faint and his hands were shaking. He got this sensation sometimes when he forgot to eat on a really busy day in the office, when hunger would mug him mid-afternoon and when he would have to run out, buy three Mars bars and stuff them down one after another. Even then he would only feel okay about half an hour later.

He frowned as he took a deep breath and the air

travelled down into his lungs and flushed his body with oxygen. As he breathed out he tried to make sense of his shakes.

Something recognisable, yet altogether new, travelled from his body to his brain. It was an old enemy, but infinitely more powerful.

This wasn't hunger. It was a longing for nicotine, but the pangs were so bad that they had actually woken him up.

He had had all manner of cigarette pangs in his adult life: the pang that made him irritable and short tempered; that made him imagine that he was hungry, that he needed to chew on something; that made him feel he couldn't face the day. Then there were the pleasure pangs: the one after a meal hinting that the whole marvellous experience of eating was just a waste of time without the precious nicotine to finish it off; the one that simply seemed to demand obedience, if life was to be made complete.

As with any smoker he had had them all, and he knew the tricks the addiction played. But this was different. This was actually agony.

It began as a knot in his stomach, as if he had run a marathon on a full meal, but his body was so weak, so undernourished that every pang was like a punch to a wound.

He struggled out of his seat and, holding a pound coin, staggered up the aisle of the carriage, asking people if they smoked and whether he could buy a cigarette. Eventually someone took pity on him, declined the money but gave him a cigarette and a box of matches. He rushed to the toilet.

He steadied himself in the small cubicle, cursing the old Victorian rail lines that jolted him from side to side as he attempted to get comfortable. If the nicotine had beaten him, then he at least wanted to enjoy this cigarette. In his whole life nothing had seemed so precious to him and at that moment he would have killed anyone who came between him and his first drag.

As he lit it he knew that this time it was going to be different, that there would be no bad aftertaste, because anything that relieved this agony had to be pleasurable. He wasted four matches in his haste but eventually had the cigarette lit and, with a long groan of relief, he felt the pain subside. His legs rocked to the movement of the train as he held the cigarette next to his head with the white fumes drifting upwards. The cubicle jolted again and he took a second, more satisfying drag. He sucked it in greedily, but this time the smoke seemed to solidify as a soft mush in his mouth and he tasted something rancid and vile. It was dog excrement, and he retched and threw up with violence.

When he returned to the carriage and slumped back in his seat he tried to ignore the odd curious look thrown in his direction. He took several deep breaths, then signalled the trolley and bought two bottles of water.

God that was foul. He didn't know what dog shit tasted of, but it was how he would imagine it and he had never, ever, tasted anything so disgusting. Even thinking about it he felt his stomach turning again, so he jumped up and ran back to the toilet, clinging on to his two bottles of water. Once inside he gargled both bottles and threw up so many times that his stomach felt as small as a prune. Everyone in the carriage was staring at him when he eventually staggered back.

Back in his seat he tried to breathe deeply again. He thought of the meditation article in The Shilling and imagined stepping into himself, when he was strong and confident. Yes, it was true... he could be two different people. In his mind he saw himself not too long ago, on the balcony of the duplex with Bernie, in love, enjoying life, excited by life. He knew he would never be there again.

His run of good luck had come to an end.

That was what *stop* had meant.

He was almost expecting his mobile to ring, which it did, at that moment. It was Graham, saying there was a problem with the Baron account and that he should come to the office immediately.

Part Four:
And this too shall pass

1 across	who do you bring?
2 down	to own
3 across	made the fires
3 down	do not accept it
4 across	no rooms
5 down	the process
6 down	she says
7 down	how many now?
8 across	weight hanger
9 down	The Shilling says

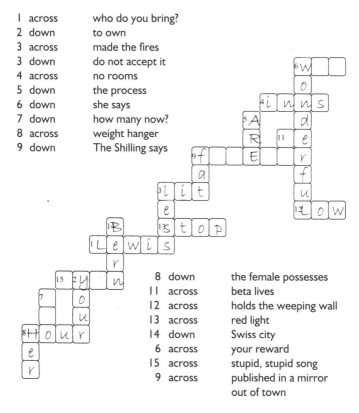

8 down	the female possesses
11 across	beta lives
12 across	holds the weeping wall
13 across	red light
14 down	Swiss city
6 across	your reward
15 across	stupid, stupid song
9 across	published in a mirror
	out of town

Lewis your lit less inns ARE wonderful

Lewis your lit less inns
ARE wonderful

Lewis ran down the steps of Harrier & O'Neill, barged through the door and came to almost a skid halt. His partners, Graham, Rhys and O'Neill, were waiting for him in reception.

"What's going on?" Lewis asked breathlessly.

"The system's down," Graham said.

"What do you mean?"

"The software that allows us access to Baron's files," Graham clarified. "It isn't responding."

"We were reluctant to call Baron ourselves," Rhys muttered, "what with the policy and everything." O'Neill said nothing, but just looked out of the window. He was watching Lewis' taxi pull away as he wondered why Lewis should be wearing a suit and carrying an attaché case when he was on holiday.

"Must be just a glitch," Lewis murmured, picking up the reception phone and tapping in Baron's number. He took a breath, then dabbed his forehead with his handkerchief.

Was it just a fault? Please God let it just be a fault.

His stomach turned as he realised that the automated call centre, which always greeted him, appeared to be defunct. The phone rang for a long while before a man picked up.

"Yes?"

"Mr Raine?" Lewis whispered, instantly recognising the barbed hook in the voice.

"Yes."

"Mr Raine, it's Lewis Coin."

There was a pause, but Lewis thought he heard a good-humoured sigh.

"Mr Coin. Did you enjoy your holiday?"

"Yes, yes thank you. Mr Raine, we're having some problems here. My people tell me that their software has frozen, that they can't access any of the claims." Out of the corner of his eye he noticed Graham and Rhys exchange a withering look at the mention of *my people*. O'Neill touched his bow tie with a thin smile, appearing to find the phrase amusing, as he turned away from the window.

"No need for concern," Raine replied. "We thought we would use your vacation to update some of our software. It has been in the planning stage for a long time, so it seemed opportune. Perhaps I should have... ah, should have told you before you left."

"You thought you'd use my vacation to update the software," Lewis repeated, turning to his three partners and putting his thumb up. The three men drifted away, Rhys and Graham muttering to each other, and Lewis found a seat and relaxed into it.

"Are you back in work now?" Raine asked.

"Monday," Lewis answered. "Is that okay?"

"Of course, of course. Where did you go?"

"London, then Italy for a short trip," Lewis answered with a raise of his eyebrows.

"Ah... the Italian air."

There was a silence, but Raine wasn't bringing the conversation to an end.

"Everything going well with you?" Lewis offered.

"Highly satisfactory. Head Office is in important talks with the American Government as we speak. They are discussing an end to the confidentiality restrictions. Production will escalate when that happens... when the process is offered to all the world."

Lewis' eyes flickered, then he smiled.

"We already have six new UK depots planned," Raine added.

"Looks like I'm going to have to recruit," Lewis remarked.

Raine made an amused sound in his throat. "Indeed," he said.

The perfunctory farewell was still nowhere in sight. Perhaps the Newport manager wasn't busy this afternoon with all the software being updated and was in the mood for conversation. "In London, I think I met someone who knows you," Lewis said, deciding to jump on the opportunity.

"Really? Who is that?"

"Oh, this ex-model."

"Dear me... what have you been doing?"

"No, nothing like that, and she's just a kid anyway. I got talking to her by accident in this bar. She used to work for a model agency called Circus and your name came up because she said that one of the backers was called Baron Finance."

"Oh yes, Baron Finance," Raine reminisced.

"So you're Baron Finance?" Lewis asked.

"We were. Baron used to finance a lot of businesses, but we abandoned that sideline when we acquired the process."

Lewis nodded with a measure of relief, considering this to be a reasonable answer. "So what happened to Circus?" he inquired.

"It was a great disappointment. The woman who ran it showed great promise, but we were forced to withdraw our support."

"Because of her drinking?" Lewis asked.

"No, the drinking was her own affair. We were obliged

to withdraw our support because of her husband."

Lewis was all ears. "Really? Because of Anton Lewinski?"

"Was that his name?" Raine asked light-heartedly.

Lewis smiled. "Yes, I think so."

"Perhaps... perhaps that was his name. We just knew him as the Jew."

Lewis' smile faded a little. "Sorry?"

Raine's voice was still cheery, but getting louder. "Her husband was a Jew, Mr Coin, a dirty, scheming son of Israel. We cautioned her, we tried to help her. Get rid of the parasite, we said. He will infect you, we said. She wouldn't listen." Raine was breathing heavily down the phone as he finished.

Lewis looked at the receiver in his hand then returned it to his ear, every sense stinging and on alert.

"Do you find us to be racist?" Raine asked quietly.

Lewis managed a laugh. "Well, I..."

"The company is not racist, Mr Coin, merely principled. Do you question our principles?"

"No, I..."

"Our principles are founded on traditional values and certain inescapable truths. In fact our principles are the foundation of our success, for we believe not only in the superiority of race, but also of class... of breeding."

It was now the old voice, the strained, unfriendly monotone.

"Principles are important," Lewis murmured.

"I am pleased you agree. All our associates are... ah, are of like mind."

It was a loaded statement and Lewis' survival antennae were spinning.

"Can you share some of your principles with us, Mr Coin?" Raine asked, his words seeping through the receiver like acid.

Two images now flashed across Lewis' mind. The first image was of Graham and Rhys, the partners waiting for him to fail, exchanging their contemptuous glances. The second image was of O'Neill, being told that Baron was taking its work elsewhere; O'Neill fixing him with his stare...

"Mr Coin?"

"Well... I agree with you about the Jews, and the like..." Lewis answered, with his eyes closed.

"But I have already revealed our policy on race. What else?"

Lewis swallowed, tasting his own revulsion. "I don't believe that children should be born out of wedlock," he murmured, muffling his answer so no one in the office could hear.

"I see. You accept that illegitimate children must have inherited their parents' tempers?"

"Yes," he answered quietly.

"Depraved tempers... contrary to all notions of self-control and moderation...?"

"Yes, yes absolutely," Lewis answered, with both a silent apology and a thank you to Bernie. He hadn't believed her in London; he suspected she was covering up a bad marriage and had reverted to her maiden name.

"Excellent, Mr Coin. I am very gratified, very gratified indeed. Miss Connor, for all her licentiousness, seems to have done well when she selected you. Business as usual on Monday... we have... ah, we have plenty still left to do."

Lewis spent the entire weekend drinking, but it didn't help him forget the conversation, or what he had done.

The reference to Jews made him think of ordinary Germans living in the Third Reich: he had sometimes wondered if he would have been a Nazi in 1930s Germany, whether he would have been taken in by the propaganda and wanted to belong. Even if he hadn't been attracted to it, whether he would simply have been too afraid to resist.

Well, now he knew.

And he hadn't needed a gun to his head, or the threat of his house being fire bombed. He just hadn't wanted to give up a £250 charging rate and lose face in front of his partners. He was disgusted with himself, his disgust all the greater in the knowledge that if he had to have the conversation again he would do exactly the same thing.

Before all this had started, he remembered having sat in the Bay Hotel, thinking how he had betrayed the person he was at twenty-one, following the money instead of his dreams. He had never dreamt the betrayal would go so deep.

On Sunday the nicotine pangs hit him again with full force and he took the precaution of having his cigarette standing over the toilet with a bottle of water close by. The water helped him when he retched and although the taste was just as bad as before the experience sobered him up.

He had problems of his own without worrying himself about Baron's politics. He needed to see a hypnotist or someone to get this idea out of his head, the idea that cigarettes tasted like dog shit, and to get rid of the bad dreams. That was enough to be going on with. So, what if Baron was the executive arm of nationalism and Victorian hypocrisy? What was that to him? He just settled personal injury claims, for God's sake, and if he didn't do it then they would find someone who would. Who would be helped? Certainly not Bernie, or her sick brother. If he was going to look after them he needed money in the bank.

Having reached this plateau of logic, he sighed with relief.

Yes, the joke would be on Baron.

If only Bernie would call.

He arrived in work late on Monday, the remnants of his hangover, on the back of two weeks of late rising, taking him through his alarm call. O'Neill and Graham were again positioned in reception as he walked in.

"Has all the software loaded?" Lewis asked brusquely. Neither man answered.

"I've got Mr Marker of the union for you," Helen said, offering the receiver across the reception desk. She was speaking to O'Neill.

"What the hell are you doing?" Lewis gasped. Graham raised a finger to his lips and O'Neill took the call, ignoring Lewis as if he was invisible.

"Stephen O'Neill here. Yes. You're the solicitor for the union?" O'Neill nodded, listening intently but with his eyes fixed on Lewis. "Is it true? I see. Yes, yes I see. Alright." He put the phone down.

"All the software's crashed," Graham explained. "It's removed everything from the memory. Pleadings, statements everything has all gone. There's nothing to show we ever had a single claim."

"It's just the new software loading," Lewis said impatiently.

"We also received an e-mail from the union first thing this morning saying that Baron was out of business," Graham went on. "Something happened over the weekend, some talks with the US Government broke down."

Lewis hesitated then turned to O'Neill. "What did Marker say?" he asked.

O'Neill's face was like stone. "The man confirmed it all. All the products are being pulled. The claims are being withdrawn and Baron's going into voluntary liquidation."

"What?"

"The process has been declared dangerous." O'Neill sniffed as he considered his errant junior partner. "Did you know it was dangerous?"

"They still owe us a packet," Graham mourned.

"Right. First things first," Lewis declared. "Where does all this come from? Is it fact or just a rumour?"

"The union have told him," O'Neill murmured back, but his attention now seemed to be elsewhere. He glanced at his watch then turned to look at Helen.

"I don't believe any of this," Lewis muttered. "I only spoke to Raine on Friday. I'm going to go up there and see what's happened. Someone's just playing a trick on us." He dashed out and headed for his car. Graham observed him from the window, while O'Neill told Helen that he wanted a meeting of all the office, everyone, in the boardroom in ten minutes. She nodded and started making the calls.

As Lewis pulled up at the Newport depot he felt a huge surge of relief. Smoke was coming out of the chimney, oh beautiful, beautiful sight, and as he walked towards the empty reception he heard the familiar banging and thumping from the old warehouse. It had always sounded rather sinister to him before, but now it was music to his ears.

Still, things clearly weren't quite right. Not only was the reception empty but even the computers were gone. Lewis walked through, shouting "Hello!" His voice echoed and no one answered.

Raine's door was unlocked and his room was empty, his desk cleared. The small picture, the one Lewis had never had the chance to properly examine, was gone.

Someone in the workshop will know what's going on, Lewis thought. He wasn't allowed in the workshop, but he would just knock on the door and speak to the nearest person he saw.

He made his way towards the sound of the banging

and arrived at a heavy wooden door with a ring handle. Again, the door was unlocked and after he had knocked a few times he tried the handle. He needed both hands to turn it.

As he stepped into the workshop he put his hands to his ears, for the noise was almost unbearable, then he grimaced as he became accustomed to it. The sound of the banging was above him, steady thumps like a giant's hammer, shaking the timber rafters in the roof. There was no one here, and the warehouse itself was featureless except for a huge smoking gas fire built into the brick of one of the walls. There was a large tape recorder nearby. He frowned as he studied it then flicked a switch on the machine.

The warehouse echoed into silence.

By the time Lewis was back behind his desk he was staring into space and hoping for a phone call, from anybody. He had rung Marker but his number was constantly engaged.

He tried to look at the whole thing logically. The claims were real, the money was real, so there must have been real work going on in that factory. Okay. Something obviously happened on the weekend... Raine did say that Head Office was at a critical stage in the talks. Obviously they went wrong, and the US Government was apparently concerned enough to demand an immediate closure and evacuation of the depots.

That gave him a ray of hope; perhaps it was a temporary political problem and next week Baron could be up and running again, with Raine giving him a breathless explanation of his most stressful week ever.

In fact, maybe nothing was wrong at all. If Baron were in some kind of transitional stage, perhaps forming into a larger operation, then they would want to give the appearance of normality. Raine had sounded very excited about the talks on Friday.

Another thought occurred, which manifested itself on Lewis' face as the beginnings of a smile.

Maybe Baron was testing its service providers, testing the confidentiality agreements. He imagined the Board saying, "Now, as we move to this critical stage, we have to be sure of the people working for us. Let's pretend, just for a few days, that we've gone out of business. Let's see what they do."

Lewis was still smiling when O'Neill appeared in his doorway, flanked by Graham and Rhys.

"You've got one hour," O'Neill said in a deadpan voice. "Clear out your desk and fuck off." He turned on his heels and returned to his room, followed by the other partners, shaking their heads.

Lewis leaned back in his chair, knowing now how it felt to be shot and wake up dead. He had always wondered how it would finally come, the moment of resolution between him and O'Neill.

Lewis sensed that everyone was avoiding walking past his door as he got his belongings together. There wasn't much he wanted to take, a few bank statements and an old photograph of himself playing the sax was all that he found, and his face was deadpan as he walked into reception and met Stuart coming in. The trainee stepped aside without looking at him and without offering his hand or saying goodbye. Lewis nodded to himself, thinking what fools they all were and how they were going to regret this. How he was going to make them regret it. As he went up the steps the last person he saw was Helen the receptionist, the public face of the firm, glancing up from her paperback. Her face was contemptuous.

Lewis didn't mind the idea of extending his holiday, and he felt oddly empowered by the time he got home.

He had around £30,000 put aside, enough to carry him through a very extended vacation, and a mass of equity in his duplex.

All the same, he supposed he had to put the duplex on the market if he was going to get an ordinary job. Maybe he should buy some rental properties and move back to something like he had in Atlantic Wharf. That wouldn't be so bad. Or, there was always Spain.

Spain... he knew that wasn't an option any more. He had changed.

He looked up at his cathedral window. He was going to miss this place though, and he was hoping against hope that his theory about Baron was right, that they were going to come back on line and give him another two years' work, enough time to make him stronger than strong.

The more he thought about it, the more he saw the tape recorder as being significant. If Baron had just gone bust they wouldn't be worried about giving the appearance that they were working. Would they?

He supposed he hoped it was true more so that he could ram O'Neill's words back down his throat. He would set up on his own... no, it could be more fun to return and negotiate a higher bonus structure, as a penalty for their impudence. Yes, he would have a lot of fun with Stuart. He'd make him jump as if the floor was on fire. Helen... well, he'd insist that she was sacked on the spot. Yes. They'd do it, too. None of those guys had a cat's chance of getting any work in by themselves and if they said no at first, he would raise the price again when they came begging. Bastards.

If Bernie would just call, it would be perfect.

He wondered whether she had e-mailed, but when he went online he was greeted by an e-mail from Farthing. com. It appeared in the same fashion as before, struggling across the screen letter by clumsy letter.

Our felicitations.

We are totally satisfied.

It is safe to reply.

Lewis, while jubilant, nevertheless considered the 'reply' option with a narrowing of his eyes. Was this their opportunity to destroy his third computer? If so, it would be a bit corny. He typed *yes?* Then clicked 'send'. His heart missed a beat as his e-mail was sent and Farthing's reply quickly materialised. The words were still being typed before his eyes, but now furiously fast.

Does The Shilling trouble you?

The photographs are on different films of paper, aren't they? They dissolve and that's what makes it smell. There's some magic ink on the crossword too. And you've filled me with some crazy drugs. Am I right?

You really are too clever.

Our relationship will be long and fruitful.

Lewis nodded. The magazine was just one big test, sort of like a MENSA exam. They weren't even angry with him, they had wanted him to do the things he did. *Why me?* he typed.

You are very special to us. What you have to offer is important to us. More important than you can imagine.

But we will talk on that subject again. First, a token of our regard. The answer to 6 across is "WIT". Write it in. You may find this a significant use for the £30,000 you have put aside.

You have our authority to use all your money, and you can even share this fortune with your friend BB. This is the reward for your efforts.

Thank you. I'm sorry about breaking the rules before. Is Baron going to contact me? Am I right in thinking that the rumour about them going out of business is just a test?

It is indeed a test.

Your office will ring you tomorrow, requesting your presence.

He beamed with pleasure and typed: *O'Neill will want to see me?*

Savour the moment of self-visualisation, when you see what you have become.

Your servants, sir.

He decided not to push his luck. There were so many questions he wanted to ask, but they were clearly signing off and he didn't want to risk another virus corruption. He switched his window. Looking through his 'old e-mails' filing cabinet he saw that the Farthing e-mails hadn't been saved and his replies weren't saved either. Nothing about Farthing's software surprised him now and during the dialogue he had being copying the exchanges onto a piece of paper. He had the smug look of a super sleuth as he re-read his notes with a big grin.

Everything he suspected was true, he had got it right every step of the way. No wonder they were impressed with him. Everything, even down to stealing Mr Dove's wallet, was probably a test. Okay, so they had some strange ideas, and they liked practical jokes, but an organisation with this type of influence and inventive know-how was going to make him a fortune. Maybe they wanted him to be their lawyer or, even better, a shareholder. Baron Enterprises could be just the beginning. Oh yes, he was relishing the prospect of his next encounter with O'Neill.

He went up to his bedroom to fetch his attaché case. The picture of him and Bernie on the balcony had been restored to his bedside cabinet and he was considering it as he clipped the case open and took out the magazine. He turned to the crossword.

6 across: *your reward.*

That one hadn't made sense before, but now it did. He wrote in *Wit*, and then decided he needed to go back online to check for companies that fitted the bill.

Wit.

Reward.

He even had an excuse to ring BB again. When he rang he would pretend that nothing had happened; BB would pretend too and everything would be okay.

As he dropped The Shilling back into the open attaché case he noticed something spiral out of it and drift slowly onto the floor. He picked it up and held it end to end. It was long, about two feet long.

It was a single strand of black hair.

He frowned and shook his head. It must have found its way into his case in that hotel room in Naples.

It must have belonged to one of the maids, he supposed. Most Italian women had black hair.

WIT

O n ringing BB, Lewis quickly offered a few pre-rehearsed lines to explain why he hadn't been in touch. Problems with the firm – he had resigned yesterday – and other stuff that had taken him out of the city. BB seemed equally anxious to smooth things over and gave Lewis an update on his tourist website that was now up and running, although it wasn't profitable yet. Lewis carefully avoided making any mention of Bernie, the real reason for their estrangement, and BB took the hint and didn't mention her either.

The ostensible reason for the call was to organise a game of squash, but Lewis slipped in his e-mail dialogue with Farthing.com and explained that he had found a company called Wild Imagining Technology – *WIT* – that had proprietary software with reasoning capabilities. BB didn't understand, so Lewis offered BB's tourist business as an example: using this software he could get all the various aspects of his business divided up into different boxes, cross-referenced, which would tell him the areas requiring priority and how that would impact upon other areas of the business. So, it could reason that Cardiff Bay was the most lucrative part of the website, but that more money needed to be spent on researching it.

"How does it do that?" BB asked.

"Well you've got to program it in first, obviously. It doesn't really think for you, it just adds clarity to your thought processes."

BB was unimpressed. "I could do a box diagram on a

piece of paper with the same result."

"Yeah, but it wouldn't be as good, would it?" Lewis said with a shake of his head. BB could be a real primitive sometimes.

"Oh I don't know. Henry Ford seemed to have no problem in building a multi-billion-dollar empire without software."

Lewis didn't comment, but went on to explain the company's history. It had been soaring high in the dot. com boom, but was one of the first casualties of the correction when the major companies had pulled in their IT spending. This was 'good times' software.

"So why buy it?" BB asked. "Sounds like a dog to me."

"That's the beauty of it. And you haven't heard the worst of it yet. The share price is so low now that it'll be thrown out of the Footsie on the next reshuffle. More importantly, it's run out of money."

"You're not convincing me to buy it," BB remarked.

Lewis chuckled. "I know, it sounds dreadful, doesn't it? Investors have been selling it in droves, because the company's got a critical meeting tomorrow with its main backers. The word on the bulletin boards is that the backers are going to pull the rug out."

"Still not convincing me."

"The backers will introduce new funding, and the share price will soar on the news."

"How do you know?"

"I just know. It's all fitting into place now. The Shilling, Baron, whoever they are... this is all about inventions. Drugs, dissolving paper, car components. I found this girl in London, she used to belong to a model agency, and Baron was experimenting with new diet techniques. They're brilliant, BB, seriously brilliant. I bet they were the real backers of all the companies they've recommended

– that's how they knew the share price was about to explode, because they tipped me just before a major announcement."

"Wild Imagining Technology," BB mused. "So you think that Farthing, the network or whoever they are, are the backers of this company?"

"Yep."

"That they know full well that they're going to hand over the funding tomorrow?"

"Yep."

"So why tell you?"

Lewis settled back into his armchair with the phone at his ear, as if he were slipping contentedly into a hot bath. His trousers were too tight and as his free hand undid his belt, then his top button, he sighed with relief. "Well that's the puzzle, isn't it? They need me for something. I suppose that passing on the information, in code, enables them to call in favours. I'm guessing that they have a whole network of people working for them, in every sphere of life, and they draw on the collective intelligence. And they leave no trace behind them. Even their e-mails can't be traced."

"Okay, I get it, but no disrespect Lew: again, why you?"

Lewis was stroking his stomach as he spoke. He was sure that he was getting fatter by the day. "I don't know. Not yet, anyway, they haven't told me. Perhaps they need a good lawyer. I think that all these tricks they've been playing is just to show me how powerful they are."

"There are lots of good lawyers out there, Lew," BB remarked.

"Well, loyalty and discretion are important to them too. Far more important, perhaps; anyone can keep their mouth shut when the money's rolling in, but people show their true colours when things go sour. I think they've been testing me in the past few days."

"So you want me to buy these shares for you?" BB asked, uneasily.

"No, it's okay, Farthing have given me the green light. I bought thirty thousand worth first thing this morning. I'm just passing on the tip."

BB continued to ask questions about the company which Lewis did his best to answer. Eventually BB agreed to place an order, using what was left of his profits from the Hour Glass and some other money he had put aside for the next six months of funding for his tourist website. They arranged squash for Thursday, but Lewis was a little peeved that BB didn't even say thank you. He was thinking that he could have done without the forty-five minutes of inquisition and that this was the last tip BB would ever get from him.

The phone rang immediately after he had put it down. It was O'Neill, saying that he had been trying to get through to him for the last half-hour. Lewis smiled, stretched, and again settled into his armchair.

"What can I do for you Stephen? How are things at the firm?" Lewis inquired in a polite voice. O'Neill didn't seem interested in playing the game and came straight to the point.

"I need to see you. Can you come in tomorrow, first thing?"

Lewis closed his eyes and nodded. "Baron Enterprises?" he asked.

"Yes."

"Something's happened?"

"Yes."

Lewis shrugged. "Alright, I'll be there, for old time's sake. But I'm not sure we've got much to talk about."

O'Neill put the phone down without comment.

Lewis bought a new suit for the meeting for the waistbands on his other suits, all virtually new, were pinching. As he looked in the mirror after he had dressed he considered the alien folds of flesh under his neck and around his eyes, and his slovenly posture. Cutting down on the curries hadn't been enough and he was going to have to join a gym.

At reception Helen informed him that O'Neill was waiting for him downstairs in the boardroom. She looked away, with disdain, as he shuffled past.

You're for the chop, my girl, Lewis thought, relishing the prospect of his revenge. He had a need for revenge, to assuage the fact that he was so hated; he hadn't known how hated he was until he had made that walk out of the office two days ago.

He paused on the stairs.

The uncomfortable truth was like a cool breeze that cleared his head.

I am hated. That's why I'm so angry.

He found himself changing his mind about what he was going to say to O'Neill and the other partners. Perhaps he had been too hard on everyone; in past months he had become just like O'Neill, worse than O'Neill, in fact. O'Neill had never sacked anyone. O'Neill could be impossible, but when it came down to it he was loyal and fair. Even when the bad times arrived, when the work was falling off, O'Neill wouldn't have made any cold decisions on restructuring personnel. He would have shouted and ranted, but would have gone down with the sinking ship.

Clarity turned into shame. He wasn't going to sack Helen, he decided, and he was going to apologise to Stuart. He was even going to suggest a more equitable profit share with the partners – that's what partnership was, wasn't it? If he were married, he wouldn't say to his wife *this is mine and this is yours*. O'Neill had taken him on when he was fresh out of law school, and made him his partner long before Baron came on the scene, or any of the insurance clients for that matter. Graham and Rhys may not have had his success with clients, the trick for securing new work, but they had always done their best.

He finished the walk down the stairs then took a deep breath as he stood outside the boardroom door. The typing pool in the room to his right was as quiet as a morgue, for the secretaries knew he was here.

Perhaps he should even tell Baron what he thought of their policies. Perhaps they would respect him for it and even if they didn't at least he would be able to sleep at night.

He nodded to himself and smiled, then knocked and opened the door.

O'Neill stood up and gestured to two men sitting at the far end of the table, who were studying Lewis carefully as he paused in the doorway.

"This is Detective Inspector Cole and Detective Inspector Fleet," O'Neill announced, "of the CID."

Cole and Fleet asked Lewis about the Baron account, while effortlessly deflecting his own questions.

These were seasoned officers, used to dealing with people a lot tougher than he was, so he went along without protest. Both men were in their late forties, senior men for their vocation, and Lewis told them as much as he had told the firm, that Baron had a unique inventive process, which was subject to strict confidentiality.

"Why are there so many claims?" Fleet asked, the rugged officer with a crew cut doing most of the talking. Cole was spending his time observing. He was thinning on top and this was obviously worrying him from the way he constantly ran a finger along his hairline.

Lewis shrugged. "There's a large manual aspect to the production side, and I think some elements of the process are unreliable, or at least experimental. That's why there are so many accidents. I can't tell you any more, because I've never been in the workshop."

"You're their lawyer, defending employer liability claims, but you've never been in the workshop?" Fleet asked casually. Cole's eyes flickered as he studied his finger.

"That's right," Lewis said.

"How do you know how to defend the claims, if you don't know how the... how did you put it?... the *process* works?"

Lewis nodded at a fair question. "The company always admitted liability. I was only instructed on quantum, the valuation of the claims." He smiled, expecting this explanation to satisfy them.

Fleet raised his eyebrows. "Admitted liability did they? Always paid out?"

Lewis nodded again. He knew now that the rumour was true, that Baron were out of business: there must be some inquiry going on as to whether the process was dangerous, just as Marker had said on Monday. Surprisingly, he didn't feel too disheartened. Baron would be moving on to new ventures and would contact him with something new.

"Was the workshop very busy?" Fleet asked.

"Yes."

"How did you know?"

"Well you could hear it going on," Lewis answered uncomfortably.

"You mean the banging and thumping?"

"Right."

Cole's finger returned to his hairline.

"And do you still believe there was a lot of work going on in there?"

"Absolutely. The claims prove it, don't they?"

Fleet's face was blank. "Would it surprise you if I told

you that the warehouse in Newport has always been empty. That the noise is just a tape recording?"

"Yes it would," Lewis answered, his stomach twitching.

"Really?"

"Of course."

"We have you on film," Fleet said, "visiting the plant on Monday. You were the only person in there. While you were inside the building the noise stopped for about a minute or so. You turned the tape recorder off, didn't you? And then you turned it back on again before you left."

O'Neill shook his head and looked down at the table, disappointed with Lewis for falling into this trap. The officers had already briefed him on the tape recorder.

"I did see the tape recorder on Monday," Lewis admitted, "but I just thought it was some kind of joke. Look, there are the claims..."

"What is this process, exactly?" Fleet asked, happily banking his winnings and moving on. Cole was wearing a faint smile now and had stopped touching his hairline. Lewis wondered if that had just been a ploy, to distract him.

"I... I can't really tell you that," Lewis answered.

"Why not?"

"Confidentiality. I've signed an agreement."

Fleet nodded, then shrugged. "It's up to you, Mr Coin, if you want to play it that way. I'm happy to put all of this on a more formal footing. The reason we're talking here, and not down the station, is because of Mr O'Neill's personal intervention. My colleague here simply wanted to charge you. Mr O'Neill has assured us of your good character and he believes that this must be a genuine misunderstanding."

Lewis glanced at O'Neill. "Tell them what you know, Lewis," O'Neill whispered encouragingly and with a sad smile.

Lewis took a deep breath. "Actually I don't know that much," he said. "The process involved making components for vehicles. The components had some kind of resistance powered into them, which reduced, even extinguished, the need for fuel."

He didn't like the way his words came out, didn't like the sound of his own description. Metal components that stored energy... he had never questioned it before, had hardly even thought about it, all that mattered was the work and the charging rate. Now, in the strained atmosphere of the boardroom interrogation, his explanation sounded ludicrous.

Both Fleet and Cole were suppressing smiles. O'Neill adjusted his bow tie uncomfortably.

"Don't take my word for it," Lewis protested, "ask the customers. They were selling the components by the bucket load."

"There are no customers," Fleet returned.

"Of course there are. They've just signed confidentiality agreements, that's all, so they can't speak to you."

"Ah, the famous confidentiality agreement again."

"Well the claims are there as the proof..."

Cole smiled now as Fleet pulled out some papers. "Mr O'Neill has kindly supplied us with your office account ledgers. You're a junior partner here, aren't you Mr Coin?"

"That's right."

"But you seem to making more than the other partners put together."

"That's what we negotiated," Lewis replied quietly.

"I see. Did you know that all these claims have been removed from your computer memory banks?"

"Baron were installing new software, there's been a glitch."

"No glitch, Mr Coin. The software did exactly what it was meant to do. It removed all trace of Baron and the so-called claims."

"What do you mean *so-called*?"

"Do you have any paper records of these claims?"

"No."

Fleet turned to O'Neill for corroboration. "No records were kept, of any description," O'Neill confirmed.

"On whose instruction?"

O'Neill didn't answer. Fleet and Cole both found broad smiles and turned back to Lewis.

Lewis shook his head, finding the line of questioning incredible. Surely this whole thing could be easily put to bed. "Look, it's simple. There was special software that filtered the materials from my computer to everyone else's, but everyone in the firm as least knew the surnames of the claimants. You can find the claimants and they'll confirm that they worked for Baron. Okay?"

"Any addresses?"

"No, of course not. We turned these claims over quickly and anyway their addresses were *care of* the union solicitor. By the way, have you spoken to him yet?"

"We can't find him," Fleet replied quickly, not wanting to be sidetracked.

"Well, anyway, get the names and you get the claimants and you get the employees."

"Ah yes, the names. Thank you for your suggestion, Mr Coin, but believe it or not we'd already thought of that. Every surname the members of your firm can remember are written down here." He held up a sheet of paper. "I've never seen so many Williams, Jones, and Smiths. Not an uncommon name amongst them, in fact. Where do you suggest we start looking?"

Lewis' heart missed a beat. Fleet was right, they were all called Williams or Jones or some other name which any Welsh phone book would devote pages to, assuming that these men were even listed. He had to code the claims when he worked on them. *Williams 12… Jones 42.*

And there was another oddity. The Welsh names continued even when he got the UK account. Maybe the employees all changed their surnames to deliberately make themselves inconspicuous, to cement the confidentiality.

"The Health and Safety Executive…" Lewis began, then frowned as he realised he was going up another dead end.

"Have never heard of Baron Enterprises," Fleet said. His eyes twinkled. "I suspect you've never seen any HSE documentation, have you? You didn't have to, because the cases settled."

"What are you saying?" Lewis asked. "What's this all about?" He was trying to remember his conversation with Bernie, when she was puzzled when he explained about the Health and Safety Executive. They won't fight the claims, she had said.

"Let me give you my theory," Fleet said, "a theory which we all happen to believe. Let's say that nothing went on at Baron at all. The warehouse had a tape recorder and a smoke fire to give the appearance that it was a busy factory, but the company was just a shell for receiving money from lawyers in America. You with me so far?"

Lewis nodded.

"Now let's assume, just for a moment, that this money can't be declared for some reason or other. Best case scenario, someone's avoiding the taxman. Worst case scenario, this is drug money that has to be laundered."

"Laundered?" Lewis whispered, now wondering whom Raine was referring to when he talked about Head Office in the States and imagining a breakfast bar in Little Italy. Cole seemed to recognise the thought process, for his eyes narrowed.

"Now the money has to be distributed. Why not distribute it in damages and legal costs? All you need to do is to invent hundreds of claimants and have the damages paid into fictitious accounts. The money's left there for a while and then picked up by nominees. All the money goes back into circulation, and it's even tax deductible."

Lewis thought about this. He didn't answer.

"Baron had no problem with paying out large awards, did they?" It was Cole speaking now in a bored voice.

"I did have a few successes for them," Lewis countered. "I brought the claims down."

"But none actually went to trial? They all settled without being issued?"

Lewis nodded uncomfortably. "You said damages and legal costs," he remarked. "Why legal costs?"

"Well that's what we're trying to find out," Fleet said. "You see it puzzles us why Baron paid their lawyers so well. What was it, two hundred and fifty an hour? Is that usual for this type of work?"

"No, but they were impressed with me." Lewis realised his answer sounded a little pathetic, but Fleet spared him a rejoinder.

"It's not unheard of," O'Neill offered. "In London, for example. Or for commercial work."

"But this isn't London, and the work wasn't commercial," Fleet remarked. "We've asked around and the best going rate for bulk instruction personal injury work is around one hundred and twenty. Usually less. And this type of work was like shelling peas, because as you said they all settled."

"They paid extra for the confidentiality," Lewis said.

"I'm sure they did," Fleet remarked. "Another question we're asking ourselves is why *you* were paid so much, as opposed to your partners."

"I told you… it was negotiated."

"Yes, you were rather greedy, weren't you? We're surprised given your appetite for money that you didn't set up on your own. Did you fancy the idea of working inside Mr O'Neill's firm, so hiding your own involvement?"

"Now come on…"

"But you still took precautions, didn't you? We've taken a statement from the first employee that you sacked. You sacked anyone who you thought might have a loose tongue."

"That was good management," Lewis protested, looking round at O'Neill for support. O'Neill was looking away.

"And we've done some research on you, Mr Coin," Cole added. "We don't think the hourly rate was the only reward Baron were giving you for the little part you were playing in the distribution." He had an impish grin as his finger tapped another sheet of paper. "You've had a few share successes too, haven't you?"

"So?" Lewis asked, trying to read the sheet of paper.

"Tips were they? I've never seen such a run of good luck."

Before Lewis could answer Fleet slid a copy of an official document down the table. It was an ex-parte injunction preventing the sale of his duplex.

"We got that this morning," Fleet declared. "If we're right, the equity in your property will be confiscated as the proceeds of crime. In the meantime, we want the number of your mobile and we expect you to carry it with you at all times. You're to stay in the Cardiff area and we're installing a tracer that can pinpoint your movements. There are still some lines of enquiry left before we put it to the CPS for a final decision. But we can charge you now and put you on bail, if you prefer."

"I can prove that the claims were real," Lewis muttered. "And even if they weren't, I can prove that I wasn't involved." He nodded to himself, his head a storage file of information that he was now desperately rummaging through.

He signed on to his e-mail as soon as he got home. He was in a daze, there was too much to think about, too many old conversations to examine.

For the first time in his life he was using all his lawyer's skills, locating evidence and finding corroboration, for his own defence. But he had one advantage: he knew he was telling the truth, and the truth would always out.

There was an announcement on the backers' meeting with Wild Imagining Technology. He opened it, hungry for some good news, and read the announcement, then read it again. The backers had refused to invest any more money. The company was going into liquidation. It was debt ridden, the likely payout was to be 2p in every pound: his shares were virtually worthless.

He looked at the screen for an age, unable to comprehend the news. He was expecting a new announcement to appear, saying that it had all been a mistake or that the backers had changed their mind. It didn't change. The screen stared back at him uselessly like a squashed animal on the road.

The phone was ringing, but he let it ring and after it stopped he dialled 1471 to discover that it was BB calling. He wasn't ready to speak to BB yet; he had to think this through.

All his spare cash was gone and his duplex was subject to an injunction. He was holding back the urge to panic and scream.

"Okay, calm down," he whispered to himself. So he had lost £30,000 in the share sale but most of his wealth was still in his duplex. He would convince the CID of his innocence, get the injunction lifted, sell up and move on. Perhaps Farthing weren't involved with Wild Imagining Technology, maybe they weren't the backers. It could have been just a bad tip. He re-read his transcript of their e-mails: *our relationship will be long and fruitful.* They were going to feel bad about him losing his money. They might even reimburse him, him and BB.

Yes, in fact he was going to insist on it. After all, **BB** had used the money for his tourist website.

But right now he needed cash. After taking a quick inventory in his head he drove to the Mercedes garage and sold his car. The price he obtained reflected his need for an immediate banker's draft which he could cash, because he suspected the CID were monitoring his bank accounts. He took two taxis home, stopping off to buy a wall safe, which he secured at the far end of his bedroom, next to his bed. He placed his cash inside, all in crisp fifty-pound notes.

Then he signed on again, and watched the screen for hours. Eventually, when it was getting dark, an e-mail arrived from Farthing.com. The page was blank and no words appeared. He waited. After a while the white page turned bright red and the words arrived, slowly at first, in white ink.

Ha.

Ha ha.

Ha ha ha ha ha ha ha ha ha ha ha ha ha
ha ha ha ha ha ha ha ha ha ha ha ha ha
ha ha ha ha ha ha ha ha ha ha ha ha ha
ha ha ha ha ha ha

The words were now whizzing across the page, filling it then moving onto the next page. He tried to reply but the computer didn't respond, then tried to sign off, but that failed too. The computer was refusing to shut down. Cursing, he unplugged it, but the computer kept on going and his jaw dropped as he looked at the plug. The screen was filled with the laughing epithets, a third page now being overrun.

"Big joke," he whispered. "Big fucking joke."

Wit.

WIT!!!

He was still holding the plug in his hand when the screen started to blur, and the computer groaned with electrical discharge as whatever energy was inside it began to falter. Like a headless chicken, which finally flops to the floor, it shut down with a bump.

Lewis had been on the balcony for an hour playing with one of his old cigarette lighters, trying to decide whether or not to burn The Shilling.

It wasn't an easy decision. Would they just send him another one? In fact, perhaps they wanted him to destroy it so they could get a new one in place, a new copy with new tricks.

If they really did change them, for he still had that nagging doubt in his mind over the spray mark around the poodle's head, the mark that told him that the magazine upstairs was the same magazine Emily had left at his Atlantic Wharf apartment.

With a sigh he went back inside, flicking his cigarette lighter on and off, unsure of what he was going to do. He went upstairs, opened his attaché case, and as he was expecting, a new clue in the crossword had been written in. 'Wit' had been superseded because the joke was over. He recognised the pattern now, even before it happened.

The new clue was: *how many now?*

The new answer was: *Two.*

Two? What did that mean?

As he turned the pages tufts of black hair slipped out of the front of the magazine. Mary Stone was crater-faced again, her smile becoming a sneer, but this time her scalp was clearly visible.

He collected a tuft of the hair and rubbed it between his fingers. It was warm and lustrous, the sort of hair you would sweep up from the floor of a fashionable ladies' stylist. There was a faint smell of perfume, or expensive shampoo.

Dissolving pages, magic ink and drugs he could explain, but he couldn't put together a theory for this. No one had been in this attaché case apart from him and not even specially treated pages could make real hair.

He instinctively checked his wall safe, but the money was still there. Where the hell did the hair come from?

You really are too clever.

It is indeed a test.

Was Farthing being sarcastic with those e-mails? Were his theories about the magazine all wrong? A knocking on his door interrupted his thoughts.

That will be BB, he realised. He sighed. Well, he couldn't avoid him forever.

He was making his way down his spiral staircase as the door knocked again.

"Coming," he said irritably. He had decided that he had problems enough without BB offloading on him about his share losses. BB was a big boy and he was going to tell him "if you play, you pay". He opened the door and stepped back in surprise.

The moment was long and glorious before he was able to speak.

"Oh thank God," he whispered, "thank God."

It was Bernie. She didn't say anything, but just smiled. Her eyes were welling up as they embraced in the doorway.

Two

ernie brushed aside his blurted apologies and after
a quick and tearful reconciliation she recovered
herself and spoke calmly and slowly.

"I believe you now," she assured him. "Don't worry, I
believe you."

The photocopies hadn't convinced her, she explained,
she thought that he had just doctored them in some way.
As she sat next to him on the sofa she glanced a few times
at his waistline and he put a hand to his stomach, feeling
self-conscious.

"They've pumped me with some kind of drug," he said.
"I get these really bad nicotine pangs too." The blood
rushed from his face; with all his attempts to get Bernie
to forgive him it hadn't occurred to him that she might
not find him attractive any more. She seemed to read his
thoughts and smiled, shaking her head.

"Lewis, I don't care about your appearance. You look
just fine. I loved you before you put on the weight, and I
love you now."

"Really?"

"Really. But we'll do something about those drugs. We'll
get you to a doctor."

She continued with her story. The photocopies had
been stolen from her bed-sit. No, she hadn't rung the
police because there was absolutely no sign of a forced
entry. There hadn't been any visitors; no one had been
inside apart from her and her brother. She shook her head,
unable to offer any explanation.

"That's when I knew," she said. "Lewis, what's going on?"

He collected the attaché case and showed her Mary Stone and the tufts of hair. He told her everything he knew, and offered up all his theories. He even told her about the dreams. She recalled that lame pick-up line he used on their first date then nodded thoughtfully.

"I can't work out the latest trick with this hair," he admitted.

"There's no trick," she said. "Someone's got to the magazine."

"That's impossible. No one's been in here, and anyway this case is impregnable."

"They got into my flat," she reminded him. "Lewis, I don't know why you're so surprised. If they can do all the things that you've said, they can certainly manage a little cat burglary, can't they?"

He thought about this, then nodded.

"What's the next clue?" she asked.

"*Two*," he replied, showing her the crossword.

"What does that mean?"

"I've no idea."

She studied the crossword, her face a mask of concentration notwithstanding the smell of dog excrement, or that touching the pages left a soggy stain on the fingers. The magazine seemed to be rotting.

"*Beta lives*," she said eventually. "That's *Be*."

"That's what I thought, but I'm not so sure now. I think maybe it's *i.e.*".

"Why?"

"Because it joins up with 'Bern' to make 'Bernie'. Be Ta: i.e. Bernie Tate."

She shook her head and said, "I don't understand..."

"You're involved in this somehow, Bernie. Look, Mary Stone's wearing your diamond pendant. I think... I think they wanted me to give you the magazine at the end, just like Emily gave me the magazine."

"To start the cycle again, but with me this time?" she mused.

"Could be. Who knows what it would have involved? I'm betting they would have offered you a cure for your brother. One of the first companies I bought was a pharmaceutical company. They're into everything."

Bernie nodded thoughtfully. "And maybe they're not as clever as you think," she remarked. "I bet the cure they would have offered my brother would have been a fake. After all, your nicotine pangs have come back, so they obviously couldn't sell that on the open market, and I couldn't see much demand for torture machines." She winced as she recalled Lewis' description of the Hour invention.

"Good software, though," he remarked.

"Yes, but it wrecks the computer."

He shrugged and said, "Well, whatever joke they're playing, I think we've poleaxed them. You see, on their little cycle, when things started going wrong for me I was meant to lose you. Perhaps at the end I'd have been persuaded to enrol you as the price of getting you back."

"But I've already come back to you," she said.

"You've come back," he agreed, with a tear starting again in his eye.

Bernie took his hand and squeezed it. She returned to the crossword as Lewis got up to make them a coffee. "But *Be* could still be the right answer," she pondered. Her finger traced the box on the crossword, across, then down. She frowned as her finger performed the movements again. Now she spoke to herself, performing the movements once more. "Across... *Be*... down... *Be*. The word reads twice. Be... Be."

"What's that?" Lewis asked, returning with the coffee.

"Nothing," she said.

"No, you were working something out. What was it?"

"Seriously, Lewis, it was nothing." She took her coffee and held the mug in both hands, smiling as she felt the heat radiate into her palms.

Lewis glanced at the crossword as he sat back down. "Bernie, there's something else I've got to tell you. I think you're right when you say that all these inventions are fakes, or useless or whatever. The process that Baron used didn't even exist."

"What do you mean?"

He now told her about his encounter with the CID and Bernie's jaw dropped as she heard about the fictitious claims. As he finished she was shaking her head, speechless.

"Bernie, did you ever go into the workshop?" he asked.

"No, no. I wasn't allowed."

"But you must have seen the workers, going in or out?"

She appeared troubled. "Well, no. But that's because the shifts began early in the morning. Only Mr Booker went in there. There was a bus which collected them all, from a back entrance in the warehouse, but I never saw it."

"Why not?"

"Mr Raine always had me in his office when the first shift ended, to check through the payroll."

Lewis groaned. "Then it could be true."

"No, it's impossible."

He nodded and was silent for a few moments. Then he smiled and said, "You know, that's what I think. I've been thinking about all those contacts you had in Baron. Any organisation that was so large couldn't just manufacture a fraud like this and then disappear off the face of the earth. Thank God you knew all those people. Look, let's just ring up some of your contacts and find out what's going on." He reached for the phone, but she was looking away, embarrassed.

"Bernie?"

She squeezed his hand again. "Please don't be angry, Lewis, but there aren't any contacts."

"But you said..."

"I just did it to impress you. To make you think that I knew people, that I had an influential job. Truth is Mr Raine didn't let me meet anyone apart from you, and the lawyer in London."

He considered her for a few moments then closed his eyes. He remembered his suspicions on their first date, when he wondered what she really did at Baron, whether she really had any responsibilities.

"I found that girl in Circus myself," Bernie admitted. She smiled sadly. "It took me ages. I'm sorry, I just wanted to impress you."

He opened his eyes. "Then I'm flattered, but it looks like I'm in the frame."

"No, no, I'll go and see the police right now. I'll tell them that I recruited you, I'll tell them everything."

"As a last resort perhaps, but I want you to stay out of it if possible."

"Why?"

"Because you're in the frame too. Won't the CID ask why you were receiving such a high salary for doing so little? Rather than being my alibi, you might be charged with me."

She put a hand to her mouth. "Oh God. What would happen to Jamey?"

"I know. I think they'll also find it significant that you changed your name to get the job."

"Why?"

"It's a way of covering your tracks, isn't it?"

"But…" She didn't finish her sentence, but nodded, horrified. "What can we do?" she asked.

"Go and see that lawyer you used to use. At least he can corroborate some of my story. I can't go as far as London; I've got a police tracer in my mobile. Check out the doctor as well, the one who did the reports for all of the claims."

"What are you going to do?"

He let out a long sigh, then something occurred to him and his expression changed. "Wait a minute," he murmured. "Wait just a minute. How could I have been so stupid?"

"What? Tell me."

He was grinning. "Vernon Jones. Good old back pain Vernon Jones."

She made a puzzled face.

"You remember he was the first claim I settled. I've seen him. I mean I've actually seen him, playing football. He had back pain."

"Vernon Jones… I remember." She now adopted a mock serious expression. "You were very naughty with him."

"I know, I know, but he exists, that's the important thing."

Her eyes widened in recognition. "Wait a minute, that means…"

"It means that the CID are wrong. There *were* workers, there *were* genuine claims."

Bernie stayed the night but had to leave very early in the morning to get back to London. She had taken a day's leave, the precious leave which she needed for her brother; she couldn't afford a carer now, so even her weekends were committed as Jamey had to have his hospital treatment while she was in work.

The alarm woke them at 4 a.m. but they still managed

to make love. Bernie had been resistant the night before in spite of their reconciliation, her passion vulnerable and under protection, for she was still nursing the wounds that were healing. The night's sleep in each other's arms had helped, and in the morning she had shaken off these burdens and the act was totally intimate.

"Will that keep her away?" she whispered. "That woman you dream of, I mean?"

"She's never coming back, ever. I love you Bernie."

"I love you too."

She was quiet as she dressed. Something seemed to be worrying her as she carefully pinned her hair in the mirror.

"Bernie, is everything okay?" he asked.

"I'm just thinking, that's all."

"About what?"

"What kind of drug can make you dream like that?"

"My metabolism is all to pot, what with the smoking thing and the weight gain. They probably didn't know I'd have these dreams; it's just a weird side effect. It's falling in love with you, that's what's done it."

"So why not dream about *me*?" There was something indignant in her tone, as if she was jealous of Mary Stone.

"Well I can't imagine you raping me, or cutting bits off me, can I?" he joked.

She huffed, not amused. "Okay, but why that woman?"

He lay back to consider the same question he had asked himself many times. "I suppose she reminds me of you, in a way. You've got the same figure, and you even look alike. Perhaps it's the way you wear your hair up."

She turned round, wide eyed. "But she's hideous!"

"She wasn't in the beginning. When I first saw her she was beautiful. She took my breath away."

Without a word she returned to the mirror, seemingly

unmoved by the implied compliment. "I still don't like it," she said. "Dissolving paper I can believe, burglars I can believe, but dreams… I just don't know. I think you're on the wrong side of something."

"Oh rubbish."

"Seriously. What about her saying that you were… what was it?… *all spent*. And then you read those exact words, buried in an article."

Lewis had described all the dreams to her in detail, they were still so clear in his mind. He had gone through them again in bed last night, and in spite of her revulsion he could feel her becoming aroused. They aroused him too.

"I agree," he said. "It's a strange coincidence."

"Coincidence?"

"Maybe I read that bit in the article… you know… subconsciously, before the dream. Anyway, I'm not prepared to believe that the network can engineer a drug that makes me dream about specific things, right down to the dialogue."

She had a wistful air as she put on her fusty blue jacket. "I don't know what to think, Lewis," she admitted, "but I do think you're on the wrong side of something."

His eyes narrowed. "So you keep saying. You think I should see someone, don't you?"

She glanced round at him then returned to the mirror to check the spring in her lace collar. She nodded.

He threw on his towel robe. "How did you put it, when we were together before? Oh yeah… *someone qualified*. No way. I'm not seeing a psychiatrist, not even for you."

She laughed.

"It's not funny!"

"Lewis, I wasn't referring to a psychiatrist when I said that you should see someone qualified."

"Who then?"

"I think you should see someone in the Church."

"In the what?"

"In the Church. That thing is evil, Lewis. It's evil, I tell you."

He held back a smile as he realised that she was deadly serious. "I didn't know you believed in God," he muttered. He hadn't heard her talk about religion before, but then again, she had a brother who would die soon; perhaps she needed to draw strength and comfort from anywhere she could. With this assessment made, he still had trouble in keeping a straight face.

"You're saying the magazine's possessed?"

She sighed as she made one final check in the mirror. There was a kind of smile, one that told of weary resignation. "Now, if you're going to make fun of me I won't speak to you."

He nodded. "So what are you saying?" he asked.

"I just believe that you could do with some guidance, Lewis. I don't care about the burglars or the share tips, but your dreams worry me. Will you at least think about it?"

"You're serious, aren't you?" he murmured.

"I do know that not everything can be explained."

"And what does *that* mean?"

"Lewis, just promise me you'll think about it."

"Alright, I promise," he said, thinking that he preferred the idea of the psychiatrist. He was quiet as he walked to the door, but the atmosphere melted as soon as it was opened. They kissed then he drew back and screwed his face up. "I have to go," he groaned.

"Nicotine pangs?" she whispered. He nodded without making any explanation, for this was the third occasion during her visit that she had witnessed the vomiting fits. "Poor love," she purred, touching his cheek. "There are three water bottles next to the downstairs toilet." As he rushed back into the duplex she waved goodbye, then walked forlornly down the corridor towards the lift.

In a six-year-old Golf GTI, purchased with cash, Lewis returned to Vernon Jones' football association. There was a members' club, with a foyer and an unmanned table, and after walking around awhile he found a bar, which smelled of stale beer and sweat.

No one was serving, and as he waited he was trying to come up with a good reason for asking for Vernon's address. Whoever he spoke to would be suspicious, perhaps thinking he was from the DSS or something.

A few old men were at a table in the corner of the club, drinking Brains SA and observing him with indifference. They didn't look away, even when he caught their eye and he fiddled uneasily with a beer mat. In his jeans and T-shirt he still felt hopelessly out of place, just as when he had watched the football match here last year.

The young barman who eventually emerged from the back was wiping a glass with a bar towel. He reached down to a barrel beneath the counter, cursed and rubbed his back as he straightened up. Lewis fought back a look of surprise as he recognised the blond crew cut. It was Vernon Jones.

"Mr Jones?" Lewis asked. "Vernon Jones?"

"That's me," the barman muttered. Lewis found himself ordering a Guinness with an even voice, even though his mind was aflutter, and he considered Vernon carefully as he poured the drink. "Do I know you then?" Vernon asked in a rich Valley accent.

"You know *of* me, I think. I'm a solicitor. I was at one of your matches last year."

Vernon paused then studied the head on the drink. He decided to top it up a little. "Did you give a friend of my dad one of your cards?" he asked.

"Yes. I'm Lewis Coin."

Vernon nodded and passed him his drink. "Yeah I remember, because that was the game that put my back out. Some bastard had rung up and said he was a talent scout and wanted to see me play. I used to have hopes a few years back, you know. My dad warned me not to play."

"I'm sorry about that," Lewis said, taking the pint with a look of genuine regret. He glanced round at the three old men. If he had to make a run for it he should be okay: three old codgers and a barman with a bad back.

"Not your fault, is it?" Vernon remarked.

Lewis raised his eyebrows, realising that Vernon hadn't put two and two together yet and worked out that the lawyer with the bag was the same person who had tricked him onto the pitch in the first place. But it was odd, for Vernon still knew that he was the lawyer who had hammered down his claim from £150,000 to £15,000, squeezing him with the threat of video evidence. Why wasn't he angry?

"So you're working here now?" Lewis asked cautiously.

Vernon shrugged, then touched his lower back and muttered something under his breath. "Until my back gets better. Doctors say it'll be at least another twelve months. My bloody fault."

"Are you planning to go back and work for Baron?" Lewis asked, casually sipping at his Guinness.

"Who?"

"Baron Enterprises."

"Who are they then?"

"Vernon, you used to work for them remember? That's how you got your back injury."

Vernon gave him an odd look. "I did my back when I was jumped outside a nightclub in Caerphilly. I think you're confusing me with someone else."

"But you got my card?"

"Sure. But I thought you wanted to do a compensation claim for me or something."

Lewis thought about this. "Why didn't you ring me then?"

"No point, was there? I didn't know who jumped me, did I? Besides, I got compensation from the Criminal Injuries Board."

Lewis put down his drink, his heart pounding. "Vernon, did you receive fifteen thousand pounds from anyone? Did you speak to anyone called Mr Marker?"

"Don't know what you're talking about."

"Did you ever work in a factory in Newport?"

"Now why d'you want to know? Who are you?" There was irritation in his voice now, as he decided that the conversation had gone beyond acceptable bar patter.

Lewis was wondering whether Vernon was lying because he was also under a confidentiality agreement. "Vernon, I'll be frank with you," he said. "I used to work for Baron Enterprises. I settled a claim that you brought when you were working there in the early part of last year. The CID is investigating the company, and they're investigating me. They're saying that it's all a big racket."

"Don't follow you."

"Look, Vernon, they're saying that the claims are fictitious. I know that you've probably signed something but you've got to tell them about Baron and the money you received." He paused. "I've seen your personnel file so I know you worked for Baron. I'm going to have to put them on to you, I've got no choice."

The threat made Vernon smile, and he looked over to one of the old men in the corner. "Da, this man wants to know who I was working for last year."

"Does he?" muttered one of the men, without looking over.

"Tell him."

Vernon's dad was now engrossed in a game of dominoes. "Vernon was in his first year in the army," he said. "He did his back when he was on leave."

"I... don't believe you," Lewis muttered helplessly.

"D'you want to see my service card?" Vernon snapped. He produced his wallet and opened it for Lewis; the card in the clear plastic holder placed him in Germany in 2001.

Lewis hesitated, the silence in his brain only broken by the occasional click of dominoes finding their position. He felt as if blank white pages were flicking one by one across his eyes.

"I'm sorry about your back, Mr Jones," he offered eventually. "I hope you get back into the army". He left his Guinness two thirds full at the bar.

He rang Bernie as soon as he got home.

There was more bad news: the lawyer in London was missing and the orthopaedic consultant couldn't be traced. The British Medical Association hadn't even heard of him.

"I'm worried, Lewis," Bernie moaned, after he had told her about Vernon Jones.

"Well, the CID were right," he said. "The claims were fictitious. Baron must have known that I'd go hell for leather on the first claim so they found a real Vernon Jones with a back injury. Or maybe they were the ones who jumped him, who knows? They simply put together a fake personnel file. That means Marker was in on it." He reflected upon Marker's indignation during the settlement negotiations, then upon Raine and Booker as they congratulated him on his success. They had played him like a child.

"If Mr Marker was in on it, then why did he ring your boss when everything started going wrong?" she asked.

"I don't know. Perhaps to throw everyone off the scent, but Marker must have been in on it."

"How can you be so sure?"

"Because I remember how angry he got when I gave him the clue about the surveillance, when I said 'the ball's in your court'. If he hadn't spoken to Vernon Jones, and we know he couldn't have, then Raine or Booker must have told him what I had up my sleeve. They probably also told him to accept the fifteen grand on the last day possible, just to make me sweat."

"Seriously, Lewis, I'm really worried about you," Bernie repeated.

"Who is there left we can talk to?" Lewis asked.

"No one. I'm going to have to go to the police and just hope they believe me," she sighed. "There's just the two of us now, no one else."

There was a pause.

"*Two*," they said together.

When Lewis met up with BB for their squash game he immediately beckoned him out of the sports centre and led him to his car. They sat in the front seats and Lewis locked the doors.

"So much for your share tip," BB muttered. He gave Lewis a scrutinising look.

"Put on some weight," Lewis muttered, touching his stomach. "Yeah, sorry about the tip. I'll get all the money back to you when I sell my place. It's my fault. But BB, listen to me, I'm in trouble and I need your help."

"What's going on?" BB asked. "What happened to your Mercedes?"

Lewis told him everything, and it took most of the period booked for the squash court. The only thing he left out was Bernie. He left her out completely, recounting neither the break-up nor the reunion.

"Bloody hell, Lew," BB said when he was finished, "what have you got yourself into?"

Lewis glanced at his rear-view mirror and BB looked

round to see two men walking by with holdalls. He turned back round with a big grin. "Relax…" he suggested.

Lewis shook his head then took a deep breath. "The London lawyer is missing," he said. "I don't like the sound of that. What if Baron are covering their tracks… you know… removing the evidence?"

BB laughed. "You're shitting me, right?"

"BB, I'm serious."

"Nah, you're wrong. It's not the Mafia or anything like that."

"How do you know?"

"You watch too many films, Lew. It's just a tax scam or something."

"You think so?"

BB had the squash ball in his hand and was compressing it between thumb and middle finger. "Well, think about it," he said. "First of all, you're still here. Believe it or not, the Mafia get rid of witnesses *before* they speak to the police, not afterwards. Second, why would the Mafia or any other criminal organisation give you share tips, or give you drugs that make you give up smoking? Why would they e-mail you? Third, there are plenty of crooked lawyers out there. It's much easier to find a crooked lawyer than to go to elaborate lengths to fool an honest one."

Lewis squirmed in his seat for a few seconds, then sighed. "That's true," he said. Thank God BB was street-wise and always talked sense, although he still couldn't understand why he didn't like Bernie.

"This money laundering thing is a good theory," BB continued, "but it doesn't explain everything, does it?" The squash ball changed hands. "There must be a reason why the network or whatever they are have gone to so much trouble over you. They probably went to a lot of trouble over Emily, too."

"Emily was killed."

"She was drunk at the wheel, Lew. There's no proof that she was killed. They obviously want something from you, though, so when they contact you again, record it on one of your Dictaphones."

"You think they'll get in touch again?"

BB shrugged. "They're bound to. They've gone to too much trouble not to finish what they've started."

Lewis nodded as he thought about this. "BB, you made a good point on the phone the other day. Why me? There are plenty of good lawyers out there. Why have they chosen me?"

BB shrugged as he turned the squash ball around in his hand. "I don't know. Maybe you can think of a reason. I'm glad you didn't burn the magazine. Whatever you do, keep it safe."

"Why?"

"The CID will be able to examine the pages, like you said, see that they've been treated. And the magazine can at least support your story on the share tips. Perhaps they can even link it to this Rever of London."

"Bernie says it doesn't exist."

BB's expression changed. "Bernie? You're not still with her are you?"

"Sort of," Lewis admitted.

"Christ, Lewis…"

"BB, did she say something to upset you, in the duplex that time?"

BB didn't answer and Lewis thought it politic not to probe any further.

"Anyway, hang on to the magazine," BB said eventually, "because it's the only evidence you've got."

Lewis had forgotten to tell BB about the photocopies he had stored in the Paddington lock up. The network had stolen Bernie's copies, no doubt because they realised they were concrete proof that the magazine changed, but they wouldn't be aware that he had a second set.

"That's right, isn't it?" BB pressed. "It is your only evidence?"

Lewis smiled. "BB, can you do me a favour? You still know all those people down in Butetown from the band days. Can you get me a gun?"

"Fuck no, Lewis, forget about it."

Lewis produced £500, in £20 notes, and dropped it in BB's lap. "Do me this favour, BB, it's just to help me sleep better."

When Lewis got home the phone was ringing.

"Lewis, get the crossword," Bernie gasped as soon as he picked up.

He retrieved The Shilling from his bedroom and a few more strands of black hair floated out of the magazine as he twisted his way back down the spiral staircase. He caught one and was holding it when he returned to the phone.

"Christ, Bernie, they've been in here again," he whispered breathlessly. "They've planted more of that bloody hair."

"Change your locks tomorrow, and put in the best alarms money can buy," she said sternly. "Who's been in your duplex, apart from me?"

"Just BB, when he took our photograph that time."

"Are you sure?" she pressed.

"Yes, I'm sure." Lewis was lying. Girls from Encounters had visited, to help him fend off the dreams, but he wasn't going to tell Bernie that. He made a mental note to ring Janet, just in case she decided to ring him with a special offer or something.

"Okay," Bernie said, "now do this for me. Don't even tell BB that you're changing the locks. I know I'm being stupid and irrational, but let's just keep it between ourselves."

"Okay," Lewis said, with a lump in his throat.

"Right, have you got the crossword?"

"Got it."

"That sequence you wrote out, with those first few answers, I've been studying it."

He looked at his handwriting under the crossword. *"Lewis your lit less inns are wonderful,"* he read.

"That's it."

"What about it?"

"Got a pen?"

He found one of his black felt tips. "Yep," he said, "go ahead."

"On 'Less', put a line before the two s's. Okay? Now, join up *Lit* with *Less*. Done that? Now, join up the last 's' of *Less* with *Inns*."

Lewis did the doodling, then considered his handiwork.

Lewis your lit less inns ARE wonderful

"What does that say?" Bernie asked, her voice trembling.

Lewis your little sins
are wonderful

L ewis planned an early start for his drive to Kent. It was barely six a.m. as he was making his way out of the door.

He was in search of Anton Lewinski, Emily's husband, his last lead.

As Lewis walked out of the large mirrored lift of his apartment complex he took a long fix of the cold and crisp morning air through his nostrils. It felt good to be on the move, before anyone else was awake.

He couldn't hear a sound, anywhere. Not the twitter or squawk of a bird, or even the distant rumble of a lorry at the end of a long night's haul. His hand was on the handle of his car door, he was now seated inside, his seatbelt was secured, the morning air still energising him. His engine started up noiselessly and the security gate of the apartment complex rose without his having to use his pass. The roads were empty.

At the traffic lights he stopped and lit a cigarette. He smoked it all as he waited for the lights to change, then turned on the radio as he powered up the long stretch of road that adjoined the long wharf dock where he used to live. It was a rough area and early morning joggers ran at their peril, for bushes dotted the side of the road where tramps and more unsavoury characters were easily concealed. He turned the radio up and lit another cigarette. The street lamps switched off as a computer somewhere decided that daylight had arrived, but the road sank into murky twilight for the loss of the artificial lighting.

He had finished his cigarette, but he was still on the road travelling along the wharf dock. He didn't remember the road being this long and was yet to see a single vehicle, a single person, or hear a single noise apart from the chiming, synthesised music coming out of his radio.

No, there was someone, standing in the road ahead waving to him. The figure waved more frantically as he approached: it was Bernie, calling to him, screaming at him to stop. He slammed on the brakes but the car accelerated, and as he collided he heard her pelvis breaking and her spine snapping as she was thrown over the bonnet and onto his windscreen. Her face was pressed up against the glass, which was greasy with her blood. She was staring at him, but there was no life in her eyes.

His car drained of power and he came to a stop at the side of the road.

He couldn't catch his breath, couldn't get up from his seat.

"Now you didn't think I'd let you forget about me? You're my little soldjar, that's what you are."

Mary Stone was sitting next to him, as beautiful as when he first saw her, examining her diamond pendant between two long fingers. In his rear-view mirror he caught the reflection of the twins, but he couldn't move his head, couldn't take his eyes off Bernie, dead on his windscreen.

"What do you want?" he groaned.

"I wants you, and you wants me. Don'tcha?"

"No, I want Bernie."

The twins in the back seat giggled. Mary Stone touched the radio and the music increased in volume.

"We're both the same, her and me."

"No you're not."

"In your 'ead, we're both the same."

Out of the corner of his eye he saw red spots appear in the white sheen of her skin. The red spots turned grey. The grey spots became craters.

"I had the small pox. Look what it did to me. Shame, innit? Lost me hair too. But I didn't mind, 'cos I survived. No one gets rid of me." She reached between his legs and unzipped his trousers.

He was still staring at Bernie's face as he went into extremis, but Mary Stone pulled her hand away at the last.

"Did you like that? You did, didn'tcha?" She tut-tutted. "And with your ladylove looking on too. Well, you are a naughty boy. You're my naughty little soldjar." Her white teeth glinted like knives as she went down on him and the twins raised themselves up in their seats, excited and wanting to watch.

He was screaming as his blood sprayed up onto the inside of the windscreen, obscuring Bernie's face in a haze of misty red.

Lewis rang Bernie constantly from around midday. At just after 2 p.m. she picked up.

"Bernie, thank God, you have to come and see me."

"You know I can't," she answered gently. "What's wrong, Lewis? What's happened?"

He told her about the dream, the worst dream he had ever had, although he left out her part in it.

"I thought you said the dreams would go away now?" she murmured. She sounded as if she was taking off her coat.

"I know. They did last time. And this dream was so real, I had no idea that I was dreaming until… until the car stopped and Mary Stone appeared. I've always woken up when the violence starts, but I didn't this time. I saw my own blood. Even in the dream I felt the pain, or what seemed like pain."

"Oh, poor baby."

"Bernie, you've got to help me. I need you here."

"Maybe it won't help, Lewis."

"It will. I know it will. Nothing's changed, I just need a bigger fix, that's all, to keep her away…"

"Lewis, I'll do anything to help, but I can't leave Jamey."

"I know, I know, but I've got an idea. Has your computer got a scanner?"

"Well yes, I think so. I don't know how to use it though." He knew that Bernie worked from home in the afternoon by arrangement with her employers, and they had supplied her with a linked computer system.

"Good. Got a camera?"

"No. Why do you ask?"

"Please, Bernie, go and buy one. A Polaroid. Ring me as soon as you get back."

"Lewis… I don't like where this is going."

"Please, Bernie, I couldn't face another dream like the one I had last night. I'm going to top myself if I have another dream like that."

Bernie didn't answer.

"Bernie?"

"The drugs will wear off eventually," she said, "you must believe that. What did the hospital say?" He had checked himself in for tests over the past few days at her insistence.

He shook his head in exasperation. "All clear. They couldn't find any trace of anything inside me."

"Well that's good, isn't it? That means it must be almost all out."

"Maybe. But then maybe it's all in my head. Maybe it was always in my head."

"I still think you should go and see someone in

the Church. Look at the crossword: *your little sins are wonderful*. Sins. There's a religious angle to this."

"Or it's what they want me to think. They're just trying to freak me out."

There was a pause. "Has another clue been written in the crossword?" she asked eventually.

"No. We're still on *two*."

"You've changed your locks, fitted the alarm?"

"Yeah."

"Anything else changed in the magazine?"

"The pages seem a little soggy, or soft, I don't know. They leave a brown stain when you touch them, but they're not fragile or anything, as wet pages would be. The shears woman has cockroaches swarming all over her. Mary Stone's getting uglier."

"But she hasn't lost any more hair? No real hair, I mean, falling out of the pages?"

"No."

"Good. Lewis, don't leave the duplex. Don't let the magazine out of your sight."

Half an hour later he printed out the scanned photograph that Bernie had downloaded via e-mail, after she had followed his step-by-step instructions. On the bottom of the photograph she had written: *Lewis, if you show this to anyone I'll kill you!*

Bernie was standing in nervous poise, one leg forward, and smiling shyly at the camera. Her diamond pendant was settled in the crease of her cleavage. She wasn't naked, as he had asked, but wearing her underwear. He had decided not to press the point and was thankful for what he had got; he supposed that nothing could make Bernie strip completely in front of a camera, not even if their lives depended on it. He smiled. God she looked good.

He took the photograph to bed with him that night and he didn't dream.

He woke to the sound of banging on his door, and moaning, found his watch. It was nearly 11 a.m. He had never slept this late and had the disturbing notion that the dream in the car had lasted a lot longer than he remembered. He had been exhausted last night and went out like a light as soon as his head touched the pillow.

"Who is it?" he called from behind his bolted door.

"It's me, BB."

Lewis put on his chain and opened the door to see BB standing there with something in a brown paper bag. "I've got that thing you asked for," BB said, peaking through the gap in the door. He considered the chain lock. "You going to let me in?"

Lewis took off the chain but stood in the doorway as he took the package and felt the weight of the gun. "Thanks BB," he whispered. "Hope you don't mind, but Bernie's upstairs. I don't want to wake her."

"Oh, right." BB's eyes wandered up to the ceiling, then returned to the package in Lewis' hands. "It's all there. Do you know how to use it?"

"I've seen films," Lewis offered.

"Christ," BB muttered. He regarded Lewis with misgiving. "Listen to me, Lewis, don't load it, okay?"

"Don't load it?"

"Right. Just keep it as a deterrent. You'll probably end up killing yourself otherwise. And if you don't, and you get lucky, the CID will really have you banged to rights. Keep the bullets separate from the gun, okay?" He took a small box out of his jacket, which contained the bullets, and he handed it over reluctantly.

"Okay." Lewis smiled, taking the box. He closed the door quietly with the eyes of a conspirator, then listened for BB's footsteps going down the corridor and waited for the sound of the lift door opening.

As he was making himself a coffee the door banged again and he went to open it angrily. He would have to be more direct with BB this time, and didn't bother to fix the chain.

Fleet and Cole were towering in the doorway. He hadn't realised how tall they were at the meeting in the boardroom and his stomach turned as he considered their dour countenances.

"Can we come in?" Fleet asked. Lewis opened the door cautiously and they filed through into the lounge. Both men remarked on the cathedral window and planted themselves in armchairs on opposite sides of the room. They beckoned to Lewis to sit on the settee between them.

Lewis was wondering whether they had a search warrant. On his bed upstairs were The Shilling, a gun, and Bernie's photograph; he wasn't sure which of the three he was most afraid of them finding, which of the three taboo items he would hide first. Although they seemed to be expecting it, he didn't offer them anything to drink. He wasn't going to let them out of his sight.

"You've put on weight since we last met," Fleet opened abruptly. "Are you drinking?"

"No, I just haven't been doing much exercise." Lewis nursed the bulge over his belt protectively. "It's your damn tracer, I'm afraid to go anywhere," he added.

"You said at our last meeting that you'd be able to prove that you weren't involved with the fictitious claims," Fleet remarked, taking out his notebook. "We're surprised that you haven't been in touch."

Lewis' eyes narrowed; he was wondering whether they really had enough to charge him.

"Is the injunction still on my property?" he asked.

Fleet nodded. "Even if you're innocent, Mr Coin, the equity in your house may still be the proceeds of crime.

No… the injunction stays put for the time being."

"What about the tracer in my mobile?"

Fleet didn't answer.

"I demand to know," Lewis said.

"The tracer's been turned off," Fleet murmured. The CID officer was clearly unhappy at the thought of Lewis being able to leave the city, but now that he had been asked he was obliged to declare the position. "So, is there anyone who can corroborate your story?"

Lewis shook his head. "No one," he said. "They've all vanished. Raine, Booker, Marker, the orthopaedic consultant. Even the London lawyer Baron instructed before me."

"London lawyer? What London lawyer?"

Lewis' heart missed a beat. "I don't know his name," he said.

"So how do you know he's missing?"

"I just know. It's… it's a hunch."

Damn!

To his relief, Fleet didn't move in for the kill but instead looked around him appreciatively. "This is a cracking place," he remarked. "I know someone who's got a place in this building, but it's not as big as this. Did you buy it off the plans?"

"Yes, off the plans."

"Smart move. They've gone up in price, haven't they?"

"I think so, yes."

"It really is fantastic," Fleet whispered, gazing up at the window, then turning to consider the platform on the first floor that led into the bedrooms. "Would you mind if we had a look around? I'm just curious to see how big it is."

"Well I would really," Lewis answered. "No offence, but when you lift the injunction I'll be a bit more co-operative." He looked at Cole who appeared set to get out of his chair.

Cole settled back.

Thank God. No search warrant.

"We had a look at those companies you bought," Fleet announced with a shrug.

"And?"

"We're satisfied that *they're* genuine, at least."

"Are you sure? You investigated the backers? The financiers?"

"All reputable," Fleet answered, finding it curious that Lewis didn't seem to want to accept good news. "Mostly financed by the major banks and long established investment houses. Why? Have you other information?"

Lewis shook his head. If Farthing didn't have some sort of stake in the companies, then how did they know they were going to bounce? Was it possible that they were just exceptionally good stock pickers?

"So where does that leave us?" Lewis asked. "Do you really believe I'd risk being struck off and going to prison for a two hundred and fifty pound charging rate?"

Fleet smiled. "No, I don't," he admitted. "But something's been going on here. We do know that you've had a string of good luck that started from the moment that Baron Enterprises came on the scene. We also find it odd that you're the only one left holding the baby. Is there someone else we can speak to, someone you're trying to protect?"

"There's no one else."

"How did you know this London lawyer was missing? Who told you?"

Lewis shook his head and didn't answer. The CID men smiled and nodded.

"You're going to have to talk soon," Cole reflected, "because pretty soon we'll have all the pieces to the puzzle. Do you understand?" He glanced at Fleet and they both got up together.

"It's still just the two of us," Lewis told Bernie on the phone that evening, "but at least I can move around now. We have to get some corroboration from somewhere." He had confessed to his slip-up with the CID officers, that it wouldn't be long before their enquiries lead them to her.

"Anton?" she suggested.

"Anton," he agreed.

They made arrangements to travel to Kent that weekend; she would arrange a carer if he could pick her up straight from work on Friday, but she had to get back for Saturday midday.

"I still think Emily is the key to all this," he remarked.

"I agree. Lewis, you haven't really explained what Emily was doing at your apartment. Is there anything you haven't told me?"

Lewis sighed and told Bernie the truth. He hoped their relationship was strong enough now to withstand his admission that he had been with a prostitute, and he was right, for Bernie just encouraged him with an "I see" and a "go on, it's okay". He still wasn't going to tell her about the others though.

"So Emily was at rock bottom when you met her," Bernie mused.

"I suppose so."

"And Jasmine said that Emily had a copy of The Shilling?"

"Not my copy, but a copy."

"And Baron financed Circus?"

"Right. But with Emily, it was booze that brought her down."

"I bet there was something in her magazine that started her drinking."

"What do you mean?"

"Lewis, The Shilling is responsible for everything that's happened. It made Emily wealthy and famous, for a short time anyway, and then she lost everything: her money, her business, her man, and eventually even her self-respect. Now look what's happened to *you*. I think… I think, we should stop trying to work out what Baron are up to, and start concentrating on the magazine. Baron… the claims… it's just scenery. If we find out what the magazine is, then everything else will fall into place."

He grinned with admiration as he nodded his agreement. Bernie was much smarter than he had given her credit for. "We've got one advantage, as I see it," he said. "I was meant to lose you. When The Shilling wrote in that clue they knew that I'd suspect you. Then Baron made sure you were fired. They figured you'd never forgive me." He remembered now that Raine had asked for proof, proof that Bernie had been in his apartment.

Had Raine already known about the photograph?

"Do you really think so?" she asked.

"Yeah, I think it's de-railed them. Bernie, listen. Imagine where I'd be now if you hadn't come back to me. I'd be alone… having lost everything… under investigation by the CID. I'd have this physical problem with cigarettes and I'd have lost all my self-confidence because I've put on weight. And, worst of all, I'd be having dreams… horrific dreams… that I could do absolutely nothing about."

"God…"

"I'd be lost, completely lost. I'd just think that the world was caving in on me, wouldn't I? I'd be like Emily, at rock bottom, on the point of suicide."

She seemed touched by this. "We'll get through it together, Lewis. Has my photograph… has it helped?"

"Yes. No dreams."

"I'm scared Lewis."

"Me too," he murmured, but he wasn't scared for himself, he was scared for her. A vision of Bernie, dead on his windscreen, flashed in his mind.

"I think we should try and do the rest of the sequence," she said. "Lewis, get the crossword."

"I've already got it." The crossword was open in front of him. Bernie's photograph was nearby.

"The two-letter word, the one we're not entirely sure of, let's assume it's *Be*," she resolved in a businesslike voice. "Don't write it in, let's just assume, okay?"

"Okay."

"Read the sequence out to me. I'm going to write it down and have a think about it. Perhaps we can work it out on the drive to Kent tomorrow."

Lewis read out the sequence. They were still missing the last two answers.

two hour fat her (be?) low stop Bern wit

"Lewis, why do you think it's called *The Shilling*?" she asked.

"Emily said it was old."

"Like *Farthing*," she reflected. "Old money."

"So?"

"Look, think it through. What is money?"

"A means of making payment…"

"Right. The Shilling gave you those share tips. It gave you the power in your firm. It gave you the duplex, the Mercedes. It even let you give up cigarettes and put on weight. Well it's taking it all back, isn't it?"

"Just like Emily, and her model agency," Lewis agreed. "I know. I've already thought of that."

"Yes, but there's something else, isn't there?"

"What?"

"That model you met, she hated Emily, didn't she?"

"Yes, I suppose so…"

"You said the firm hated you, when they threw you out."

"Bernie, what are you saying?"

280

She sighed, and he had the feeling she had been waiting for the right moment to say what was on her mind. "Lewis, you will take this the right way, won't you? I'm only trying to help, to make sense of this."

"It's okay. Go on."

She sighed again. "When I first met you, I knew you were an honest man. I've met a lot of dishonest ones. You were honest."

"You're thinking of Vernon Jones aren't you? That stunt I played with the videotape. I did it for you, Bernie."

"Maybe you did. But it was still wrong. You knew it was wrong."

"Well the claim was fictitious anyway."

"But you didn't know that at the time. Then the way you treated the people in your firm. You turned into your boss. You became worse than him."

"I just wanted to get out of the rat race," he answered defensively. "Being efficient and working hard seemed the best way."

"I'm sorry, Lewis, but it was greed. You could have let all your partners share the profits. They'd have loved you for it. You would have saved the firm."

She was right. He felt ashamed as he considered how O'Neill had tried to protect him during that meeting with the CID, even after everything that had happened.

"Bernie…"

"You bought shares knowing it was insider trading. You stole someone's wallet. You tried to trick Farthing by buying the shares through BB. Then the way you were prepared to believe that I'd betrayed you, the way you threw me to the wolves."

"Bernie, you know how sorry I am about that…"

"And finally, when you heard Mr Raine talking about Baron's policies, agreeing with him. Actually agreeing with him."

Lewis wondered if she was harbouring resentment over that, and other things, but her voice was gentle and controlled. "You're right, Bernie," he said, "The Shilling changed me. I thought I was being so smart, but it changed me."

"Lewis, please believe me, I'm not trying to hurt you. But you have to see the big picture. The Shilling brought out the worst in you. You could never be bad, really bad, but it brought out what you were capable of, I think."

He nodded as he struggled to grasp what she was telling him. "When I was last at the firm... I wanted revenge at first, but I changed my mind. I was going to make it up with O'Neill; I was going to make it up with all of them. I was even thinking of telling Baron where to go. But it was too late."

"At least you wanted to make up," she said encouragingly. "That's got to be a good sign, hasn't it?"

He nodded to himself. What had that e-mail said? *Savour the moment, the moment of self-visualisation, when you see what you have become.*

Our relationship will be long and fruitful.

"Your little sins..." she whispered. "Sins have to be paid for, don't they? Old money..."

Lewis was looking at the crossword. "What do you think they want?" he murmured.

"One thing I do know," she said, "is that the magazine was designed for you and no one else. The crossword... that legal advert at the back..."

"The Carbolic Smoke Ball," he agreed.

"Yes, what is that?"

"The Smoke Ball? Oh, famous nineteenth century case. This company advertised a reward of a hundred pounds – lot of cash in those days – if anyone used their smoke ball thing, some kind of medical preparation, and caught the flu. A woman caught flu and they refused to pay. She won."

"So what was the point of the case? Why is it so famous?"

"The company said there was no individual contract with the woman, but the courts found they had made an 'offer to all the world'."

"A what?"

"An offer to all the world. She accepted the offer by performing the action, using the smoke ball."

Bernie didn't speak, but he could hear her breathing.

"Bernie?"

"An offer to all the world," she repeated slowly.

There was a pause.

"They're making you an offer," she said.

Part Five:
Mary Stone

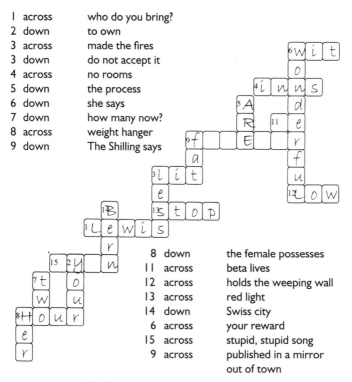

1	across	who do you bring?
2	down	to own
3	across	made the fires
3	down	do not accept it
4	across	no rooms
5	down	the process
6	down	she says
7	down	how many now?
8	across	weight hanger
9	down	The Shilling says

8	down	the female possesses
11	across	beta lives
12	across	holds the weeping wall
13	across	red light
14	down	Swiss city
6	across	your reward
15	across	stupid, stupid song
9	across	published in a mirror out of town

Lewis your lit less inns ARE wonderful two Hour fat her (be?) low stop Bern wit

Lewis your little sins are wonderful

Two hour fat her (be?) low stop Bern wit

The village in the Kent countryside, the nearest map reference to Anton's home, had as its focal point a large and carefully maintained pond. The pond was clearly loved by the residents for the water was free of any rubbish, with only the leaves of the nearby sycamores floating peacefully on its obsidian surface. Lewis parked next to it with a grunt of appreciation.

"Isn't that beautiful?" Bernie sighed.

He grunted again. "Bet the council tax is sky high," he muttered.

"Oh Lewis!"

He was smiling as he got out of the car. He strolled casually into the nearby grocer's and in seeking directions he used Anton's name, rather than the address; the grocer told him that he knew Mr Lewinski well, a nice chap who kept himself to himself but who popped in twice a week for his pre-ordered crates of wine. Lewis bought a large bottle of water in gratitude for the information, while hungrily eyeing the cigarettes stacked behind the counter.

"Looks like Anton is still drinking," he said as he got back into the car. He handed Bernie his scribbled directions and pulled out to find the dirt lane, next to the letterbox, which would take them to Anton's cottage.

"I can see why Emily liked to live here," she said as they drove off. "You could forget all your problems in a place like this." She glanced behind her. "I saw a nice pub back there."

He nodded half-heartedly as he swung the car into the dirt track. He wasn't keen on the country.

"What are you going to ask him?" she asked.

"Everything. Whatever he's prepared to tell me."

She took a deep breath. "Lewis, I've worked out the next part of the sequence, on the crossword I mean. The *Two Hour Fat* thing..."

They drove on in silence. "So have I," he murmured after a time. Neither of them had discussed the crossword on the way down.

The cottage shortly coming into view seemed to be part of a farm, but the animal shelters were empty, their doors unlocked and creaking in the wind. An old Mercedes sat in the mud of the track leading off the lane, one tyre parked off the track and lost in the overgrown grass. Empty wine bottles were stacked near the cottage door and the curtains were drawn.

The doorbell didn't work so Lewis knocked. On the fifth knock he was using his fist and the oak door was shaking.

"Maybe he's not in," Bernie whispered.

"He's in. His car is here."

"So? He could be out for a walk."

He raised his fist to knock again just as the lock clicked and the door opened slowly. A small, fragile-looking man in late middle age, with a shock of grey hair and hamster cheeks, peered around the door. His eyes were weary and bloodshot.

"What do you want?" he muttered in a tone that wasn't so much a question but a tired code for "go away you're disturbing me". He had an accent that rolled the vowels on the tongue, which Lewis took to be Polish.

"Mr Lewinski?" he asked.

"Yes." The short answer had almost a lyrical quality in

the man's throat. He was struggling to stand up straight and using the door as support, he was so drunk.

"My name is Lewis Coin. This is Bernice Tate. Could you spare a little time to speak to us?"

Anton looked suspiciously at Bernie then silently formed the name *Tate* on his lips.

"It's about your wife, Mr Lewinski," Lewis added.

"My wife?" Anton's head lowered slowly and he was looking at the ground, in the manner of drunks when they can't find the energy to support their neck muscles.

"Yes, I'm afraid she's dead."

Anton nodded abstractly. "Is she…? Is she…"

"I'm sorry. Can we come in?"

Anton didn't reply. He was drawing upon the strength in his body and preparing to shut the door.

"I didn't know her well," Lewis persisted, "but there are a few things I'd like to discuss with you. It won't take long." Anton slowly shook his head.

"Mr Lewinski," Bernie piped up, "we do need to speak to you. I was a friend of Emily's and she has an important message for you." Lewis threw Bernie a sideways glance that conveyed his puzzlement and concern.

"A message… for me?" Anton muttered, forcing his head up.

"Yes… from *her*…"

Anton shambled towards Bernie, then lunged at her and with a scream she barely escaped his hands. Lewis angrily grabbed Anton's arm and forced him back into the house, but immediately regretted being so rough as he realised how frail the man was. Anton slumped to the floor, muttering incoherently, and after several unsuccessful attempts at rousing him Lewis gently closed the door.

They went back to the car. "What the hell was that about?" Lewis gasped as he turned over the ignition.

She looked out of the window and didn't say anything.

"Bernie?"

"Don't be angry, Lewis, I was just trying to help. I thought he might speak to us if I said I was a friend of Emily's, anything to stop him closing the door."

He was still perplexed as they drove off. "What was this important message you were going to give him?"

She was clearly embarrassed. "Oh I don't know, I was going to make something up. I wouldn't make a very good private eye, would I?"

He sighed and said, "Well, we wouldn't have got much sense out of him anyway. Did you see the state he was in? Look, let's go back to that pub you saw and get a room. Anton's bound to be sober some of the time. He drives to the village, after all. I'll go back first thing tomorrow morning."

"Can't I come?"

"I think you've blown that," he remarked. "He may have been drunk but he clearly doesn't like you."

"Stupid," she muttered, "why did I have to open my big mouth? He must have known I was lying about being a friend of Emily's."

Lewis nodded. "Don't worry, I'll give you a full report." His eyes narrowed. "What did you think of him?"

She thought long and hard about the question then smiled in spite of herself. "I thought he was a sweetie," she admitted.

"But he attacked you."

"I know. But he was drunk, wasn't he? I still think he was a sweetie."

She met his sideways glance with a shrug, which said, *this is who I am*. He was smiling by the time they were heading back down the village road.

Bernie stayed in the car to ring her brother as Lewis booked them into the pub. As he filled in his details he remarked on the great smells coming out of the bar. He booked a table for 7.30 and a glance inside revealed immaculately laid tables, a sawdust floor and a low-beamed roof. He sighed with genuine appreciation; rural ponds were all very well, but this was the real thing.

Going back out to the car he saw that Bernie was upset. "Is Jamey okay?" he asked.

She shrugged instead of answering, then wiped a tear from her eye. He decided that an inspection of the restaurant could wait for the moment.

Their room had a quaint en suite and as he took a much needed shower he reflected on how he was enjoying his first break away with Bernie, how he was looking forward to their pub meal, their first meal in public. He emerged wet and invigorated to find Bernie curled up on the bed, asleep.

He went to wake her then decided against it. She had mentioned on the drive down that she had been up all night with her brother, who had had a serious breathing attack. She had mentioned these attacks before, which seemed to be getting more frequent.

Lewis had never had any dependants, not even any pets. As he stroked her hair he realised that he had never fully appreciated how hard it must have been for her, commuting to Wales to be with him. This little trip would have been another drama in her tight schedule.

He telephoned reception to cancel dinner and to order some sandwiches for the room then carefully got on the bed next to her, content for the morning to arrive. When the sandwiches came he ate half of them quietly and at some point he put a sheet over Bernie, undressed and got into bed. Sleep came quickly.

When he awoke Bernie was already up, sitting on the bed.

"Sorry about dinner," she murmured, "I was so tired."

"No problem. Anyway, I was out not long after you. What's the time?" he asked with a yawn and a stretch.

"It's about nine."

"Right. Time I was going."

When he had showered and dressed she was still sitting on the bed, feebly attempting a smile. "Look, Bernie, why don't you come along?" he said. "He's probably forgotten all about you by now."

She shook her head. "No, you're right. You've got a better chance of speaking to him on your own." She paused. "Are you taking it with you?" she asked with a glance at the attaché case, which was on the floor. During the trip down he had given her the combination to the lock and told her to memorise it.

"No, I'll leave it here. I don't want to risk upsetting him again. If he wants to see it then I'll come back for it."

"Why don't you leave it in the car?"

"No, I don't want it out of our sight."

She nodded forlornly.

"Bernie, don't open it," he said.

She nodded once more.

Anton, sober, acknowledged Lewis with a smile and beckoned him inside. As Lewis had returned down the dirt lane he had come up with half a dozen stratagems for forcing his way through Anton's door, from half-truths to downright lies, so he followed him inside in surprise and relief.

Anton walked a little unsteadily but was perfectly lucid and had a soft, deliberate voice, which Lewis thought couldn't be a vehicle for obscenities or unordered dialogue; his immediate assessment was that Anton was a gentle soul who must have been putty in Emily's hands. A sweetie, as

Bernie had said.

Anton put up his arms in a gesture that asked him to forgive the mess. The cottage was littered with books, newspapers and too much furniture and Lewis had to position an armchair and clear away the remains of a TV dinner to sit down opposite what he perceived to be Anton's chair, the only one free of clutter. A few beautiful examples of marble sculpture and canvas art could be seen amongst the debris of the front room.

"I obtained your address from the hotel in Capri," Lewis explained as he spied another lovely objet d'art, a three-foot porcelain detail of the Three Graces. One of the Graces had red wine-stained hair.

"Yes, yes," Anton murmured, as if it mattered not.

"Thank you for seeing me."

Anton sat down and brought his hands together. He appeared very tired. "You must forgive me for my outburst yesterday," he said.

"You remember it then?"

"Vaguely." He seemed embarrassed.

"Why *did* you attack my friend?" Lewis asked.

"Is that what I did? Oh dear. Something she said perhaps…"

"That she was a friend of Emily's?"

Anton rose in his seat at the mention of his wife's name, and then deflated sadly.

"I'm sorry about your wife, Mr Lewinski."

Anton made a philosophical face. "I already knew that she was dead. The police found me from her records. They told me she was drunk… drunk at the wheel."

Lewis thought that he detected just the flicker of a smile and remembered the passion with which Jasmine had hated Emily Lewinski. "Forgive me for saying so, Mr Lewinski," he ventured, "but you don't seem to be too sorry she's dead. Did you dislike her that much, at the end?"

Anton smiled good-naturedly. "No, no, you misunderstand me. I loved my wife. She was everything to me. And please, call me Anton."

Lewis nodded with a bemused expression. "She told me a little about you... Anton. She mentioned that you worked together in a model agency called Circus. I was hoping you'd tell me something about it."

"What would you like to know?"

"Oh, anything really. How did you meet?"

Anton settled back. "Well, well, I was an aspiring haute couture designer in my younger days but that didn't work out. I don't think designers can be Polish Jews in this industry, but Emily always said that was my paranoia speaking." He smiled briefly at a private memory, then continued. "I set up the Circus agency and I recruited Emily as a model. She modelled for a time but her heart wasn't in it. She wanted to help with the business." His voice tailed off sadly.

"How did she help you?" Lewis inquired, hardly believing his luck. Anton was talking freely with hardly any prompting; he never imagined it would be so easy.

"She became a talent scout and... well... we became wealthy indeed. Circus moved up from being a low key supplier of fresh-faced girls for conservative mail order catalogues to supplying daring creations for the catwalks." As he said *creations* his fingers danced above his head as if he were offering a mime for alchemy.

"I don't know much about the fashion industry," Lewis said, "but don't the organisers of the shows supply the... creations? You know, the designers?"

"The clothes, yes, but that's not what I mean by the creations. I am talking about the girls' hair and make-up. The physical look, you see. That was why no one could compete."

"Why not?" Lewis asked, remembering Jasmine's

photograph and the starved, alien appearance.

"Find a beautiful model," Anton replied, "and a rival agency can poach her with their chequebook, yes? Not so with the Circus girls. That was Emily's trick. She found plain girls and transformed them." He spread out his hands expressively. "I hate to describe them so, but it's true I'm afraid. I don't know how she did it. One of the girls defected in the early days… a review had made her think she was a little special, you know how it is… but she was unable to find work. She begged Emily to take her back and that sent a message to the others. They were plain girls, as I said."

"When did things start going wrong?"

"The girls kept getting thinner, too thin, far too thin, and eventually there was a backlash in the trade press. When that happened all the enemies came out of the woodwork and we had made many, many enemies. I was to blame in part, because I took the criticism to heart and I sued a lot of people. And I started to drink. I think Emily joined me at first just to keep me company. I think she felt guilty."

"Why guilty?"

"She knew how upset I used to get about how the girls looked. Everything went wrong when we started drinking."

"I think I should explain why I'm here," Lewis said quietly. Anton hadn't asked him a single question so far, hadn't questioned him at all over the purpose of his visit; it was as if they were old friends and he had just popped in for a chat. He was now starting to find it a little odd.

"Oh I know why you're here," Anton murmured.

"You do?"

"Yes, yes," he said. "You see Emily and I also tried to track down the person who gave *her* The Shilling. Your name is Lewis Coin, is it not?"

Lewis nodded slowly. He had told Anton his name at the door yesterday, but he was impressed that he remembered, given the state he was in. "So you know about The Shilling?" he asked.

Anton didn't seem to have the energy to laugh and he satisfied himself with a pat of his hand on his thin chest as he nodded.

"Who was it that you tried to find?" Lewis asked.

"Does it really matter?" Anton sighed, as if the question was unnecessarily wearisome.

"Indulge me," Lewis said with a smile.

Anton took a deep breath and said, "Emily came across The Shilling at an industry party in London, a huge affair organised by a very rich Afro-American lady."

"Afro-American?"

"She sang at the party, she had a wonderful voice. She'd been a soul singer with Stax records for a time... something like that. She must have been very beautiful when she was young."

"How old was she?"

"In her fifties, I would say, although I suspect..."

"Suspect what?"

"That she was much older. She had an older sister, and her sister must have been in her seventies, but they had the same features..."

"Twins?" Lewis pressed.

"If it hadn't been for the age difference I would have sworn they were twins," Anton confirmed. "The older sister lived in London, they were estranged and I think the party was some sort of reunion. I saw them hugging and kissing at the end of the night and Emily said that they hadn't spoken for many, many years."

"What were their names?"

"They gave false names, we found out later on," Anton replied.

"So this black singer gave Emily The Shilling?" Lewis asked.

"No, no, it was the older sister."

"What did they talk about... Emily and this older woman, I mean?"

Anton shook his head. "Emily never really said, she only mentioned that the woman had lost her family years before, in the Depression." He nodded to himself. "That would have struck a chord with her."

Lewis nodded too, remembering Emily saying that she had returned to Vale to find her family. Jasmine was certain that she had no family. "The sisters *are* twins," he declared, "and I've seen them."

"You have?"

"Yes, but as young women in The Shilling. Anton, is the older sister still in London?"

"After the party she and her sister went to Italy for an extended vacation. We tried to find them many times and eventually tracked them down to Capri, but they wouldn't see us."

"Is that why you and Emily travelled so much?"

"It was my idea mostly. Emily knew it was useless."

"Are they still in Capri?" Lewis queried, getting out his notepad.

Anton shook his head. "You won't find them now, my friend. If they are in The Shilling then they are both dead."

As Lewis took this in he was overcome with nicotine pangs and he reached for his coat to find the small bottle of water that he kept for emergencies. His hands were shaking as he held it close to his chest.

"The toilet is the second door to the left." Anton murmured, making no further comment.

Lewis had a green pallor when he returned and Anton waved off the need for explanations.

"You're saying that all the models in my magazine are dead?" Lewis asked, swallowing uncomfortably.

"Yes, it is impossible to be in there otherwise. Haven't you worked that out yet?"

Lewis swallowed again, but this time tasted his fear. "Anton, are they going to kill me?" he whispered.

Anton offered him a curious look, appearing to find the suggestion humorous. "No, no," he said simply. "You don't have to worry about that. They can't kill you. They can't kill anyone." He shrugged. "The sisters would have died of natural causes."

Lewis felt a surge of relief. So it wasn't the Mafia...

"Anton," he said, "there's so much I need to ask you and I don't really know where to begin. Why, for example, does The Shilling... Farthing.com... the network... make all these inventions?"

"Inventions?"

"Puzzles... computer and photography tricks..."

"I think, I think that this is an area of interest for you? Puzzles and inventions?"

Lewis didn't answer and merely frowned.

"They always find the things that move you, my friend," Anton said. "That's how they reveal themselves. With Emily it was children in Third World countries. She was passionate on the subject. There was an article, a very nasty article, about it in The Shilling. Or rather, something buried inside an article. That's what made her break away from Baron Investments, but she was drinking by then and it was too late."

"Didn't she break away from Baron because of their anti-Semitism?" Lewis asked.

"Anti-Semitism?" Anton queried.

"Yes, I know that they hated you."

Anton gave him a quizzical look. "Did they hate me?"

Lewis opened his mouth to speak, but the words were

lost. He had the feeling of walking through a maze and constantly meeting a dead end.

Anton said, "I think this is another point of interest for you: prejudice, historical prejudice, yes?"

Lewis shook his head. "I don't understand..."

"You're confused because you're trying to work out what's happening to you by learning about Emily. There are no clues, my friend. Emily realised that sooner than I did. This is all about *you* now, and they will find the things that move you, as I said."

"Was there a crossword in Emily's copy of The Shilling?" Lewis asked, persisting in spite of what he was being told.

"No," Anton replied with a sigh.

"No?"

"So you have a crossword? I see that you do like solving puzzles."

Lewis touched his stomach uncomfortably. "So what did Emily have?" he asked, a little irritably.

"Recipes," Anton said and made a gesture above his head as if he were releasing birds from his fists.

"Jasmine told me about the recipes," Lewis remarked, his eyes following the imaginary birds.

"Well, well, Jasmine Stimple. You've met her? She was a nice girl."

"She has an eating disorder now. She's very overweight."

Anton nodded to himself and was silent awhile. "We all have our scars, my friend," he said eventually.

"Scars? I don't understand. Emily had the magazine, not you. Why do *you* drink, Anton?"

"No one who is touched by The Shilling escapes completely."

"What do you mean?"

He shrugged. "I enjoyed the money. Jasmine enjoyed

the attention. Both were gifts of The Shilling."

"Is that why Jasmine has her eating disorder?" Lewis asked. He was recalling their meeting in the front room and now remembered she had also needed to have all the windows open. The traffic was deafening, but she had insisted.

"The silly girl became too curious about the magazine," Anton returned. "That's why Emily pretended to be so angry with her."

"Pretended?" Lewis asked, looking around the cottage. All the windows were shut, the curtains drawn, the air stale and he sighed inwardly at meeting another dead end. There was no pattern, no link.

"Emily loved all the girls, but Jasmine especially. She became afraid for Jasmine when she got her hands on The Shilling, I think she believed..."

"That Jasmine was the next recipient," Lewis suggested.

"Well, well, she was wrong, wasn't she? Or perhaps she wasn't wrong, but allowed Jasmine to escape. Who can say?" Anton turned round now and sniffed, as if he could smell the wine that was stacked and bottled by the door. He didn't store his alcohol, he just dragged it inside and Lewis briefly contemplated his own addiction, the cigarette that he had to smoke even though it made him retch.

"These recipes," Lewis pondered, "were they actual written recipes, like out of a cookbook?"

Anton nodded. "Emily loved to cook, and for the girls in particular. It made her feel as if she had a family, but the recipes were very complicated and required a great deal of preparation. She did them one by one."

"Did... how can I put this?... did these recipes follow the events in her life?"

Anton nodded once more. "The recipes made the girls thinner, and the later recipes required alcohol. But sometimes the names of the recipes were also significant. Some were named after the girls she was about to find. There was one named Jasmine Pie. Emily would say that when she met an ordinary looking girl in a club or somewhere she would know that the girl was the one. The recipe would have told her, you see."

Lewis tried to make sense of this information, but failed for he had been expecting Anton to tell him about puzzles, inventions, computer software and insider trading. And he had the notion that Anton was fencing with him. "Anton," he said, "I've got the feeling that I'm asking you the wrong questions. What can you tell me? Help me."

Anton clenched and unclenched his fists in an addict's mantra. "Anything I say, anything, will be useless to you, my friend. Do you think they'd let me speak to you if it was otherwise?"

Lewis leaned forward. "Who's *they*?"

Anton groaned wearily. "As I said, this is all about *you*, my friend." He considered Lewis awhile then sighed. "Well, well, I can see you're not convinced, so I will do you a trade. I will give you something, something that you think you need, if you will help me satisfy myself on one subject... about Emily. I think I know the answer already, but I need to be sure."

"Ask me anything," Lewis encouraged him.

"As you have The Shilling..." Anton opened, "I suspect that Emily was sober when you met her, when she gave it to you. Am I correct?"

"Completely sober. How did you know?"

The colour had drained from Anton's face. "She couldn't have stopped drinking by herself," he said. "The guilt becomes something real, a physical need that is irresistible. That's the way they work. They find the dreams in your mind, the desires in your heart, and make them monsters in your body."

Lewis pondered this as he waited for Anton to collect his thoughts. Emily had been sober during their evening together. Could it be that The Shilling had cured her, cured her completely? But if so, why was she drunk the following evening?

Once more the image of Emily looking down, as the lift doors closed, flashed in his mind. Did she regret at that moment giving him the magazine? Did she start drinking again to go back on the deal? Was that why Anton wasn't sorry that she was dead, because he knew she had been drunk?

"Here's the trade," Anton said, his voice faltering. "Is there a picture of Emily in your magazine?"

Lewis shook his head.

Anton audibly gasped his relief. "An article, a mention, anything... anything at all?"

Such was the vehemence in his tone that Lewis considered he should go through the motions of thinking carefully. He paused for a few seconds then firmly shook his head. Anton looked down and breathed out heavily.

"Why do you want to know?" Lewis asked.

"The publication serves as a sort of obituary, for the subscribers. The sisters wouldn't see us in Capri, but they sent Emily a note saying that she should look for them in the magazine. They must have known they were dying."

Lewis nodded thoughtfully. "Jasmine mentioned some models, skinny ones, in Emily's magazine. So, were they dead subscribers too?"

Anton shook his head, his eyes still directed towards the floor. "No, no, I don't believe the models were subscribers, although I have no doubt they were dead. Jasmine couldn't have looked at the models very carefully, I think, because if she had she would have seen that they were children."

"Children?"

Anton looked up, now seeming to regain his composure.

"Wasted, emaciated children, in rags and make-up. They were called *the Farthing children* and Emily just became more determined as they got thinner, insisting that she could help them. She said her experiments with diet would help children all over the world."

"Really? So that was her motivation?"

"That's what… what that *bitch* told her…"

"Bitch? What bitch?"

"I complained bitterly about the pictures," Anton said, ignoring the question. "I was very sensitive about it. My grandparents were in a concentration camp, you see. I thought… I used to say… that the pictures were ways of taunting me… taunting my family. I left, in fact… but I came back."

"But she left *you*, eventually?"

"Near the end we tried to rebuild our lives. We'd lost nearly everything through the lawsuits. We stayed here for a month, hiding out, just going for walks in the village. Have you seen the village pond? We would sit there for hours. Emily had this new idea for starting afresh, moving away from the agency and pushing me as a designer instead. It was exciting, planning this new start, and it kept us sober."

Anton glanced at his door again and went quiet. Lewis suspected that this was about the time he had his first drink. "Go on, Anton, I'm interested," he urged.

Anton shrugged. "We sold what we had left to arrange this launch, and spent most of it inviting minor celebrities." He twiddled his fingers next to his ears at the word *celebrities*. "But I messed it up. One of the press people mentioned something about starvation diets and I got into this argument. Then I got very drunk. I think I fell over the table with the Thai seafood and passed out. The celebrities did what they'd been paid to do and stayed until the end, but it was over. I didn't see Emily again after that night."

"You think she left you because she was angry you ruined the party?"

"No, no. She left because she knew it was useless. Emily loved me. The Shilling had given her the idea for the launch, you see, in one of the articles. She had even used one of the recipes, the last one, for Thai seafood as it happened. She realised then that The Shilling had tricked her, building her hopes up in that way. She left the party with Celia."

"Celia?"

"Celia Maidstone. They were very close."

"Jasmine mentioned an older woman involved with the finance side. Is Celia Maidstone *the bitch* you referred to just now?"

Anton nodded and fought back a smile as he observed Lewis jot down the name. "Celia encouraged Emily in the early days," Anton murmured. "She was with her all along."

Lewis' eyes flitted around the room. "Anton, do you have The Shilling here? Can I look at it?"

"The Shilling is yours now, my friend," came the muted response.

"No, can I see *Emily's* copy of The Shilling?"

Anton was about to say something, but decided against it. Instead, he turned once more to consider the wine at his door, with a sniff of impatience. His thoughts seemed far away now.

Lewis raised his eyebrows as he returned his notepad to his jacket pocket, wondering whether he could really trust anything this man had said. Perhaps everything he had been told was just the figment of an alcoholic's imagination. "You mentioned a trade," he muttered suspiciously.

A shard of sadness splintered Anton's face as he touched

his chest. His nostrils were flaring as if the room had suddenly been flooded with perfume.

"Anton?"

Anton nodded and with difficulty reached across to a side table. He found a photograph under a carriage clock and handed it to Lewis. The monochrome photograph, which was brown and crinkled, was of Mary Stone, her hair pinned up on one side with a hatpin and with her swanlike neck nestling in the lace of her floral dress. She was standing under a sign, which read 'The Farthing Works', the slight tilt of her head and a thin smile conveying her pride and an aloof strength of purpose.

"You know this woman, I take it," Anton said. "The older twin delivered this to Emily in Capri, with her note."

"Who is she? Please Anton, tell me," Lewis whispered.

"I think that Emily was meant to give this to you," Anton mused. "But it has fallen to me instead."

"Anton..."

"You will pass it on in your turn."

"Anton, I dream of this woman and I believe she's very real. I believe that she knows me, that she's the centre of the network."

Anton coughed and patted his chest. "You must go now," he gasped. He seemed to be having trouble swallowing and was looking longingly at his wine bottles.

"Just tell me who she is and where I can find her."

"You really don't understand, do you?"

"What do you mean?"

"The photograph that you are holding is over a hundred years old."

When Lewis returned to the pub he found Bernie sitting on the corner of the bed, shaking. The Shilling was on the floor, the crossword open.

"It started about ten minutes ago," she whispered. "I heard it scratching. I opened the case because I heard it scratching."

Lewis sat next to her and reached for the magazine.

"Don't touch it!" she cried. He hesitated then put his arm around her as she started sobbing. She was trembling, he guessed on the verge of hysteria.

The four-letter answer of 15 across, which had the clue *stupid, stupid song*, was being spelt out. The second letter 'Y' and the fourth letter 'N' were in place from before, but the first letter 'H' had now appeared. The third letter 'M' was in the process of being inscribed. The letter was being slowly scratched into the box, the lines drawn thinly then thickened gradually with short precise scribbles. It was Lewis' handwriting.

"That's not magic ink," she sobbed. "You said it was magic ink! Someone's writing it in. Look!"

He tried to hug her but she was shaking uncontrollably.

"I heard it scratching..." she moaned into his shoulder.

Stupid, stupid song.

Hymn.

"Bernie, it's okay, it's okay..."

She didn't speak for a long while and eventually she stiffened in his arm. "I want to get out of here," she declared and her hand, which had previously been behind her, was now resting on her lap. In her palm was the last of Mary Stone's long black hair.

HYMN

Lewis scrabbled together most of his conversation with Anton on their drive back to London.

"The Shilling is passed on like a baton in a relay race," he explained. "If you pass it on then you're rewarded, but I'm guessing that Emily went back on the deal for some reason. They bring you up, then bring you down again, to soften you up for the pitch."

"What pitch?" Bernie asked.

"As I said, passing it on the next person. I still believe it's some kind of collective intelligence and they've got this weird thing about showcasing the subscribers when they die. The twins died recently. One of them seems to have led a charmed life."

"Only one of them?"

"Yeah, but the other one was clearly a late convert."

"But what about this Mary Stone woman?" Bernie asked, the photograph in her hand. "She didn't die recently, did she?"

He didn't answer.

"You're right," she murmured as she considered the photograph, "she *was* beautiful."

"We've only got Anton's word for it that the photograph is so old," he suggested.

"Why would he lie?"

"Well, we'll find out. There must be plenty of records that we can check, but even if Mary Stone did live all the way back then, it's easily explained."

"Easily explained that she appears in a magazine with

a colour photograph?"

He shook his head and said, "You can perform all sorts of tricks with computer graphics."

"Oh for goodness's sake, Lewis, you're still not... look, you were there, you saw the crossword write itself..."

He nodded. "Okay, I admit I was wrong about the dissolving film on the pages and the magic ink. But what happened in the pub only seemed weird because we were looking at a page in a magazine, and paper isn't meant to behave that way."

"What are you talking about?"

"Look, if you saw that crossword on my computer and then the writing appeared by itself, you wouldn't be shocked at all, would you? You'd just think it was some fancy software."

"So?"

"I still think it's significant that those pages are so thick. What if... what if the network has made an invention, which is basically a computer screen, but which looks and feels like a piece of paper? Now think about it, they could control what happens to it from another computer, send it signals and stuff."

She shook her head. "Alright, how do you explain the smell? How do you explain the hair?"

He didn't answer.

"Haven't got an explanation for that, have you?" she said.

"That doesn't mean that there isn't one," he returned irritably.

"Well, have it your way. But I want you to go and see someone in the Church as soon as you drop me off. See if you can make sense of this *hymn* thing."

"No, we've got to find Mary Stone."

"I'll find Mary Stone, as soon as I've dropped Jamey off at the hospital. Do you know anyone you can speak to?"

"The only person that I can think of is my old pastor."

"Pastor? What's that?"

"Sort of a vicar… an Evangelical minister."

"You go to church then?"

"When I was younger. My parents did."

"Why didn't you mention this before?"

He looked uncomfortable. "Well, long time ago now, Bernie; too long. I don't think the pastor would approve of me, the way I turned out."

"You turned out just fine. What are you talking about?"

"All the same, I'd rather find someone in London."

"No, you need someone that you can trust. Someone that you know. Go back to Cardiff as soon as you drop me off."

"Bernie…"

"Do it, Lewis. I've been asking you for long enough."

The pastor was Elfed Hopkins; he was Welsh Evangelical and if anything would make Lewis believe in the power of God then it would be this man whose every thought, every action, was dictated by the certain contemplation of the afterlife. He was in his late seventies now, worn out but still preaching, and revered by his congregation.

Lewis tracked him down from the phone book to a humble semi-detached house, and shyly knocked on his door. The pastor didn't remember him at first, but eventually his memory was jogged. "You're David and Gwen's son," he declared gently, always pleased to see a face from the past. "They were lovely people." Lewis had come very late in the day and his parents had used to say it was like that miracle in the Old Testament story.

They sat in a small front room with chintz chairs and countless photographs of the Hopkins clan. Lewis had his attaché case at his feet and was thinking how frail the pastor looked, how tired, and that he shouldn't be bothering him with this.

"It is good to see you again, Lewis," the pastor said quietly, sitting upright with his hands on his knees. "Is the Lord in your life?"

Lewis shrugged uncomfortably and felt the old conflict: the desire to be in the Faith, but the contradiction of reason and logic. Evangelicals were straightforward: there was no 'my son' or any other form of ritual in speech or action. The pastor could have been any normal old man, but the bonds that Evangelicals wove were tighter than any ritual, for it was a complete devotion in word and action to the Faith. It was this inflexibility that had made him defect, years ago. Lewis believed in God, but wanted to lead a full life.

He knew of course that his terms were completely unrealistic. If he believed in judgment in the afterlife, which lasted an eternity, then everything he did in the fraction of a second that was *life* should be in preparation for that. That was what allowed the Christians to sing as they faced the lions in the Arena.

It also justified the Inquisition burning people at the stake.

"Pastor, I have to be honest," Lewis opened, "it was my girlfriend's idea that I come and see you. She thinks you may be able to help."

The pastor nodded and brought his hands together with an air of disappointment. Lewis took a deep breath and gave him a potted version of his dealings with The Shilling. He had rehearsed it in the car: he left out anything which involved sex, although he gave a 'U'-rated version of his dreams with Mary Stone. The thought of even making a reference to anything lewd would be unthinkable; he would imagine the pastor withering away.

"It sounds as if you are very much in the world, Lewis," the pastor remarked. "I have been to London and I have seen how fast everything moves, with everyone rushing somewhere or other, following their man-made idols. I think... I think how can the word of God ever breach these high walls?"

Lewis nodded and said, "But do you think I'm mad, Pastor, do you think I'm imagining all this?"

The pastor paused before answering. "Do you really want my opinion, Lewis? Is it important to you?"

Lewis took a deep breath. The pastor was right of course, for he didn't really know why he was here.

"I'm sorry, Pastor, I don't know what to believe. I've always tried to be a good person. I just have a problem sometimes with the... the logic of Christianity."

"The Devil knows that, Lewis," the pastor replied in a slow and serious voice. Evangelicals had no problem with making reference to 'the Devil' and they didn't have any sympathy with modern notions of an afterlife without judgment.

"I've tried to make sense out of everything that's happened," Lewis said, "but whenever I come up with a plausible theory something happens..."

The pastor now smiled in sympathy. "The Devil will use logic to misguide you. His greatest weapon is that in this age of reason and technology it must seem impossible for him to exist."

"But I believe in God, Pastor."

The pastor closed his eyes sadly then opened them again. "Lewis, the Devil believes in God. That's not enough."

Lewis was unnerved by this statement and didn't speak for a time. "Pastor," he said at length, "I've told you my story. Do you believe any of it?"

"The Devil shows himself in many forms," the pastor returned.

"Has anything like this ever happened to you?"

The pastor's hands returned to his knees. "I remember when I was very young, in my early thirties, I was driving to my church. A young man on a motorcycle was swerving in and out of my lane, trying to make me crash. I slowed down and beeped him, but he wouldn't relent. Eventually he raced off by himself. When I got to church, was giving my sermon, the same young man wandered in, still wearing his helmet. He sat in the front pew and tried to distract me all the way through, making signals at me and muttering obscenities. Afterwards, when I complained to the ushers, no one would confirm that he was there. Only I saw him."

Lewis had heard this story before, for it was famous in his church. "But the Devil couldn't shake your faith, Pastor, so why did he send that person?"

"It is because he couldn't shake my faith. The Devil is a bad loser, Lewis. He had nothing further to lose by revealing himself to me, but the last thing he will do is reveal himself to the weak of faith. If you believe in the Devil, you run to God..."

Lewis now became animated. "So why am I going through all this? If I'm going to Hell anyway, why bother with me? Why not just leave me to it in the big bad world?"

The pastor sighed. "Lewis, perhaps your path would have eventually led you to the Lord. You said at the beginning of your story that you were sick of the rat race, as you describe it. You were going to Spain. Perhaps you would have seen things more clearly out there, and come back. Come back to church."

Lewis thought about this. Spain! It seemed so long ago now. "So, you think this was... his way of keeping me here?" He couldn't quite bring himself to say *the Devil*.

"Perhaps you are being tested, Lewis, but you must

understand that the Devil has very little power in the final scheme of things. He'd be running amok down here otherwise. The Lord allows him to exist because he tests our faith, and for no other reason. But the Devil is clever, and he's a trickster. He knows that the temptations of the world are very powerful. You say this thing is a fashion magazine?"

"A kind of fashion magazine," Lewis qualified.

"What could be a more appropriate vehicle for him?" the pastor mused. "Temptation, unobtainable temptation, with all the vanities of the world paraded. Do you want to show it to me?"

Lewis nodded, then rubbed his stomach. "I'm sorry, I have to have a cigarette first." He looked at the pastor imploringly.

"Would you like to go into the garden?"

"No, that's no good. I have to use your toilet." He checked his jacket and grimaced. "And can I have a large glass of water?"

The Shilling was the same as when he had first seen it and Mary Stone, beautiful once more, was smiling serenely at the camera. The pages had no smell, the paper no rotting texture and the articles were not reading backwards. Only the crossword, almost complete, was as he last saw it.

"I don't understand," Lewis muttered, discovering that even his air freshener mark over the poodle's head had disappeared. He turned to Mary Stone and left the page open, her face feigning innocence on the pastor's coffee table. "This is the woman I dream of," Lewis said. "Someone told me that she lived a long time ago."

The pastor nodded and leaned forward, keeping his hands on his knees.

"The pages have changed again," Lewis explained. "She's pockmarked normally, and her hair's falling out. I think maybe they've developed some computer software that makes the pages change. You have to believe me."

"She is an evil woman," the pastor said.

Lewis shook his head once more before the statement registered. He turned to the pastor with a raise of his eyebrows. "How do you know?" he asked.

"I know. Put the thing away."

Lewis reached for The Shilling but snatched his hand back. Mary Stone, now crater-faced, was snarling and hissing.

"Did you hear that?" Lewis whispered. The pastor nodded, but his face remained impassive. The smell of dog excrement filled the room for a moment like a fog, then retreated.

"Leave it alone," the pastor said calmly. "It's excited. I think it's excited because you've brought it here."

The pages flipped over, backwards and forwards until the magazine lay open at the twins, who had turned to face the camera and to look into Lewis' eyes. The smell of excrement returned, and the hissing was all around the room, as if it were coming out of imaginary speakers in the ceiling. The pastor looked down and muttered something to himself.

"Oh God," Lewis groaned, feeling nauseous.

The magazine jumped a few inches into the air, as if it was being pulled on strings, and landed upside down. The back cover showed skeletal women walking down a catwalk. It flipped again. This time horoscopes were revealed. Another flip, a syringe, flip, a saxophone. The Shilling was flipping quickly now, only offering glimpses of the new covers. Lewis saw the word 'fascism', a design for artillery shells, a chimney, with smoke billowing out. Then it flipped open to the front page and presented an enlargement of Anton's photograph of Mary Stone, the same photograph that Bernie was touting around the hall of records as they sat here.

The page flicked over. Blueprints for a factory; flick, an article entitled 'The Means of Production'; flick, a picture of young children carrying bales of wool, they looked emaciated. Flick, a recipe for salt, water and bran: a complicated formula for bulking up the three ingredients to make a mash. Flick, a business ledger in two columns: on the right were sales figures with nineteenth century denominations; on the left were expenses. Salt, water and bran: 2d. Orphanage retainer: one guinea. Constabulary: one pound six shillings (estimated).

Flick, an article on small pox; flick, make-up treatments, with an advert for Pear's soap. Flick, a 'who's who' of wealthy landowners and a list entitled 'eligible widowers'. Flick, some kind of contract, set out in elegant calligraphy, the words so tiny that a magnifying glass would be needed to read them. The magazine snapped shut.

Another smell appeared, this time an overpowering aroma of porridge, so salty that it seemed as if the room was under the sea. The smell subsided but traces of salt lingered in the air.

"Take it away," the pastor whispered. Neither man had moved as the magazine revealed itself to them. Lewis started, collected up the magazine, and silver shillings fell from inside the pages, clattering onto the coffee table. He gathered them up, his face white as a sheet, and slid them into his attaché case along with the magazine. He closed the case with shaking hands.

"It's possessed, isn't it?" he groaned. "I should destroy it, shouldn't I?"

"You can't destroy it. The malice of Hell is in this thing."

"The malice of…?"

"The Devil is a trickster, but he is also vain and frustrated. He needs to show his power in some manner or other, just as God in his majesty shows his power in everything around us. But the Devil cannot create, Lewis, he can only corrupt. He shows himself in war, and in cruelty, and in every other vice that he nurtures within us."

"But why this magazine?"

"Stop thinking of it as a magazine. It presents itself in a form you can understand, and will take the shape of your desires, or rather the things you *think* you desire. There is no greater triumph for the Devil than to tempt you, but to make the prize meaningless and hollow when you achieve it."

"You don't think it's a magazine? Then what is it?"

"I don't know if I saw the same things as you, Lewis. What did *you* see?"

Lewis gave a recap as best as he could but his recollection was already starting to fade, like a dream.

"I didn't see the magazine change," the pastor admitted. "I merely heard obscenities. I think… I think perhaps it is wary of me."

Lewis nodded slowly, mortified with fear. "But you said the Devil would never physically show himself?"

The pastor sighed. "Yes… there must be a reason for all this. This Mary Stone, this woman, in life she must have been very strong, very strong willed. Lewis, do you believe that a house can have an atmosphere? If something very bad has happened? That people can leave behind a stain… a stain of their grief, or perhaps their anger?"

"Yes I believe that… I think I do."

"This woman wanted something very badly, I believe, and the Devil gave it to her. But the force of will was so great, the prize so dearly bought, that this document of her life has survived."

"Pastor, what can I do? Someone very close to me is in danger."

The pastor shook his head. "You're in no physical danger, not you or anyone you know. You must remember that you belong to God, and the Devil cannot harm you. He can only tempt you."

Lewis swallowed, starting to recover his composure. "Someone else said something similar... that I was in no physical danger, I mean."

The pastor nodded. "There are rules, Lewis, and the Devil is forced to follow them."

"Rules?" Lewis mused. "I saw a contract, in the nineteenth century magazine, in Mary Stone's magazine."

"There are millions of contracts with the Devil. Anyone who chases the material pleasures of the world makes such a contract and the Devil rejoices because the true Word is there in front of us, yet we choose to ignore it. There lies his victory."

"Pastor, you don't think perhaps that this is a big conspiracy, some sort of satanic cult or something?"

The pastor took his hands. "Stop trying to find explanations, Lewis. You're not clever enough... no one is. You are playing on his terms if you attempt that. Trust in the Lord, that is your only hope of salvation. Pray with me now..."

Lewis was driving away some twenty minutes later, his memories of what he had seen already vague and incomplete. As he had carried the attaché case out to his car he had heard no rattle of coins.

His prayers had been sincere, but already he felt the tug of reason and logic. The Devil! The pastor made it all sound so reasonable but he shuddered with embarrassment at the prospect of having to explain all this to Bernie.

Lewis shook his head and tried to rationalise.

The pastor hadn't seen what he saw. That had to be significant.

"Yes," Lewis murmured to himself, agreeing with the rational voice in his head. Within the small confines of the pastor's sitting room they had both witnessed the infernal power of this magazine as it plumbed the depths of their consciousness and attacked their senses. The pastor had inevitably explained the experience to himself as a holy fight versus good and evil; it was altogether logical that he would do so, but the fact remained they had seen *different things*.

"Different..." Lewis whispered. He frowned as he negotiated a corner. Then, as he straightened the wheel, he smiled and nodded.

What if the magazine contained an hallucinogen?

That would explain a great deal. It would explain the way Mary Stone's face changed when he dropped the magazine in the lift that time; perhaps he hadn't imagined it, perhaps it was the hallucinogen kicking in.

The hair... Mary Stone's hair... always seemed to get lost, to disappear. Bernie had already lost the clump that appeared in the pub and he knew the silver shillings would be gone when he opened the attaché case.

Thinking about it, he hallucinated about Mary Stone after he had collected it from the rubbish, when it had started to smell. The smell could have been caused by the hallucinogen.

He still believed the bin men were involved, somehow. He was still in the centre of a conspiracy, a very real and mortal conspiracy, and he knew that Bernie was in danger, physical danger, no matter what the pastor said.

His phone was ringing as he walked through the door early in the evening and he was relieved to hear Bernie's voice.

"Bernie, what did you find out?"

Bernie seemed out of breath. "She existed, Lewis,

Mary Stone existed. She lived in London in the nineteenth century. I've found these old newspaper clippings."

"Okay, Bernie, calm down. Is Jamey okay?"

"He's staying overnight at the hospital," she explained quickly, not wanting to be distracted. "She had smallpox, just as she told you in the dream."

"Is that what she died of?"

"No… she outlived three husbands."

"How did *they* die?"

"Natural causes, I think, although there was something in one of the articles… oh bother, I can't put my finger on it now…"

"Never mind, what else do you know?"

"Well, she died very wealthy and left her fortune to a publishing house."

"I think I can guess what it was called," he said.

"Well you're wrong, because it's not Rever of London."

"What then?"

She sighed. "Baron Publishing."

"Jesus."

"I know. And I found out how she made her money, before she started marrying it, I mean."

"Child labour?" he asked.

She paused. "How do you know?" she whispered.

"I'll tell you in a minute. Go on."

She paused again. "The first reference to her is in a medical journal. Doctors said it was a miracle that she survived. There's a picture of her, Lewis. She'd lost all her hair, her face looked terrible. Her address was given as Mile End; I think that was a slum district then. No family alive. The article said that she had no occupation, but was known to the magistrates."

"Prostitute?" he suggested.

"Well, she was poor and probably starving…"

Lewis nodded.

You like that, don'tcha, my little soldjar?

"Go on, Bernie," he said.

"There's loads more, but that can wait. Lewis, I've worked something out. I think I know where we should look next."

"You do?"

"Rever of London," she began meaningfully.

He waited expectantly, but she didn't finish her sentence.

"Bernie?"

"There's someone at the door," she said distractedly. "I'll be back in a sec."

He nodded reluctantly. So, Mary Stone was a prostitute, but disfigured by small pox and with no family or welfare state. It put his problems with falling share prices into perspective and he felt a begrudging sense of admiration for this nineteenth-century woman, the way she defied fate.

No one gets rid of me.

And even her money was still around, in the form of the Baron trust, temptation money, the means to make dreams come true. It was a kind of immortality.

Taken the shilling, ain'tcha?

A few minutes had passed and Bernie still hadn't come back to the phone.

"Bernie?" he said. "Bernie, are you there?"

He grunted irritably as he glanced at his watch. Who was she talking to? How could it be more important than this? Perhaps something had happened to her brother... "Bernie?" he called, hoping she might hear him.

More time passed and gradually a cold feeling found a home in his stomach, the realisation that Bernie wasn't going to return to the phone.

Lewis made London in just under an hour and thirty minutes, fully calling upon the fuel injection his Volkswagen Golf had hidden under its bonnet, but it was still dark by the time he pulled up outside Bernie's terraced house in Acton. Now he was here he wasn't sure what he was going to do and the only things he had brought with him were his attaché case and his gun.

He had loaded the gun, in spite of BB's warning, loaded it slowly while holding it as far away from him as his arm would allow. He had considered calling the police, but instinctively knew that it would be the wrong thing to do. What would he tell them? That a satanic cult had orchestrated his destruction and now he was sure his girlfriend had been kidnapped... no he didn't hear a struggle but she hadn't come back to the phone. And how did he know there was a conspiracy? Well, there was this magazine and the pictures were changing... and he had talked to a teenager who was an ex-model... and an alcoholic... and an Evangelical minister...

The grim realisation that no one would believe him made him thank his lucky stars that he had stored those photocopies in the Paddington strongbox. At least they gave him a fighting chance.

Bernie's door was open and he entered quietly, one hand on the roomy jacket pocket that held his gun. This was his first time inside Bernie's home. Standing in the narrow hall of the terrace, to his right he saw the living room that had been converted into a bedroom, with a saline drip set up on the side of the bed: Jamey's room. He walked through to the kitchen. A mug of coffee had been prepared but was awaiting hot water and a microwave meal was open nearby. The phone was off the hook, engaged.

He quickly went upstairs, but the house was empty. Coming back down to the kitchen he replaced the phone and on the counter he saw the photocopies of the newspaper articles Bernie had referred to.

A clock was ticking in his head as he imagined Bernie tied up somewhere, in distress. But where was he to go? He could think of nothing else to do but to look through the articles.

The article on the top of the pile was from a local medical journal, entitled 'New miracle treatment for smallpox and advanced alopecia'. The photograph of the woman was taken in profile, but the skull with the pitted skin could have been Mary Stone. The doctor's name was Booker.

Lewis frowned. Mary Stone's name wasn't mentioned in the article, so how had Bernie found this? Had someone else compiled all this information already? He supposed that would explain how she had come up with so many articles in so little time.

Stapled to the article was a column from *The Lancet*, the journal for the medical profession, announcing that Dr Booker had been struck off. It was stated that the claims he had made in an article a year earlier for curing skin conditions had been completely discredited.

Lewis frowned. Booker… He sat down at the breakfast bar, the kitchen being too small to hold a table, and skimmed through the clippings as quickly as he could.

An article from a financial paper; a local businessman, who preferred to remain unnamed, was financing a workhouse in the poorest area of Mile End. The workhouse was called the Farthing Works and would generate cloth for garment factories.

Six months later, the same publication reported that the Farthing Works was a great success and that its credit history was exemplary.

A later article in the publication announced that a woman, Miss Mary Stone, in fact ran the Farthing Works. For the purpose of not discouraging suppliers and credit in the early days it had been held out that a man ran it. This man was in fact Miss Stone's accountant, one Howard Raine Esquire, formerly of the East India Company.

Lewis paused, studied the article awhile then smiled as he pulled three fingers though his hair. It could no longer be a simple coincidence that the doctor was called Booker: it was now clear to him that the two men he knew as Raine and Booker had read these articles and changed their names. Perhaps it was some sort of personality cult built around this Mary Stone woman.

He flicked quickly through the next set of articles. A sorority ball, a charity opera, events, events, events... a marriage. Mary Stone became Mary Strathmere as she married a wealthy landowner and local magistrate, John Strathmere. There was a photograph of John Strathmere, with a note that Miss Stone declined to be photographed. Strathmere didn't appear to be too happy with the idea either, for the photograph showed him stepping out of a hackney and gesturing at the camera with his cane.

A later article offered an explanation as to why Mary Strathmere always refused to be photographed. Lewis suspected that he had now come across the article that Bernie had mentioned on the telephone, for it was an expose and it was from *The Times*.

The article voiced the growing rumours about Mary Stone's working-class origins, challenging her assertion that she had worked abroad as a governess. 'Customers' of her early vocation, which could be said to be amongst the oldest of vocations, had been located. There were other rumours about her working practices, her misuse of child labour, with a hint that the local constabulary had sabotaged an investigation by Scotland Yard.

Lewis took a deep breath. This was in an age when child labour was commonplace and orphans ten a penny. What abuses would have caused a Scotland Yard investigation?

The article gave no clues.

Questions were even being raised over the death of her first husband, John Strathmere. His body had been burned, allegedly as his dying request, before the autopsy.

Lewis turned to the next article and saw that it was from a rival paper. Mrs Mary Strathmere had sued the editor of *The Times* for defamation and the newspaper's witnesses either hadn't come forward or had been discredited in cross-examination. Her legal team was said to be formidable, Mrs Strathmere herself possessing more than just a working knowledge of the law. She had obtained a substantial amount in damages.

As Lewis continued through the photocopied clippings he smiled the smile of a knowing lawyer. After the court case the allegations had come to an end.

He stopped at an article in a local paper. The editor, in the course of praising her charity work, announced that Mrs Strathmere was now taking her second husband and reverting to her maiden name of Stone.

Three years later she was married again, once more retaining her surname. That must have been unusual in the nineteenth century, he thought, and would have required some creative legal paperwork.

He turned to the next article. After her death in 1901, the year Queen Victoria died, the Suffragette movement had picked up on her, liking the idea that she had kept her maiden name after marriage. Well, not the movement itself, he saw on closer examination, but one particular suffragette, Miss Ruth Keenes.

The next photocopied page was a very short announcement in *The Times*. The Suffragette movement no longer associated itself with Miss Keenes, describing her methods as "too extreme".

He came to an obituary notice that carried the rarest of treasures – a photograph of Mary Stone. It was the portrait photograph that was on the first page of The Shilling, but in monochrome. He read that it was taken to celebrate her sixtieth birthday.

So she was sixty in that photograph, he realised. He had thought she had been in her early forties, at the most.

Mary Stone had died peacefully in her sleep. The funeral had been a private one, attended only by her accountant and her doctor, and the body had been cremated. The article praised her achievements, especially her work in the regeneration of the district of Mile End. It was said that she had only two lifelong ambitions that remained unfulfilled: the first was to dance with the Prince of Wales; the second was to take afternoon tea with his mother.

That was the last article and he put it down in dismay. What was the thing Bernie had mentioned before the doorbell rang? Bernie had worked something out, and maybe it was coincidental that she had collected all these materials at the same time. *Rever of London*, she had said.

Rever of London published The Shilling. There was a crossword clue dealing with publishing and he knew it word for word: *Published in a mirror out of town.*

That was it... Bernie had worked out the answer to the clue and that was where he had to look: it was the place where The Shilling was published.

He closed his eyes and concentrated as he had never concentrated before.

Out of town. So, the publishing house wasn't in London.

No... no... the clue was cryptic. *Out of town. Rever of London*. Remove London and what was left was *Rever of*.

Published in a mirror. A mirror put words in reverse...

Rever of. Fo rever.

Forever.

He reached into his attaché case, took out The Shilling and saw that *Forever* was being scratched into the crossword.

FOREVER

orever Publishing was listed in the phone book under mail order, in Mile End. As Lewis walked down the long side street, past the warehouses and tenements, he knew instinctively that this was where they had taken Bernie. Every window was boarded up; there were no streetlights, the entire street seemingly derelict and forgotten.

Purchased simply to remain empty?

Held in trust?

His thoughts were as vagabonds on the road, wandering aimlessly.

Orphaned children could easily be hidden here, kept alive on salt gruel.

Bernie, be alive. Please be alive.

Half way down the street, reading the numbers, he came to a stop. It was raining heavily and he had to rub the small metal plate to read the faded inscription, *Forever Publishing*. The door was a thick wooden beast, but it was unlocked.

Please Bernie, be alive. Be alive.

His anger consumed him as he imagined Bernie locked up in this place, frightened, possibly hurt and he took a deep breath, knowing he had the will to commit murder. BB's gun waited like a treacherous fate in his pocket. As he stepped inside and closed the door behind him the heavy wood swallowed the patter of the rain. The sudden silence was abrupt and his breathing, coming short and strained, was like a foghorn.

He saw row upon row of empty shelving, the room resembling a fusty library that had been stripped and emptied. There was a faint light in the room, catching the edges of the shelves; he was unaware of its origin but the ceiling was in pitch darkness and he wondered whether it was coming from the floor. Somewhere in the distance he heard the echo of voices and his hand wandered to his gun, but the voices seemed far away. He guessed that there were rooms leading off from this street entrance, although he hadn't seen any doors.

"Where are you?" he whispered, negotiating carefully through the shelves and nearly tripping over something under his feet. It was an open trap door that had risen out of the floor in a cloud of dust. A modern padlock was cast aside nearby. Crouching down he saw that he was right: the light was coming from below, underneath the floor.

Steep wooden steps led down to a cellar, which was lit with candles placed at regular intervals at the foot of the walls. Evaporated salt crystals hung in the air and he was reminded of the smell of gruel at the pastor's house, although this aroma was fresh and invigorating. As he lowered himself down the steps Lewis noticed that the cellar itself was a perfect square and three of the walls had as their sole purpose the presentation of a framed picture, each hanging dead centre at eye level. The fourth wall boasted a rosewood chest of drawers, carved with the ivy pattern from the cover of The Shilling, and above this chest hung a wall plaque cast in bronze with writing set in a beautiful gold calligraphy. The plaque would not have looked out of place in a very select golf club, as a trophy record, for it seemed to display a list of names. In the corner of this wall was a heavy wooden door with a ring handle, the handle identical to the one at the factory in the Newport depot.

A huge enlargement of The Shilling's photograph of

Mary Stone hung on the wall opposite, the portrait from the first page of the magazine.

He considered the candles, tall and white, standing in their own wax and only recently lit.

This is a shrine...

To his left was an oil painting set in an elaborate frame. It was a portrait of a man. On the next wall was something he recognised immediately: the long angled photograph of a warehouse, the one from Howard Raine's office. With a grunt of curiosity he went up to it to study the three distant figures and on closer examination of the setting he now saw that bales of wool were being loaded from the warehouse onto a horse and cart. An inscription near the bottom right of the photograph read: *The Farthing Works, 1888.*

The faces of the three people were difficult to make out, little more than pinpricks on the faded monochrome, although the figure in the centre was definitely a woman. He flicked his lighter and almost touched the photograph with his forehead, as he looked closer. Yes, he was sure of it: the centre figure was Mary Stone and at her sides were Raine and Booker. All three were looking very serious and correct.

Lewis frowned. From the newspaper clippings he knew that Mary Stone existed, so this must be a genuine photograph. The two men must have superimposed their faces somehow. He stepped back and shook his head.

He needed his lighter again for the wall plaque as he considered the three columns of names carved in the tiny writing. There must have been a hundred names at least. At the top left the first name was Dr. Cecil Booker MD, then Mr. Howard Raine Esq. He only recognised one other name, a little way down the first column, Miss Ruth Keenes.

He pulled three fingers through his hair. Ruth Keenes

was the suffragette he had read about in the newspaper article. Next to her name was written: *With our Father, 2001.*

With our Father. Did that mean she was dead?

He searched for names with similar epitaphs, but they were rare and of the deceased only two more bore the date 2001. They were Prissy and Ellie Maine, Prissy near the top of the second column, Ellie the very last name of the third column.

These could be the twins, he realised. So, Anton was right, they were dead, and they were in The Shilling. That meant... well, it followed logically... that the suffragette Ruth Keenes should be in The Shilling too.

She was the shears woman, the woman who despised him, who dared him to even look at her.

His heart skipped a beat. How old could she have been when she died?

He checked the list again, carefully. There was no sign of Marker or Dove, but he guessed that didn't mean anything as they were bound to be using pseudonyms; a money-laundering lawyer and an applicant for a patent torture machine would hardly use their real names. He closed his eyes and concentrated, trying to picture the inside of Dove's wallet and the name on the credit cards. It was *S Warner.* Lewis studied the list again and found a *Saul Warner* near the centre of the third column.

Marker's up there too, somewhere, he thought, nodding grimly to himself.

He scanned the columns of names for a final time, this time looking for Celia Maidstone, but he didn't find her. A guilty thought ran through his mind, the thought being that he only had BB's word for it that his closely-guarded real name was genuine.

The ornate rosewood chest was in front of him and he opened one of the drawers. It was crawling with cockroaches and he slammed it shut. He had the impression that one of the names on the plaque, he believed it was Ruth Keenes, had momentarily glowed white as he had been startled into a gasp.

He steadied his breathing, knowing that his imagination was going into overdrive. Steadying himself, he tried another drawer. It contained a photograph album, beautifully presented in velvet and with heart and flowers flitting around the title *In Loving Memory*. He pulled the drawer out to its limit, ready to slam it back and return the album to the chest if necessary, but the plaque didn't react. He turned the cover with the album still in the drawer; it was heavy and as the album was opened he detected the rank smell of mildewed clothes.

He recognised the first photograph, which was a man stepping out of a hackney, gesturing angrily with his cane. This was John Strathmere, Mary Stone's first husband.

The second photograph was a close up portrait of Strathmere, sneering as if he had just soundly beaten a school fag. The oil painting was of the same man, Lewis realised, although in the painting Strathmere's mouth was open in an 'O', his eyes in a fearful stare.

"The widow..." Lewis murmured, recalling her short letters to the editor in The Shilling. The widow had said that her husband had his portrait painted, as he died.

The third photograph was another close-up of Strathmere, but now his expression resembled the one in the oil painting. Lewis turned to the next photograph, which showed Strathmere in bed, attended by Mary Stone and Booker.

Lewis frowned. *Booker? How...?*

Larger photographs now, with pressed flowers on the pages opposite, yet the stale wardrobe smell persisted. Mary Stone with a cloth to her husband's forehead, her hair tied back in the manner of an efficient nurse; Booker holding Strathmere's wrist, checking his pulse.

A photograph taken from another angle, wife and doctor in the same pose, but Strathmere's face visible, his eyes staring.

Wife and doctor helping Strathmere out of bed. Strathmere was naked, his body shaved and grossly overweight; a far cry from the tall, thin rake stepping out of the hackney. His arms were at his side, his legs straight and he was stiff, as if he was in rigor mortis.

Many photographs followed, all showing Booker and Mary Stone carefully positioning the stiffened Strathmere up against the wall, as if he were a newly delivered grandfather clock. Lewis was turning the album leaves quickly now and the photographs almost created a moving picture. Strathmere's expression changed from horror to resignation, then back to horror. Lewis realised that not only was Strathmere clearly alive, but he was alert.

The positioning over, Booker now looked at the camera, holding aloft a jar of cocaine, as Mary Stone dabbed her husband's forehead once more.

Lewis imagined he almost heard the flash of the camera as they both stepped away to leave Strathmere standing rigidly against the wall.

A long scar travelled down Strathmere's body, beginning at his right shoulder, down through the right side of his groin, into his right leg and stopping just above his kneecap.

Lewis looked closer. No, the line wasn't a scar, but carefully interwoven black stitching, with the flesh pressing outwards. The stitches were straining in spite of the folds of obesity. Something long and hard and stiff had been stitched into the right front side of his body.

Lewis took a breath of air, feeling nauseous. What was it? Some kind of stick or pole?

His eyes narrowed as he recalled the letters from *the*

Widow. She had mentioned that her husband had a silver-topped cane, he called it *his ferule*, which he kept beside him on their wedding night. Lewis switched back to the first photograph, the one of Strathmere gesturing angrily with his cane, then closed the drawer quickly.

For the first time since he had arrived here he felt truly afraid. He supposed he had believed Anton, had believed the pastor, when he had been told that neither he nor Bernie were in physical danger. Seeing the way that the network had taken care of Strathmere he didn't believe that any more and that was definitely Cecil Booker, Baron's so called Health and Safety Manager, in those photographs.

Had the modern day Booker had plastic surgery?

There were two more drawers. The first held a full set of the newspaper clippings Bernie had collected. The second held a book, or rather pages held together with treasury tags. The plain paper cover simply read: *Lewis Coin*.

The first page contained a resume in large type. His date of birth, educational history, his qualifications, his employment history.

Some personal details, but going beyond what would be found in a curriculum vitae. A romantic, essentially monogamous, heterosexual male. Reluctant smoker. Weight problem, painfully thin. Modern music enthusiast, amateur musician, dreams abandoned. Interested in history and other forms of escapism. Shortly to emigrate, which he sees as a means of escape. Lost everything in a stock market crash, crippling debt. Unhappy in his work, feels undervalued and unable to assert himself. Unaware of it, but likes solving puzzles…

He raised his eyebrows at this sketch summary of himself and wondered who had compiled this information.

He continued to flick through but there were hundreds of pages, double-sided with tiny writing. It was a record of his adult life. All of the addresses he had ever lived at. All of the telephone numbers he had ever had. A detailed transaction of all his financial dealings, not only his share purchases but the balances in his current account. Then the type went even smaller. Things he had bought: videos, CDs, items of clothing, holidays. Now a list of everyone he had ever known or even met on a casual basis. Next to certain people an italicised remark keyed in their significance.

He is jealous of this person's success with women... he has difficulty communicating with this person and so distrusts him accordingly...

Every girlfriend was listed, casual or otherwise, together with an attached reason, again in italics, for the failure of the relationship.

Girl found him unappealing, physically... girl found his personality lacking... he was embarrassed by a physical defect... he was unfaithful...

He blanched, now ignoring the italics as he read on.

As he came to the end of the list he scanned the names again. Some of the names made him smile or frown, depending on the memory that had been lost or buried. It took him a long time, but he found no mention of Bernie, Jasmine, Emily, Anton, or even Vernon Jones. He scanned back up to the top of the list. BB wasn't named either, with his nickname or his real name.

At the bottom of the last page he noticed a paperclip. Turning the page he saw that the paperclip secured a small photograph of BB.

"BB," he murmured to himself, then shut the drawer as he heard a voice. He looked round, breathing in through his nose, for the salt had increased in density. The voice became a muffled scream and he recognised it as Bernie's voice, through the wall. He darted to the door and pulled at the ring handle; the door was unlocked but stiff and jammed, the wood having swollen on its hinges over many damp and neglected years. With difficulty he forced it open and as he stepped through into the adjoining room the smell of salt gruel smothered him.

"Found me then, my little detective? My little Sherlock?"

The salt was so heavy it was a mist and he struggled to make out the bodies slumped against the walls of the circular stone room, children so emaciated that they barely had the strength to turn their heads to look at him. They were eating with their fingers, balancing bowls on their laps, their arms and knees not so much human limbs but bone levers. A cauldron was bubbling in the centre of the cellar and Mary Stone emerged from behind it.

"They're on a break, see. Just like I told the beak, I doesn't work them all the time." She surveyed her little charges with pride and tenderness before turning back to Lewis. "Are you looking for that Bernie Tate?" she asked, wiping her hands with a cloth.

"Where is she?" he murmured. "What have you done with her?"

She let the cloth fall to the floor and rubbed her forehead. Her hand was wet from the salt steam coming from the cauldron and greasy pockmarks were revealed above one of her eyebrows.

"She'll be gone soon," she remarked.

"What do you mean? Where is she?"

She didn't answer, for something had caught her eye. She walked over to one of the children, Lewis thought it might be a little girl; it was difficult to say as the child was little more than a cadaver of wrinkled skin. Mary Stone put her hand to the child's forehead and closed her eyes with two gentle fingers. Carefully putting aside the bowl she lifted the child tenderly over her shoulder then returned to the cauldron. With a slight sigh of effort, she tipped the dead child into the pot, and the porridge gruel bubbled with appreciation.

"Oh God..." Lewis groaned. His eyes narrowed with hatred and he strode up to her and swung a fist. With a yelp she staggered back, clutching at her face, then collapsed to the floor. He turned to the children, but they had gone. The salt mist had also retreated, and now he saw that the cauldron had vanished.

Bernie was lying on the floor clutching her eye, her cheek already beginning to swell. She looked at him fearfully, then, slowly, her expression changed.

"Lewis?" she whispered.

His stomach turned over. "Oh God, Bernie, what have I done?"

"I thought you were BB," she said, painfully. "I was talking to BB..."

He ran over to her and helped her up. "It's the hallucinogen," he explained. "I thought you were Mary Stone. Oh God, I'm so sorry."

She shook her head to say it didn't matter. "You came for me," she said, "that's the important thing."

"What happened?" he asked.

"I don't know," she answered helplessly. "I opened the door and then I woke up here."

"You don't remember anything at all?"

She shook her head weakly. "I thought you were BB," she repeated. "He wanted to know where you were. I wouldn't tell him. He hit me."

"It's okay, Bernie, it's okay."

She touched her left cheek and her eyes watered. "Where are we?" she asked.

He sighed as he stroked her hair. "This is the headquarters for some kind of cult... a sadistic cult. Don't worry, there's enough evidence next door to put them away for years. All of them."

As he helped her through the door they were confronted with Raine and Booker descending the steps. The two men stiffened with surprise, then carefully stepped down into the cellar as they saw that Lewis was pointing a gun in their direction. Their hands were up, but Booker was smiling, a large cigar in his hand. Lewis could almost hear his brain ticking.

"Now we can talk about this, Lewis," Booker wheezed, his voice like gravel in its croaked baritone. "We can explain everything."

Bernie squeezed Lewis' shoulder. "Let's go," she whispered.

"What and just let them find us again?" Lewis whispered back.

"Please, Lewis, don't do anything," she implored.

"Now I think you should listen to her," Booker agreed. "This isn't what you think. It is true that we're interested in you, of course. You should hear us out, hear our proposal."

Lewis had noticed that Raine was looking at the floor and his hands had lowered somewhat.

"Now if we had wanted to kill you, you'd be dead already," Booker pointed out.

"Lewis, let's go," Bernie insisted. Raine's hands were getting lower.

"Do you think we would have put the answer in the crossword if we didn't want you to find us here?" Booker continued. "Think about it Lewis, you're a clever man... a logical, reasonable man. That's why we chose you. That's why you were chosen."

Lewis glanced at the rosewood chest, then at the steps. He considered the two men blocking his path and his eyes narrowed. He aimed the gun at Raine's thigh, held it steady for a moment then pulled the trigger. The gun came back swiftly with the recoil, the smell of cordite filling the small room and Raine fell to the floor, screaming and clutching at his leg.

"Lewis, stop!" Bernie cried.

Booker looked at his stricken associate with horrified surprise and dropped his cigar. A second bullet was pumped into Booker's thigh and he dropped too.

Lewis kept the gun levelled at Booker, who was writhing in agony on the floor, and used his free hand to take his mobile out of his jacket. He pushed a pre set with his thumb and put the handset to his ear.

"Who are you ringing?" she cried.

"BB," he replied.

"Lewis, no... don't..."

"It's okay, I know what I'm doing – BB? Hi, it's me. Look you have to help me. Ring the police as soon as you get off the phone. Tell them to go to Forever Publishing, Mile End, London. Get a pen."

She tugged at his sleeve and shook her head, horrified. Lewis ignored her as he gave BB the full address. "Tell them to make contact with officers Fleet or Cole, Cardiff CID, tell them that I've found the centre of the network. Yes, yes the network. There are two wounded men, they kidnapped Bernie." Lewis paused for a moment to let BB say something but then cut him short. "Listen, BB, this is important. Behind the reception desk there's a trapdoor to the cellar. Everything's downstairs in the cellar. Tell them to look in a chest of drawers. There's a photo album. There's also a small photograph on the wall... they'll recognise two of the men in it."

He cast a grim smile at Raine and Booker, who were clutching at their wounds. Booker had found a handkerchief and it was stained red.

"Lewis, please..." Bernie implored.

He waved his hand impatiently. "I'm going to lock the trapdoor to keep the two men down here," he continued.

"They're both injured so ring 999 first to get the police here, then explain everything afterwards." He paused again and shook his head. "No, it's better if you call. I've got to pick something up… it doesn't matter… I have to get this stuff and I just haven't got time to be questioned by the local force. Tell Fleet I'll be waiting for him back home, so we can give full statements. Okay BB? You'll ring 999 now? You've got the address?" He ended the call and looked up at the trap door. "Okay, let's go," he said.

As they got into the car Lewis turned the engine over, but kept the gear in neutral. He still had the mobile in his hand.

"You shouldn't have rung BB," Bernie moaned. "I was trying to tell you. Lewis, I don't trust him."

He nodded and checked his watch. "Five minutes, maximum, for the police to arrive," he murmured.

"What do you mean?"

He turned to her with a troubled expression. "If BB has made the call then the police will be here any minute. If he hasn't, he'll think I'm driving back to Cardiff and the network will arrive instead. Either way, I'll know. I'll give it another two minutes before I ring the police myself."

Her jaw dropped. "You… you don't trust him either?"

His expression darkened. "No. But I have to be sure. The answer to *Beta Lives* goes across and down. *Be… Be…*"

"You saw that too?"

"He knew about the photograph of the two of us on the balcony. I think Raine knew I had that photograph, when I… you know. Coincidence?"

"You think he told Mr Raine?" she asked.

"He kept throwing me bum steers on the magazine, as well. Asking me what I thought about it. The network knew that he bought shares on my behalf. I always told him what I was about to do…"

"So you think…?"

He shook his head quickly and said, "I don't know. None of this is concrete proof that BB's involved. Maybe the network wants me to think he's involved, just like they wanted me to think that you were in on it, at the beginning. Perhaps they want me to lose everyone I care about."

"Someone close to you must have given them all your information, Lewis," she said. "Don't you see that? That's why I thought…"

"Is that why you wanted to meet him?" he asked.

She looked away then nodded.

"Do you think that's why he didn't like you?" he pressed. "Because he guessed you were trying to sum him up?"

"I don't know why he didn't like me," she admitted.

He thought about this awhile, his mobile still in his hand. "It could be that guy BB's working with on the tourist website," he mused. "The computer whizz guy, I mean. He came along when all this started to happen. Maybe he's tricked the info out of BB."

She didn't comment and simply shook her head. He was patiently looking at the empty street in his rear-view mirror, but his faith was faltering. "Come on BB," he muttered, "come on."

"Ring the police, Lewis," she said.

"A few more minutes…"

"Lewis, ring them."

He sighed and regarded his mobile. He dialled the first 9. She glanced over at him and nodded sadly. He dialled the second 9, then put the mobile down as he saw two police cars drive up the street and screech to a stop. Four uniformed officers jumped out and entered the building. He shoved into gear and slammed on the accelerator. "I knew it couldn't be BB, I knew it!" he exclaimed jubilantly.

As Bernie buckled up she looked back at the street, confused.

"We're going back to Cardiff?" she asked shortly.

"I've got to make a stop first, at Paddington station. That's where my strongbox is."

"Strongbox?"

"I've got another set of photocopies in there, photocopies of The Shilling I mean. I'll be able to show them to the CID to prove that the magazine changes. They'll be able to link that up with all the stuff in the cellar, won't they?" He nodded grimly. "They'll believe me."

She didn't speak for a time. "You didn't tell me about this strongbox," she said eventually.

"I know. I'm sorry."

"You still don't trust me?"

"Bernie, of course I trust you."

"No you don't. You would have told me." She winced as she touched her cheek, which was coming up purple. A tear started in her eye.

He made a pained face. "Bernie, listen. What if the duplex is bugged? Have you thought about that? Wouldn't that make sense, the way they tricked me all the way along, the way they always seem to know my every move? If it is bugged then the strongbox would be empty now. They stole your photocopies, remember?"

"You could have written me a note," she murmured.

"I didn't tell BB either," he offered lamely.

"I'm flattered," she said, touching her swollen cheek again. "You really hurt me," she muttered.

"I know, I'm sorry." He glanced at her and attempted a reassuring smile. "I'm sorry for everything," he added.

It was some time before she spoke again. "Maybe the photocopies have changed as well," she said, her tone suggesting that she had forgiven him. "Maybe they're just

340

like the ones in the attaché case."

"I don't understand," he said. "What are you saying? That the photocopies can change?"

"Why not?"

"Because the photocopies are taken from an old machine in a London library. It was a Canon, I think, though I'm not sure of the model."

"Are you being sarcastic?"

"Yeah, sorry."

"Lewis, that magazine isn't natural."

"I agree. But that doesn't mean it can't be explained."

"Lewis, you can't still believe..."

"If you showed a man from the Middle Ages television, he'd think you were a demon or something. Agreed?"

She didn't answer.

He threw her a smile. "Agreed?" he asked.

She looked out of the window, showing annoyance at seeing the lawyer side of him come out. At length she shrugged.

"Bernie, it's just clever technology, that's all," he continued, "no matter how they're trying to dress it up. My guess is that hallucinogen is soaked into the pages of the magazine. Some sort of intelligent drug... the network probably triggers the illusions with a computer programme. I should have realised that when they first contacted me on the Internet... when my computer crashed."

She didn't comment, but as she stared out of the window she mouthed the word *technology* to herself with mistrust.

It was raining heavily by the time they reached Paddington and he returned to the car later soaked through, but with the photocopies of The Shilling safely protected in their plastic wrapping. He rolled them up to put them in the glove box.

"No, Lewis, take them out and look at them," she said.

"We have to go," he said, with a shake of his head.

"Take them out!" she ordered, her voice shaking.

He hesitated, then sighed and took out the photocopied pages, which were as he had packed them. Mary Stone was in transition, her skin failing and starting to lose her hair.

"Same as the ones I sent to you?" he queried.

She took the pages suspiciously and felt their texture. It was plain A4. She handed them back and nodded.

"Alright," she said reluctantly, "tell me your theory."

"Well they have all this crazy technology…"

"No, I mean *why*," she said. "Why are they doing all this?"

He shrugged. "It's some sort of personality cult… they're all crazy… I saw everything in the cellar. It was a shrine to this Mary Stone woman. I think she set up some sort of trust fund…"

"Trust fund?" Bernie gasped.

"Something similar to a trust. She just started something and had the money to make it possible for it to continue. The network recruits; perhaps it's a generation-by-generation thing. They research their subjects extensively, very extensively, believe me, and The Shilling – the magazine itself – is some sort of initiation ceremony."

She thought about this. "Recruit? Why? For what reason?"

"I don't know," he conceded.

"And what did your pastor say?"

He waved the question away in exasperation.

"Lewis?"

"Look, forget about the pastor, that was a stupid idea you making me go and see him. This is a criminal organisation we're dealing with."

"Criminal? Criminal how?"

He returned the pages to the plastic wrapping, which he fitted into his glove box. "Maybe the CID were on the right track," he reflected. "Maybe it is something to do with money laundering."

"Oh Lewis!"

"Seriously, think about it. Look at all the money that's changing hands."

"Why haven't they killed us then?" she asked.

"What do you mean? They tried, didn't they? They kidnapped you…"

"And gave us the clue where to find me," she returned. "And let you rescue me," she added.

"What do you mean, *let* me?" He was hurt. For a few moments back there he had felt like Bruce Willis.

"It was a bit easy, wasn't it?" she said.

"Easy?"

"I think they've planned everything that has happened so far. This isn't a crime ring. Lewis, you have the last answer to the crossword sequence. *Forever* is the last answer to the sequence. Do you know what the sequence says? I've worked it out. Have you?"

He considered the steering wheel.

"Lewis? Have you worked it out?"

He slowly nodded his head.

She was looking downcast as she buckled her seatbelt. "Where on earth did you get a gun from?" she asked, shaking her head despondently. "You shouldn't have shot those two men."

Back in the duplex in the early hours, waiting for the call from either BB or the CID, they laid out the magazine on the floor. *Be* had found its way into the crossword, the remaining empty box being filled with the letter 'B'.

Lewis made a few scribbles as he wrote out the rest of the sequence.

(full)
two hour fat her (be?) low stop Bern wit hymn forever
to our father below. Burn with him forever

"*Be* was the right answer," he said. "Not *ie*. Be. The network must have written it in on our drive back."

"*Lewis your little sins are wonderful to our father below. Burn with him forever,*" Bernie read.

"It sounds like some sort of satanic cult," he said, then found a reluctant smile.

"What's funny?" she asked.

"I always thought *Bern* was part of your name, because it had a capital B, but it has the capital because it comes after a full stop. And Bern is a capital city."

"Clever isn't it?" she remarked.

He threw her a curious glance. She had also laid out the photograph of herself, posing shyly in her underwear.

"I keep that in the attaché case because I don't want anyone to find it," he explained quickly.

"And for emergencies," she added. "To stop the dreams, I mean. I remind you of her, don't I?"

He was puzzled now. She was talking as if she were drunk.

"Bernie, are you okay?" he asked.

She offered a contented moan in reply, smiling as she flattened out her photograph and the crossword with her hands.

"Bernie, perhaps we should get you to a doctor. You could be in shock."

"In shock?"

"You've been abducted, seen two men shot…"

"No, I'm okay."

"Maybe the network has slipped you something,

344

drugged you."

She touched the face of her photograph with her fingernail. "Make love to me," she muttered. She reached over to him and stroked his collar. Her purple cheek, now so swollen that her left eye was almost closed, gave her request a certain ferocity.

"Perhaps you should ring the hospital, see if your brother is okay," he suggested. He knew that if anything would bring her to her senses it would be the mention of her brother.

"Don't worry about him," she purred, then ripped open his shirt.

She was sitting quietly in an armchair as he emerged from the bathroom. His expression was one of incredulity.

"I don't know what came over me," she admitted.

"They've drugged you," he said, sitting down on the floor with difficulty. His groin was sore.

"Drugged me?"

"My libido went crazy in the early days too," he murmured then winced as he discovered a few bruises on his sides and on his legs. He was reminded of when he used to wake from his dreams.

"I think you're right," she agreed, "I'm not myself."

"You were like *her*," he said. "It was as if you hated me."

"I don't hate you, Lewis. I love you."

"You slapped me."

"I know."

"You called me... you called me your *fat pig*."

"Oh dear. Did I?"

He closed his eyes, finding the memory painful. "Like *her*, that look I saw in her eyes, as if I was just a tool, a toy..."

"Did it turn you on?"

"What?"

She shook her head and looked at the crossword. "What does *Be* mean?" she mused. "The answer goes across and down…"

Lewis hesitated, then sighed and sat down next to her. "I know," he said. "It must mean BB but I don't know how he fits into this."

As if on cue, the phone rang.

"Lewis, what's going on?" BB barked as soon as the phone was answered.

"Did the police find everything?" Lewis asked, a little unsettled by BB's tone.

"They found two men shot in the leg. Fuck, I told you not to load that gun."

"It's okay, they're Howard Raine and Cecil Booker, the men I was telling you about."

"They're *who*?"

"Raine and Booker. Baron Enterprises."

"They're two local businessmen, Lew. They use that place as a warehouse. They said they went downstairs because they heard a noise and then you just shot them."

Lewis chuckled. "Nice try. What did the police make of the shrine?"

"The *what*?"

"The pictures, the paintings," Lewis said irritably. "There's a photo album showing a ritual murder…"

"Lew, the place was empty. There's a back room leading off from the cellar but that was just filled with comic books. That's what they do, they sell comic books."

"I don't understand," Lewis said, his voice faltering.

"What have you done? The police think this is some sort of racist attack."

"Racist?"

"Christ, Lew, stop mumbling and listen. You didn't get

the gun from me, okay? You got lost, somehow, and you were downstairs trying to find someone so you could ask for directions. Those two men came down and startled you. You panicked and rang me, okay?"

"BB... don't you believe me?"

"What I believe is that you're in serious trouble. This thing with the magazine is all in your head. I've been telling you that all along..."

Lewis put the phone down, not letting BB finish.

Bernie was shaking her head. "Oh no, oh no," she moaned, "I told you not to ring him. I told you..."

"We've still got your newspaper clippings," he said, his voice shaking. "We can show they've taken the names of the doctor and accountant. You can confirm that they were part of Baron. Anyway, Raine and Booker won't dare press charges."

"Who?"

"Raine and Booker," he repeated.

"Who?"

"Bernie, what are you going on about? Raine and Booker are pretending to be these comic book retailers, and when I shot them..."

"You didn't shoot Mr Raine or Mr Booker," she whispered.

"What?"

She had a horrified expression. "You shot two Indian men. I assumed that you knew they were part of the network."

He opened his mouth to speak, but no words came.

"Oh Lewis, what have you done?"

"I must have been hallucinating," he gasped. "I thought I saw Raine and Booker."

"But...?"

"Didn't you think you saw me as BB?" he snapped. "Didn't I see you as Mary Stone?"

She thought about this, then nodded. "What are we going to do?" she asked.

He regarded the gun on his table. "BB set this all up. He must have rung the network and cleared out the shrine. Those policemen, they were network people dressed up. I'm finished."

"No, no, you've still got the photocopies."

In desperation he snatched up the plastic wrapping and turned it over in his hands. "Perhaps they'll still believe me," he agreed. "They can analyse The Shilling, do tests on it and stuff, can't they?" He ripped it open and the photocopies snarled at him. Dog excrement wafted from the pages. On the pages Mary Stone's skin was flawless and she had a full head of hair. The photocopies had changed.

He dropped them, his expression stunned as he turned to Bernie. She was holding up her photograph where she was posing shyly in her underwear, but the woman in the photograph had the face of Mary Stone.

"Bernie?" he whispered.

"BB hasn't betrayed you, Lewis," Bernie said. "You're going to betray *him*. You're going to give him The Shilling, *that's* why his name was the last answer in the crossword."

"Who are you?" he murmured.

Bernie gave him a sympathetic look as she fiddled with her hair. Then she took a deep breath and her hair turned as black as pitch. She took another deep breath, looking up and stretching her long neck as far as it would go, and Bernie's face changed. The features remained the same but she was older and her face was pumped with a lustful energy and proud disdain. As she turned to look at him her eyes had turned a deep and piercing green.

"Ah, my poor little soldjar," she declared, with a slight tilt of her head.

He found himself nodding as he retrieved a memory that he had discarded as being impossible.

That face from behind the clothes dummy, the woman in the mountain lift. Someone he thought he had seen but who couldn't be there, couldn't possibly be there, following him though Italy.

It *was* Bernie he had seen in Capri.

BE

Instinctively, he looked at The Shilling. It had changed. He turned to face the woman still sitting comfortably in the armchair and the blood drained from his face.

"You're... Mary Stone?"

"Of course I'm Mary Stone. Miss Mary Stone of the Farthing Works, Mile End, London Town, if you wish to be particular. Who else did you expect? Or did you reckon it was a coincidence that only Bernie could stop you dreaming of me? That I was wearing her diamond?"

"But... you're dead."

She raised her hands in the manner of a party trick then offered him her half smile. It was proud and ruthless.

"You're dead," he repeated.

"Well if you ain't going to kiss me then you might as well sit yourself down." Her eyes narrowed into slits as she leant forward. "We needs to talk."

At some point he made the decision to sit down. Time seemed to have lost its beat. "Be Bernie again," he whispered.

"You're not going to run?" she asked. Bernie had returned, but she seemed a little different, somehow more punctuated. Her skin, free of the powdery make-up, was flawless and her Titian hair, which before had sometimes seemed rather lifeless, was now thick and lustrous. Her hourglass figure was exaggerated, almost like a cartoon, the buttons of her shirt were straining, yet she still possessed that feminine frailty, conveyed through every word and action, that he found irresistible.

His mind registered certain facts: the room was silent and there was no salt or excrement in the air. With a certainty that came from his stomach he knew this was no dream or hallucination.

"No, I want answers," he said. He was less afraid now that Bernie had returned and he was recalling something that Anton told him, and the pastor. That he couldn't be harmed.

"So have you run out of theories?" she inquired. Her tone was gentle, understanding.

"Yes," he admitted. "I want answers now."

"Yes... answers... they always want answers."

"Are you a ghost?" he asked.

She clapped her hands politely. "At least you admit that I'm talking to you? That I'm not an hallucination? That I'm not an invention of your... your wild technology?"

"You're real," he droned, "I know that now. Well... are you a ghost?"

"Lewis, you've touched me, held me, made love to me." She closed her eyes briefly as if to recall the memories. "How could I be a ghost? For you, I'm as real as anything can be. But only you can see me, if that's what you mean."

He sat back and pulled his three fingers through his hair. She smiled, finding this particular habit of his significant.

"I can see that you're thinking, but there's no need to be worried," she said.

He looked down. When he had first met Bernie it was in the boardroom and he later gave Helen the receptionist a bawling out for not telling him that she was down there waiting for him. She had protested, as he recalled. Thinking back on it now he was certain he hadn't seen

Bernie when he walked into the boardroom. At the time he had put it down to his being miles away... miles away because he was thinking what he was going to say to O'Neill, when he handed in his notice. Everything changed after that meeting...

The next time Bernie was in his office she was sitting in reception, with O'Neill having one of his moments and flailing his arms around. He remembered thinking how rude O'Neill was to act that way in front of a client. When Bernie ran off, after he had kissed her, Tracy had asked him who he had been talking to. He had mistaken Tracy's curious smile for jealousy.

The secretaries must have thought he was mad, talking to himself like that in the boardroom.

Months later, when he stopped her in the street outside her office in Holborn, begged her to come back to him, those passers-by had given him odd looks. A madman in the street, pleading with the air...

Then there had been all her strategies for not being able to go out in public: the fraternisation rule with Baron, falling asleep in that pub in Kent – she had stayed in the car when he booked in – and, above all, the sick brother she couldn't leave.

"I take it there is no sick brother?" he asked, looking up at last.

"Poor little Jamey was your idea," she replied sweetly.

"My idea?"

She threw up her hands with good-natured exasperation. "You created me, Lewis. Haven't you realised that yet?"

"I created Mary Stone?"

"No, silly boy. You created Bernie. Your need was for a perfect woman. In your subconscious your perfect woman was totally feminine, something out of a period novel, innocent, vulnerable yet voluptuous. It made sense that such a woman would have a sick brother to make her love and sacrifice manifest. Isn't that what happens to beautiful young things in romantic novels? When I visited you in the boardroom I had no control over what you saw."

"So… you were Celia Maidstone as well, weren't you? The older woman who worked with Emily."

"Of course. Emily created me as a mother figure. She was orphaned very young and needed a family, that's why she fell for an older man. So, I appeared to her as an older woman who understood her needs, encouraged her in her endeavour, a surrogate mother. I give everyone exactly what they need… what they think they need. But if you're expecting me to show you Celia Maidstone then you'll be disappointed. Celia was for Emily. *I* don't even know what she looks like."

"But Anton recognised you. And Jasmine saw you too."

"Yes, they both saw me as Celia Maidstone because they were intimately involved in Emily's experience. But you were very lonely, Lewis. Bernie was only for your eyes."

Yes, I was lonely, he thought. I'm lonely now, more lonely than I've ever been.

"Anton and Emily were in love," she added, "while Jasmine was her favourite. She was very protective towards Jasmine…"

"Was Jasmine destined to have The Shilling?" he asked.

She shrugged and didn't answer, but something around her eyes, a twitch of annoyance, seemed to send a subliminal message to his brain.

The nosy mare, the horse-faced missy…

"What?" he said.

She shrugged and shook her head.

"Who did BB see?" he asked. He was remembering their conversation, the difficult one here in the duplex.

"The woman who will shortly have a great influence on his life," she answered gravely. "She's a music executive. I can't tell you what she looks like, but I suspect she's rather plain. She has a brutal tongue, though, which is just what he needs. She told him a few home truths, that he was a quitter... a loser."

"But he hated you. Whoever he saw, you can't be his dream woman."

She sighed. "Oh my. Stop seeing everything from your perspective, Lewis. BB isn't searching for a dream woman. He wants someone who can give meaning to his life, who can help him succeed." She smiled playfully. "I'm going to enjoy playing that role. No, he didn't like what I had to say but the words hit their mark. He went home wondering if he should give his music career one final go."

He tried to piece together BB's conversation with Bernie. His replies were odd, connecting awkwardly with the questions he heard being asked.

Then there was Anton lunging at Bernie, at his front door. He had seen Celia Maidstone, coming back to taunt him.

"Raine could see you," Lewis pointed out, trying to find some sense, some logic some pattern that he could grasp. He felt adrift.

"Of course. We go back a long way, Howard and I. And Cecil too, Dr Cecil Booker that is. They set up Baron, a hundred years ago. They administer the Trust."

She raised her eyebrows to offer him a sudden image, which she pasted in front of his eyes liking a moving photograph. He was in the Newport branch, it was his first visit, for Raine was wearing his cravat, mulling over the Vernon Jones file while belittling Bernie. Lewis was feeling protective towards the nervous woman sitting a little way from the desk. The photograph scanned left and Mary Stone was leering at him with puzzled satisfaction.

Her face was pockmarked.

"Are you the Devil?" he asked, his voice shaking. She laughed, genuinely amused.

"They always ask me that," she chuckled, "and I always find it amusing. Every time. Lewis, we wouldn't be having this conversation if that were so. You cannot even *comprehend* the Devil, or any of the higher management for that matter. Neither can I," she conceded.

"Why not?"

She shook her head. "Let it go, Lewis. See this little intrigue as challenge enough."

"No, I won't let it go. I want to know."

"Lewis, I can't help you with this. Don't be fooled by The Shilling, I don't have that kind of rank. Management barely knows I exist, in fact. I'm simply moving around in the meagre smallholding I've been leased, that I'm renting, as are you."

"So who are you?"

Her eyes darkened. "I'm just a woman who refused to accept what life handed out to me. Refused it, absolutely. Refused to accept poverty and an illness that disfigured me. After I had been created so beautiful. If God made me that way, which he surely did, then why did he take it away? Wasn't our Father Below more merciful?"

He hesitated then said, "But it was at a price, wasn't it? That's why it's called *The Shilling*, isn't it? And *Farthing*. Everything is at a price. You live in this publication, for eternity."

She chuckled again. *"The Devil... eternity.* These are words that you cannot possibly understand. How can any of us comprehend *eternity*? We think that by labelling and naming a thing, that we understand it. Remember that night, under the museum, when the centuries just ticked by? Your brain couldn't comprehend it. You'd virtually forgotten it even as you woke up. I've been an observer for over a hundred years and seen many wonderful things, and if I go another hundred years then I'll be content. But I have no yearning for eternity." She paused. "You could join me," she added.

"What, swarming with cockroaches?"

She shrugged off the question. "My little Ruth just wanted to scare you, to upset you," she said. "Ruth hates men, all men, I can't do anything about that. What I can guarantee is my love. We'd be together and you would be happy. You see I know all your fantasies, all your desires and I can fulfil them. Bernie can fulfil them."

In his head he put this information to one side, for the lawyer in him was in play now. That was a bargaining card, freely offered. He could get more. More than anything, he wanted answers.

"Why did you appear to me as Bernie?"

"I told you…"

"No, I mean why appear to me at *all*?"

"Because I can, but also, to make sure you reached the end."

He thought about this. Everything that had happened to him had concerned Bernie; his decision not to emigrate, wishing to succeed with the Baron account, his suspicion, his betrayal, trying to get her back. He had an overwhelming need for her in order to stop the dreams. Finally, his fear for her, which eventually led him to Forever Publishing, where he shot two men…

"You played the part of the knight in shining armour," she clarified. "Bernie brought that out in you and took you to the end, in lust, in shame and in fear. Still, the journey was shorter than I would have liked. You were, I confess, something of a disappointment."

"What do you mean… a *disappointment*?"

"You were doing so well in the beginning. When you lied about that videotape and became a little tyrant in the office, I was so proud of you, had such high hopes for you. Then when you went along with Howard's ideology, oh that was wonderful. You'd become so ambitious!"

"So how did I disappoint you?"

"You were walking down the steps to the boardroom, to see O'Neill after he'd sacked you. You were going to make him grovel, make him pay, but you had a crisis of conscience." She sighed. "Well, I had to let you go then. I was hoping you'd take your law practice nationwide, performing wonderful things with Baron Enterprises, before I had to call you in."

"The CID were in the boardroom, waiting for me. I was in trouble no matter *what* I thought."

She shook her head. "The CID wouldn't have been there. O'Neill and the partners would have been waiting for you because Baron had restored the instruction. The shares you had just bought would have gone up."

He frowned.

"You see, you can't even get your head around *that*, can you?" she said. "You're still seeing everything in cause and effect, in days and minutes. And you talk about eternity..."

"So how would it have ended? Would I still be talking to you now?"

"At some point. But your fall would have been postponed, and would have been from a much greater height. As it turned out you only managed a little drama."

"Then I'm glad," he said.

She puckered her nose, which for Bernie was the closest she could get to a sneer. "In the way that someone at a funfair is glad he didn't go on the biggest ride. You were just scared, Lewis. Scared of what you might become. You were a very little soul, with little sins."

"But they're still wonderful to you, aren't they?" he

murmured, quoting the crossword sequence.

She shook a finger insistently. "Not to me," she clarified. "The crossword sequence is part of my contract with the Father. Your sins... all your sins... are wonderful to Him." Her eyes narrowed. "I have to tell you that... that's one of the rules."

"Rules?"

She didn't amplify and he was reminded of that conversation with Emily, when she was playing the question and answer game.

"Is it in the rules that you have to bring out the worst out in me? Is that why The Shilling exists?"

"I think you have guessed that. I have had and will have far better successes, but I still had more entertainment than I expected."

"Entertainment?"

She was smiling as she talked. "I couldn't believe how many mind defences you put up, how you struggled for explanations. They usually realise when the pictures change, but no... you always had a theory. When I returned The Shilling to you, completely changed but with the exact air freshener mark, I thought *now he'll understand*... but oh no. It must be the bin men... you and your bin men! Even when I gave you my hair, when I dropped the shillings out of the magazine, still you didn't believe..."

He took her teasing in good humour, for she was as sweet and as gentle as ever, but he tried to remember that this wasn't Mary Stone talking, just his mind fantasy who he had named *Bernie* and Bernie would say things in a way that pleased him. So what was Mary Stone saying? Was it the same thing?

He was trying to grapple with this as Bernie said, "You have a little too much faith in technology, don't you Lewis?"

Think you're educated, don'tcha, penny clerk?

The echo in his mind passed quickly.

"Emily wasn't fooled," Bernie conceded, nodding to herself. "She understood very early, but she didn't care. Even when I appeared to her after the launch, when she left Anton, I don't think she was really surprised. She knew who I was, I think, early into the recipes."

"Why the recipes?" he asked. "Why the crossword?"

"The Shilling is where I live," she explained. "You need to understand that. I didn't want to die and I wanted to be beautiful. The Father sympathised with that. But The Shilling is also the contract, the contract that I made with Him. Within those parameters I can only appear to people who have taken The Shilling or are destined to take it, and those very close to them. And I can only direct events through it."

"That's why everything that happened to me was prompted by the answers in the crossword?"

"The crossword was for you. It appealed to you, because you like solving problems. Emily liked to create, and cooking comforted her, was important to her. It gave her a sense of family, of home. And I gave her the little girls, the rather ugly little girls who she dressed up and made beautiful. I gave her the family she wanted."

"The Shilling isn't just about me," he returned. "Three of the subscribers were pictured, the ones who have died.

"Of old age, of contented old age," she qualified. "Yes, they have an entitlement to appear. But no one is left out. The subscribers who have already passed prepare the articles and write the letters. Anything to trigger a reaction along the route we plan out. Many of them are creative, you know. They devised the recipes for Emily, and they've already written some songs for BB. We haven't got a lawyer yet," she added as an aside. "It's still early days and most of the subscribers are still alive. As they die I suspect The Shilling will become more ambitious in its scope."

"But only the pictured subscribers, and Raine and Booker, are allowed to step out of it?"

"Cecil and Howard are the founding members," she agreed. "There has to be a ranking priority. That's only correct. Higher management believes in the privilege of rank. Recent additions are allowed in the dreams, but only for a time. They're slowly weaned off the life experience."

"So they're just eventually lost in the magazine... never leaving..."

She shook her head. "You're seeing this from the wrong perspective, Lewis. They're happy; they're just working in the back office, that's all. Tired of being in the field. When did you last travel anywhere? You're happy here, in front of your TV." She saw he wasn't convinced. "Actual experience is overrated," she said. "You'll appreciate that one day. The twins in The Shilling are already realising it, they're already looking forward to their retirement."

"Why did the older twin take The Shilling?" he asked. "She was going to die soon, it was too late to enjoy..."

"So you've guessed that the younger looking twin took it many years ago?" She hesitated. "Don't believe that everyone wants the same things as you, Lewis. She didn't care about riches, or her looks."

He felt a knife in his ribs at this implied criticism and his subconscious trawled over the summary of his life contained in that book in the rosewood chest. He had hated what he had read, the incriminating evidence of a wasted, unfulfilled life: the DNA blueprint of his soul.

"Ellie simply wanted to be re-united with her sister before they died," Bernie explained. "The estranged sister she had worshipped from afar."

Time passed and neither of them spoke. He was whipping through the events of the last eighteen months in his head, struggling to tie up the loose ends. He knew it didn't really matter now but to finish the jigsaw was in his nature. "What about Marker? What about the London lawyer?" he asked at length.

"Well the London lawyer doesn't exist, obviously. Only I told you about him… as part of the reason why I needed to be protected."

He shook his head. "No, wait a minute. This wasn't all in my head. The money was real." He looked around him. "I bought this place with it."

She nodded. "The Trust is very rich, as you would imagine," she said.

"But what about the factory?"

"We're allowed to make certain things real. The tape recording of the banging in the factory was real, wasn't it? That's in the rules and we're allowed some latitude on that. Not as much as we'd like, but some. Baron, that's the Trust, is only allowed to operate out of nineteenth century warehouses, and then it can only use its original furniture."

"Why?"

"It's the rules, as I said. We're only made real by what was important to us, in life. With Baron it was the warehouse, and the money. Raine and Booker are still fascinated by money." She raised her eyebrows whimsically to imply that she regarded them as children playing with their toys. "Oh, and technology," she added. "Baron began as a patenting company. They love the new software, this so-called communications age. I admit some difficulty with understanding their excitement, I have always preferred a more personal approach."

"They were talking to me on the Internet? They were Farthing.com?"

She nodded, patient and happy to answer all his questions, seeming in no hurry to go anywhere. Their conversation was so natural he almost thought he should ask her if she wanted coffee.

If she wanted sex…

This is Mary Stone, not Bernie, he kept reminding himself.

"Money was important to Baron," he mused. "What was important to you?"

She smiled, but didn't reply, for he knew the answer. The rage against her disfigurement, her acquired sexual power, sustained her in life and allowed her to step out of The Shilling; not as the fantasy constructs of her subjects, which was part of her contract, but as herself.

"That's how you stretch your legs," he murmured.

"Pardon me?" she said playfully.

"With sex, and with pain."

"Dear me, you have such a poor opinion of me."

A hiss sounded inside his ear, as if a tongue was licking at his eardrum.

My little soldjar…

"I love you, Lewis," Bernie whispered. "Nothing can change that."

He suspected that about an hour had passed by the time he spoke again. Somewhere as he drifted he thought he had heard a telephone ring, perhaps there had even been knocking at the door. He felt as if he were in a capsule where only his questions and her answers were real.

"Inventions," he murmured. "Mr Dove, that man I had lunch with, the inventor of the Hour machine… he was real. His name is Saul Warner. The waiter saw him… gave him his coat."

"He is real," Bernie confirmed. "He's a subscriber who's still alive. And he does make inventions, but they're only used in the Third World and some parts of Asia. He's very rich. We call in our subscribers now and again for favours. Mr Marker is another subscriber, in case you hadn't guessed."

"Both of those men took The Shilling?"

"And passed it on. Mr Marker lives in the Bahamas. He runs health clinics. Rich women go into his clinic at sixteen stone and leave at nine stone. But they always have to go back…"

"Yes, nothing really lasts with your inventions, does it?" he mused. "Marker and Dove… no doubt you ruined their lives before you forced them to join you? Just like you ruined my life."

She looked offended. "Ruined your life? You have nothing, but you started with nothing, remember? I simply took you on a journey and then brought you back. That's another rule: I can only take away what I've given. That's fair, isn't it? But the journey is important because it gives you a taste of what you are capable of. And a taste of what you can have," she added enticingly.

He shook his head. "That's not true. I didn't start under investigation by the CID and facing a criminal assault charge."

"There are inevitably some variations," she conceded, "but you brought all that on yourself, didn't you? Your partners asked you to share the Baron account, and I pleaded with you not the shoot those two men."

"I didn't start overweight and throwing up whenever I smoked."

"Why is being overweight worse than being underweight? And at least I cured you of your smoking habit. You're healthier, now, aren't you?"

He nodded grimly. *Rules*, he thought. Who laid down these rules? Not Mary Stone, that was for sure. She was too keen on breaking them, or at least interpreting them in her favour. Bernie… the old Bernie… had warned him that he was changing, that he was being punished for his sins. Incredibly, now he thought about it, she had insisted that he see the pastor. Was *that* in the rules too? A rule of full disclosure?

She was looking at him suspiciously, as if she guessed at his thought processes.

So why would the Devil limit her power? he wondered. Perhaps the contract wasn't as powerful as either of them cared to believe. Perhaps the Devil's power was limited. Or then again, maybe this was a game that God had invented, a game of faith, and the Devil and Mary Stone were unwitting pawns.

As he considered Bernie he decided against making such a suggestion, guessing it wouldn't be received favourably. Even behind the shield of Bernie's personality he detected the enormous ego of Mary Stone.

"Are there any other rules?" he asked.

She nodded. "I have to make an offer to you now," she said.

"The offer to all the world?" he suggested.

She chuckled. "The carbolic smoke ball," she reflected, "yes I thought that was rather apt."

"On whose authority do you make this offer?" he asked, finding strength in his voice. Perhaps it was the mention of a legal case authority, the reminder that he was a lawyer, which steeled his resolve. He was allowed to ask her anything; he could even cross-examine her.

She had noticed the change in his tone and was smiling.

"On whose authority…" he repeated.

"On behalf of the Father," she said, still smiling.

"So I can burn with him… forever?" he answered wryly.

"I see the crossword is worrying you," she said. "Well, that wasn't my idea, I have no control over such things. The Father must have his say, but *this* is real, Lewis, you and me. Here and now."

He weighed her words carefully. He suspected that one of the rules was that she couldn't lie to him on this subject, that he had to exercise free will. She hadn't denied the fact of damnation. "Go on," he said cautiously.

"You'll have a wonderful life, Lewis, starting from... well... now. All your problems will disappear. I promise. Those two men you shot won't press charges. The CID will find evidence of your innocence: Mr Marker will get it to them. You will go to Spain, but we'll give you some more share tips to make you rich. I'll restore your appearance to that time when women found you irresistible. Do you remember those few months?" She paused. "Picture yourself as that person, Lewis, walking along the beach, handsome, and rich. But that's nothing. Bernie will live with you in your dreams. Bernie is my gift to you."

"Go on," he urged, cutting through the sales pitch.

"You'll succeed at everything. Why don't you take up the saxophone again? You'll be surprised at how good you are. Or perhaps try your hand at writing historical articles. You'll get published. Why not be a movie critic? Even a director of films. Acting, perhaps? The world is large and wondrous, Lewis, and it belongs to you now."

"They wouldn't be my achievements," he said, "they'd be yours."

"What does it matter?"

"It matters."

She threw him a puzzled glance, as if he was talking gibberish. "Are you denying that with a little more luck, with a different upbringing, that these things *couldn't* have been yours?"

He smiled at her silky logic. "Is that what you offered Emily?"

"No... money and fame never interested her. She wanted a family. She wanted to find her family..."

"Her parents were dead."

"When I say her family, I mean her children. She couldn't have them, you know."

"You... you could have given her children? Cured her sterility?"

She hesitated, reluctantly. "No," she conceded.

"No, you can't create life, can you?" he murmured.

"She wanted to adopt," she remarked, ignoring the taunt. "That was impossible with her alcoholism and the concerns over the agency, the allegations of anorexia."

"Problems you created," he muttered.

"She would have adopted, we had arranged it," she said, still patiently refusing to rise to him. "There were beautiful twins, a boy and girl. She was going to see them on the Monday... the Monday after she visited you. Then she would have returned to Anton."

He nodded slowly. "But now you make Anton suffer, because she went back on the deal? Because she killed herself?"

He visualised Emily once more, looking down as the lift door closed.

It was as if she had left that memory behind for him. Perhaps as a warning of what was to come, perhaps also as a parting gift, borne out of regret.

"If I don't pass The Shilling on, is that the end of the line?" he asked. "Is that the end of *you*?"

She raised her eyebrows. "Oh my, you do have a high opinion of yourself, don't you? No, I'll be around for a long time yet, with or without you. But BB will be bypassed." Her last sentence was said quietly, reluctantly.

Was this another rule of disclosure?

"And what happens if I refuse?" he asked.

She seemed disappointed that he should even ask this question. "That's your prerogative," she said. "There's nothing that I can do now to influence you one way or another."

"I'll go to prison?"

"As I said, I have no control over that. You certainly have problems, problems of your own making I might add. But that's nothing. What's important is that you'll condemn yourself to a life of mediocrity, Lewis. There will be no second chance, you won't be able to change your mind and find me. Even after you die, you'll be mediocre. Have you thought about that? Is that what you want? Whether you're prepared to admit it or not, you've found all this exciting. I chose you because you're special, Lewis. All the subscribers are special, in their own way. They have potential, unfulfilled potential..."

He took some deep breaths, the attack on his subconscious having wounded him. It was true... he hadn't fulfilled himself. That book in the rosewood drawer, with its bland jumble of worthless facts, was still haunting him.

"Remember all your ambitions when you were young?" she asked gently. "They should have come true, you were entitled to have them come true. God planted your dreams then denied you the pleasure of them. He put you in a place where you hated yourself."

"It might have been different," he returned. "The pastor said that going to Spain might have changed me."

Her eyes narrowed. "What does he know?" she murmured.

Interfering little POPE FUCK!

"This is real. What I'm offering you is real," Bernie said quickly, sensing the intrusion, the echo of Mary Stone.

"This isn't about mediocrity," he protested, "and don't try and pretend you're doing this for *me*. This is about souls. That's your contract. You're collecting souls for the Devil."

She sighed, exasperated. "That name again," she grumbled. "Lewis, grow up. Do you think anyone down

there, or up there, really cares? It's just a game to them."
She effected a serious expression as she collected her
thoughts. "Imagine two people playing cards, over
countless millenniums. Let's say they're playing trumps.
Every trump is a soul, billions and billions of souls. But
the game to them is nothing, just one outlet for their
competitiveness, for their hatred of each other. When
they've finished trumps they'll move on to something
else. Think about that and you'll realise how completely
pointless you are in the final scheme of things. So stop
worrying and at least get something out of it for yourself,"
she suggested reasonably.

"It may be that way for the Devil," he muttered, "but
it's not that way for God. You can't speak for God."

She shrugged and one of the buttons on her shirt that
had been straining now sprang away. Blood rushed to her
lips and he went weak at the sight of her, every fibre in his
body keyed into a passion for her. It was as if Bernie had
been built out of a blueprint of his desires. Even now, he
could forgive her anything. "But will you do it?" she asked.
"Will you give The Shilling to your friend?"

Lewis stared at her in silence, afraid to answer.

It was the essence of temptation: the immediate need
was so attractive, so appealing, outweighing any future
consideration.

And Bernie had a point, the lawyer in him argued. The
next forty to fifty years were real, and as she said *eternity*
was just a word, just a word that no one could understand.
And perhaps Hell didn't exist at all.

"Believe that if it comforts you," she said quietly,
reading his mind.

He picked up The Shilling. It had changed, completely
changed, save that the same portrait of Mary Stone occupied
the first page. It looked like a rock music magazine.

"BB hasn't told you but he lost everything with that last share tip you gave him," she remarked cruelly. "His tourist website has closed down and he's being chased by the bank. But now his luck's about to turn as Baron Enterprises becomes Baron Records." He was flicking through the magazine and stopped at a picture of a three-piece music combo, recognising the twins, now a rhythm section, with the shears woman, the suffragette Ruth Keenes, sitting at a piano. He suspected that Prissy Maine, the twin sporting the double bass, would be the singer. Turning the pages he came across song sheets and musical scores.

"They're wonderful songs, Lewis," she said. "Well, they're derivations on some old classics, actually. Mozart and Schubert chamber music mostly. But it'll take some time before anybody works that out and BB will go a long way on them before they do."

"But I have to give it to him," he murmured. He felt broken, but also, in a strange way, relieved. Relieved that it was all over. "Mozart and Schubert," he mused. "Couldn't think up any new material, could you? It's just as the pastor said. You can't create, you can only corrupt."

She raised her eyebrows in protest, but didn't answer.

"Baron," he said. "*Barren*. Where nothing grows. Maybe *higher management* isn't as clever as you think." He put The Shilling back on the coffee table, not wanting to look at it any more.

"You're being very cynical, Lewis," she said, feigning indignation. "You shouldn't belittle my achievements. They're all little miracles. You'll create miracles too."

"Let me think," he muttered and he got up and walked out onto the balcony. He needed fresh air.

"We'll be together, Lewis," she called after him. "Now and in death. Isn't that romantic? Isn't that so exciting?"

He gripped the balcony rail. "Do you love me, Bernie? Really?"

"Really. I can't lie about that Lewis. I wouldn't have chosen you otherwise."

"How can I believe you?"

"Because I'm asking you to live with me. I do love you. Lewis, I do."

He looked out at the water. "You had a very hard life, didn't you?" he said.

"I was starving. Disfigured, a freak, a joke for the doctors. Do you blame me for turning to the Father?"

"No," he conceded. "My life has been very easy."

"Don't think that the Father values you any less for that," she said. "It makes you no less worthy."

He gripped the balcony rails tighter. His knuckles were white.

"Is there really so much you have to think about?" she called. "You know what you want, Lewis, you *know*. You just feel guilty for wanting it."

He nodded, acknowledging the truth in her words, knowing that he couldn't refuse her. That he was too weak to resist this ultimate temptation. The Shilling was part of him now, and so was Bernie... Mary Stone.

Bernie tested the hooks and pulled them tight. "Those old photographs of me... that was my real skin, Lewis, and my real hair. Do you see now how merciful the Father is? How good He was to me? I had a wonderful life. I was rich and admired. I went everywhere, knew everyone. I outlived three husbands. And the twentieth century was wild and the next century is going to be even better. We'll be there together, Lewis, all the way through."

He sighed. "Why did you murder children?" he whispered. His words were reflective and as quiet as words could be but he knew that Bernie heard him.

"What did you say?"

He was still gazing out to sea. "I asked you why you killed the children."

"What makes you think I killed them?"

"I know," he said simply.

"I didn't kill no one. It's like I told the beak, they was all just accidents, see? I loved those little…"

Bernie stopped mid sentence.

"Lewis?" she asked, her voice loaded with tension. For a moment the smell of dog excrement had wafted through the balcony doors.

He considered the balcony rails, finding it curious that destinies could so easily find their metaphors. With Emily it had been an empty bottle of Bell's whisky. With him, it was a set of balcony rails, and a view that he always believed he needed.

"Lewis, what are you doing?"

He climbed over the balcony rails and jumped off.

1 across	who do you bring?
2 down	to own
3 across	made the fires
3 down	do not accept it
4 across	no rooms
5 down	the process
6 down	she says
7 down	how many now?
8 across	weight hanger
9 down	The Shilling says

8 down	the female possesses
11 across	beta lives
12 across	holds the weeping wall
13 across	red light
14 down	Swiss city
6 across	your reward
15 across	stupid, stupid song
9 across	published in a mirror
	out of town

(full)

Lewis your lit less inns ARE wonderful two Hour fat her (be?) low stop

Bern wit hymn forever

Lewis your little sins are wonderful to our father below.

Burn with him forever

Epilogue

The police investigation into the death of Lewis Coin began energetically but ended up as a routine paper-filing exercise.

Two officers of the CID took an interest and checked for signs of an intruder and foul play, but none were found. They told the coroner's court that they were due to visit the deceased the next day to confirm that an investigation they were following was about to be dropped for lack of evidence, and that the injunction they had put on his apartment had been lifted. They conceded however that the investigation might have had an adverse effect on him, because he had been involved in an incident the night before where two men were shot and wounded. The Indian businessmen involved could no longer be traced, and it was believed they had left the country. A search of the warehouse in Mile End had uncovered certain narcotic substances and it was suspected that the comic book business was a front for a drug ring. A friend of Mr Coin's, who had tipped them off about the shooting, had insisted that the whole warehouse be searched from top to bottom. This was in spite of the owners' protestations, and the two businessmen were gone by the time the search was over.

The coroner, in making his assessment, recorded that while Mr Coin had nothing to fear from either of the two police investigations, he wouldn't have been aware of this when he was standing on his balcony contemplating ending his life. His state of mind was further put into sharp focus from the evidence of members of the law firm where he used to work. Secretaries had testified that they had heard him talking to himself in the boardroom. His ex-partners had described a personality change in the last eighteen months, which had transformed him from being one of the best-liked and most respected lawyers in the firm to being hated and feared. No psychiatrists had been called but the coroner commented that Mr Coin might have been having some mental difficulties.

A photograph had been introduced into evidence that further supported this proposition. It was a framed photograph that the police said was on his bedside table. It showed him alone, smiling on the balcony, his left arm outstretched as if he wanted to believe that someone was with him. In addition to being depressed, Mr Coin was almost certainly very lonely.

The coroner's jury was unanimous in its verdict: suicide, caused by depression possibly while the balance of his mind was disturbed.

Stephen O'Neill gave evidence. He said that Lewis Coin was a fine young man, an able lawyer and notwithstanding some recent disagreements he had always been very fond of him. He had agreed to deal with the probate; Lewis hadn't left a will and so he was in the process of tracking down the nearest surviving relative and which wasn't proving to be easy for Lewis was an only child and his parents had died some years ago. The apartment had sold quickly with all of the contents.

O'Neill shook his head when he was asked whether he had found anything in the apartment when he had carried out the probate inventory which could further cast light on Mr Coin's state of mind.

This wasn't strictly true, but O'Neill had felt uncomfortable about giving an honest answer. There were in fact two things that he had considered unusual.

The first was that there was a packet of cigarettes and a pint of water next to each of the three toilets.

The second was a piece of computer software on the coffee table, which he had briefly studied before putting it back where he found it. He didn't recognise the software and nothing on the cover gave any clue as to its purpose.

The software was called, oddly enough, *The Shilling*. Perhaps it was a money management package, but it was clearly some kind of bootleg as there were no credits or symbol of any major company on the sleeve.

The picture sleeve was unusual. A striking woman with black hair seemed to be talking to someone.

But she was talking to thin air. The sleeve cover almost seemed improvised, as if one of the models had decided to walk out of the camera angle leaving the woman to fend for herself. The woman's sense of professionalism had kept her smiling, but her eyes betrayed her anger and dismay.

O'Neill remembered that sleeve so well because it haunted his dreams. Before he left the apartment, his inventory complete, he picked it up again. His imagination was playing tricks on him because he was certain the dark haired woman was glancing sideways at him... that is to say, at the camera.

His fascination to find out what was on the program urged him to place it discreetly in his pocket, but this sudden compulsion triggered a moral dilemma. Even if the item was innocuous, not important enough to appear on the inventory, it still belonged to Lewis, and now it belonged to the purchaser of the apartment.

The moral debate in his head seemed out of all proportion to what was at stake. This was just another CD-ROM, a piece of twenty-first century junk, which would no doubt be the first thing thrown into the new owner's black bag.

But he decided to leave it, all the same.